CHAPTER ONE

A melia Watkins couldn't believe what she was seeing. She frowned, slowing the car instinctively as her eyes took in the scene ahead of her. *What the—!*

She reached out automatically to silence the radio, her eyes glued to the layby in the quiet country lane, and in that moment she wished she was anywhere but here … driving down a deserted country road in the early hours of the evening, witnessing what looked horribly like a kidnap attempt.

But, *really?* Even as her eyes logged the fact, her brain was dismissing it. Her family would be laughing at her, telling her it was her overactive imagination at work again. And yet …

Her first thought that she should stop and help the heavily pregnant woman being dragged towards a car by two men, was quickly overridden by her second, which was that she should get the hell out of there and call the police from a safe distance. She was almost on them now and, hearing the car, one of the men turned to look at her. It was that that made her stop. If he hadn't looked, she would have driven past – but making eye contact suddenly made it impossible to ignore what she was witnessing.

She pulled up alongside them and clicked on the button

1

to open her window. 'Is everything alright? What's going on? Are you okay, love?'

'No, help me. They're holding me against my will.'

'It's not true,' the man said with a tense smile. 'She's my wife and we're just helping her get home – her pregnancy triggered a psychotic episode recently and she hasn't been herself since.'

That was an understatement, Amelia thought, taking in the wild eyes and gasping sobs of the heavily pregnant woman they were holding – but she seemed to quieten suddenly, slumping in their hold as if she'd lost all her energy.

Amelia absorbed it all uneasily. It didn't feel right. On impulse, she reached for her bag and said. 'I'm sorry but I'm calling the police. If this is genuine, you can sort it out with them.'

'There's no need for that, Amelia. Really.'

The voice was familiar and as Amelia's gaze turned in the direction of the second man, her eyes rounded in shock.

'Hang on a moment,' he said. 'Let me just help him get her back in the car and then I'll be with you. It's fine though, nothing to worry about.'

Relief surged through her and she watched as between them they managed to manoeuvre the by-now barely conscious woman back into the car and strap her in. Once she was safely secured, the man said something to his companion, patted him on the shoulder and then headed over to where she was waiting.

'What's going on?' she asked. 'That poor woman looks distraught.'

His expression was tense but he smiled, diffusing the situation. 'She'll be fine. They're friends of mine and he called me because she'd run off again. He'll get her home

2

now and call their doctor as soon as he gets back. I knew she'd had problems before, but her pregnancy's made her psychotic episodes worse and she's convinced everyone's out to harm her.' He shook his head. 'It's a terrible thing to see, especially when it's people you know.'

Amelia's eyes darted towards the car, then back to his face, her expression uncertain. 'You're not kidding. It was scary for me too. I thought she was being kidnapped.'

He reached out and opened her driver's door, and even as her brain was computing that that was rather an odd thing to do, he said pleasantly. 'Get out of the car, Amelia, will you?'

'What?'

She blinked at him.

'I said, get out of the car.'

His tone had hardened, and from nowhere it seemed, he had drawn a knife. She stared down at it in shock and gave a nervous laugh.

'Is this some sort of joke?'

'I'm sorry. This is the last thing I would have chosen to happen.' His tone sounded genuinely regretful as he leant in and swiftly withdrew her keys from the ignition.

'*What are you doing?*' The other man's voice rose in disbelief as he realised what was happening.

The man responded without turning around. 'What do you think I'm doing? I'm clearing up the mess you've made. I haven't got us to where we are now to risk having it all blow up in our faces. Just learn your lesson from this and stick to what you know in future. Now come and give me a hand. We need to get her out of sight before someone comes.'

Realising that this was definitely *not* a joke, Amelia made

3

a frantic grab for the door handle. But it was too late. He was quicker and far stronger than her, as he seized her by the arm and hauled her out of the car.

'Come on. Out you get…'

NO ESCAPE

CAROLYN MAHONY

ACKNOWLEDGEMENT

To my amazing Advance Reader Group for the incredible support and time you so generously give to me. Your feedback on the final version of this book (and its cover) undoubtedly made it a far more polished product than it might otherwise have been.

Thank you all – you know who you are!

CHAPTER TWO

Two weeks later

I've never known fear like this. The need to escape spurs me on as I stumble through the trees, my heart pumping so heavily it feels like it's going to burst.

'*Keep going. Keep going. Keep going,*'

I repeat the mantra over and over, clinging on to it as I force one leg in front of the other. I don't know where I'm going, and I don't care. All I know is that I must keep running if I want to stay alive.

Up ahead I see space beyond the trees. A road? A field? Where *am* I? I bolt for that space, and when I get there I sob my relief. I know where I am now. And it's not far to the village. If I can just get there …

I hear a car, and without even looking to see who it is, throw myself down into the leaves. I hold my breath, not moving as it drives past, then I raise my head cautiously to get a better view. It's a red Volkswagen Polo – not a car I recognise … and now I wish I'd flagged it down. I've missed my chance.

I lie on the ground, breath rasping as I try to clear the fog in my head. *Think!*

Should I stay where I am, hidden in this ditch, until night-time – move under cover of darkness? I'm so tempted to do it.

But *no*, stupid to think they aren't searching the surrounding area for me even now. I have to get away from here.

Scrabbling up from the ground, I take off again, hugging the trees, keeping low as I bolt up the road. It seems to take forever but, finally, rounding a bend, I sob my relief as people come into view. The market is on and there are crowds of them. It must be Saturday. I race across the road and head for the pub on the corner of the square. I can get help inside – call the police.

But outside the entrance, I freeze, my gaze locking with another pair of eyes that are surveying me predatorily from the doorway. A bolt of electricity shoots through me. I don't give myself time to think. Spinning round on my heels, I sprint for the market square.

The pavements are hectic with people and I fly past them all, adrenalin spurring me on. If I stop now to ask for help, he'll kill me, I know it. My only hope is to lose myself in the crowds so he can't find me.

'*Oi*,' one indignant voice shouts as I race past, but I keep my head down, bent only on escape.

'Sorry,' I gasp, colliding into a young mother and nearly knocking her over. 'I'm being chased.'

Why had I said that? I take a left and belt across the road, ducking and diving, keeping low to conceal myself from my pursuer. The crowds are thicker now, slowing my progress, but suddenly I see my chance. To the right is a stall full of clothes and instinctively I dive towards it and tuck down behind one of the rails. I try to quieten my breathing, terrified that despite the noise of the market, the man chasing

6

me will hear it. From beneath the clothes rack, I see a pair of legs run swiftly past. Then they halt and turn, as their owner obviously looks back the way he's come. Is he looking towards me? *Can he see my feet like I can see his?* I smother a sob, fighting the urge to bolt as I press myself against the soft materials.

Then the feet are turning again, moving forward at a slower pace, but nonetheless, moving forward.

'Everything alright, love?'

The man's voice behind me makes me jump.

'Sorry,' I mumble, grabbing a couple of tee shirts off the rail. 'Is there somewhere I can try these?'

He looks at me oddly, but shrugs his shoulders. 'Through there, behind the mirror. There's not much space…'

I'm gone before he can finish his sentence, quickly drawing the cubicle curtain closed behind me. Once inside, I sink onto the small wooden stool and lean against the canvas backing, trying to regain control of my shaking limbs. It's not an over-reaction, they have every reason to be shaking. Because I know that today I could die.

If only I had my phone.

'Excuse me, you haven't seen my girlfriend around have you? Fair hair … blue and white stripy top?'

I freeze at the sound of that voice, jumping up from my stool and looking desperately around for a means of escape as I hear the response. 'Yeah, she's in there, I think, trying on some clothes. Should be out in a minute.'

I dive down onto the floor yanking desperately at the canvas backing of the changing room. Thank God, I can lift it just enough to lie flat on my stomach and wriggle beneath it. Then I'm running like a bat out of hell again, slipping up a narrow alleyway back towards the road. But as I reach the end of that alleyway, I collide with another figure. I clutch onto the solid strength of an arm, knowing I must tell someone what's happening.

'Please help me,' I say desperately, looking up into his face.

And then I see who it is and catch the briefest glint of a knife.

And I know it's over.

⤻

Time passes. People … voices … sirens. I'm only vaguely aware of the hands easing gently beneath my body, shifting me from my position on the ground to the stretcher. I'm weak as a kitten. Blood … so much of it. I remember how it sprung from the wound like an unstoppable river, the warm stickiness oozing through my fingers as I tried to stem the flow. But no pain that I could remember, just shock as I stared up at that face and fell to the ground.

There are other memories too as they carry me off, but for some reason my brain can't process them. I claw desperately through the fog, trying to clear the debris that's blocking them, but nothing shifts. It seems that every time I clutch at one, it's like a wisp of air … gone before it's had time to form and take shape.

The man's voice is loud and rousing, disturbing my concentration, stopping me from slipping into the deep sleep my body craves.

'Come on, my love, stay with us. Stay awake. We're going to get you to the hospital so they can sort you out, but you need to stay awake, okay?'

Theo. Pain lurches in my heart. I try desperately to turn my head to speak to the man at my side … to communicate

8

the urgent need for them to find my son, but nothing in my body is working. Not even a gurgle escapes my lips. The man's voice is coming from further and further away and no matter how hard I try to cling onto that sound, it's seeping away with the rest of my consciousness.

Theo needs me. How will they find him if I can't tell them? Stay with us, my love.

I'm trying … I really am. How can I let him down like this? I need to stay alive for the sake of my son.

But it's no good. I'm so tired. The man's voice has become a distant, incoherent mumble, barely a ripple in the silent ocean of peace that beckons. It calls me deeper – and I follow.

And I know there's no stopping the sleep that finally claims me.

CHAPTER THREE

DI Harry Briscombe stepped out of his car and cast a quick glance about him before making his way swiftly through the crowd that had gathered to where the scene of the crime was sectioned off with tape.

'Young woman with life-threatening injuries,' DC Beth Macaskill informed him, thrusting some protective clothing at him as she filled him in. 'She was stabbed in the stomach and cracked her head on the kerb as she fell. She's been rushed to the hospital but it's not looking good.'

'Anyone see what happened?'

'Not from the few people I've spoken to so far. We've sealed both ends of this street off while Forensics do their stuff but the market's in full swing just down that alleyway there.'

'We'll need to question everyone we can before they all disappear.'

'Geoff's already on it. I said we'd join him when we're finished here.'

'Right …' Harry applied the final bit of protective covering to his shoes and lifted the tape to make his way over to where one of the SOCO team, a tall, lanky man, in his mid-forties, was painstakingly taking samples from the bloodstained area in the road.

'Hi Tim, anything useful?'

The man looked up and shook his head. 'Morning, Harry. Not a lot to go on at the moment, I'm afraid. Single stab wound to the stomach and an unfortunately severe head injury apparently, probably caused by hitting her head on the kerb.'

'Did you see her before she was taken off?'

'No – ambulance had been and gone by the time I arrived.'

'Weapon?'

'As I say, she was stabbed, but whoever it was took the knife with them.'

'Great …' Harry cast a brief glance around, observing that there was really very little to note. 'Well, if you come up with anything?'

'I wouldn't hold your breath. Doesn't look like the perp left much behind him. I think all we'll find here will be confirmation of the victim's blood group. Sorry.'

'We should question this lot,' Harry said, turning to Beth and indicating the small crowd that had gathered. 'Someone may have seen something. Then you can join Geoff down in the market and I'll head over to the hospital and see what's happening there. Do we know the woman's name?'

Beth shook her head. 'No ID. She didn't even have a handbag – though her attacker may have taken that, of course.'

'Sounds more than likely, what woman goes out without her bag?'

'Not many, I'll grant you,' Beth agreed, pulling out her notebook and heading back towards the crowd of spectators.

Harry followed her, and once they were on the other side of the tape they removed their protective clothing.

'Right now,' Beth said, addressing the crowd. 'Anyone

11

see what happened? Anything at all – no matter how irrelevant it might seem?'

Amazing how quickly people scarpered at the thought of the spotlight being on them, she thought, as the group started to rapidly break up and drift away. But one woman with a buggy was approaching them purposefully.

'Yeah,' she said, coming to a halt in front of Beth and rocking her child's buggy as she did so. 'I saw her down in the market, running as if she'd got half an army after her. She barged into me, said she was sorry, and then she was gone.'

'Was someone chasing her, do you think?' Beth asked, scribbling in her notebook.

'You sure you're a cop? You don't look like one to me.'

Beth sighed, it was a common enough reaction – prompted, she knew, by the somewhat extreme hairstyle she sported. Short, spiky auburn hair wasn't your usual DC image. She was beginning to get just a little bit fed up with the comments and slowly coming round to thinking that a major makeover was required.

'Quite sure,' she said, and the woman sniffed her response.

'Yeah, well … no, I didn't see anyone chasing her, but she said they were, and she was definitely in a hurry.'

'Did she say anything else? Who was chasing her, maybe?' Beth knew it was a long shot and wasn't surprised when the woman shook her head.

'No … no time for anything like that. She just apologised for barging into me and said she was being chased.'

'Did she look frightened – or more like it was a game?' Beth asked.

'It weren't no game,' the woman said straight away. 'She looked desperate. I did turn around to see if someone was after her, but I didn't see anything. It was so crowded though.

Next thing I know, I'm walking home up the alleyway, and—' She broke off, the look on her face reflecting her horror at what she'd seen. '…I recognised her from the blue-and-white top she was wearing,' she added.

'Did you see anyone else in the alleyway when you were walking up it?'

'A couple of people, but now you mention it … there was someone came out at a bit of a pace, just as I turned in.'

'Did you see a face?'

'No. I think it was a man, but he had his hood up.'

'Whereabouts was she when she bumped into you?'

'Just near Joe's veg stall. I can show you, if you like?'

'Thanks, that would be good. Did you notice if she had a handbag of any sort?'

The woman thought about it and shook her head slowly. 'I don't remember seeing one. But she could have, I suppose.'

'Okay, thanks. Can you give me your details? Someone will be in touch about taking a formal statement?'

After she'd finished writing it down, Beth turned to Harry, who was talking to a middle-aged man who claimed to have seen the attacker. 'It was quick,' the man was saying. 'She literally came running out of that alleyway there, and collided with this fella. Next thing I know, she's down on the ground and he's taken off up the same alleyway. I ran up to see what had happened and saw the blood. She was a mess. Most of it was coming from her head but then I saw her stomach too. All I could do was try to stem it as best I could while someone called the ambulance and you lot. Didn't know what else to do.'

'You did well,' Harry responded, noticing that the man's hands and clothes were heavily stained with blood. 'Did you see what he looked like? Would you recognise him again if you saw him?'

The man pulled a face. 'I'm not sure – he was wearing a jacket with the hood up, like they all do. I got a quick flash of his face 'cos he turned round to see if there were any witnesses, I reckon, but only enough to see that he was white. Couldn't even make a stab at his age – though he was a man, not a lad. I shouted out but he wasn't hanging around for anyone.'

'Did you see if he grabbed her bag, or anything?'

He shook his head. 'No. Don't think so, but couldn't say for sure.'

'I'd be grateful if you'd give your details to my colleague here and at some point it would be useful if you could come down to the station and have a go at drawing a photofit of the guy? The sooner the better if you can, while it's fresh in your mind's eye. We'll probably need to take your DNA too, to exclude you from the forensics.'

'I can come later this afternoon, if you want, but I'm not sure I saw enough of him to give you much to go on.'

'Every bit helps,' Harry said, snapping his notebook shut and turning to Beth. 'You okay to take Mr Riley's details and then cover the market with Geoff? I'll head up to the hospital and see how our victim's getting on. I'll catch up with you later.'

〜

At the hospital, Harry made his way up to the ICU reception. He was always struck by how quiet and unhurried the intensive care unit was, compared to the hustle and bustle of other departments in the hospital, but he never underestimated the life-saving activities that went on here.

'Young woman … stabbing victim … brought in about

an hour ago?'

The nurse at the desk was talking to a female doctor and they both looked up as Harry joined them.

The doctor nodded towards one of the rooms. 'She's in there but you can't go in I'm afraid. She's very poorly.'

Harry pulled out his card. 'DI Briscombe, Hertfordshire Police. Is she conscious? I'll keep it to a minimum but we really do need to speak to her.'

The doctor shook her head. 'She's out of it – in a coma. You'll get nothing out of her at the moment – we're not even sure she'll last the night. I'm Dr Reed by the way.'

She was a young woman in her late twenties and the shadows around her eyes suggested she'd had a run of late nights. 'Do you know who she is? It would be helpful to pull her medical records if we've got some for her.'

Harry shook his head. 'We're working on it. I understand there was no ID on her?'

'Nope, nothing.'

'What sort of age is she?'

'Difficult to say … late teens, early twenties? She was in a state when they brought her in and not just from the stab and head wounds. There's bruising to her body and arms suggestive of physical restraint and she's got significant marks across her back as if she's been lashed. I don't know what's gone on with her, but it hasn't been good.' She hesitated. 'And one other thing … she's had a baby very recently.'

'A baby?'

Shit – that wasn't good news. Hopefully, it was safe at home with its father, but if it wasn't … it wouldn't be the first time someone had nipped out while a baby was safely sleeping in its cot. And of course no one ever factored in the possibility that they might end up in hospital in a coma.

'How recent?' he asked.

'Certainly within the last month, possibly two to three weeks? The chances are she'd have had it here. Patient Liaison are looking to see if we can trace her from that.'

'That would be helpful, thanks. Can you pass my details over to them so they can let me know as soon as they come up with anything?'

'Of course, I'll mark it in the handover notes.'

'We need to find out who she is, urgently,' he added. 'I'd be grateful if you could stress that to whoever's in charge of identifying her? It's not impossible that the baby could be alone somewhere, unattended.'

The doctor looked shocked. 'I hadn't thought of that. I'll get on to Patient Liaison right away, see what we can do. Poor girl…' She looked at the woman through the glass window. 'Whatever can she have done to deserve this?'

'Nothing she could have done deserves this,' Harry said.

'No, you're right – there are some evil people out there, that's for sure. Let's hope you catch them.' She flashed him the briefest of smiles. 'Good thing we've got the strong arm of the law looking out for us.'

He returned her smile with a wry one of his own. 'Now, if everyone else shared your faith, it would make my job a lot easier,' he said.

Back in his car, he pulled out his phone and called Beth.

'How's it going down there?'

'All good.'

'Anything useful?'

'Yup. One of the younger stallholders thought he might have seen her before, but not for a few weeks, he said. And wait for it …' She left a dramatic pause. 'He reckoned she was pregnant at that time.'

'I'm one step ahead of you on that one. The hospital's confirmed that she's recently had a baby. They're checking their records to see if that might help us trace who she is.'

'Oh.' Beth sounded a bit miffed that her news wasn't quite as groundbreaking as she'd thought it was. 'So, where's the baby then?'

'That's what we need to find out. Do you need my help down there?'

'No, Geoff and I are doing okay but the market's winding up for the day. Reckon we'll be through in about half an hour, but we'll need to come back tomorrow to catch the ones who packed up earlier.'

'Right … well in that case I'll head back to the station and get the incident room up and running. I'll see you both there.'

'Okay, and if it's not too cheeky asking a DI … get that kettle on can you, we're gasping!'

Harry smiled as he hung up. Beth could be spiky at times and from what little she'd said, he put that down to her family life which he knew hadn't been good. But she was a great member of the team and was shaping up well as his DC. He was lucky to have her on board.

⌐

It was late afternoon and a smattering of people had gathered in the incident room, some sitting on the few chairs provided, the rest standing, or perching on the edge of a desk.

Harry looked around the room, making sure he had everyone's attention, before switching his gaze to the few scraps of information he'd scraped together for the board.

'Right now,' he said. 'This is the first briefing on what

we'll call Operation Market Square – an investigation into the attempted murder today of a young woman at Bowman's Market. The victim was stabbed and suffered a severe head injury as she fell. She's now in a coma fighting for her life. So far we have no ID on her, and that presents a problem because she's had a baby very recently and we can't know for sure where that baby is. According to the hospital, it looks as though her hands had been tied, and she had marks on her back suggesting she'd been beaten, possibly with a belt. Now that suggests to me that she was either caught up in a very abusive relationship or she was being held somewhere against her will. Either way, if she had a baby on top of all that, I can't see it being good news for her or the baby. Hopefully, someone will come forward and report her missing in the next few hours. But if that doesn't happen, we need to make identifying her and finding her baby our top priority. For all we know, the child could have been abducted or is lying somewhere unattended on its own. Beth, Geoff … did you learn anything from the people you questioned at the market?'

It was Beth who responded. 'Not much. The guy I was telling you about – the one who said she was pregnant? He said he'd seen her a couple of times – noticed her because she was so pretty – but not for a couple of months, he reckoned.'

She moved forward, closer to the incident board. 'The bloke you spoke to this morning came down and had a go at doing a description of the attacker, and this' – she pinned a drawing of a figure onto the board – 'is apparently what he came up with.' She pulled a face. 'Not much use, I know – no identifying features, just an outline in a jacket with the hood pulled up, as you can see. In fact it could even be a tall woman when you look at it. But assuming it's a man, he's about 5'11, slim rather than bulky and this description matches the one given by another person of the man seen running down the alleyway. We're checking the CCTV in the area in the hope that it might have picked him up either just before the incident, or just after it. And obviously we've still got a few stall-holders left to interview, but that will have to wait until tomorrow now.'

'Well, it's a long shot, but I guess it's worth showing the photo-fit around the market people and local residents to see if it rings any bells,' Harry said. 'Have we established which direction she was running from?'

'According to the woman she collided with, she was coming from the direction of the pub. There's still a long way to go on the house-to-house enquiries. It's a built-up area.'

'And you might as well take in the pub while you're at it? Beth nodded.

'It's still very early,' Harry said, 'plenty of time for someone to come forward and report her missing. But if no one's done it by tomorrow morning, I'll get a photo-fit of the victim released for the press first thing. We need to find that baby, make sure it's safe. In the meantime, I want people back out there today and tomorrow, asking questions. Someone must have seen something. And someone knows who she is. Okay … that's all for now. There'll be another briefing first thing in the morning, unless anyone comes up with anything significant before then. In which case I want to know straight away. I know it's Sunday tomorrow, but we're going to need all hands on deck for the foreseeable future, I'm afraid.'

CHAPTER FOUR

'*Oh, Juliet ... where are you?*'

It was only as Marie Sanderson spoke the words out loud, hearing the anguish in her own voice, that the subtle irony of them hit her. Only it wasn't the memory of some romantic Shakespeare play that had wrenched them from her – but the deep, burning ache in her gut that every now and then threatened to completely submerge her. Like today, Sunday, 10th November ... Juliet's twentieth birthday. It seemed she'd divided her life into two segments now – life before her darling daughter had gone, and life after.

Life before had been taken for granted; her existence consumed by the petty day-to-day trials and tribulations of family life that had driven her to distraction more often than not, but at the same time, had wrapped her in a cocoon of love that felt unbreakable. The constant nagging at her children to wake up and get ready for school; the arguments over make-up plastered on too heavily, clothes that were too short, too tight, too skimpy ... all of it was a ritual that every parent went through with a philosophical shrug of the shoulders and a fond, '*Teenagers ... who'd have 'em,*' attitude. It had never occurred to her that one day that life would be gone, snatched away from her without warning or any chance to prepare for it.

And as for life after … it had been one huge empty crater. An unfillable void that came from nowhere and stayed.

She wandered around the bedroom, trying to feel some sort of connection with her daughter as she touched things aimlessly – the geometric duvet cover they'd chosen together when she'd finally outgrown her favourite Peter Rabbit one; her sketch pad crammed with drawings of random people who caught her interest; the picture of the four of them, Mike, her, Juliet and Lisa, squashed into the photo-booth at her niece's wedding, seeing who could pull the ugliest face. She picked this last item up and stared at it intently, remembering how they'd shrieked with laughter when they'd seen the photo, but instead of laughter now, she felt the tears wetting her cheeks. How could Juliet have *done* this to them? Walked out of their lives without a backward glance? Marie's emotions see-sawed from disbelief at her daughter's selfish actions, to shameful guilt at her own – knowing that she was the cause of her daughter's decision to go. A simple act, like offering to tidy up her mother's filing system. Who'd have thought it could lead to such tumultuous events? And how could she have been so stupid as to let her do it? What must it have felt like for Juliet, learning the truth like that?

'*Mum?*'

It was Lisa calling loudly up the stairs, and she resented the intrusion from her older daughter. She wanted this time to herself, to remember … even indulge in a little hope that today of all days, they might hear from Juliet. But there was an urgency to Lisa's voice that caught her, plucked at her hypersensitive state. She rushed out onto the landing.

'What's the matter?'

21

'Come quickly,' Lisa's voice was panicked. 'There's a news report on the telly. I think it might be Jules.'

⤶

Harry could feel his frustration rising. It didn't look good for the DI in charge of the case to expect everyone to come in early on a Sunday morning and then be late himself, but he'd overslept, and now he was rushing around his grandmother's house like a lunatic trying to find his keys.

It struck him that even though she'd died over six months ago and he'd been living here ever since, he still thought of it as her house. But he guessed it took a bit longer than that to replace a lifetime of memories – he'd lived here with her for most of his life, after all. Maybe it would always be 'Gran's house' to him, and he didn't have a problem with that. In fact, he rather liked the idea.

Ah, there they were. He pounced on the bunch of keys half hidden by the newspaper on the coffee table and vowed to buy himself a new key board like the one he'd had in his flat. The one that Beth now used. Weird to think of her there, using stuff that had once been a part of his life, but he was glad it had worked out, and much preferred the idea of her as a tenant, than some random stranger.

At police HQ he took the stairs two at a time, only observing the two people sitting quietly in the reception area out of the corner of his eye. His mind was already sifting through what little information they'd picked up yesterday – working on a plan for the day. Up in the open-plan office, where he still sat by the window despite his recent elevation in status to DI, he was pounced on by DS Geoff Peterson the moment he appeared.

'Did you see the couple downstairs in reception?'

'Yes.'

'They want to speak to you, and only you, about the unidentified girl. They apparently saw the news this morning and think it could be their daughter.'

Harry's eyes lit up.

'*Right*. Bring them up. The DCI's not back until tomorrow, I'll use his office. It's less intimidating than the interview rooms.'

A few minutes later, Geoff showed the couple in. They looked to be late thirties or early forties and both were clearly in a state of high tension.

Harry stood up and offered them a seat. 'Good morning. I'm DI Harry Briscombe, and you are…?'

'Mike Sanderson, and this is my wife, Marie,' the man replied succinctly as they sat.

'We're separated though,' the woman said, flashing a quick look at her husband.

'Ah, okay. Can we maybe get you a drink before we start?'

Marie Sanderson nodded agitatedly. 'A cup of tea if you've got one. Thanks.'

She was wringing her hands in her lap, her eyes anxious as she looked at him. 'We needed to speak to you. Your name was mentioned in the news report and we wanted to speak to the person in charge.'

Harry could tell the tears weren't far off.

'How can I help you? My sergeant tells me you've come about the girl we're trying to identify?'

'Yes … we think it might be Juliet, our daughter. Is she still alive?'

She blurted the words out in such a rush that he had difficulty catching them, but there was no doubting what she'd said.

'She's alive,' Harry reassured her quickly, 'but … she's not in a good way, I'm afraid. She's in a coma, though the hospital are hopeful she'll come out of it. What makes you think it might be her?' he added gently.

'The photo-fit on the news this morning. It's her, I know it is.'

'Okay … let's take this slowly. Excuse me just one moment.'

He picked up the phone on Murray's desk and dialed a number. 'Beth? Can you bring the file in please on the young girl in the market stall incident? And could we maybe have some tea in here? Thanks.' He put the phone down and smiled across the desk. 'If it does turn out to be her, we'll get you straight over to the hospital to see her, okay?'

'They said on the news she'd been stabbed?' Marie Sanderson was looking at him in horror. 'What happened?'

Harry hesitated. 'Before I answer that, do you by any chance have a photo of your daughter on you? If you have, I can probably tell you straight away if it's her or not.'

The woman nodded and opened her bag. She went straight to an inner pocket and pulled out a 6x4 photo. 'This was taken about a month before we lost contact with her. Nearly a year and a half ago now.'

She handed Harry the photo and he knew straight away that it was the young girl he'd seen in the hospital. There was no mistaking her. She was striking, with a mass of long blonde hair framing a perfectly oval-shaped face, and mischievous eyes that you somehow weren't expecting to be quite so blue. She looked very different now, fighting for her life in the intensive care unit – things had clearly taken a turn for the worse – but it was her, and he felt his heart go out to the couple in front of him.

Marie Sanderson was watching his face. 'It's her, isn't it?'

His eyes met hers just as Beth arrived with two cups of tea on a tray and a manila folder tucked under her arm.

'I'm afraid I think it could be,' he acknowledged quietly, waiting as Beth put the cups down on the desk and then handed him the folder. His eyes were sympathetic. 'But we'll need you to confirm that when we take you to the hospital? Do you mind if I hang on to this for a while? I'll let you have it back.'

The woman broke down, burying her face in her hands as she sobbed quietly. 'It's all my fault,' she said brokenly. 'All my fault.'

Her husband, Harry noticed, didn't comment.

'Here you go,' Beth said, handing them their tea. 'Would either of you like sugar? It might help a bit with the shock.'

Michael Sanderson looked at his wife who had pulled a tissue out of her bag and was blowing her nose vigorously. 'None for me, but Marie takes one, thanks.'

'So, can you tell me your daughter's full name?' Harry asked, picking up a pen. 'And would you mind filling us in on what's gone on? It might help shed some light on a few things that are puzzling us at the moment.'

'Juliet Anna Sanderson,' Michael Sanderson said, and shook his head. 'It's a complicated story, but I'm not sure there's much we can say that'll be of any use to you.'

'You say you haven't seen Juliet in quite a while?'

'We argued. Over a year ago now.'

'And she's how old?'

'It's her twentieth birthday today.'

'Do you mind me asking what you argued about?'

Michael Sanderson hesitated, looking at his wife. 'I think we need to tell them everything, Marie, if we want justice for Jules.'

She nodded. 'It's complicated,' she said. 'If I had my time over, I'd do it differently, that's for sure.'

She sighed. 'We married because I got pregnant at eighteen. Mike was twenty-one. Neither of us was really ready to settle down, we were both so young. Then he had an affair when our older daughter was two years old … and I was so angry, that I retaliated by doing the same. It was only a brief fling; it meant nothing … over before it had begun. When I discovered I was pregnant, the bloke involved didn't want anything to do with it. Not that I would have wanted him to. I think that's partly why I chose him, because I knew he wouldn't want anything permanent. It was a terrible time and a terrible mistake, but somehow my husband and I came through it, and Mike's always had a brilliant relationship with Juliet – treated her as if she were his own. And … we never told her that she wasn't.'

'I take it she found out the truth?' Harry prompted as she trailed into silence.

She nodded. 'My filing system was in a terrible state and Juliet offered to tidy it for me … if I paid her.' She managed a small smile at that memory, then shook her head. 'I can't believe I was so stupid. I completely forgot there were letters in there from me and Mike over that time, trying to work our way through it all. She confronted us with them. She was devastated. Mike told her it didn't matter who her genetic father was; he was the one who'd brought her up, the one who'd loved her all these years – but she was distraught. Wouldn't listen to anything we said. The next thing we knew she was upstairs packing, saying she couldn't trust us, couldn't believe she'd been living such a lie all these years. She said she was going to stay with her friend while she

26

thought everything through. She'd just done her A levels and was eighteen. There wasn't much we could do except hope she'd calm down. We'd always had such a good relationship we thought she'd come round once she'd had a bit of time to think about it, you know? Only she didn't. I think she was just devastated to know that Mike wasn't her real dad.'

The tears were leaking out of the corners of her eyes and Beth handed her a box of tissues.

'What happened then?' Harry probed gently.

'We knew she was okay because we knew who she was with, so although we were upset, we didn't worry too much. We could tell sometimes that she'd been back to the house to pick stuff up while we were out – clothes, photos, even a couple of her old teddy bears. Then one day, a few weeks after she'd gone, her friend's mother contacted us. She thought we ought to know that Juliet had moved out – hooked up with a man and got involved in some sort of religious community. Mike and I were concerned, obviously, so we tracked her down. The people there were quite open and welcoming, but she wanted nothing to do with us. Just stood there and said she didn't want to see either of us ever again. She'd got a new family now.'

Her voice broke.

'That must have been hard,' Harry said.

'It broke us up,' Mike said, picking up where his wife had left off. 'We argued all the time after that. I just wanted to drag her out of there and bring her home, but Marie wouldn't let me. She said we needed to respect her privacy.'

'I was convinced she'd come back when she'd had a chance to calm down,' Marie responded. 'And I thought it better that she did it of her own free will. She knew we loved her – I didn't believe she could stay away forever. She was signed up to go to university and everything. She must really hate us to turn her back on all that.'

The tears spilled over and she rubbed at them with her tissue.

'I'm sure she doesn't.' It was Beth who spoke, stepping into the strained silence that followed, and Harry was grateful to her. She rolled her eyes. 'I remember what I was like as a teenager, a nightmare … but the trouble is, you feel everything so deeply at that age. I had a friend so committed to saving the world that she dragged me off on a walk for global peace, and never told me that it was for five days!'

'That was it exactly,' Marie said, switching her gaze and grabbing at the lifeline Beth was offering. 'Juliet was passionate about everything. The brother of a friend of hers was killed in Afghanistan – any peace march and she'd be on it. She wanted to save the world. That's why she liked the idea of the commune, I think. Everyone looking out for each other and trying to spread good will across the globe. And I don't have a problem with that. It just breaks our heart that she turned against us so completely. How can she not *know* how much we love her?'

'She does,' Beth said. 'It's the sort of thing you know instinctively, even when you're angry. Just like when you're not loved … you know that too.'

Her voice had altered ever so slightly and Marie shot her a quick look before saying gratefully. 'Thanks, love … I hope you're right.'

'Do you remember what this community was called that she joined? Where it was?' Harry asked.

'It's called the Brethren of Serenity,' Michael Sanderson said quickly. 'They're quite active around the country – always on pro-life marches and the like. They've got a big place out Borehamwood way. The women wear awful grey tunic dresses. You must have seen them.'

'And that was the last time you saw your daughter or had any contact with her? When you went to visit her there?'

They both nodded.

Marie looked at Harry. 'Can we see her now?'

'I'll take you myself,' he said, rising from his desk. 'If you wouldn't mind just going back down to reception for a few minutes with Beth, I'll phone Watford hospital – let them know we're coming. '

'We've got our own cars. We'll meet you there, if that's okay? That way we can pick up our other daughter on the way.'

'That's fine.'

Out in the office, Harry cornered Geoff Peterson. 'We've had a lead. The victim's name is Juliet Sanderson and she left home over a year ago to join that commune in Borehamwood. You know the one … the Brethren of Serenity? I'm taking the parents over to the hospital now to see their daughter, and then Beth and I will head straight over to the commune to see what we can find out there. Meanwhile, can you supervise the door-to-doors, and check the market stalls again, for any that might have closed early yesterday?' He handed him the photograph Marie Sanderson had given him. 'This is her photo. Get some copies made up and see if anyone recognises her or saw her with her baby. Chances are her child's at the commune, but we need to know where that baby is and what's gone on.'

CHAPTER FIVE

Juliet

I can't move.

It's been a while now and nothing is changing. I can't even open my eyes.

My heart's pumping with anxiety, and I try to push down the fear as I make myself concentrate. The ringing in my ears is drowning everything out, but gradually, through the din, I'm aware of other noises – muffled and distorted. But I can't identify any of them. I put every inch of effort I possess into raising my hand – it doesn't budge. A ton weight, impossible to move.

I try to call out, desperate for someone to come and help me – but my voice doesn't work either, and in that moment I realise with sudden, awful clarity that I'm paralysed. The only thing that's working is my brain … locked inside a body that can't move. I can't keep the panic at bay as I make one last desperate attempt to break free of those invisible binds constraining me.

Nothing.

Help me, someone! Why can't I move?

Harry stood to the back of the room as Marie Sanderson and her daughter, Lisa, sat on either side of the bed, each holding one of Juliet's hands. Michael Sanderson stood a little aloof at the foot of the bed. They were all distraught and it got to Harry as it always did. He didn't have that close a relationship with his own parents but he could imagine them being equally devastated in this sort of situation. It felt intrusive witnessing such deep, personal grief.

He watched as Marie stared at her daughter for a long moment, then leaned forward to place a gentle kiss on her forehead. 'I'm so sorry, love,' he heard her say in a low, broken voice. 'We did what we thought was best for you. Please believe that.'

'Hey, Jules, it's me, Lisa,' her sister said softly, stroking her hand. 'We're with you now and we're not going to leave you, okay? We're going to find out who did this. You just make sure you get well quickly. We've missed you.'

There was no response and Harry didn't miss the anxious looks that passed between them all.

Outside the room ten minutes later, while they were waiting for the doctor to come and talk to them, Harry bought some coffees from the machine.

'I've got a couple more questions, if you don't mind?' he said, handing the drinks around. 'Then I'll head off and leave you in peace.' He hesitated, but knew it had to be asked. 'I wonder … were you aware that Juliet had recently had a baby?'

Three pairs of eyes swung to his in shock.

'*A baby?*' Marie exclaimed. '*No.* Where is it?' She looked around, as if half expecting someone to suddenly materialise with it in their arms.

'I'm sorry, but we don't know the answer to that. All we do know is that she's given birth in the last two to three weeks. Now we've identified her, hopefully it will be easier to track down her last movements. You mentioned a boyfriend earlier? Do you have a name?'

'No, she wasn't speaking to us at that point,' Marie said. 'We heard about him from Melanie – the friend she was staying with.' She turned to her husband, her expression bemused. 'A *baby*. Why didn't she tell us?'

Her gaze returned to Harry. 'You'll let us know when you find it? You understand, in the circumstances—' She broke off, emotion clouding her voice.

'As soon as we know anything, we'll let you know.'

It seemed the possibility that the baby might be lying alone, abandoned somewhere, hadn't even entered their minds, and he certainly wasn't going to be the one to plant the thought.

'This friend of hers … the one who told you about the boyfriend. Can you tell me her full name?'

'Melanie Brent,' Marie said straight away.

'Do you have her contact details?'

'I've got her mobile number as long as she hasn't changed it and we'll have her address at home if you need it.'

She pulled her phone from her pocket and scrolled the numbers. 'This is it.'

She watched as Harry jotted it down. 'Thanks. We'll give her a call. I'll leave you with your daughter now. If there's any change?'

'We'll let you know,' Michael said.

Back in the car, Beth was busy on her phone when Harry joined her. She looked up. 'How did it go?'

He shrugged. 'I've left them there. She's still unconscious.

32

How about you? Anything new?'

She shook her head. 'Nothing yet, but I've been googling the Brethren of Serenity. They're in Little Ashton.'

'And?'

'They occupy a big old house called Serenity Hall – thirty acres and a community of about fifty people, who live off the land and preach good deeds. One big, happy clappy family. Their ethos is to promote world peace and do unto others as they'd have done unto themselves. They keep pretty low under the radar – nothing negative showing up – and they apparently pride themselves on living a clean, healthy and avarice-free life. That's what the website says anyway.'

'Sounds idyllic! Are you happy to drive?'

'Of course,' Beth said promptly, and Harry grinned. She always said that, no matter whose turn it really was, because the simple fact was she loved driving and he didn't. He saw it as a necessary chore to get from A to B.

'Let's go then,' he said. 'And see what the good Brethren of Serenity have got to say about Juliet Sanderson.

Serenity Hall was impressive – a large country pile with big wrought-iron gates and a long sweeping drive bordered on both sides by greenery, which culminated in a circular parking area outside the main house. It was low-key but remarkably well maintained.

'We do most of the maintenance here ourselves,' Joshua Jarvis told them, not without an element of pride, as they sat in his comfortable office, sipping coffee.

Harry judged him to be in his late forties, a confident, good-looking man, in possession of that extra something usually defined as *charisma*. Not for him the baggy, pale grey 'Serenity Brings Peace' tee shirt and black jeans they'd seen several of the men wearing downstairs. He was wearing blue jeans and a smart round-necked designer sweatshirt that framed his muscular physique in a way that showed it off, rather than hid it.

'It's a beautiful old place,' Harry said. 'How long have you lived here?'

'All my life. Serenity was started over forty years ago by my father, Damian Jarvis. You may have heard of him?'

Harry shook his head.

'Ah well … his name's big in our world but I accept that has limited reach. He died about ten years ago and I took over. Now … what can I do for you?'

'We're trying to track this woman … Juliet Sanderson?' Harry fished the photo out of his pocket. 'We think she may be a member here?'

'Juliet?' Joshua's expression was startled as he looked at the picture. 'Yes, I know her. She was one of our members until quite recently, but she left here a couple of months ago. What's this about? Is she okay?'

'She's in a coma in intensive care at the moment. She was stabbed in Bowman's Market yesterday.'

Joshua looked horrified. 'That's terrible. Who'd do that to her?'

'That's what we're trying to find out. You say she left here a couple of months back, where did she go?'

Joshua shook his head, still looking shocked. 'We don't know – she never left a forwarding address. It was unexpected, but we suspected she may have gone back to her boyfriend.'

'Who was that? Was he local?'

'I have no idea. She joined us a little over a year ago, I'd

34

guess – I remember she'd been deeply disturbed by some issue that had estranged her from her family. They came to visit her here once and after that she asked for a transfer. We arranged for her to go to our community in Northumberland and she seemed happy enough up there for a while. But then she asked to come back.'

'We've been told by her family that she had a boyfriend before she came here? Someone through Serenity, they thought?'

'I believe she was seeing someone at that time, but it wasn't a member of our community. She came here alone after attending several of our meetings. She was very troubled and we gave her some space to find herself. People are free to come and go – she could have been seeing someone on the outside and we wouldn't have known.'

'How long was she up in Northumberland for?'

'Two or three months. She came back to us the early part of this year … around Easter time, I think it was.'

'And she lived here in this house?'

'To start with, but then she moved into one of the cottages.'

'She was pregnant, we understand?'

'Yes.'

'When did you realise that?'

'Not long after she got back from Northumberland. She confided in one of the women and they came and told me. She said she was worried we'd throw her out but of course we don't work like that. I assured her that her baby was very welcome in our community. I did ask her about the father but she didn't want to tell me, she said it was over. I remember doing some maths in my head and working out that it could either have been just before she left here that she fell pregnant, or soon after she got to Northumberland, but either way, she told us that the man was no longer involved in her life and we had no reason, at that time, to disbelieve her.'

'But then you weren't so sure?'

'There was something going on, something that was making her unhappy, but we never got to the bottom of it. Then, a couple of months ago, as I say, she just disappeared and we haven't heard from her since.'

'What do you mean, she disappeared?'

'Well, that's maybe a dramatic way of putting it, but she left without telling us. Just packed her bags one day and left a note thanking me for giving her some space. She gave us a generous cash donation of a hundred pounds and that was the last we saw of her.'

'That sounds like quite a lot of money for someone in her situation?'

'It was, but we assumed she'd paired up with her boyfriend and thought maybe he'd given it to her.'

'And she didn't leave a forwarding address?'

Joshua gave a little smile. 'She'd come here to get away from people. To start a new life, she said. There was no forwarding address.'

'Who was her GP, do you know?'

'She never told us who her family doctor was because he was apparently a good friend of her parents and she didn't want them to know about the pregnancy. But we use a mixture of NHS and private resources here anyway. Dr Janner's our GP, he's attached to the Acorn House surgery but also runs a small private practice, and he normally monitors our members through their pregnancies. We also have access to a consultant obstetrician-gynaecologist at the Oakfield Private Hospital if need be.'

'And did Juliet see him?'

'Yes, she would have had shared care between him and Dr Janner.'

'His name?'

'Jonathan Anderson.'

'Do all your members get such good, private treatment?'

'Most of them – unless they have a serious or chronic illness, in which case we use the NHS. Juliet was due to have a home birth here, all being well. We have members who are qualified midwives and Mr. Anderson would have come himself, if he was available. It makes it a very relaxed environment for the expectant mother.'

'So when she left here, she was still pregnant?'

'Oh, yes. She still had several weeks to go.'

'What would have happened then about her care?'

'I don't know. I assume she signed on with another surgery.'

'Well, she had her baby two or three weeks back, but so far we have no idea where it was born or where it is now.'

'Right. I can see that would be a worry, although hopefully it will be with the father?'

For a moment Harry wondered whether to let on that they suspected Juliet might have been held somewhere against her will, but he decided against releasing that information just yet.

'We hope so but he hasn't come forward yet, so we need to find her baby … make sure it's okay.'

He looked around the room, assimilating the numerous pro-life, anti war and 'We Are One' posters on the walls. 'So, how does all this work? What exactly do you do here? Are you a commune? A religious sect? A political pressure group?'

'A bit of a mix of all those, I'd say. Religion plays the

biggest part in what we do – everything is geared towards doing God's will and achieving the highest order in the after-life. It's difficult to lead a simple existence in this modern age – we've lost sight of the truly important things in life. Everything's about money and power – without giving much thought as to how it's been achieved.'

There might be some truth in that, but Harry couldn't imagine himself dedicating his life to spreading the message like Joshua Jarvis obviously had.

'And somebody like Juliet … how would she pass her time?'

'However she chose. At first she spent a lot of time on her own, I remember, staying upstairs in her room, just coming down for meals, but gradually we drew her out and she became more interested and involved in our work. When she came back from Northumberland and moved into the cottage, she seemed to quite enjoy going out on the streets, attending meetings and handing out pamphlets to people – engaging them in conversations about the state of the world. She was good at that – people liked her. We were sad to lose her.'

'Could we take a look at the room she had here?'

'Well, you're welcome to, but there'll be nothing there relating to her. There's someone else using it now. You'd be better off talking to the people she shared the cottage with, although I wonder if that's something you could come back a bit later to do?' Joshua Jarvis glanced briefly at his watch. 'Two of our members fully initiated this morning and we have a big celebration lunch planned for them. It'll be starting soon – we're holding it outside in the barn. I doubt anyone will be in the cottages.'

Harry hesitated, but it would give them time to check a

couple of things out and he'd rather conduct the interviews in the house where she'd lived.

'Okay, but I'd like to speak to the people she shared the house with, today. What time would you suggest we come back?'

'Well, the lunch starts in half an hour and will take a couple of hours. Shall we say mid-afternoon, around three o'clock? She was in cottage four. I'll let them know you're coming.'

Harry nodded.

'One more thing. You say she went to your organisation in Northumberland for a while. Maybe she met a new boyfriend up there? Can you let me have the name of a contact? We're trying to trace her exact movements since she left home and it would help.'

'Of course. She went to one of our Newcastle houses, I remember. The brother there is Thomas White, I'll give you his number.'

Joshua reached for an address book and copied a number and address onto the back of a visiting card. 'My details are on there too if you need any more help.'

Harry took the card and rose from his chair. 'Thanks.'

'You're welcome. Do you still want to see Juliet's room upstairs?'

'Please.'

But Joshua Jarvis was right. When they knocked on the door to what had been Juliet's room, there was a man in his twenties lying on the bed, reading a book. He jumped up and showed them his drawers and wardrobe when Joshua explained why they were there, but a quick glance around the plain room had been enough to convince Harry they'd find nothing of significance relating to Juliet here.

'I'll see you out,' Joshua said, leading the way back down the stairs.

The large hall had become a hive of activity since Harry and Beth's arrival, with several people chatting and laughing excitedly as they made their way outside for the celebrations. The women all wore a standard grey pinafore dress that did nothing to enhance their shape; their hair tied up in a knot on their heads. It gave an uncanny uniformity to their appearance that was unsettling. Out on the drive there were even more people, mostly standing in clusters talking amongst themselves while presumably awaiting the newly initiated members. Their chatter fell to silence as they stood aside to let Harry and Beth make their way back to the car.

'Well, this feels a bit weird,' Harry said, observing how they still stared as he fastened his seat belt.

'Yeah, isn't it? They all look a bit zombie-like, if you ask me.'

'What did you think of Joshua Jarvis then?'

'Interesting character. Macho-man, definitely!'

'I agree.'

'He seemed genuine enough – a bit whacky – but then you'd have to be to run a place like this, wouldn't you?'

'Yeah, I guess so. How do you feel about going to Newcastle? It needs to be done I think, but I can take Geoff if you'd rather not come?'

He knew she hadn't been back to her home since joining the police, and from what little she'd shared, it wouldn't surprise him if she rejected the idea. But …

'No, that's fine, I'll come.'

'I'll fix that up for tomorrow then. We'll need to head off early.'

'No problem. I never sleep in after six.'

Harry's phone rang in the central console between them. He clicked it on to loudspeaker as Beth started to pull away down the drive.

'DI Briscombe's phone.'

'Ah … hello. It's the patient liaison officer here, at Watford Hospital. You asked us to do a patient record search on Juliet Sanderson?'

'Yes, that's right.'

'We've got nothing on her, I'm afraid. No record before this current admission.'

'Oh, right. Well thanks for looking. We've just found out that she was being seen privately, which might explain it. '

'Oh, good … I'm glad you've traced her. If there's anything else we can help you with, just call, won't you? There's apparently no change in her condition and none expected in the immediate future.'

'Will do, and thanks for the update,' Harry said.

He terminated the call and pulled out his notebook. 'We'll need to check out the GP he mentioned when we get back, and the consultant,' he said to Beth. 'See if you can get appointments to see them, will you?'

'I doubt we'll catch them at work on a Sunday. But we could get their home addresses and call on them there?'

'Good idea. One of us can do that while the other comes back here to talk to the occupants of cottage number four.'

'Would you like me to do that?'

Harry threw her a look. 'What are you saying? That you'll do a better job than I will of wheedling information out of them?'

'No … although you have quite often said that's one of my strengths.'

'You're right, I'll probably only put their backs up. And

41

while that can be useful at times—'

'A softly, softly approach might work better initially?'

Back at the office, Harry and Beth joined Susie Evans, one of the PC's from uniform, who was going through the video footage.

'Anything worth seeing?' Harry asked.

'We've covered all the market and surrounding streets,' Susie said, 'and we've found him, but he's kept his jacket hood well down and there's not a single picture of his face. But we've sort of got a trail for him.' She flicked back a few frames. 'This is where we first see him, approaching from the north side of the market and talking to someone on his phone. Then, here' – she flicked to another scene – 'he's still on his phone, only now he's picking up pace, heading away from the market, possibly because he's received some information on where she is and is acting on it?' She moved on again. 'We've got the back of him on this one, clear as anything, bumping into Juliet Sanderson as she exits the alleyway … and look at her face as she looks up at him. She's terrified. It's obvious she knows him. And then …'

She didn't need to finish her sentence as Harry watched Juliet Sanderson's expression change to one of disbelief as she suddenly clutched her stomach and slumped to the ground, her head hitting the kerb sickeningly as she went down. The man didn't wait to see the results of his handiwork, as he quickly tucked something inside his jacket and slipped swiftly down the same alleyway she'd emerged from.

'Well, if we get our man he'll find it difficult talking himself out of that one,' Harry said. 'It's obvious what he's done.'

'Oh yeah, and if you slow it down, you can even see the glint of the knife he had no compunction sticking into her. And a small logo on the handle. That could come in useful – we'll try to trace that.'

'So who is he?' Harry studied the frozen picture for a bit longer, before shaking his head and straightening up. 'Well done, keep trawling through it. I'm going to grab a quick bite to eat in the canteen before I head off. You coming?' he said to Beth.

'Yeah, I'm hungry and I could be a while at Serenity.'

Geoff Peterson was already down in the canteen and he waved at them to join him.

'How's the market going?' Harry asked, sitting down with his plate of food.

'Slowly. I thought I had a bit of a breakthrough. One of the stallholders reckoned he'd seen her – said she'd tried some clothes on, and when some guy asked if he'd seen his girlfriend and described her clothes, he'd said yes. But apparently by the time the boyfriend went to the changing area, she'd scarpered. At which point he disappeared off in a hurry too.'

'Description of the boyfriend?'

Geoff shook his head. 'Useless. Usual thing – he was wearing a jacket with the hood up, but white and a bit older than the girl he reckoned. Said he might be able to identify him if he saw or heard him again.'

'Nothing else?'

'Not so far. But I'll head back down there later, see how the others are getting on.'

Harry pulled a piece of paper out of his pocket and passed it to Geoff. 'See if you can contact this girl, Melanie Brent, and her mother. She's a friend of Juliet Sanderson's and apparently Juliet stayed with them after she fell out with her parents. They're probably the last people to see Juliet before she joined the commune.'

'Will do.' Geoff took the piece of paper and tucked it in his pocket. 'I'll catch up with you later.'

CHAPTER SIX

Beth pulled up outside cottage number four on the Serenity estate and got out of the car. It all looked rather idyllic. The houses were tucked away in a little enclave off the approach road to the main hall – six terraced cottages that had clearly been occupied by farm labourers in the days when it had been a working estate. There were no front gardens, but the paved area had several little tables and chairs set out, where people obviously sat and mingled. She knocked on the door and waited.

It was opened by a woman in her early fifties, who introduced herself as Sheila Bates. 'Come in,' she said. 'Joshua said you'd be calling.'

She led the way through the narrow hall into a room on the right, where a middle-aged man was sitting quietly in a chair reading the paper.

'Terence, it's the police,' Sheila Bates said.

The man looked up. He looked like he'd been in the wars with a large pad covering a wound to the side of his head. 'Excuse me if I don't get up? I fell down the stairs yesterday and took a crack to my head. I'm not feeling quite myself.'

'No worries,' Beth said, walking into the room. 'That can't have been pleasant.'

'Could have done without it, that's for sure; it's a busy time for us at the moment. Where are Paula and Victoria?' he asked Sheila. 'I expect you'd like to talk to us all?' he added, turning back to Beth.

'Please.'

Sheila disappeared off to get them.

'They'll be doing their prayers at this time of day, I expect,' Terence said. He touched his wound gently and gave a rueful little smile. 'Should have prayed a bit harder myself and this might not have happened. Still … no use crying over spilt milk. Joshua tells me it's about Juliet that you've come?'

'That's right.'

'Terrible business. Why would anyone want to hurt her? She's a great kid.'

His gaze slid past her to the door as Sheila walked back into the room, followed by two young women. Like her, they were dressed in the standard uniform grey dress.

'Paula and Victoria,' Terence introduced them. 'So … we're a full house now, how can we help you? Can we get you a drink of anything, by the way?'

'No, I'm fine thanks.' Beth pulled out her notebook. 'As you know, we're investigating the stabbing of Juliet Sanderson.'

'I can't believe it. If only she hadn't left … she was safe here.'

'Was there any reason that you knew of why she wouldn't be safe if she left here?'

'Not specifically. But she had quite a lot of dramas going on in her family life. She used to tell us about it in the early days, but then she seemed to settle in and we assumed it had quietened down.'

'What sort of dramas?'

'Rows with her parents mostly, her father in particular I seem to remember.'

'And her boyfriend?'

'We never met him. I mean, obviously there'd been someone – but she was very cagey about it. Never said who it was. And that was her right. We didn't press her.'

'Were you surprised when she left? Did you think she was going to settle in the community?'

'Yes … definitely. It came as a real shock.'

'And when did she leave?'

'A couple of months back now, I'd say.'

Beth looked at the women, all of whom nodded.

'So she was still pregnant?'

More nods.

'Was it one of you that would accompany her on her ante-natal visits?'

'It was me usually,' Sheila said. 'She was fine – fit and healthy. No problems.'

'And she never confided in you who the father was?'

'No.' Sheila's eyes flicked to Terence, then dipped away again and Beth studied her for a moment longer, before asking. 'Was she happy about being pregnant?'

'No.'

'Yes.'

Terence and Sheila both spoke at the same time.

Terence smiled. 'She was worried to start with,' he clarified, 'because she felt she was too young and anxious about the responsibility of bringing a child up on her own. But then when she realised we raise all the children here together in a little community, she became a lot happier about it.'

Beth turned her attention to the two younger women, who were clearly quite nervous. 'Is there anything either of you can add that might help us get a better idea of where Juliet's been living these last few weeks?'

They both shook their heads.

'And you never suspected she was thinking of leaving?' More shakes.

'Could one of you show me her room, please?'

'I'll show you,' the older of the two, Paula, offered.

She led the way out of the room and Beth followed. 'How long have you been here?' she asked conversationally as they headed up the stairs.

'I came when I was eighteen … ten years ago. I'd been in and out of foster care since I was thirteen and there was only one way I was heading at that point. Then I went to a few Serenity meetings and came to one of the weekend sessions. I joined up after that.'

She didn't sound particularly enthusiastic, but then again, Beth suspected that enthusiasm wasn't the Serenity way. Not for the women at any rate. From what she'd seen of them so far, they all looked very subdued.

She followed the woman into a good-sized bedroom, bare of any decoration apart from a few religious paintings on the walls. She snatched a quick look around, observing the double bed and further single bed beneath the window. It all looked fairly characterless.

'Are you married? Do you have children?' She asked. 'Sorry, but I don't know how the set-up works here.'

'We don't marry. We can choose to co-join if we like but most people don't bother and pairing is quite flexible. I have a son and a daughter – they live in the nursery hall where all the kids are raised.'

48

'Right.' Beth wasn't quite sure what to make of that or how to phrase her next question delicately.

'When you say flexible, does that mean you can form relationships with more than one person in the community?'

Paula nodded. Her expression had relaxed a little, and Beth got the impression that now they were further away from prying ears, she was happier to open up a bit.

'Sometimes we choose who we pair with ourselves and at other times it's pre-arranged by Terence or Joshua.'

If Beth had had a cup of tea in her mouth she'd have choked on it. Yet Paula seemed totally oblivious to how bizarre and unnatural that sounded.

Somehow she managed to keep her expression neutral. 'Right,' she said again. 'And your children have the same father?'

'No. Terence is father to my daughter, and another man fathered my son,' Paula confirmed and looked sheepish as she added. 'But it doesn't really matter who the parents are … we're all one big family here and they'll be looked after, come what may.'

She looked a little crestfallen as she spoke about her children, moving Beth to prompt gently.

'But they don't live with you here?'

'No. They're being brought up by the elders in what used to be the old stable block, up near the main house – you may have noticed it? It's been converted to a boarding house and nursery for the children, and they get their schooling and everything there. I get to see them quite regularly though, and they usually come here for lunch on Sundays.'

'Isn't that hard for you, not having them with you?'

Paula braced her shoulders and said briskly. 'It's for the best. This way they grow up with the right values in life and a true faith in God – perfect followers. With the life I had, how could I expect to be a good mother to them? I wouldn't know how to be. I'd do more harm than good.'

It was stated with such conviction that Beth suspected it was a mantra that had been drilled into her over a very long period of time – though whether that was a Serenity influence or one from her previous life, was anyone's guess. Either way, it was an indoctrination she could relate to, even though she knew the reasoning behind it was nonsense.

'I'm sure that's not true' she said. 'More often than not, we learn from our experiences and benefit from them.'

Paula shook her head. 'I've had a lot of counselling. I'm damaged goods, and there's no getting away from it. The Serenity mother hens, as we call them' – she allowed herself a little smile as she said this – 'are much better trained and equipped to do a good job. Was there anything in particular you wanted to see in here? I'm sorry it's not very tidy. I'm using it now and I've been sorting some of my things out.'

Her eyes darted around the nooks and crannies nervously, settling with embarrassment on a pile of underwear sitting on her bed.

'Don't worry, I've seen a lot worse. Do you mind if I take a quick look in the wardrobe and drawers?'

Beth moved over to the large double wardrobe and opened it up. There was very little inside, just a couple of the grey pinafore dresses hanging from the rail and two cardigans.

'So, what's the set-up here? Did Juliet have this room to herself?'

'Most of the time. I shared with her sometimes, if we had visitors or anything.'

'But she didn't share it with her boyfriend?'

Paula looked flustered as if suddenly remembering the

reason for Beth's visit. 'No,' she said.

'I don't need to remind you that it's a crime to withhold relevant information in a police investigation?'

'We don't know who her boyfriend was.'

Paula clamped her lips firmly together and it was obvious she'd said all she was going to – was probably already chastising herself for talking too much.

Beth sighed and reached into her pocket. 'This is my card. If you remember anything, Paula, anything at all, you can call me in confidence, okay? Obviously we're worried about Juliet, but even more important maybe, is that we don't know the whereabouts or safety of her baby, and I don't know about you, but the thought of that really upsets me.'

Paula took the card and tucked it into her pocket. Her eyes, as she looked at Beth, had tears in them.

'Juliet and I were close. I hope you find who did this to her. It's terrible.'

'Yes, it is.'

'Will she be alright?'

'We hope so, but she's in a coma at the moment.'

'I'd like to see her when she's better.'

'Maybe that can be arranged but it won't be for a while.'

As Beth turned to go, something crunched beneath her feet and she looked down at the piece of pottery she'd trodden on.

'Sorry,' she said, standing back. 'I hope I haven't broken anything valuable.' She bent down and picked it up, but already, Paula was holding her hand out to take the fractured pieces from her.

'It's all right. It's just a piece of the bedside lamp. It fell off the table and broke yesterday, I thought I'd swept it all up. Was there anything else you wanted to ask?'

'You say you were close to Juliet. Did she make no mention of the fact that she was intending to leave? It seems odd that she'd go off like that without saying anything to anyone. Was she happy here?'

'Why wouldn't she be?'

'That's not what I asked.'

The woman looked fidgety. 'She was happy most of the time.' She shrugged. 'I think she sometimes missed her old life but she didn't want to go back to it she said, and I knew what she meant. This way of life is challenging when you first come into it, but if you persevere …'

'Yes?' Beth prompted.

'The benefits of being part of a large family like this, far outweigh the limitations. You find inner peace, you know? Putting yourself into the hands of God and the community – it takes all the stress away. You don't need to worry about anything other than trying to lead a good life.'

And that *was* the appeal of it, Beth knew – the ability to hand over responsibility for your life to someone else. Her friend Bryony had got involved with a commune several years back during a stressful period, and Beth had read up on it. In fact … she frowned as the realisation hit her. No wonder Serenity had sounded familiar. It was the same organisation – only Bryony's branch had been up in Northumberland, where they'd both lived at the time – where she and Harry were going tomorrow. There was no denying that Bryony had found them supportive over a difficult period and for that Beth had been grateful. Bryony had always been banging on about how much less stressful her life had become since her involvement with them, and how Beth should come along one of their meetings because they were designed for people like them – people with crap backgrounds who needed an anchor in their life. Still … they hadn't stopped her friend from committing suicide in the end, had they?

'Okay, I think I've seen all I need to here, but I'd like to take a quick look around the nursery before I go?'

Beth didn't know what more to say as she followed Paula back down the stairs. It felt that quite a bit had been revealed – and not revealed – in the conversation they'd had. She needed to talk it through with Harry.

It was Sheila who accompanied her to the nursery block and if the whole idea of removing children from their mothers hadn't been so unnatural, Beth would have found the set-up quite impressive. The converted stable block had been turned into a mini boarding house and school, with a nursery for the babies, bigger dormitories for the older children, several classrooms, a large dining room and a couple of what were termed 'rest rooms' where children could relax and play. There was no television that she could see and most of the older children's books seemed to be about Serenity's teaching or religion. But the children there all seemed happy enough and a quick tour of the entire premises revealed no babies under the age of about six months.

'Most mothers stay here with their babies until they're weaned,' Sheila explained. 'Then the mothers move back to one of the cottages.'

'Well, thanks for showing me around.'

'I can see you find it all very strange.'

'Different, certainly.'

'It works well. We're all part of one big family and the children are loved by us all. But I understand it must seem alien to you.'

'And Juliet? Did it feel alien to her? Might that be why she left?'

'I don't know. She was … mixed up. Sometimes very happy, sometimes a bit depressed. But she was a good person and brought light into our lives. I hate to think of her—' She broke off, clearly upset.

'We'll find out who did this to her,' Beth said. 'Don't you worry about that. It's only a question of time.'

CHAPTER SEVEN

Juliet

I'm *so scared.*

How long have I been lying here trapped in my body, awake yet unable to move? It feels like only a few hours but maybe it's been days or weeks. Or even months? I'm in a constant state of panic just thinking about it.

Images bombard me non-stop, but I can never make sense of them. They're like fragmented puzzle pieces refusing to take shape, taunting me. I settle on one, but before I can grasp it, it's gone – elusive memories fluttering around like butterflies that I just can't catch.

But then, suddenly, one is staying with me and taking form. I clutch at it, like a drowning man, desperate not to lose it.

I'm walking down the High Street to the bus stop, smiling. My blonde hair bobs gently around my neck and I touch it, loving the soft, light feel of the strands now they've been cut. I'm not going to worry about the money I spent at the hairdressers because it was worth it and because occasionally, just occasionally, I miss the frivolity of my old life. And really, what harm is there in looking nice?

'Hey, Jules … hold up.'

I look across the road to see one of my old school friends hurrying towards me.

'Mel! How are you doing?'

'I'm good.'

'How's uni?'

We exchange hugs and she feels so familiar that for a moment, I don't want to let go.

'Great! I'm loving it. You don't know what you're missing.'

I think back to not that long ago, when I was at school, studying for my A levels. My friends had been so shocked when I'd joined Serenity, and most of them thought I was mad – but I wouldn't swap the life I've got now for anything.

'So, what are *you* up to now?' Mel asks.

'I've got a boyfriend and I've been living up in Northumberland but I'm back down here now.'

'Cool. Have you patched things up with your mum and dad?'

Her eyes keep flicking back to the bus stop, ready to make a dash for it if her bus comes.

'No.'

She looks at the tunic dress I'm wearing. 'You're still involved with that cult thing, then? Is he one of them?'

'It's not a cult, it's a commune.'

'Yeah, well same thing really, isn't it? Jules, I can't believe you've settled for that sort of life.'

It annoys me how judgmental people are about Serenity. Even Mel, who's probably my closest friend, never got how totally devastated I was when I found out about Dad. But Serenity did, straight away, when I opened up to them about it. And they gave me shelter, picked up the broken pieces and slowly put me back together again. I've found peace there in a way I've never experienced before.

'A commune and a cult aren't the same thing, actually,' I say, trying to hide my annoyance. 'But, whatever ... we just try to do good in the world, help people out and give them a safe refuge when they need it. A better life. What's wrong with that?'

I've heard the words said so many times they trip off my tongue with ease and I'm pleased with myself. The Brothers would be proud of me.

My friend, though, is looking at me as if I've got two heads and I can just imagine her going back to our other mates and saying, 'Bumped into Jules today ... she was *so* weird. And you should have seen what she was wearing – that drab grey dress thing they all wear. She wouldn't have been seen dead in something like that before.'

And of course she's right, I wouldn't, so I can hardly blame her for thinking that. Just for a moment I'm remembering the hours we spent together experimenting with different make-ups, putting fake tattoos on our arms and generally trying to be as outrageous and controversial as we could. But that was before my life fell apart. Though I miss my friends, I know it's a price I have to pay.

'Your mum rang me the other day; she's worried about you.'

'I can't deal with it, Mel...'

'I know ... just thought you'd want to know that your family's missing you.'

'Serenity's my family now. I know you don't get it and it's not easy to explain, but they fill a gap inside me that I never even knew existed. I don't have to worry about anything anymore. My life has direction.'

She gives me a hug. 'Then I'm happy for you, babe. I

just hope you know what you're doing. It doesn't feel right that you've dropped off the radar like you have. I miss you so much – we all do. *Damn*, my bus! Look out for yourself, you know where I am if you need me or want to go for a girlie catch-up.'

She's gone before I have time to tell her that I don't do girlie nights anymore – before I have time to dwell too fully on the loss of our friendship.

My phone rings at the same time as my friend bolts across the road, and I look at the screen and grin. I click the button. 'Hiya.'

'Jules, where are you?'

'On my way back. Just catching the bus, I'll be about half an hour.'

'Right. Just checking you're okay. I was getting worried.'

'Couldn't be better,' I respond. 'See ya soon.'

Sometimes his overprotectiveness irritates me, because even though he's older than me, I'm by far the more streetwise one. But I've learnt to suck it up, because it's kinda cool too that he cares enough to worry about me.

∽

'What have you done to your hair?'

He's looking at my head as if I've suddenly grown an extra one, and I sigh. 'What does it look like? I've had it cut short. Don't you like it?'

'Yeah, but … you know how it makes me feel when you break the rules. How are we going to explain it?'

Sod the rules, I feel like saying – but know I can't. Instead I smile at him cheekily. 'Put it down to my rebellious nature. Tell them I have these weird, uncontrollable moments and you're working on me. What are they gonna do, hang me?'

But he isn't smiling with me, joining in my banter. He's looking worried and it's a look I'm seeing quite often these days. I get how difficult it is for him, having known no other life but this one, I do. But *seriously*, does he really think we'll be banished from the afterlife for cutting our hair?

'You'll have to wear your head scarf when we're out and about ... just until it's long enough to tie back,' he adds quickly, clocking my look.

His arm slips around my waist, drawing me to him, and I begin to feel mollified as his expression eases. 'Sorry. There aren't many rules here, you know that, but singling yourself out to look special is committing the sin of vanity. It's as if you're shouting out to everyone, *Hey, look at me ... I'm so much better and prettier than you are.*'

I've never thought of it like that and I find myself considering whether there could be some truth in what he's saying. And he certainly practices what he preaches. It's one of the things I love about him. He's so fit and good-looking but he doesn't seem to realise it and never swaggers around like some of the boys at school did. He's so much more grown up than I am – in a bit of an old-fashioned way that I've come to love. He's taught me what a relationship's really about. He makes me feel special.

He trails his hand loosely down my side, and I shiver at his touch.

'It's another hour until lunch. Let's go upstairs and make the most of it, eh?' he whispers, nuzzling my neck and the soft hair that some would apparently find so offensive.

As he bends down to kiss me, properly kiss me, I find myself melting into his arms, knowing that this is what it's all about. He's my reason for living now. Between us, we'll work it out. I know we will.

Afterwards, as we lie folded in each other's arms, he places his hand gently on my stomach. 'Shall we tell them today, at the gathering…?'

⁓

That simple memory of his hand on my stomach, jolts me into awareness as I lie in that hospital bed. *I'm pregnant.*

My instinct is to place my own hand on my stomach, to check my baby's alright, but I'm reminded only too brutally that I can't. Is the baby still there? Have I had it? I've felt no movements all the time I've been lying here, but then again, I feel nothing anywhere else, so maybe I can't feel it moving. The panic's threatening to spill over again, and I calm myself by concentrating fiercely on that one memory I do have – and slowly the scene returns.

'I'm not ready to tell everyone yet,' I tell him in answer to his question.

I feel his withdrawal as he draws back to look at me. 'You're not having second thoughts … about having it?'

'No.'

And I'm not, not really. I just feel so confused about everything, and how can I even begin to explain my feelings to him when I can't make sense of them myself? I'd been horrified when I'd realised I was pregnant. And angry. What was the point of using contraceptives when they let you down like that?

And I nearly hadn't told him at all, knowing what his views were. But he'd guessed straight up that something wasn't right and had chipped away at me until finally I'd broken down and told him.

'How many weeks?'

'I don't know. Very early. How can it have happened?

60

You promised you were being careful … and I don't want a baby. I'm not ready for all that yet.'

'Look, calm down. I get how you feel, I feel the same, but ... it looks like it's been taken out of our hands now. I know it's a bit earlier than you might have planned …'

'I can't do it.'

'Of course you can. Lots of girls younger than you have babies.'

'But they're not me. I won't be pushed into it. I won't.'

I was surprised by my own stubbornness and I knew my voice had risen, but I was remembering why I'd left home – how Mum had ruined everything with one careless mistake – me. I didn't want to bring a baby into the world until I was sure I wanted one – knew what sort of life I'd be able to give it. And even though I loved it here, loved him, everything was still so new.

He was staring back at me in shock. 'That's my child in there too, don't forget. Don't I have a say in anything? What are you planning on doing then? Killing it?'

I blanched. 'Don't—'

'Don't what? Say it as it is? You know Serenity's views on abortion. You know mine. We've been on the pro-life marches together – argued our cause on street corners. Are you telling me now that was all lies? That the sanctity of life means nothing to you? That you're prepared to murder our baby?'

'*No.*'

Put like that, I was horrified at myself for secretly harbouring such thoughts. 'Of course not.'

'Well, that's what it's sounding like to me. I can't believe you'd even consider it.'

'I'm sorry … I …'

He was looking at me as if he hardly knew me, and I hated that.

'I need to get my head around this,' he said. 'I get that you're upset, I do, and I know we hadn't planned for it – but I don't believe in abortion and I can't let you have one.'

I nearly retorted that he couldn't stop me if I chose to go ahead, but that wasn't the sort of relationship I wanted. I wanted one where we talked everything through together – like we did in the Serenity sessions we attended. It was what I loved about my new life … the way everyone treated me with respect, as if my view counted. I didn't want to lose all that, and I didn't want to lose him…

Now, as I lie here, my anxiety level rises to a new pitch as I try to remember what happened to my baby. Have I had it? Or – a terrible thought clutches at me. If I'm still pregnant, did it survive whatever the trauma was that has had such a devastating effect on me? Why can't I feel it moving?

The need to know my baby's safe and well is overwhelming, a physical pain slicing through me. I'm trying so hard to think ahead of all this to the final outcome, but I'm exhausted and my brain won't let me. It seems to be making me work through my memories step by frustrating step and as I feel them slipping away, back into the fog of my brain, my last conscious image is one of me cradling a tiny infant in my arms, close to my heart.

Please let my baby be alright.

CHAPTER EIGHT

'Who's going first?' Harry asked looking around the incident room later that afternoon. He directed his gaze at Beth. 'Beth, how did you get on at Serenity?'

'I can't say I learnt anything significant about Juliet, but it was certainly an eye-opener.'

She filled them in on her visit to the cottage and nursery. 'It's just not natural, is it?' she asked when she'd finished. 'Those kids must become completely insitutionalised.'

'Makes them easier to mould, I guess.' Harry said.

'The whole set-up is so weird though. That Terence chap even decides who the women have sex with. I mean, come on, that's gross isn't it?'

'But nothing new on Juliet?'

Beth shook her head. 'Sorry, although it may be worth another visit once we get more info in. I just felt really sorry for the women there. They seem to live entirely in Terence's shadow and I don't think they even realise it.'

'Were they being completely open, do you think? Or did you feel they might be hiding something?'

'Difficult to say because they seem to look to Terence for permission to breathe … and even if they had nothing to hide I think they'd come over as being evasive. There was nothing obvious to make me feel they were lying or trying to cover something up.'

'Geoff, how did you get on?'

'I spoke to Juliet's friend, Melanie Brent. She's at Nottingham University so I haven't seen her in person but we had a good chat on the phone. She was shocked to hear about Juliet – hadn't seen the news, apparently.' He shook his head. 'She didn't have much to offer except to confirm what we already know. She said that Juliet was devastated when she found out the truth about her dad and she stayed at Melanie's house until Melanie headed off to uni, and that's when she moved into the commune. She apparently changed over that time – got heavily involved with Serenity and said she wasn't going to go to university. Melanie said she suspected there was a man on the scene but Juliet was quite evasive about him. All she knew was that Juliet had met him at one of the meetings, but she didn't know if he was a member of Serenity or someone like Juliet, who'd gone along to the session. She apparently bumped into Juliet in the Easter break this year and said Juliet seemed happy. She was still in the commune and had definitely got a boyfriend then. Melanie didn't know if it was the same one or not.'

'That must have been just after she got back from Northumberland then,' Harry said. 'So chances are, whoever that was, he was the father of her baby.'

'I agree.'

'So who was he? And where is he now? Has he got her baby? We need to find out.'

'The trouble is, there's no one obvious we can ask,' Geoff said. 'From what Melanie said, it doesn't look like she kept in touch with any of her old mates or family, so this man, whoever he is, is likely to be either someone she met before she joined the commune or someone in the commune.'

'Which Joshua Jordan denied when I interviewed him, but we need to keep an open mind on that one. How are the door-to-doors coming on?'

'Haven't turned anything up yet. No one recognised her or said they'd seen her with her baby. No one in the pub saw anything. It's a dead end.'

'We'll have to widen the search then. If we could even find out where she *had* the baby it would be a start. We know she didn't have it at Watford, so check all the other hospitals in the area – start with Barnet and move wider from there. Also check any hospitals around Newcastle, in case she went back there.'

'We could also look at baby clinics? New mums often go to those to get their babies weighed and checked?' Beth said.

'Good idea. Get someone on to it asap, can you, Geoff? Beth and I are heading up to Newcastle first thing tomorrow, to check out the address she was living at, there. Obviously, it's Beth's old stomping ground, which could come in useful.' He hesitated. 'I've been holding off doing an appeal about the baby, but it's been twenty-four hours now and no one's come forward. I think we need to release the photo we've got of Juliet, and put out an appeal that we're worried about the whereabouts of her baby. I'll draft a statement and Beth, maybe you can get that sorted with the media and news programmes? Someone somewhere *must* have seen them at some point and know where that baby is.'

'Okay,' Beth said. 'What about you? How did you get on with the GP and consultant?'

'I didn't. Called on them both and neither of them were in. I left messages asking them to contact us urgently, but obviously I won't be around tomorrow. Maybe you could chase them up, Geoff, if we don't hear from them today? Right' – he looked around at the assembled group – 'does everyone know what they're working on? Anyone not know what they're doing? Good. Anything significant, I want to hear about it straight away. Otherwise, we'll compare notes tomorrow evening or Tuesday morning, depending what time Beth and I get back from Northumberland. Oh, and Geoff, one more thing … see if you can get the name of Juliet's real father and pay him a visit. Check if he's had any contact with her.'

∽

That night, as Beth cleared away her dinner plates and stacked the dishwasher, she felt unsettled. Maybe it was the thought of going back home to Newcastle tomorrow, or maybe it was because that, together with thinking about Bryony today, had transported her back to a dark period in her life. She didn't usually allow herself to go there, it was never a positive experience, but when she'd finished clearing the kitchen she found herself in her bedroom, rummaging through her bedside drawer. Ah, there it was.

As she reread her sister's last letter, she couldn't stop her eyes from welling up, just as they had the first time she'd read it ten months ago.

Dear Beth,

Thanks for the Xmas present, but as you can see I'm returning it.

This is a hard letter for me to write, because there was a time when I couldn't have imagined life without you. You were the mother that Mum never was, and the only person to show me love. I thought we were so close. But then you walked away from me. I was eleven, how could you do that?

The reason I'm writing now, after all this time, is because, like you, I'm leaving home. Mitch has said I can move into his house for a bit, and I know you won't be happy about that, but he'll look out for me until I get myself sorted with a job. You've banged on about him in the past, but at least he's still here and in my life.

Don't try to get in touch. I'm making a new start and I'll do it my way.

Have a good life.

Isi

Beth put the letter down on the bedside table beside her and reached for the glass of wine. At least she'd come prepared this time, and it was numbing her nicely.

Or was it? If that was the case, why was she still blubbing over the damned letter ten months down the line? Her father would have scoffed that it was because she was being hormonal and perhaps she was, but it went a lot deeper than that. Isi was right, she *had* abandoned her. She'd tried to stay in touch but her parents had made it impossible and, at the time, she hadn't been in a strong enough place herself to take them on.

She remembered the conversation she'd had with her sister as if it were yesterday.

〜

'But *why* are you going?'

They were lying next to each other on the bed they still shared and Beth was feeling utterly miserable. How to explain that if she didn't leave, she'd go mad, or worse, have a complete mental breakdown?

67

She was eighteen, nearly nineteen, she needed her own space. Needed to get out of the corrosive atmosphere that was home. Needed to deal with her grief.

'I know it's hard for you to understand, Isi, but … I just need to get away. You know how awful it's been for me since Andy and Briony died. I need to make something of my life. It's what Andy wanted for me and if I don't do it now, I never will.'

'But what about me? Who will I have to talk to?'

'You'll still have me. We can talk on the phone whenever you like. I'll call you all the time. And maybe when I'm trained and sorted, you can come and live with me.'

But how naïve she'd been. As she'd come to realise only too quickly, her parents were never going to let that happen.

'You're selfish, Beth, always were,' her mother said. Beth could almost see her dragging on her cigarette and blowing it out down the line. 'You made your choice and we weren't good enough for you. Best stay away, believe me. Now you're a copper your dad and brothers want nothing to do with you. Don't call again.'

And though she'd tried on numerous occasions to call Isi, she'd been blocked at every turn, and the occasional home visit she'd made had been equally disastrous as it became more and more obvious that comments such as they weren't *good enough* for her, were beginning to stick with her little sister, reinforced by the rest of her family.

She moved into the kitchen and put the kettle on, knowing that wine wasn't the answer. She'd made her choice and she had to live with the consequences of it. And much as she hated herself for letting her sister down, Isi was eighteen now and needed to make her own choices too. Maybe one day they'd both be in a better place to work things out, but it wouldn't be today and it probably wouldn't be in the foreseeable future. Beth needed to accept that.

She looked at her watch, glad to see that it was almost time to turn in for the night, especially as she had an early start in the morning. The thought of heading back to her hometown might not be filling her with pleasure, but with a bit of luck, by the time they returned tomorrow afternoon, they'd have some answers and that would make it worthwhile.

Having made her tea, she took her cup through to the lounge and pulled out her box set. One episode of *Game of Thrones* to unwind, then bed.

Just what the doctor ordered.

CHAPTER NINE

Harry arrived promptly at six thirty. Beth led the way through to the lounge and observed him looking with interest at the eclectic mix of throws and cushions and the array of paintings and cartoon sketches on the walls. It looked very different to when he'd been living there, she knew.

'You've made it look good.'

'Thanks. It wasn't hard. The furniture you left me is way better than anything I can afford. It meant I could indulge myself and buy a few knick-knacks.'

Harry shrugged. 'Well, my gran's house had so much clutter in it I wasn't exactly short of stuff. Have you settled in okay?'

'Love it.'

'Not lonely on your own?'

'Nope. It's great to come back to my own space. Do you want a quick drink of anything before we head off?'

'No. We'd better get on. Not sure how long it'll take to drive to Newcastle.'

'Four hours plus, I reckon. I googled it. Just give me a minute to grab a jacket, and I'll be with you.'

When she returned to the room, Harry was studying a couple of photos on the bookcase.

'Are these your grandparents?'

'Yeah. I see them quite often now. In fact they're coming over for lunch next Sunday.'

'I'm glad that all worked out.'

Beth nodded. 'It's good to have *some* family around who don't mind being associated with me.'

'Who's the young girl?'

She hesitated. 'My sister.'

'I didn't know you had one.'

'Yeah, well, I don't tell you everything, Harry. She's a lot younger than me and I don't see much of my family, as you know.' She grabbed her bag. 'Come on, let's hit the road – we can share the driving, but I'll start if you like.'

In the car, Harry strapped himself in and turned to Beth. 'Everything alright with the press release?'

'Yup. It will be on the news today and in the papers.'

'Good. I'm worried about that baby. As far as I can see, there are three possible reasons why no one's come forward. One, which is the worst scenario, it's been left somewhere on its own; two it's been kidnapped by whoever might have been holding her prisoner; or three, she was stabbed by her partner who still has the baby with him. None of them are good outcomes, but as far as the baby's concerned the last one's probably the best case scenario.'

'Let's hope Geoff turns something up while we're in Newcastle.'

'Yeah. Maybe the GP or consultant will have something to add. Which reminds me, the consultant rang last night. He has an all-day operating list today and is on call this evening. I left it that, depending what time we got back from Newcastle, we'd either catch up with him tonight, or see him tomorrow morning at the Oakfield before his private clinic

71

starts. I might need to get you to do that if it's in the morning. I'll need to get up to speed with what's gone on while we're away today and I want to do some research on Serenity.'

'No worries.'

Harry switched his attention to the address for Thomas White on the card he'd been given yesterday.

'28 Portland Road, Gosforth. Do you know it?'

'Yeah. Nice part of Newcastle, about fifteen minutes from the town centre.'

'Whereabouts did you grow up?'

'Not there, that's for sure. A bit further out. One of the smaller villages.'

'No one you'd like to see while we're up here? You're entitled to a lunch break.'

'Nah.'

⤶

Thomas White lived in a large, detached house in a street of similar residences. Harry took it all in as they waited for someone to answer the door.

'Ah think the police are here,' they heard a woman's voice call out in a broad Northumberland accent. 'Will ah let them in?'

'Aye. I'll be down in a minute,' another voice responded.

When the door opened, a woman in her mid-thirties, dressed in the standard three-quarter-length grey dress, welcomed them in. 'Thomas'll be with you in a minute,' she said, showing them into an orderly, spacious lounge. 'Can I be getting you a drink?'

Harry shook his head, but Beth said, 'A cup of tea would be great; milk, no sugar. Thanks. It's been a long drive,' she defended herself, catching Harry's smile. He knew she loved her cup of tea.

After the woman went out, they both looked around the room. It was plainly decorated in neutral colours, but what stood out was the number of wooden bookcases hugging the walls, all of which were packed from top to bottom with books and pamphlets. Harry wandered over to take a look. They were nearly all either of a religious content or self-help of some kind, and he marvelled at the enormous selection on offer. Did anyone actually read this stuff?

'Hi there, sorry to have kept ye waiting … Thomas White. How can I help?'

The accent was broad Northumberland and he was a burly, overweight man, who Harry guessed to be in his mid-fifties. He knew he shouldn't judge from appearances, but he didn't trust people with narrow, shifty eyes and he reckoned this man had them in spades, his beady gaze darting constantly from him to Beth, a smile pinned to his mouth.

'DI Briscombe,' Harry said, showing his card. 'And this is DC Macaskill. We're here about Juliet Sanderson?'

The man's brows had raised in surprise at the mention of Beth's name and he fixed his eyes on her now, ignoring Harry's question.

'Macaskill is it? Are ye any relation at all to Mitch Macaskill?'

Harry caught the quick, nervous glance she threw at him before responding to the man's question. 'Er, yeah … but we're not here about him.'

'Glad to hear it.' The man grinned, nodding his head slowly. 'I know Mitch quite well. Wouldn't want to be hearing he's in any trouble, mind. You be seeing him any time soon? Be sure to pass on my best, won't you, Pet?'

'Juliet Sanderson?' Harry interrupted, bringing the

73

subject back on track.

'Ah, Juliet. Yeah. Joshua told me what happened to her. Dreadful business. I remember her well. She wasn't with us long, mind – three months, mebbe? She'd fallen out with her family and been to a couple of our meetings down South. Found the solace she needed, I'm glad to say.'

'But she moved from down South to here?'

'For a while.'

'Why was that?'

'Because her mam and dad had been to see her. Wanted her to go home. She didn't want to be with 'em and was worried they'd start putting pressure on her. She asked to come up here for a bit. To get away from them, like. Her dad in particular, I'm remembering.'

'Did she have a boyfriend while she was up here?'

'Not that I'm aware of. May have had. We don't pry into people's lives when they take refuge with us. They're free to come and go as they want.'

'Why did she go back South?'

'Found our ways a bit too different to what she was used to, ah reckon. At the end of the day, she was a Southerner and we're not so posh up here as you are down there.' This was delivered with a sardonic smile.

'And that was the last you saw of her?'

'Aye.'

He broke off at the sound of the front door slamming, and a few seconds later, the door to the lounge was flung open as a younger man burst into the room.

'Thomas – we need to talk—'

He stopped mid-sentence when he saw Harry and Beth standing there. 'Oh, sorry … didn't know you had company.'

'No matter, Dean. This is the police. They're just asking

74

me a couple of questions.'

'Right. Sorry. I can wait.'

He hovered for a moment, looking uncomfortable, then looked up as the woman entered with Beth's tea.

'Any more of that left in the pot, Mary? I'll go help myself, if that's okay? I've only got five minutes before I need to be out again.' He was already sidling past her. 'I can catch you later, Thomas, it's not urgent. I just need your advice on something.'

'Sorry about that,' Thomas said as he exited the room. 'Now, where were we?'

The answer to that was a big fat nowhere, Harry thought irritably. They'd come all this way for bugger all, by the looks of it.

'When exactly did she leave? Do you have a record of the date?'

'Well, no. Why would I need one? I can tell you roughly, though … it was around Easter time this year. So … March, April?'

'Did you know she was pregnant at that time?'

'No. She never said.'

'What about boyfriends? She must have had one. Was it someone from here?'

'Nope. Can't say she ever spoke of anyone. I were surprised when Joshua told me she were expecting.'

'So what do people do when they come here? Can you give me a bit of background?'

'Well, we've got a few houses like this around the town – little communities if you like – where some of us live together, and a small meeting hall in the centre of Newcastle where we meet three times a week for worship and to welcome new members. A lot of our day is about getting out on the streets and spreading the word. There's eight of us live here and we have prayer meetings and gatherings every day. We also have a much larger house outside Hexham – not as big as Serenity Hall, mind, but it's our main hub of activity. We grow a lot of our own produce there, for example, and any big meetings or seminars are held there. A lot of our supporters are more casual of course – living independent lives and going about their daily business, but giving donations, attending services and promoting our beliefs where they can.'

'Do Serenity own their properties or are they rented?'

'A mixture. This one's rented, for example, but some are owned.'

'So, if you don't mind me asking, how do you make the money to finance yourselves?'

'You'd have to speak to Joshua for anything to do with big finance. But Serenity's quite a big organisation now; it's been going a number of years. Some of our members aren't short of a bob or two and we all contribute to the fund. And we have a business arm, like, specialising in selling self-improvement techniques for businesses and individuals, teaching people how to make the most of themselves. Here, this is one of our leaflets, if you're interested? We've got a seminar going on in a couple of weeks' time, as it happens.' He handed Harry a small, colourful poster of a team playing rugby, with the heading: *KICK YEARS OF SELF-DOUBT INTO TOUCH! Are you being held back in life through lack of self-confidence? Attend our Weekend Seminar and change your life forever...*

'Sold out,' Thomas said. 'We're very diverse as an organisation but always at the heart of what we do is trying to help people improve their lot. People like the courses and therapy sessions that we run – and they're open to anyone.

Even you guys could benefit with the stressful job you do.'

'Would you describe your organisation as a cult?'

Thomas White laughed. 'Not at all! More a commune – we live together in harmony. But people are free to come and go here, and there's no pressure to keep them with us if they're wanting to move on.'

'You say there are eight people living here. Are any of them here now, to have a quick word with?'

'Aye, I can give them a call if you like. There's only five, mind, that were here in Juliet's time, the others are newer.'

'Okay, if I could speak to them all please?'

But half an hour later, he and Beth were taking their leave, realising they'd sucked the essential goodness out of the residents of 28 Portland Road. No one had anything to add to what Thomas had already told them, and no one apparently knew anything about Juliet's mysterious boyfriend.

'Thanks for your time,' he said at the door. 'This is my card if anything else comes to light about Juliet that you think might help us with our enquiries?'

'Sure. I'll get back to you if I hear anything. And 'ah hope you find who did for her. She was a great girl.'

'*Is* a great girl,' Harry clarified. 'She's not dead, and hopefully she'll make a full recovery.'

⌒

'Well, that was interesting, wasn't it?' Beth said, as they climbed back into the car. 'Wouldn't trust him as far as I could kick him, as my gran would say.'

Harry laughed, handing her the leaflet he'd been given, before starting the engine. 'What happened to police impartiality? But as it happens, I agree. Here, check them out when we get back. We need to find out as much as we can about Serenity – they're the only lead we've got so far.' He looked at the clock on the dashboard. 'Any suggestions where we can go for lunch? I think while we're up here, we might as well check out the place he mentioned near Hexham, but – I don't know about you – I need some food in me before we hit that and the return journey home.'

Beth hesitated, not sure she wanted to revisit old haunts. 'Yeah,' she said coming to a decision. 'There's a bistro not far from here. I don't know if it's any good still, but … go up to the crossroads and turn left.'

'You sure you don't want to see anyone while we're up here? We can easily ask them some questions about Serenity to justify the visit?'

'I don't think so. Thanks, though.'

But in the bistro, as Harry took himself off to the gents, Beth found herself wavering. She remembered Marie Sanderson and Lisa's anguish over the guilt they felt at having lost contact with Juliet; it was exactly how she felt about her little sister. But Isi, at eighteen, wasn't going to be talked around to anything in the space of a lunch break. Was she? Maybe it was worth one more try.

She slipped outside to make the call, reluctant to have anyone overhear their conversation if she did get through.

She found she was nervous as she waited for it to be picked up. She was deliberately using her police phone so that her name wouldn't show up on Isi's call log.

'Hello?' Her sister sounded curious.

'Hey, Isi, it's Beth.'

Silence.

'Look, don't hang up – please. I just want to talk.'

'I don't want to talk to you though, Beth.'

'I know,' Beth said quickly, desperate to keep her sister

on the line. 'And I know why – that you feel I abandoned you. And you're right, I did. But I'm really sorry for that – I didn't mean to, I swear. I tried to keep in touch, you know I did … but Mum and Dad made it impossible. They hate me for leaving and for what I've become. Surely you can see that – that they poisoned your mind against me?'

There was a long silence.

'Isi? I just want you to know that I love you and that I'm sorry I left you. I was in a mess over Andy and Briony dying and I didn't really know what I was doing. I just knew I had to get out of there if I was going to make anything of my life.'

'And I was the casualty of that decision,' her sister stormed angrily. 'You don't know what it was like after you went.'

'I can imagine. Look, I'm in Newcastle at the moment … I could swing by for a quick meet up wherever you are—'

'No! I'm catching up on some work and I'm busy. I don't want to see you.'

Beth hesitated. 'Okay, pet, but just think about it, will you? You know what Mam and Dad are like. I'm sure they had plenty of bad things to say about me – and maybe some of them stuck? Please just know that I love you and I want to be here for you. Did you get the new address I texted you?'

A pause. 'Yeah.'

'Well then, you know where I am. Are you still living with Mitch?'

'No.'

Silently, Beth heaved a huge sigh of relief, but she didn't comment.

'Well, if you want to text me your new address any time – just so I know where you are?'

'I've gotta go, Beth.'

'Okay … just—'

But the line had already clicked off. Beth stared at her phone for a moment longer, then slipping it into her pocket, she turned back into the bistro to rejoin Harry.

'Everything okay?' he asked, as she took her seat.

She nodded. 'Fine. I just gave my sister a quick call.'

'The one that's a lot younger than you?'

'Yeah. We're not close.'

'Want to tell me about it?'

She hesitated. Even though the conversation hadn't gone well, she felt quite elated that she'd actually managed to even speak to her sister. It felt like a breakthrough, even if she was kidding herself.

'Maybe, but let's order first shall we? I don't know about you, but I'm starving.

⌐

It was gone eight o'clock by the time Harry pulled up outside Beth's flat, and they were both mighty glad to be back. The visit to the larger Serenity community had been a complete waste of time, as no one there even remembered Juliet.

'If she was with Thomas in Newcastle, there'd have been no need for her to come here for anything other than the bigger community meetings,' Mathew Fraser, Lead Brother, told them. 'She would have been one of many. Sorry. I don't recall her at all.'

It had been worth a try but the only result for their pains had been an extra couple of hours added on to their journey and they were both more than a little weary.

'Do you want to come in for some cheese on toast?' Beth asked, unclipping her seatbelt.

'Tempting though that is, no thanks; I'll head off,' Harry said. 'See you tomorrow.'

'Yeah, okay.'

He watched her enter her flat then, on impulse, changed his mind. Why had he said no? It wasn't as if he had anything more exciting beckoning him home. And he was maybe getting a bit too used to spending his evenings on his own.

'Hold up,' he called after her, getting out of the car. 'Can I change my mind on that?'

Once they were in the kitchen, she passed him a couple of glasses. 'There's an opened bottle of white wine in the fridge, or I've got some beer if you'd rather? It's in the door. What do you want – cheese on toast or cheese and tomato omelette?'

'Whatever's easier. I'll be grateful for what I get.'

A quarter of an hour later they were tucking into their omelettes. 'Sorry it's only toast with it, but it's filling if nothing else.'

'I'm not knocking it. I'd probably have ended up eating crisps and peanuts if I'd gone home.'

Beth grinned. 'Not much of a social life with our job, is there?' She waved her glass at him. 'Do you get out much?'

'Not really.'

'What happened to that Claire girl you were seeing a few months back? Do you ever see her now?'

'What's this, twenty questions?'

'No. But I reckon you owe me one after me telling you about my sister today. I thought at the time you were quite keen on Claire?'

'I was, but—' He broke off.

'I was kidding, Harry. You don't need to tell me if you don't want to.'

Harry found himself wondering what Claire was up to – and not for the first time these days. It had been six months since they'd gone their separate ways and it was weird how, even though they'd done no more than kiss, he seemed to spend a disproportionate amount of time thinking about her.

'I did like her,' he admitted, 'but she wasn't the sort of girl you messed around with, if you know what I mean? She'd recently come out of a relationship and made it pretty clear that she wasn't up for a meaningless fling. And I got that.'

'And is that all you wanted?'

He shrugged. 'With everything that was going on at the time, with work and my gran dying, I didn't know what I wanted. I don't think I was in the right head space.'

'It must be six months now since your gran died?'

'Yeah, and I've thought about Claire quite a lot, I can't deny it.'

'So what's holding you back?'

He hesitated. 'I guess I don't want to mess her around. I worry what would happen if we started seeing each other and it didn't work out.'

'Then you'd call it a day. I can only speak from my own experience. I loved my Andy, but I didn't know that straight away. It takes time for a relationship to grow, and if she's got any sense at all, I'm sure your Claire realises that. There's a difference between a meaningless fling and two people taking time to explore a relationship.'

Harry took a swig from his beer. 'You're quite wise for one so young.'

'Yeah, well, we weren't all born with a silver spoon in our mouths, Harry. I learned my wisdom the hard way from an early age.' She grinned, robbing the words of offence. 'But seriously. If you like the girl, call her. What have you got to lose?'

'She might have a boyfriend by now.'

'And she might not.'

'Ever thought about being an agony aunt if being a detective doesn't work out?'

Beth laughed. 'I'm far too screwed up for that. Although, I'll let you into a secret … I haven't been out with a bloke since I moved into this flat. Haven't felt the need. Now what would an agony aunt make of that? You know how I was when I first started working down here. Couldn't bear to be on my own.'

'You get used to it after a while.'

'Which isn't always a good thing. Call her, what's the worst that can happen?'

She's right, he thought, when she finally waved him off. What was the worst that could happen?

But he still didn't make the call.

CHAPTER TEN

Harry walked across the car park the following morning. He was late and flustered because he'd spent the last ten minutes trying to reassure a hysterical Marie Sanderson, who just seemed to have realised that her daughter's baby could be lying abandoned somewhere with no one looking after it. As if the thought that the child had been left to die didn't already make his stomach churn enough. He ended the call and walked briskly into the building. It was seven forty-five and he'd scheduled a briefing for nine sharp following a terse conversation with his boss, DCI Murray, who'd called him first thing that morning to announce that he was coming back to work earlier than planned after a short break.

'Where are you at with this attack on the girl and missing baby?' he'd said. 'I've got Region breathing down my neck demanding that we show them we're not sitting back on our arses doing nothing.'

'You know we're not doing that, Sir.'

'Yeah. Well come and see me first thing for a catch up, before your team meeting. Get me up to speed.'

In the building, Harry took the stairs two at a time, knowing that Murray would already be in his office submerged in paperwork.

He was right. His boss's thickset frame was bent over his desk as he sat in his chair frowning at the papers in his hand. He looked glad of the interruption, as Harry knocked on his door and entered.

He tossed his pen down on the desk and leaned cautiously back in his chair, enabling Harry to see for the first time the thick walking boot encasing his ankle.

'What happened to you?' Harry asked.

'Missed the kerb when I was crossing the road. I got off lightly apparently, though I've still got to wear this bloody thing for several weeks.'

'God, that's not much fun.'

'No it bloody isn't. And nor have I been since I did it, which is why my wife's booted me back out to work – if you'll pardon the pun. So … tell me something that's going to cheer me up.'

'I can give you an update, but I doubt it'll cheer you up.'

'Try me. It can't be more depressing than the stuff I've got here from Region on our strategic objectives. Any developments?'

'I wish I could say yes, but we seem to be hitting stone walls at the moment.'

Briefly, Harry filled him in on what they knew so far.

'So, the long and the short of it is you still don't know where she's been living this past couple of months, or who with?' Murray said when he'd finished. 'Nor where the baby is?'

'That's about it. No one's come forward from the appeal we did yesterday, which I find strange – you'd have thought someone would have recognised her. A neighbour at the very least.'

'You're right, and I think if that remains the case, you

have to move more to the possibility that she was being held captive somewhere. If so, where and why? If the commune was the last known address, then I'm sure you don't need me to suggest you dig a little deeper into them. At least it gives you somewhere to start.'

'That's my job for today … looking into their background. In the meantime, we just have to work with what we've got. Beth's interviewing the obs & gynae specialist Juliet was under and Geoff tracked the GP down yesterday so I'm hoping that one of them might be able to throw some light on the last few weeks of her pregnancy, and where she moved to. Maybe they even met the boyfriend. But none of this is helping us find her child. We're doing our best but we can't just magic it up out of thin air.'

'Who's handling the action book?'

'Geoff. He's really organised at that sort of thing. I feel comfortable handing it to him.'

'Well, keep an eye on it to make sure every action's followed up. You were pretty good at that yourself, I seem to remember, but I still had to call you out occasionally.'

'Point taken.'

'Are you managing for manpower?'

'Not too bad. I'll shout if it gets too much.'

'Do that. I'm happy to take a more active role if you need it, rather than have people drafted in from Region but it will need to be desk-bound work. Which reminds me, I've got a meeting upstairs at three tomorrow, it would be good if I had something to report.'

Harry nodded but kept his mouth firmly shut. He couldn't see that happening in a hurry.

Out in the main office, he bumped into Beth.

'You're an early bird.'

'Tell me about it,' she said. 'I was in at seven this morning. I'm about to grab myself a quick fry-up before I head off to see Juliet's consultant. Want to join me?'

'Okay.'

Once they were seated with their food, Beth opened the decorative little notebook that was her pride and joy. 'I've been doing some digging on Serenity.'

'I was going to do some of that myself today.'

She looked up. 'Well, I couldn't help noticing while I was trawling the market on Saturday, that there was a poster advertising a seminar for tomorrow evening – like the one Thomas White was telling us about yesterday. You know … the one about being held back in life through lack of self-confidence? This must be an abbreviated version because it only lasts a couple of hours, but I thought I might go – pretend I'm a potential customer interested in what they do.'

Harry looked dubious.

'What?' Beth said. 'Why not?'

'They'll recognise you straight away for a start. Your hair's a dead give-away every time. What do you think they're going to do … suddenly decide that they've remembered something, and tell all?'

'I'm not stupid, Harry. It just feels too good an opportunity to miss. I can get a real inside view of what goes on if I go undercover, and I guarantee they won't recognise me, okay?'

Harry still looked doubtful.

'Anyway, I'm not sure you've got any jurisdiction over what I do in my spare time, as long as it's not illegal?' she said. 'As it happens, I probably do have issues with self-confidence, and who knows, I might learn something.'

Harry sighed, suspecting that she was right thinking he couldn't stop her. 'Let me think on it,' he said.

Beth looked at her watch and jumped up from her chair.

'Oops, I'd better get moving if I want to catch this very busy consultant at the hospital.'

⌒

As she waited in the reception area of the private hospital for Jonathan Anderson's secretary to come and get her, she scribbled a couple of notes in her pad – just in case her mind went blank like it sometimes did when she was agitated. She couldn't help it. Hospitals always did that to her – even posh ones like this – stemming, she knew, from several childhood visits when one or other of her parents had been over-zealous in their dishing out of discipline. She'd always been terrified that the doctors would find out the truth – that she hadn't been playing with a 'live' cigarette butt and burnt herself, or fallen off a climbing frame and broken her leg, when in fact it had been such a vicious kicking from her father that it had fractured her shin in two places. But now it angered her that no one had questioned what was going on and made her parents answerable for their actions. The latter incident, she'd realised later, had raised suspicions, as she was taken aside a couple of times and questioned about how it had happened. But she'd stuck resolutely to the story she'd been fed, terrified that she might be taken away from her parents and put into a home. Now, as an adult, she couldn't help feeling that would probably have been a better outcome for her.

As she sat there, watching several pregnant women walk past, she wondered how many of those babies would be coming into the same sort of corrosive family life she'd been born into. The thought triggered her conscience even more over Isi. How could she have deserted her sister like that?

'DC Macaskill?'

She looked up, jerked out of her reverie by the friendly voice of the young woman standing in front of her.

'Mr Anderson can see you now, if you'd like to come through.'

She followed the woman through some swing doors and into a clinic reception area, before they headed down a quieter passageway with offices feeding off both sides.

The secretary tapped on one of the doors and opened it. 'DC Macaskill.'

The man sitting at the desk was fiftyish, of medium height, with an engaging smile that didn't quite hide the stress lines on his face as he rose from his seat and extended a hand. 'Jonathan Anderson. What can I do for you?'

'Sorry to bother you – I know you're busy, but we're looking into the stabbing a few days ago of a young woman called Juliet Sanderson?' She pulled a photo out of her pocket. 'We understand she was one of your patients.'

'God, that doesn't sound good.' Jonathan Anderson looked shocked as he took the photo she handed him and studied it, nodding slowly as he handed it back to her. 'Yes, I remember her. Poor girl … what happened?'

'That's what we're trying to find out. She was a member of the religious community, Serenity? We understand you were seeing her privately through them?'

'Yes, that's right.'

'Did you deliver her baby?'

'No. She was down for a home birth there, but she left the commune a few weeks before she was due, and she hasn't been back to me since. I assumed she'd transferred her care to another hospital. I did prepare a medical report in case anyone got in touch, but as far as I'm aware, no one did.'

'Do you have a copy of her records that we could take a look at?'

'Of course. I'll get them copied and sent over to you.'

They both looked up as his secretary walked in. 'This is Juliet Sanderson's hospital number if you want to check her appointment dates,' she said, handing him a piece of paper. 'Can I get either of you a drink?'

'Not for me, thanks,' Beth said.

'Jonathan?'

'Coffee would be great, thanks.' He was already typing something into his computer. He quickly scanned the screen that came up, then looked at Beth. 'As I thought, everything was straightforward. No complications at all – not that you'd particularly expect them in someone of her age. Her last scan was at twenty weeks. It showed she was having a little boy.'

Beth sighed. 'Well, that's one piece of information, I suppose. Does it say when her due date was?'

'Twenty-ninth of October.'

'So that's over two weeks ago … and we know she's had it. What we don't know is where.'

'I remember she liked the idea of a home birth. She could still have gone for that. How's she doing? She was stabbed, you say?'

'Yes, she's in a coma at Watford. Fortunately, they missed her vital organs with the knife, but not so good was that she cracked her head on the kerb as she fell. We're hoping she'll come round okay, though. When she came to see you, was she ever accompanied by her partner?'

'Not that I remember. She always came with Sheila from the commune, but of course I only saw her two or three times. She'd have seen her GP on the other occasions.'

'Did she ever talk about her boyfriend? Mention a name?'

He shook his head. 'The only thing I remember her saying is that he wanted to be at the birth. I told her we encouraged that.'

'So when was the last time you saw her?'

He consulted the computer screen. 'The twentieth of August when she was thirty weeks. Everything was fine and it was left that I'd see her again at thirty-six weeks. That's the appointment that never happened because Serenity rang to say that she'd left the commune.'

'Right. Well, thanks for your help.' Beth signed off on her notebook and rose from her seat.

'It doesn't feel like I've been very useful,' Anderson said, rising with her. 'Do you want to leave details of where I should send her notes to?'

'Yes.' Beth handed him a card. 'And could I have a quick word with your secretary before I leave?'

'Sure, although the secretaries here don't actually do my work. One of my colleagues and I share a private secretary who works for us both from home. She's on holiday at the moment, so Emma, who you just saw, is standing in for her.'

'So Juliet's records are here? Or your other secretary would hold them?'

'The main system here would show any appointments she's had at the hospital or any tests she's had done and then I use a system called PML which is a completely transferrable practice management system for storing her notes and any letters I might write. I have it installed on my personal laptop, my secretary has it on hers, and it's also set up on the system here, so I can access my patients' notes virtually wherever I am. As well as that, I do still keep paper records in a secure cabinet at my home – just in case anything goes wrong with the technology.'

He smiled. 'My wife says it's overkill and she's probably right, but it's hard changing the habits of a lifetime. Sometimes it's just easier to pick up a file and flick through it.'

Beth got that. The computerization of everything at work drove her nuts at times and she wouldn't be without her own personal little notebook for anything.

'Do you want me to ask Emma to come in?'

'No, it's alright, I'll catch her on my way out. When's your usual secretary back from her holiday? We'll need to speak to her to see if she had any further contact with Juliet.'

'She's due back on Saturday. I'll send her details over to you with Juliet Sanderson's notes. I can let you have it all by this afternoon.'

'Thanks, that would be great.'

He shook her hand and his handshake was firm. 'I hope you find whoever did this. It feels like the world's gone crazy with all the knife crime around. God knows what the answer is though.'

CHAPTER ELEVEN

'Right,' Harry said, walking into the incident room at nine o'clock sharp and setting his coffee down on a desk. 'What have we got? Geoff … are you okay to update the Action book as we go along?'

'Sure. I've already got it here.' Geoff Peterson pulled out his own notes and scanned them briefly. 'I did what you asked and tracked down the victim's biological father, Roy Woolman, yesterday. He lives in Highgate – claimed not to have seen the news or heard anything about it, if you can believe that. He said that he and Marie Sanderson had been at school together, which was how they knew each other, and Juliet had tracked him down via Michael Sanderson about three months ago. She asked for a meeting and at first, he said no … he didn't see any point in that, but when she threatened to turn up on his front doorstep he changed his tune and arranged to meet her in a pub at Kings Cross, where they apparently had words. He says he told her he wasn't convinced he was her father and at any rate, he already had two other children, and wasn't keen to take on any more – especially when Michael Sanderson had been only too happy to acknowledge her as his own and bring her up. She apparently demanded he do a paternity test, telling him that her baby deserved to know who its family was, and he flatly refused. She then threatened to confront his wife and kids who, according to him, know nothing about her existence.'

Harry had already added the man's name to the board. 'So what do we know about him and his circumstances? What does he do?'

'He's a taxi driver and his wife's a solicitor. Two children, a boy at university, and a girl doing A levels. He's apparently always been the househusband – running around after the kids, picking up, dropping off, while she worked in the City. Nice house, nice cars … I doubt they were financed from his earnings.'

'So his wife didn't know about his fling with Marie Sanderson?'

'Nope. That was the thing that most concerned him when I asked to see him – that I didn't tell her.'

'Did you ask him where he was Saturday morning?'

'He said his wife's away with girlfriends at the moment and he'd dropped her at Stansted airport at nine o'clock in the morning and was then out and about getting food and shopping for himself and his daughter. A normal Saturday he said, and he got home mid-afternoon. And before you ask – no witnesses that he could remember and he says he was nowhere near Bowman's Market. We're rechecking the CCTV at the market just in case he shows up on it.'

'But a possible suspect, bearing in mind Juliet had the power to ruin his cushy little set-up at home. Anything else?'

'Yes, and this is interesting. He said that Juliet told him that she'd had a massive row with Michael Sanderson when she'd asked him for Roy's address, and that Michael had accused her of destroying their whole family with her behaviour. She told Roy that she'd never seen him lose it

94

like that and he could tell it had really upset her.'

'Funny that Michael didn't mention that or the fact he'd given her the father's address.'

'Yeah ... or the fact that he knew she was pregnant, which he must have noticed.'

'I think it merits another chat with him. Do we have contact details for him?'

'They're on file.'

'Run a background check on him. Anything else?'

'I spoke to Juliet's bank yesterday. She had a cash payment of three thousand pounds into her account in June this year and made very few withdrawals until recently. In the last couple of weeks her account's gradually been emptied, bar twenty pounds.'

'Credits?'

'None. Not receiving benefits, certainly no salary from anywhere.'

'So has she been using that money to support herself? Was it her who took it out, or someone else. Do we know?'

'Not yet. They were ATM withdrawals. Susie's on it.'

'Okay. Beth's seeing the consultant at the moment, but what about the GP? How did you get on with him?'

'He's basically confirmed what everyone else has said, that Juliet dropped off the radar a couple of months ago – she apparently left a message saying she was moving areas and having her baby elsewhere. He assumed they'd get a request from her new GP but that never happened. Fit and healthy, normal pregnancy, blah, blah ... no need for them to be particularly worried about her.'

'Anyone else got anything to add? What about the hospital checks?'

Susie Evans chipped in. 'I've contacted all the local

hospitals and the ones further afield, including around the Newcastle area. She's not registered with any of them. I asked them to give us the names and details of any babies born in the last month just to make sure, but it doesn't look like she registered with a new GP or hospital. I also checked the baby clinics attached to the surgeries – nothing so far.'

'Well, keep looking,' Harry said. 'Geoff, I want you to take over the search for that baby as your personal responsibility. Do whatever you have to do, but we need to find it. In any normal relationship, the partner would have contacted us by now with the press coverage this case has had, and I think we have to assume there's a good reason why he hasn't.'

'You're thinking it was him who stabbed her?'

'It's certainly possible and if that's the case then we need to know that baby's safe. What doesn't sit right is that why, if they were living together, no one else has come forward saying they recognise her: a neighbour, a shopkeeper. We should know where she's been living by now. Was he keeping her prisoner, out of sight somewhere or was she in hiding? I tried to reassure her mother this morning about the baby, but I just hope to God I was right, and that someone's taking care of it. Okay … unless anyone else has anything to add?' He looked around expectantly, but no one stepped up to the mark. 'In that case, you all know what you're doing and if you don't, then just ask Geoff. I'm going to do a bit of research on Serenity.'

⁓

Harry was working at his desk when Beth returned. He looked up. 'How did it go?'

He could tell from her expression what the answer was.

'Sorry,' she said, slumping into the chair next to him.

'Nothing significant. He's sending her medical records over this afternoon but I can't think there'll be anything riveting there.'

She filled him in on what the consultant had told her and Harry sighed his frustration. 'Geoff spoke to the GP yesterday. He hasn't seen her since she left Serenity either.'

'How's the research into them going?' Beth asked.

He turned back to his screen. 'A couple of interesting things are coming out. It seems Juliet Sanderson's parents aren't the only ones to have concerns about them. Several families have lodged complaints, accusing the commune of manipulating their loved ones and encouraging them to break all contact with their families and friends. Some, who were traced, turned out to genuinely want to stay in the community but there are three or four still unaccounted for – people who joined Serenity but then apparently left without a trace for their families to follow. We need to follow those up – see if they're still missing and what the story is behind them. One of them disappeared very recently, a few weeks before Juliet by the sound of it. Her name's Cara Swift. I think we should start with her. Can you do that? Interview the parents this afternoon if you can.' He handed her a piece of paper. 'This is their address and the other families' details are on there too. While you're doing that, I'll head over to Michael Sanderson and see what he's got to say about his argument with Juliet and the fact that he knew she was pregnant.'

⌐

When Harry finally tracked Michael Sanderson down, he was surprised to discover him at the hospital with his estranged wife.

97

'Your office said they thought you might be here.'

'Yes. A lot of my work's client based. I can do it on the hoof and I wanted to be with Jules.'

'How's she doing?'

'No change, but we're staying hopeful. We've brought some of her music along to play and recordings of some of the poems she wrote. Maybe it'll help.' He shrugged and Harry got the impression he was saying it more for his wife's benefit than his own.

'I have a couple of questions for you Mr Sanderson. Would you rather talk outside?'

Michael hesitated. 'I'm not sure … might be better, I suppose.'

'Can I come?' his wife asked, looking at Harry.

'Of course.'

There was a little side room next to the reception desk – the relatives' room the nurse had told him – and he'd already been told they could use that. Once they were seated, he got straight to the point, directing his question at Michael.

'One of my team met with Roy Woolman this morning. It turns out that Juliet visited him a few months back and she told him that you and she had had a big bust-up a few days previously. Can you tell me what that row was about?'

'Mike?' Marie Sanderson looked shocked as she stared at her husband. 'You never told me you'd seen her.' And then as the penny dropped. 'You *knew* she was pregnant?'

Her husband looked uncomfortable. 'She was upset when she found out that you and I had split. She said she'd only come to the flat if I promised not to tell you. I hated the idea of that and I told her so, but in the end I figured it was better to meet up with her than not. I hoped I'd get her to come home from her own choice.'

'And the argument?' Harry asked.

The other man hesitated, his gaze shifting to his wife.

'I'm not going anywhere,' she said. 'Whatever you've got to say, you say it in front of me.'

'It has no relevance to what's going on now.'

'I need to be the judge of that,' Harry said.

Mike sighed. 'Yes, we rowed. She wanted Roy's address and when I wouldn't give it to her, she screamed at me and said I had no right withholding it. She said he was her father – that she had a right to at least meet him. I said he'd had plenty of opportunity to get to know her and he'd never been interested. Why should that change now? She said …'

Harry could tell that whatever was coming next, it had been a bitter pill to swallow.

'She said that maybe the fact he was going to be a grandfather might change things. Might make him want to be a part of her life. I was shocked – not only that she was pregnant, because she was wearing a loose dress and I hadn't realised – but that she wanted to get to know him. To involve him in her life. It was a kick in the teeth. I asked her why she'd want that. I was her father, always had been and always would be. I was the only grandfather her child would need. I reminded her of the special relationship we'd had. How we'd always been so close. It made no difference at all to me that she wasn't biologically mine. And then she looked at me and said—'

He broke off and Harry waited.

'Said what?' Marie asked when it became obvious he wasn't going to carry on.

He shook his head. 'It doesn't matter. It was between her and me.'

'That's not good enough, I'm afraid,' Harry said. 'This

is an attempted murder we're looking at and the possible abduction of a child. You need to tell us everything you know.'

Michael hesitated, then took a breath, his gaze locking with Harry's for a long moment before he said, 'She said that maybe I'd been *too* close for someone who wasn't really her father … inappropriately close.'

His gaze flicked briefly to Marie at her gasp, before switching resolutely back to Harry. His voice shook with remembered emotion.

'I saw red. I asked her what exactly she meant by that … who'd put such poison into her mind. She said she'd been having counselling for her emotional problems and they'd been looking into suppressed memories. I lost it then. Told her that there were no suppressed memories … that if she could believe that of me, then I never wanted to see her again. I told her she'd already done a good job of splitting the family up, that Marie and I were no longer together, so there was no reason for her not to go home to her mum – especially if she was pregnant. But she just repeated what she'd said when we saw her at that place … that she had a new family now, and someone who loved her. She didn't need anyone else. The only reason she wanted to track her real father down was to give him the opportunity to make peace with himself and her.'

He gave a short laugh. 'It was obvious she didn't know Roy … he's the last person to give a toss about any of that claptrap. I asked her if he was to be allowed to visit his grandchild when we, the parents who'd brought her up all these years, presumably weren't – and for a moment I think that stumped her. I don't think she'd thought beyond wanting her father to acknowledge her.'

There was a heavy silence. He turned his gaze to Marie

but if he was hoping for support, it wasn't forthcoming.

'You should have told me.'

'I'm sorry.'

'You had no right keeping that from me, especially now all this has happened. Why didn't you tell me?'

'Because you were going through enough, you didn't need all that crap on top of it–'

'That's always your problem, Mike – you think you know better than everyone else what's good for them, instead of treating people like adults and letting them make their own decisions. I had a right to know that Juliet was pregnant and that you'd seen her.'

'I'm *sorry*. I know I should have told you but I was so hurt that she could even *think* I might have—' He broke off.

Marie shook her head slowly. 'I don't know what to say.'

'Well, maybe you could start by showing me a bit of support and saying you don't believe it. I've done exactly the same for her as I've done for Lisa over the years, you know I have, because as far as I'm concerned, they're both my children. I wouldn't do anything like that, you know I wouldn't.'

'How did that meeting end?' Her voice was cold.

He shook his head. 'I lost it. I know I shouldn't have, but the thought of her spreading that sort of poison to the wider world – can you imagine the impact of that – how we'd have felt? I told her to get out with her filthy imagination and accusations. That if I wasn't good enough for her, then she certainly wasn't good enough for me. I should never have said that.'

This time it was Harry who broke the long silence that followed.

'And was that the last time you had contact with your

daughter, Mr Sanderson?'

Michael's eyes were still on his wife, as if willing her to look at him. When she didn't, he shrugged, turning back to Harry.

'Yes. I lost it and I shouldn't have done. I know that. I was just so hurt.'

CHAPTER TWELVE

Beth took the seat that Cara Swift's parents offered, and faced them both over the coffee table. The autumn sunlight filtering into the room was in stark contrast to the oppressive gloom that clung to them as they waited for her to speak.

'First off,' she said, 'I take it you've still heard nothing from your daughter?'

They both shook their heads but the wife looked at her hopefully. 'Have you got news? Do you know where she is?'

Beth shook her head. 'I'm sorry, we've got nothing concrete at the moment, but we're working on a case that may have a link to Cara. It would be helpful to hear from you exactly what happened with your daughter.'

The woman's eyes widened. 'Is it to do with the girl who was stabbed at the weekend? Do you think that might have happened to Cara, too?'

'I'm sure not, Mrs Swift. There's nothing to suggest that at all and it could be that your daughter's perfectly safe somewhere and simply not wanting to get in touch—'

'But that girl … she joined that cult too, didn't she? They said so on the news. It's too much of a coincidence. You have to check them out, because I'm telling you there's something not right there.'

'And we are. But there are other leads too that we're investigating and there may be no link at all to either Serenity or your daughter. But if you could just fill me in on the details that will help us when we start sifting through the information we've got. Can you just tell me what's gone on with your daughter? How long ago did she join Serenity?'

The woman sighed. 'We don't know exactly. She left home in June last year, to move in with a boyfriend we didn't like – he was trouble, you could tell, and we fell out over it. But we knew where she lived because she left a forwarding address for her mail. When we sent her a birthday card, back in April this year, Saul returned it with a note saying they'd split up and she no longer lived there – she'd moved into that commune, Serenity. We got on to them and we spoke to her a couple of times there, but she didn't want to know. She said she had a new life now and didn't want any contact with us.'

Her eyes filled with tears and she dabbed at them with a tissue. 'Sorry … it still gets to me. We'd always been so close when she was growing up. Can you imagine how that feels to a parent, to hear your child say that?'

Beth couldn't, because she knew her own parents wouldn't give a toss if they never heard from her again, but she nodded her head sympathetically and made the right noises.

'There was nothing we could do,' the woman continued. 'We just had to accept it. Then, about three months ago, she phoned from a call box near the library in Little Ashton – said she wanted to come home and would we pick her up. We were over the moon but, in the middle of taking down the details of where she was, the phone suddenly went dead. We went straight there, found the phone box … but she wasn't in it. After that, we went to the commune – spoke to one of their lead brethren or whatever they call them – a man called Joshua, but he told us she'd left the community a couple of weeks earlier. Gone back to the boyfriend, he said.'

'How did she sound when she spoke to you?'

'Anxious. I asked her if she was all right and she just said she'd tell us everything when she saw us but to please come quickly.'

'So in reality, she could have still been at Serenity or she could have been back with her boyfriend, as they said?'

'It's possible. But after we spoke to them, we went round to Saul's flat and he denied she'd moved back in, though he refused to let us in to see for ourselves. He said it was because the place was a mess, but we didn't believe him, it looked fine from what we could see. That was when we logged the missing person's report down at the police station. But they weren't interested. She's twenty-four, they said, and they had enough trouble trying to track down under-age missing persons. They agreed to keep it on file though, in case anything else came to light.' She paused, dread in her eyes as they met Beth's.

'And now, maybe it has.'

⤻

As Beth drove back to the office some three hours later she felt emotionally drained as she mentally sifted through the information she'd received. It had been harrowing seeing the unresolved anguish in all those parents' eyes as they'd only too eagerly shared every scrap of information they had on their loved ones, in the hope it would finally help track them down.

'Anything?' Harry asked, as she settled herself into a

105

chair next to his desk.

'Maybe.'

'Are you going to enlighten me?'

'Maybe.' She grinned as she pulled out her notebook and flicked to the first set of notes. 'First off, I started with Cara Swift's parents – she's the most recent one to have been reported missing. Quickly, she filled him in and when she'd finished, he was tapping two fingers on the desk, a sure sign that he was thinking.

'Did you get the boyfriend's name and address?'

'Yep.'

'Similar story to Juliet's, isn't it? Right, we'll need to check him out. What about the others?'

'A mixed bag. Next on your list was Alison Maybury. I spoke to her parents and they've not seen or heard from her in five years. She was over eighteen when she joined Serenity, but they apparently managed to persuade the police to pay the commune a visit about two years after she joined because they hadn't been allowed any contact with her. Apparently, after the police visit, Alison called them and reiterated that she was fine and didn't want any further contact. They forgot to inform us and they haven't spoken to her since.'

She consulted her list. 'Next up was Louise Riley. Her parents lost contact with her when she joined Serenity some eleven years back, aged twenty-three. She was quite an activist at the time – anti-war, anti-pollution, all that stuff. She told them that she'd found a new way of life that suited her and that it was distressing meeting up with them because the two lives could never mix. She was sorry, she loved them, but she didn't want to see them again. Her mother tried to get in touch with her about five years ago to tell her that her father was dying and Serenity told her that Louise was no longer with them – she'd moved to Spain with some bloke. Her mum says she contacted as many of Louise's friends and old work colleagues she could think of to try and track her down, but no one had heard from her. In desperation she got on to us but was told that Louise was an independent adult and there was certainly no reason to suspect anything had happened to her. However, the duty officer apparently said he'd make enquiries if he got a moment. Nothing came back from that. She was an only child and her mum said they'd always been really close. She couldn't believe that Louise would drop out of their lives like that without any contact at all, but she said she'd resigned herself to the fact that she'd go to her grave never seeing her again, just like her dad did. It was awful. It would be nice if we could at least put her mind at rest that she's okay.'

'See if you can find out who the duty officer was and chase it up. We need to establish that she's at least alive and well.'

'Okay.' She turned back to her notes. 'The last interview was with Sophie Parkhurst's parents. They were older, and her story goes back even longer – fourteen years. It's also more complicated, in that she suffered from depression and had always had a difficult relationship with her parents. Apparently she started regularly attending Serenity's meetings as a sort of self-help support group. At first, her parents thought it was helping her but then they reckoned she became too reliant on the meetings. One day she came home and said she was moving into the commune because they understood her and got what her issues were. After that they lost contact with her. They were insistent that, although she had problems, she'd never have gone this long without some sort of contact. Apparently, whenever they tried to speak to her in the early days – birthdays and Christmas mainly – she refused to talk to them and eventually they stopped trying. Then, a few years back when they tried to call again, Serenity told them that she'd left and hadn't left a forwarding address. They tried to involve the police at that point because of her depression issues, and insisted a formal record was lodged. But it sounds like nothing was followed up. She was thirty when she joined so it's not surprising. The parents said that, although she'd always been quite religious, they were worried by how quickly she'd been sucked into the cult's beliefs. Brainwashing they called it.'

'Or maybe they couldn't stomach the fact that their daughter chose another life? It does happen,' Harry said.

'Well, whatever it is … it seems their teachings are pretty powerful. If I come in after their seminar tomorrow saying I want to jack it all in and sign up with them, lock me up, will you?'

Beth grinned, but Harry sighed, shaking his head. 'I'm still not convinced that's a good idea. If they recognise you and they *have* got something to hide, it'll warn them that we're suspicious of them.'

'They won't recognise me, okay? I'm a master of disguise and I'll keep a low profile. Now, how did you get on with Juliet's dad?'

Briefly, Harry filled her in. 'It was quite a row by the sound of it.'

'Could there be any truth in her accusations, do you think?'

'Who knows? It could have been Serenity manipulating her to break the ties with her family, or there could have been some truth in what she said that he doesn't want coming out. He certainly didn't like the idea of those rumours spreading, and it didn't go down too well with his wife, as you can imagine.'

'Yeah, not good hearing something like that about your husband. I wouldn't mind being a fly on the wall when they talk that one through.'

Harry sighed. 'Okay, we need to check out and trace these girls, and someone needs to question Cara Swift's ex to see if she's moved back in with him.'

'There's still time this afternoon if you want me to head out again?'

'Yeah, why not. You do the boyfriend and I'll head back to Serenity and question Joshua Jarvis about the girls. We'll touch base here, later.'

CHAPTER THIRTEEN

'Is this going to take long?' Joshua Jarvis asked as Harry sat down opposite him in his office. 'I'm meant to be taking the service in twenty minutes.'

'Hopefully not. In the course of our enquiries into Juliet Sanderson, I'd just like to clarify the whereabouts of a few other women whose parents have expressed concern at not seeing or hearing from them since they joined your commune?'

Joshua sat back in his chair and smiled regretfully. 'That happens, I'm afraid. It's difficult to merge the two lives and once people find happiness here, they can find it difficult maintaining relationships outside the community. It's often easier in the long run for them to completely sever the ties.'

'But you can see how hard that is for the ones left behind?'

'Yes, I can. But we've tried blending the two and it just doesn't work. People on the outside can't accept that maybe their loved ones are genuinely happier here. Now, who are these people? Let me see if I can help you.'

'The most recent one is a woman called Cara Swift. She apparently left Serenity about three months ago?'

'Oh, I remember Cara, of course I do. She'd been in an abusive relationship and came to us to get away from it. Unfortunately, his hold over her was stronger than ours. She told us they were going to give things another try. We tried to talk her out of it, told her that people like that rarely change, but she was adamant that he'd reformed. Can't see it myself. I only met him once, when he came screaming and shouting round here for her to go back to him. I felt uneasy about it, but I couldn't force her to stay. That's not our way. I can give you his address, if you want? We did manage to get that off her.'

'We already have it, thanks. One of my officers is going to see him.'

'Who else is on your list?'

'A woman called Louise Riley?'

'Louise Riley?' Joshua frowned. 'I'm not sure I recall her …'

'Her parents were told she left here four or five years back, to go and live in Spain?'

'Ah yes, it's coming back to me now. I seem to remember that she met some chap while she was walking the streets handing out pamphlets. He lived in Spain she said, and she wanted to be with him. Again, nothing we could do about it. She was a mature woman, perfectly capable of making her own decisions. It happens, you know – people leave Serenity as well as join it, and that's fine. We're sorry to lose them, obviously, but you have to be fully committed to be happy here and if you aren't it's no good to either party.'

'Did she leave a forwarding address?'

'Not that I'm aware of. I can check with Brother Fabian.'

'If you would.' Harry glanced at his list. 'Alison Maybury?'

'Ah, now there I can help you, Alison is still here … I can arrange for you to see her. if you like? No problem. She just doesn't want contact with people from her past life, including her family.'

'Thank you, I would like to see her. And finally … Sophie Parkhurst? Her parents reckon they haven't heard from her in nearly fourteen years. Is that normal?'

Joshua leaned back in his chair and smiled. 'Absolutely. As I keep saying, our way of life is very different, and outsiders find that very hard to accept. They inevitably spend all their visiting time trying to persuade their loved ones to leave here and go home. They don't get that this *is* their home now.'

'Can I see Sophie?'

'Unfortunately not. Even though it was quite a long time ago, I remember Sophie's story well because it was something of a tragic one. She suffered from depression and a fondness for alcohol. At first when she came here, she seemed to find a peace and contentment that she said she hadn't experienced in a long while. But after a while, her issues became more pronounced and she suffered from severe mood swings. In those first few years, she left our community several times. Just disappeared without telling anyone where she was going. Usually she came back after a week or two. She wouldn't tell us where she'd been except to say that she hadn't returned to her parents and didn't want us reporting back to them as she was an adult and entitled to live her life as she chose.' He sighed. 'She was always in a state when she came back and my guess was that she was living on the streets. Then one time, she simply didn't come back at all. We left it a couple of months or so, and I was at the point of wondering if I should report it to the police because of her issues, when her mother rang asking to speak to her again. I explained that she seemed to have left the commune and that we hadn't heard from her in a couple of months, and her mother got very agitated and said she was going to report her to the police as missing. I welcomed that, and the police did come round to see me. They asked if she'd ever threatened to harm herself and I was forced to admit that she hadn't. That was the last I heard from anyone and, as her family were now involved, I was really quite relieved to be able to hand it over to them.'

'How long ago was this?'

'God knows. Maybe six or seven years?'

'Do you happen to remember the name of the police officer who interviewed you?'

Joshua raised an eyebrow. 'Give me a break. Would you, that long ago?'

'Okay. Would you mind telling me where you were last Saturday morning around midday?'

'That's easy. Sadly, I was at a cremation for Brother Simon, one of the older brothers. The service was at Cockfosters Crematorium at eleven o'clock and then we came back here for the wake afterwards. It went on until about two o'clock.'

'And you were there the whole time?'

'Of course, I'm Lead Brother. It's my duty to run these affairs.'

'Thank you.' Harry closed his book and stood up. 'If you could just take me to see Alison Maybury now?'

Harry didn't head straight back to the office after his session at Serenity. Instead, on exiting through the large gates, he turned right towards Little Ashton and Bowman's market a couple of miles away. The market wasn't on today and he parked his car and retraced what they knew of the route

113

Juliet had taken. The first sighting on CCTV was when she hit the market from the direction of the pub. There was a bus stop there where she could have got off and he made a note of the relevant bus numbers, but even as he did it he couldn't help thinking that, with the physical state she was in, someone on the bus would have noticed her and come forward from one of the appeals. She could have come from the direction of Serenity Hall, of course – or one of the larger houses between the market and Serenity. Not to mention the numerous residential roads surrounding the pub and market, where she could have been living. But one thing was becoming evident in Harry's mind and for the first time, he felt he was getting a sense of the situation. She'd been maltreated, that much was obvious, and bearing in mind the physical state of her, it surely had to be one of these more local options? She wouldn't have travelled far, and she wasn't some casual shopper out for a stroll buying her weekend provisions. She'd been trying to escape from somewhere.

And they needed to find out where.

CHAPTER FOURTEEN

A brand new day it may have been, but Harry felt they were getting nowhere as he exited Murray's office the following morning. His boss hadn't been too impressed that he had nothing to add for his meeting with the big wigs later that day, and who could blame him? But it wasn't as if they weren't all working their butts off trying to get a lead.

Rallying himself, he closed Murray's door and headed for his desk with a purposeful stride. He'd actually got home at a reasonable hour last night and apart from the fact that cooking himself some beans on toast had driven home to him how solitary his life had become, at least he'd got an early night and was feeling refreshed and ready to go.

His attention was caught by the side view of a rather attractive redhead talking to Geoff Peterson in the far corner of the office. Who was that? No one he knew, for sure. She seemed quite at home and authoritative as they talked and he found himself wondering if it was someone drafted in from Region, to help out with the investigation. But then he'd just met with Murray, who would have informed him of anything like that.

He saw Geoff indicate his presence to the woman and she looked over. For a moment their glances held, then with a cool nod of the head, she turned her attention back to Geoff. Harry found himself heading over in their direction.

'Geoff?' he enquired politely, waiting for an introduction.

The woman turned to face him full on, her eyes meeting his cheekily as if she knew him, but still it took a few seconds for the penny to drop.

'Beth!'

'Hey … told you, you wouldn't recognise me.'

She flicked the shoulder length red hair back with a grin. 'What do you think?'

For a moment, Harry was speechless. Then he grinned, shaking his head and holding his hands up in surrender. 'Amazing. You look totally different. What is it? A wig?'

'No, I grew it overnight and dyed it! Of course it's a wig.'

'It suits you long like that – not that short hair doesn't,' he added quickly, suddenly worried he might be stepping over the line.

She gave her head another toss. 'Yeah, I must admit I quite like it myself. So … if it took you a while to recognise me I can't think any of the Serenity lot will at the meeting tonight, but I'll be careful not to draw attention to myself if it makes you feel happier. Are you okay with me going now?'

Harry sighed. 'I guess it could be a good idea. What time does it start?'

'Seven thirty and finishes at nine. It's being held at the Imperial in one of their conference rooms.'

'Okay, just don't get converted! We're short enough staffed as it is. Anything new to report, either of you?'

'We've checked out the ATM withdrawals from Juliet's account over the last few weeks,' Geoff said. 'There have been six, each one for five hundred pounds and the CCTV footage we've got shows it's the same man every time – and he's making damn sure he can't be recognised. Jacket with a hood and sunglasses. But he's smaller than our attacker and the jacket's quite distinctive with stripes on the arm and a logo on the front. The last withdrawal was after her attack, on Monday.'

'So she's told someone her pin, or been forced to give it to them. I have to say that from the information that's coming in, or rather lack of it, I'm increasingly of the opinion that she was being held prisoner somewhere. But where and why? And where's that baby?'

Geoff shook his head. 'We're on it, believe me. We've questioned everyone at Serenity and checked out the premises there and we're now trawling through all the hospital and known home births, tracing every single one back to its home address so that uniform can follow up with a visit. We're also checking all births that have been registered in the last four weeks, but it's a slow process.'

'I suppose you'd better check stillbirths and infant deaths as well, while you're at it. Just in case.'

'On it.'

'What about you?' Harry asked, turning to Beth. 'How did you get on yesterday with Cara Swift's boyfriend?'

'I tracked him down at Mendelsons Deliveries, where he's a lorry driver. Having met him, I'm not surprised she left him. Saul Hampton's his name and he claims not to have seen her since she walked out on him over six months ago after an argument. Usual thing … couldn't remember what they argued about but swears he hasn't seen her since. He took me back to his flat in Hatfield. No women's stuff around that I could see. I also questioned a couple of the neighbours. Two of them remembered Cara from when she was there previously but both said they hadn't seen her recently, although one of them said she'd heard a woman shouting and screaming in the flat on a couple of occasions recently. According to Saul, that was probably him having an argument with his sister who's always nagging him for money. He also claimed that the reason he refused to let Cara's parents inside the flat was because he had another woman in there, some random he'd met at a pub the previous evening, and he didn't want them to see her. Says he hasn't seen her since – and can't remember her name. I visited his sister yesterday before clocking off, and she confirmed that they'd had a couple of rows round at his and she said she hadn't seen Cara in months. I'm running a check on Cara's finances which should be through any time now.'

'Good. Well, keep on it. What are you plans for today?'

'I've got a couple of things on my list but if there's anything particular you want me to do?'

'Well, I interviewed Alison Maybury at Serenity yesterday and she confirmed that she's happy there and severed ties with her family of her own free choice; but can you follow up on Louise Riley and the other girl reported missing, Sophie Parkhurst? All Serenity could tell me about them was that Louise had gone to Spain – no forwarding address, and Sophie apparently had mental health issues and they don't know where she is. We need to establish that they're both safe and accounted for.'

Harry turned to Geoff. 'Are the house-to-house enquiries done?'

'Yep.'

'How big an area did you cover?'

'The streets and buildings surrounding the market and general vicinity.'

'Extend it, can you? I think we can assume, bearing in

mind the state she was in, that she hadn't travelled far, so widen it to a mile and a half from the market. It's a lot I know but it needs to be done. See if uniform can spare any more people. Murray's not keen on bringing in anyone from Region if we can avoid it and I agree with him. Much easier working with the team we know. Right, we'll catch up later. I'm going to dig deeper into Serenity. It could be that we need to get a warrant and conduct a detailed search of the place but let's get as much info in as we can first, before heading down that route.

CHAPTER FIFTEEN

Beth looked around the crowded conference room as a tumult of applause rang out, grateful that the sound of it drowned out the noise of her stomach rumbling. God, she was hungry, but she'd been so caught up at work she hadn't had time to grab any food before shooting over to Borehamwood for the Serenity seminar.

It had been a good presentation, no denying that, and the man who co-presented it with Joshua Jarvis was his son, Dean. He was a supremely confident-looking young man in his mid- to late-twenties, who seemed to have it all: good looks and an easy-going charm that she suspected drew fans like moths to a light. But what really struck her about him was that she'd seen him before. He was the same young man who'd burst into the room when they'd been talking to Thomas White up in Northumberland.

He raised his hand to silence the applause as the seminar came to an end and held up a piece of paper.

'Thanks to my father for doing the lion's share of the work tonight. We hope you've enjoyed this seminar. Please do take a leaflet from the table here. It shows various links to our podcasts and other presentations that we give that might be useful to you, both as individuals and companies. For companies we do several presentations specifically tailored to help you get the best out of your employees, and to help them understand themselves. They begin to learn what makes them tick and how this translates to their job performance. We also provide award-winning techniques that you can employ as a company to get the best out of all your staff, and garner more engagement, and thus sales, with your client base. If you want to book a private seminar for your management staff, just give us a call. On a more personal note, for anyone here who may currently be struggling with self-confidence issues or anxiety, you may like to take a look at the residential courses we run in our beautiful country house near here, Serenity Hall. The setting alone is enough to reduce your stress and anxiety levels, and through close one-to-one mentoring over the course of just a few days, we can significantly help you to apply proven techniques to overcome these issues for good. We touched on some of the possible causes and symptoms in this talk tonight and if any of what we've said has struck a chord with you, then you're the type of person who'd most benefit from this sort of residential course. Do feel free to take a look on our website and if you feel it might be for you … do something now to change your life. Help is only a call away. Both Joshua and I are here now if anybody wants to discuss anything we've talked about tonight. And a take-away thought for you all? Just remember that Rome wasn't built in a day – but it was built. Thank you for coming.'

As people started to rise from their seats, Beth found herself remaining where she was, deep in thought. She hated to admit it, but a lot of what they'd talked about had struck a chord with her. She had issues, she knew that. And who wouldn't with the upbringing she'd had? Joshua, in one of his deliveries, had touched tonight on the effects of a violent upbringing on a child, and the subsequent adult that child became … and yes, it had hit home. She reckoned that she, more than most, understood why people signed up to an organisation like Serenity.

But she'd been one of the lucky ones. Andy had come into her life when she was just seventeen and somehow he'd seen beyond the belligerent teenage angst, digging deep and plucking out the *real* Beth, as he'd termed it, with a flourish. She knew without a trace of doubt that he'd saved her.

And then he'd died.

'Are you okay?'

She looked up to see Dean Jarvis smiling gently down at her. The room had almost cleared now, apart from a handful of people who were talking to Joshua at the front of the room.

'*No,*' she wanted to say. '*I'm not. I worry constantly about what sort of a mother I'd make, or partner, or even if I'm capable of committing to a relationship at all – which I suspect I'm not.*'

Instead, she said. 'Yes. Sorry, I was miles away. I'm fine.'

'I've done quite a few of these seminars, you know. I've learnt to look out for and recognise those they're most designed to help. If there's anything I can do? The last thing we want is to feel that we've stirred things up for people and are then sending them away with more heartache than they came in with.'

'No. No, you haven't. I was thinking about a work problem.' She didn't sound very convincing to her own ears, so she doubted she did to his, but he nodded, giving her the benefit of the doubt.

'Well, if you're sure? Here …' He handed her a leaflet. 'We have one of our three-day residential courses next

122

month. People genuinely find them helpful, you know, and they're not that expensive. It's great food and company, if nothing else.'

He smiled at her, and she felt the full impact of that smile. His hair was blonde and he had the most startlingly blue eyes she'd ever seen. It would be easy to get lost in those eyes, she found herself thinking whimsically.

'Dean?' They both turned at the sound of Joshua Jarvis's voice. 'I've got a couple of people to see in the room. I'll leave you to pack all the stuff away.'

His gaze shifted to Beth and she found herself holding her breath, but there wasn't a hint of recognition in his eyes as he acknowledged her politely. 'Sorry to interrupt your conversation.'

She smiled, not risking letting him hear her voice.

'I'll maybe see you again.' Dean said as she stood up to go, and she found herself smiling back at him.

'Maybe.'

As she walked back to her car a few minutes later, she texted Harry.

'Seminar finished and mission accomplished. No one recognised me! Over and out.'

⤶

She was getting out of the shower an hour and a half later, when she got the call from Harry. His tone was urgent.

'Can you get back to the hotel? I'll meet you there.'

'What's up?'

'Joshua Jarvis is dead.'

'*What?*'

'Looks like he's been murdered.'

Beth was back in record time. 'What happened?' she

123

asked Harry, as she hurriedly donned protective clothing and entered the room. Joshua Jarvis's body was lying on the floor amidst a pile of broken glass and scattered debris.

'We're waiting for Edwards to find out. He was apparently alive and kicking a couple of hours ago, but there's obviously been a fight here.'

Beth looked shocked. 'He spoke to me briefly after the meeting, before I left. He was fine. But he told his son, Dean, that he was meeting up with a couple of people in one of the rooms. We probably need to find out who they were.'

'Definitely. Can you get on to the front desk and see if they've got a record?'

'How did he die?'

'Stab wound by the looks of it. His son found him and is in the room next door. Did anything happen out of the ordinary at the seminar?'

'No. It went well. But there were a lot of people there – could have been any one of them. Anything missing?'

'His mobile apparently, but there's a considerable amount of money in his wallet left untouched, three thousand pounds. See if the front desk have got a list of attendees to the seminar while you're there. It's more likely Serenity will have that information, but you never know. Also find out why he booked the room, if they know, and what CCTV they've got?'

'I'll get on to it now. One other thing. Have you met the son yet?'

'No. I'm heading in there in a minute.'

'Well, his name's Dean Jarvis, and he's the same guy that came into the room when we were visiting Thomas White in Newcastle.'

'Is that so? Well, not that surprising I suppose, considering they do these conferences there too, but good to know.'

Dean Jarvis looked shaken as Harry walked into the room next door to where Joshua Jarvis was being examined. There was already a police constable standing in attendance and Harry nodded at him before approaching the chair where the man was seated.

'I'm sorry for your loss, Mr Jarvis.'

Dean shook his head. 'I can't believe it. Who'd want to kill my father? He's never done anything but good for people. Serenity was his life.'

'Is there anyone you know who might have held a grudge against him?'

'No.'

'I believe he met up with a couple of people after the meeting tonight. Do you know who they were? People from the meeting perhaps?'

Dean shook his head again. 'I don't know. He just said he was meeting up with a couple of folk and could I pack up and clear the conference room of all our stuff. That took me a while to do and then I nipped out to grab a burger. When I got back and went to find him …'

'Did you see anyone else leaving his room or in the corridor at any point?'

'Yes, someone was heading off down the corridor towards the exit as I went in.'

'What time was that?'

'I can't say exactly … but around ten fifteen?'

'Description?'

'He had his back to me, I didn't really register what he looked like, but he looked like he was in a hurry.'

'And you didn't see anyone else?'

'No – at least…' He frowned. 'I did see someone come

125

through the swing doors earlier, as I was going out to get a bite to eat. No one I knew though.'

'What time would that have been?'

'Around nine thirty?'

'Can you give us a description? Height, age, hair colour, clothes? Anything would help.'

'Well, I wasn't taking much notice, but he was definitely white, slim, similar height to me.' He frowned in concentration. 'Black hair and wearing jeans, I think.'

'Jacket? Jumper?'

'Sweatshirt, dark. But I can't say for sure that he was heading for my father's room, he just passed me through the swing doors. He might have nothing to do with this.'

'Well, that's useful. It'll help us pick him out on the CCTV with a bit of luck and if he's not involved, we can eliminate him from our enquiry. Is there anything else you can tell us?'

'I don't think so.'

'Would you recognise this man if you saw him again?'

'I might, but I remember his clothes more than I do his face.'

'Okay. Well, if you don't mind hanging on just a bit longer, we're gathering some CCTV footage together now. It would be good if you could identify him tonight to let us get on with things first thing in the morning?'

'Of course. I'll help in any way I can.'

'One other thing. I think we saw you briefly when we visited one of Serenity's houses up in Newcastle? You must have known Juliet Sanderson?'

'Yes. She was up there with us for a while.'

'You know she was attacked and is fighting for her life in intensive care?'

'Yes, my father told me. Terrible.'

'Did she ever mention who her boyfriend was? You know she was pregnant, I presume?'

'No. At least, yes … I knew she was pregnant but not who her boyfriend was.'

'Well, she's had her baby but no one seems to know where it is. I don't suppose you have any ideas on that?'

Dean shook his head. 'No. She moved back down here and last I heard, my father told me she'd left and they didn't know where she'd gone on to.'

Harry sighed. 'Well, obviously we can't rule out that there might be some link between Juliet's attack and your father's. Anything at all you can think of that might help us form a connection between them?'

'None. I can't think of any reason why anyone would want to hurt either of them.'

⌒

'What have you found out?' Harry asked Beth, joining her in the foyer.

'The hotel receptionist says that he apparently hires a room regularly once a month to meet up with what they presumed to be clients, usually on a Friday evening, but he saw two people tonight.'

'What sort of clients?'

Beth shrugged. 'Your guess is as good as mine. Personal counselling sessions maybe? They're heavily into all that stuff. Though you'd think he'd do that at Serenity where he wouldn't have to pay for a room.'

'This could be easier for people to get to – it's presumably why they held the seminar here tonight? Did the hotel have a list of attendees for that?'

Beth shook her head.

'That would be too easy,' Harry said. 'What about the CCTV?'

'We've been able to pinpoint a window of opportunity. The meeting finished just after nine so I've asked for footage of people entering and leaving the entrance and lobby areas between eight forty-five and ten fifteen, which is when his son found him. One of the other Brothers came running out to reception in a right panic apparently.'

'Okay, well let's take a look at the CCTV. The son's given me a description of someone he saw in the corridor and reckons he might be able to identify him if we showed him some pictures.'

'That looks like it could be him,' Harry said a bit later, pointing at a figure on the screen who was entering the hotel in what could only be described as a furtive manner. 'Stop the footage and let's get a look at him.'

The image was quite clear and they studied the man on the screen.

'He's keeping his head down, as if he doesn't want to be recognised,' Beth commented, 'but that's not a bad picture.'

'No, it's not and his clothes match the description Dean Jarvis gave.' Harry took out his phone and took a picture. 'I'll show it to him and see what he says.'

He turned to the receptionist who was standing behind him. 'Do you recognise him at all? Have you seen him before?'

'Yes. I don't remember his name, but he's visited Mr Jarvis on a few occasions. There should be another man on there too – the one who had the appointment after him.'

'You'd recognise him?'

'Yeah. They've both been before.'

They continued running the footage.

'There. That's him,' the receptionist said, pointing to a man with a receding hairline. 'He's definitely been in before, and I'm sure he asks to see Mr Jarvis when he comes.'

'Thanks, that's very helpful.' Harry straightened up. 'Is it okay if we take this footage? We'll let you have it back as soon as we can.'

'I suppose so. I'll tell the owner to take it up with you if he's got a problem with that. I phoned him as soon as we discovered Mr Jarvis's body. He's on holiday in Devon at the moment but he said he'll cut it short and come home tomorrow morning.'

'Could you ask him to call us? We'll need to talk to him.' He paused. 'Actually, with the CCTV … what time did the Serenity seminar start?'

'Seven thirty.'

'We'll need footage from seven o'clock then, please. No harm checking out who attended. And what about the car park, any CCTV for that? If so, we'll have that over the same time period.'

'Sure. I'll get on to it now.'

Out in the foyer, Harry turned to Beth. 'You might as well head off home. I'll just check with Dean Jarvis that the man on the CCTV is the same man he saw, then I'll let him go too and wind things down from our point of view. Not much more we can do tonight until we see what Edwards comes up with once he's examined the body. Early start in the morning though – we'll need to get over to Serenity and start trying to track down who was at that meeting.

'Do you think his death's related to Juliet Sanderson's attack?'

'Two people with Serenity in common, both attacked

129

in the same way? Too much to be coincidence in my book. Either way, Serenity seems to be popping up more and more on our radar. And that's something we can't ignore.'

CHAPTER SIXTEEN

Juliet

There's a change in my condition today, I sense it from the moment I wake up.

At least … I presume I wake up but you have to sleep to do that, and do I? There are certainly times when I'm totally shut down in my mind, unaware of anything. And it's more reassuring to call it sleeping, as what really frightens me is the thought that one day I might not have my 'awake' moments and stay shut down forever.

But today, the hissing in my ears is quieter and the awful distorted sounds are taking on more substance – indistinct voices murmuring in the background. I can't clearly make out what's being said but I can tell they're voices and it feels like progress.

I've slowly been piecing together the fragments of my life, but each new step forward is such a hurdle. It's as if my brain has decided to remember only the things it wants to, when it wants to, the memories fleeting and disjointed – and there's always this sense of foreboding that when I do remember, the knowledge might destroy me. But as thinking's the only function I have at the moment, I've told myself that it's better to do that than risk slipping into an oblivion that I never come out of.

I force myself to relax, pushing the anxiety aside to make room for the memories. I've got better at this each time I do it.

⤚

I'm looking out of the cottage window, feeling so lucky. The view is fabulous with the grounds and tree-lined avenue that leads up to the main house – and it stretches over fields and countryside for what looks like miles. I feel so blessed to be living in a place like this, with the love of my life.

'It's amazing here, we're so lucky,' I say, and Dean hugs me tight.

'I'm glad you like it. It's important that it feels as much home to you as it does to me, but equally as important, is that your baby will get the best care here – and so will you.'

'Our baby,' I remind him gently, and he smiles.

'Of course.'

Then I'm moving forward to another memory. I'm in our bedroom in the cottage, trying to hold back my tears.

'But why do you have to go? Why can't I come with you?' My sense of loss is overwhelming and he's not even gone yet. He's my strength, and when he's not here I feel lost, a piece of flotsam floating around in this exciting but unfamiliar world I now inhabit.

'Joshua's orders. I tried to talk my way out of it but he says they need me up there. It's only for a couple of weeks and I'll call you every day, I promise. Sheila and the others will look after you – I'll be back before you know it.'

'It feels like Joshua's been trying to keep you away from me ever since we got back from Northumberland. We've hardly seen each other.'

'Of course he hasn't; there's just always so much to do.'

'That's exactly right.'

We both spin around at the sound of Joshua's voice as he enters the room and I feel embarrassed at being caught out.

'This young man's talents are much needed up in Northumberland. We have a big business conference being held there with over three hundred attendees. That's significant revenue for us and I'm sure you can appreciate that we need to put all our resources into it?'

I'm cross at my own weakness as I nod and shy away from any direct challenge.

'But don't you worry, Juliet, we have plenty to be getting on with to keep you busy while he's gone. You'll be undergoing stage three of your initiation and that takes a lot of preparation and is probably best done with no distractions. Are you up to that, do you think? It can feel uncomfortable at times, challenging some of the beliefs you've held unquestioningly for so long.'

'God will help me,' I say automatically, knowing it's the right response. And he smiles.

'He will indeed,' he says gently. 'And he'll help you not miss this young man too much, as well, while he's away. How many weeks pregnant are you now?'

'Twenty-six.'

His eyes slide over the contours of my stomach. 'You'd hardly know it, you're very slim still.'

I feel uncomfortable under his penetrating gaze, even though it's the truth. There's a slight bump but not much showing yet. I look across at Dean. There's a watchfulness about him as he looks at Joshua that unsettles me, but then his eyes meet mine and he smiles. 'You'll be showing soon enough and then you'll be complaining about how big you are.'

'Speaks the expert,' I retort, grinning.

But there's no grin as I wave him off.

⌒

It's been a week since he went and despite the fact he calls me every night, I miss him so much. It's not the same here without him. Especially at the moment. It's all so unsettling. I hadn't realised how intense the final stages of my initiation would be. I've been moved out of the cottage where Dean and I shared a room, up into the big house where Joshua and the higher brethren of the community live. I spend the entire time there on my own, part of the initiation process so that I can learn and absorb everything they're teaching me. I feel so lonely and isolated that I avidly welcome my sessions where we spend hours on end analysing my issues and character flaws – praying to God to help me find the strength to identify my problems and overcome them, so that I can be a true asset to Serenity and a valued member of the community. I go on long walks every day with one or other of the elders, who talk to me about the community and how special it is – so different to the outside world where everything is about selfishness and greed. Here, our first loyalty is to each other and God. I've never been particularly religious but now I'm woken in the middle of the night to think about Him, pray to Him, and I'm exhausted. Most of my counselling sessions are with Brother Fabian, but some are with Joshua and he's good at drawing me out.

'Anything you tell me is confidential and between us,' he says.

And I find myself pouring my heart out to him, desperate

to ease the raw pain of finding out that my dad isn't my real father – desperate for someone to talk to, who can help me feel better about it.

In the evenings, he comes to my room to talk me through the day's events and any uncertainties I may still have.

⌒

'This final stage is the hardest, Juliet,' he tells me tonight, smiling. 'But you're doing so well, I know you're going to come through it with flying colours. I can see that you're the sort of person to whom the truth and honesty are paramount, and that's the sort of person we want at Serenity.'

I take a nervous sip from the cleansing elixir that is part of these sessions, a fruity mixture of herbs and spices that tastes delicious and always relaxes me, so that I feel more comfortable about opening up to him. Because I have to admit, I feel completely over-awed by his presence.

'You've told me how devastating it was for you when you realised your parents had been lying to you all these years.'

I nod, the emotions still raw. 'I felt like the rug had been pulled from beneath my feet … like everything I'd ever believed in had just blown up in my face.'

'I'm not surprised – learning that you've been deceived is one of the most soul-destroying things that can happen to a person; it robs you of your ability to trust again. That's why here in Serenity, our whole ethos is based on truth and love for our fellow brethren. Soon you'll be fully accepted into the Family, and then you need never worry again about being let down. Though your path might feel challenging at times, you'll know that there's always someone by your side, looking out for you.'

It's exactly what I want. The thought of being able to

pass over the responsibility of my life to someone else and let them get on with it; to know that I'll never be let down again. And yet his words about being fully accepted into the family panic me. I'm not sure I'm ready for that yet, it has a ring of finality that unsettles me.

'My parents do love me,' I say, not wanting him to think too badly of them. But I'm remembering some of the other things we've talked about in my earlier sessions, how maybe some of my father's love was inappropriate. Like when we'd shared baths when I was little – or when he'd sat on the bed with me, his arm around me as he read me my stories. I don't remember anything inappropriate going on, but apparently as children we can suppress those memories and he's been trying to help me dig deeper into my subconscious, to see if I'm burying anything. It feels dirty and sordid even considering it might be true, and I remember with shame how I challenged Dad with those accusations in that terrible row we had. I feel so disloyal to him. But what if Joshua's right? I feel so muddled about it all.

I'm tempted to talk to Joshua now, to tell him about the argument I had with Dad, but I find I can't. Something's holding me back – like it's held me back in previous sessions. I can't make up my mind whose pull is the strongest, who has first call on my loyalty, Dad or Joshua, and until I know that for sure, I feel I owe that loyalty to my father. Even though he isn't my father.

'Dean's coming back tomorrow,' I say, eager to change the subject, and he looks at me in surprise.

'So soon? I thought he was due back on Sunday?'

'He's got his work done and is coming back a couple of days early.'

'Right.'

136

He leans forward and refills my glass, lifting his own in a 'cheers' motion. There's a sense of purpose to his next words. 'We'll have to speed things up a bit then, so that you can greet him as a fully-fledged member of Serenity. He'll be so happy about that.'

We clink glasses and I drink. I'm aware of that weird, floaty feeling that you get when you've had too much alcohol, but it can't be that because there's no alcohol in the elixir.

'I feel a bit warm,' I mumble, rising from my seat to go to the window. I open it and breathe in the crisp, evening air. It makes me feel giddy and I clutch at the windowsill. Behind me, I sense Joshua rising from his seat.

'Are you okay?'

'Yes.' I give an embarrassed laugh. 'I feel strange.'

'I think that's because it's time. The spirit of the brethren is settling on you; it fills you with the most amazing sense of oneness. Are you experiencing that?'

He's standing right behind me now, and I nod, feeling it's expected of me.

'You're safe here, Juliet. We all love you and want you to be happy.' His hands move up to gently stroke my back, easing my tension. They're firm through my dress, as he massages my shoulders and I want to move away from him, but my legs are like ton weights. They feel sluggish and won't budge. It doesn't feel right, because it should be Dean touching me, but he's not here and I don't know how to handle this.

'I … I feel better now,' I stutter, straightening up and hoping he'll move away, but he doesn't and I can feel his breath in my hair as his arms slide down my arms and he tells me. 'This is the final part of your initiation, Juliet. Everyone loves everyone here, there's no room for the petty emotions that govern the outside world, like jealousy, possessiveness, greed. Those are the emotions that spark unrest and war, they're why there's so much conflict in the world.'

He's right, I know. We've talked about it so often in our sessions this past week that I can quote him and Brother Fabian almost word for word.

'You're carrying Dean's baby, but to make it a true disciple of the brethren, one born to go on to lead in the future, you need to be filled by my spirit too, so that it can spread to your child. You understand what I'm saying?'

His hands slide around to gently stroke my stomach and he draws me back against him, so that I'm left in no doubt as to what he's saying. 'You can have a preferred co-partner here,' he says, just so I'm in no doubt, 'but you know there's no exclusivity. We are one as a family and we give our love to all.'

His words bring back a memory of something Sheila said to me when I was talking to her about how much I missed Dean when he was away.

'Don't get too fond of him,' she'd said.

'What do you mean? Of course I'm fond of him, we love each other.'

She'd shaken her head. 'Things work differently in Serenity, Juliet. We are as one, with no boundaries separating us from each other, or binding us to one person in particular. Remember that.'

How could I forget it? There are posters and signs everywhere, with *WE ARE ONE* boldly emblazoned on them. It's our mantra.

'We're one community, one family, where everyone loves everyone,' she'd added. 'It's core to our belief. Sometimes

138

we have to make decisions … accept things … that are difficult at first.'

'What sort of things?'

'The sorts of things you'll learn about with Joshua in your sessions.'

But so far, my sessions with Joshua have consisted of talking about my childhood, my relationship with my parents and sister – helping me to come to terms with their lies and deception. Now, with his arms holding me possessively, I realise exactly what she was saying.

'I'm not ready,' I whisper. I feel confused. What happened to the opinionated, independent person I used to be? Suddenly I want my mum and dad. But only Joshua is here, still stroking my body, so that I'm almost getting used to his touch, despite the fact that I don't want to.

For a moment, there's space to breathe as he moves away from me, but he's back before I've realised it, my glass in his hand.

'Finish this,' he says, turning me around to face him, 'it'll help you relax.'

My eyes lock with his … always that startlingly deep blue like Dean's, yet never more vivid and compelling than they are now.

'Drink it,' he says again.

And I do.

Afterwards, as I lie alone in my bed, my cheek wet from my tears, all I can think is.

What have I done?

CHAPTER SEVENTEEN

When Harry was shown into one of Serenity's offices the following day, he found Dean, sitting at the desk going through some papers.

He jumped up as soon as he saw Harry. 'Have you got any news?'

'Not yet. Sorry, it takes a while for these things to come together.' He looked around the room but no one else was there. Dean indicated a visitor's chair for Harry to sit in, and sat back down himself.

'I've got a few questions for whoever's taking over here?'

'Well, it looks like that might be me, although it has to go through the Committee first. This is a lot earlier than any of us had expected.'

He seemed more composed this morning, his emotions more contained. There was a determined look on his face as he asked. 'How can I help? If I don't know the answer, I'll find someone who does.'

'You said your father had no enemies that you knew of?'

'No. Quite the opposite, he was popular – although there are people out there, of course, who think we're a bunch of nutters – and we've been targeted on the streets and the like. But murder? That's a whole different story, isn't it?'

'Nothing unusual happened in the meeting?'

Dean shook his head.

'Have you managed to find out yet, who he had the appointments with last night?'

Again, Dean shook his head. He opened a diary on the desk in front of him and pushed it towards Harry. 'This is his desk diary and there's nothing in it for last night, apart from the seminar. He does also keep a calendar with appointments on his phone, but as you know that's gone missing.'

Harry spent a couple of minutes studying the pages, then looked at Dean. 'Can I keep this?'

'Sure.'

'The hotel told us he regularly booked a room there to meet people, usually on a Friday, but there don't seem to be any corresponding entries in here? Any idea what those meetings were about?'

'I don't know for sure because I'm not involved in the day-to-day running of the place, but I think he'd sometimes see clients there for counselling sessions. He was a trained psychotherapist and hypnotherapist, as quite a few of us are. He regularly saw people on a confidential basis. Which reminds me … you asked me last night if anything had been stolen and I said his mobile. But I realised after you'd gone that he would have had his laptop with him too, if he was seeing people. I checked in here and in his room, but can't find it. So it looks like that might have been taken as well.'

'Would his client list have been on that?'

'Probably, although he has a host of physical files for clients too.' He got up from his chair and moved across the room to a large filing cabinet, pulling out the drawers one by one to reveal a string of manila folders. 'The current ones are all here but we've got a load more that have been archived if you need to see them too. I'm not sure what the legalities are surrounding client confidentiality though, and I'd like to take advice on that. People might not be happy about their private lives being passed over to you.'

'Okay, but we can get a warrant if we need to and if you want us to find your father's murderer, then the sooner we find out who he saw last night, the better. Perhaps you could just give us a note of the names and addresses – that won't be revealing anything too sensitive.'

'Okay. I'll get on to it urgently.'

'Do you have a list of the attendees for the meeting last night? I presume you have a bookings process of some sort?'

'Of course. I've already got that sorted for you.'

He moved back to his desk and handed over a list of names. Harry glanced at the total. One hundred and five of them.

His phone rang and he smiled at Dean apologetically as he reached into his pocket to pull it out. It was Beth.

'Thought you'd like to know we've got an ID on the chap Dean Jarvis saw in the corridor? We've just gone through the car park CCTV from the hotel and we managed to see him getting out of his car at nine fifteen and getting back in at ten past ten. Interestingly, there's no footage of him leaving the hotel foyer though, we just pick him up once he's approaching his car in the car park. We got the number plate and it's registered to a William Blake, of 34 Wyndsweep Drive, Borehamwood. Shall I head on over there?'

Harry scribbled the address in his notebook. 'Yes, but wait for me outside, we'll do it together. I can meet you there in about half an hour.'

'No worries. We also got an ID off the same footage on the other guy that the receptionist recognised – the bald one?

His name's Daniel Jefferson. He arrived just after nine thirty, and left about forty minutes later.'

'So he and the other chap overlapped for a while? On second thoughts, to make it more efficient, why don't you go and see him and I'll do William Blake? We can compare notes later.'

'Cool. I just spoke to Geoff and he asked me to tell you he's in the Serenity car park with Rob waiting for you to give the go-ahead for them to start trawling through Joshua Jarvis's records and computer. Are you ready for them yet?'

'Yes, tell them to come up now.'

Harry clicked his phone off and ran an eye over the list of attendees Dean had given him for the meeting last night. There was no William Blake or Daniel Jefferson that he could see.

He got up from his chair. 'Looks like we've got a lead on the guy you identified in the corridor. His name's William Blake. Ring any bells?'

Dean shook his head.

'Can I take a quick look in that filing cabinet to see if there's a file on him? We're going to interview him now. I'll let you know if we learn anything new.'

'Sure, but again … just to see if it's there? I wouldn't be happy at this stage letting you read the contents.'

'Fine.'

Dean moved back to the cabinet and flicked through the suspension files in the top drawer. 'They're in alphabetical order so Blake should be here, but …' He shook his head. 'Nope, can't see anything.'

Harry was standing at his shoulder and could see for himself that there was nothing there. 'What about a Daniel Jefferson?'

Dean opened the second drawer down and again shook his head.

'Sorry. Nothing.'

'No worries. A couple of my team are on their way up to go through Joshua's stuff. They'll want to bring back things like his desktop computer and anything they find that might produce a link to his attacker last night. Do you have any objection to that?'

'No. Not if it might help you find his murderer.'

He accompanied Harry to the door. 'I've got to start thinking about my father's funeral, I guess. Any idea when his ... he'll be released?'

'There'll be a post-mortem and it could be a while, but we'll let you know as soon as we can. In the meantime – any information you can dig out on those meetings he had after the seminar would be very helpful.'

'I'll have a word with some of the other brothers – see if they've got anything to add.'

'Thank you. One final thing.' Harry's look was penetrating. 'How well did you know Juliet Sanderson?'

'Quite well while she was up in Newcastle with us.'

'Did you have a relationship with her, by any chance?'

Dean's hesitation was almost imperceptible. 'If you mean did we pair, then yes we did, a few times ... although you have to realise that here in Serenity there's no exclusivity. It's part of our ethos that love is shared freely within the community, so although Juliet and I did pair up, she may well also have paired with one or two others, as did I.'

There wasn't a hint of awkwardness in the man's eyes. It was obvious, that to him this was nothing out of the ordinary.

'When was the last time you saw her?'

'A couple of months back, when I came back down this

way for a while.'

'Were you the father of her baby?'

The question was direct and Dean blinked, but his response was immediate. 'She wouldn't say who the father was but that wasn't seen as an issue. All the children here get brought up in the nursery community under one umbrella anyway, so who the parents are is actually of little relevance.'

'Unless your Joshua Jarvis's son – or yours perhaps – and destined for greater things?'

'I'm one of fourteen children that Joshua fathered. I don't have a divine right of passage, and although my father made it clear his preference was for me to succeed him, he never favoured me. As I said, my appointment still has to be approved.'

He smiled almost pityingly at the look on Harry's face. 'I realise that it all sounds very different to what you're used to but it's a system that's worked well for a number of years now and it certainly hasn't done me any harm.'

'You say that Juliet … paired with other people? Can you give me names?'

'I said she may have done. She never spoke about it with me and I never asked.'

'Do you think the father of her baby was someone at Serenity?'

'I only know what my father told me. That he suspected it was someone from outside and that was why she left. Is there anything else you need to know? I have got rather a lot to get on with.'

⤿

Thirty-four Wyndsweep Drive, was a modern semi-detached house in a neat little cul-de-sac. A woman was watering

145

her plants in the front garden as Harry approached, and he smiled at the sight of the little boy at her side with a watering can of his own.

'Mrs Blake?'

She looked up at him enquiringly. Now he was closer he saw she was a bit older than he'd first thought, maybe early forties.

'Who wants to know?' she said with a grin, wiping her hands down her leg.

'My name's Detective Inspector Briscombe, I was wondering if your husband's around at all?'

Her look became more guarded. 'He's working. Is everything alright?'

'Fine. I just wanted to ask him a couple of questions about a man called Joshua Jarvis? Does the name mean anything to you?'

She shook her head. 'No. Should it?'

'Not necessarily, but Mr Jarvis was killed last night and we have reason to believe that your husband may have been one of the last people to see him alive?'

'God!' She looked shocked. 'When you say killed?'

'He was murdered. I'm sorry, we'd just like to eliminate your husband from our enquiries. Were you aware that he'd seen Mr Jarvis last night?'

'Uh, he may have done … I'm not sure. Give me a minute can you … my mind's gone blank. It's not every day you have the police turn up on your doorstep.'

'Where can I find your husband?'

Her eyes flashed to the van parked on the drive and then back to Harry. 'Out in his shed in the garden, I expect. He's a carpenter and working from home today. Tommy … don't put that plant in your mouth, please. Come with Mummy,

146

we're going to show this nice man where Daddy is.'

Harry followed her down the side of the house and through a gate into the back garden. He could hear music playing, the sound coming from a large, modern shed at the bottom of the garden.

Mrs Blake walked up to the door and tapped loudly on it. 'Bill?'

The door opened and a dark-haired man looked first at his wife and then at Harry, questioningly.

'It's the police,' his wife said. 'They've got some questions about Joshua Jarvis?'

Harry would have had to be blind not to see that the name clearly registered with Bill Blake.

'What about him?'

'You saw him last night.' Harry made it sound a statement rather than a question.

'So?'

'You were one of the last people to see him alive. He was murdered last night.'

'*What?*' Bill Blake looked thunderstruck. 'Shit. Who by?'

Harry shook his head. 'We're trying to find that out. Can we maybe go into the house? I need to ask you a couple of questions.'

'Of course.'

'I'll get the kettle on,' his wife said quickly, turning to lead the way back into the house. 'You can stay out here on your bike, Tommy. But not on the climbing frame without me or Daddy watching you, poppet, okay?'

In the house Bill Blake led Harry into a large through-lounge. He was visibly disturbed, but whether by the news or Harry's presence was hard to tell. His phone rang and he glanced at the display and frowned. He looked at Harry.

'Sorry, I probably need to take this, if that's okay?'

'Sure.'

The man moved up to the other end of the room and Harry cast a quick look around him while he waited. Nothing out of the ordinary, the usual pictures of Bill, his wife and child marking various events of their lives. The conversation in the other room was brief and it was barely half a minute before Bill was clicking off his phone and returning to Harry. 'Sorry about that, a delivery issue. Where were we?'

'You saw Joshua Jarvis last night?'

Bill hesitated, then shrugged. 'I did, but I didn't kill him.'

'Do you mind telling me what your meeting was about? I believe you met up fairly regularly?'

They both looked up as Mrs Blake came in with a tray. 'Milk and sugar?' she directed at Harry.

'Just milk, thanks.'

She handed him a mug. 'Help yourself to biscuits. Am I alright to stay or do you want to talk to Bill alone?'

'I'd prefer to speak to you separately at this stage, if you don't mind? I'll let you know when I've finished with your husband.'

'Right.' She and Bill exchanged glances before, with a little shrug, she turned and left the room. She pulled the door to but didn't quite close it, and Harry couldn't help wondering if she'd be listening on the other side. Not much he could do about that.

'Your meeting?' he prompted Bill, in a quieter voice.

'Oh, yeah. Well …' he definitely looked out of his comfort zone. 'I, erm … had counselling sessions with him. You know … psychotherapy stuff.'

'And how long has that been going on?'

'I don't know … quite a while … two or three years.'

'Do you mind me asking *why* you were seeing him?'

'Yeah, I do actually. It's personal. I had some issues, that's all and Joshua was helping me tackle them.

'Did he seem any different last night? On edge in any way?'

'No.'

'We have CCTV of you entering the building. It has to be said, you're looking a bit furtive, as if you don't want to be recognised.'

'Well, you probably would too if you were having therapy sessions. It's not exactly the sort of thing you want to broadcast to the world.'

Harry got that. In fact, it touched a bit of a nerve. He'd had a few issues himself and a couple of past girlfriends had sarcastically suggested he might benefit from counselling about his commitment issues. It had only been after Claire though, six months ago, that he'd quietly taken himself off for a few sessions.

'Okay. So you arrived, had your session and left? What time was your appointment?'

'Nine twenty-five.'

'And after your session?'

The man hesitated. 'I came home. Look, this is ridiculous. I'm not a murderer.'

'Do you know a man called Daniel Jefferson? He had the appointment after you, we believe. Did you see him going in as you were coming out?'

'No.'

'How long did your session last?'

'I don't know – not long. We'd got to the point where Joshua just gave me one thing to concentrate on, we'd discuss that and then he'd send me off with some coping strategies.'

149

'Yet you didn't leave the hotel until a while after ten.'

'No … that was because I wanted a drink – only one – and I headed for the bar.'

'We have you getting into your car, but we don't actually see you leaving the hotel. Can you explain that?'

'I used the emergency exit off the corridor where I'd had my session with Joshua. I'd noticed it was open and it leads straight out onto the car park. It was quicker that way.'

'Okay.' Harry shut his notebook and got up from his chair. 'I'm going to have to ask you to come down to the station to give a formal statement, and we may need to ask you more questions. If you could bring your diary with you, please, that would be helpful. In the meantime, if I could have a quick word with your wife, so that she can verify your movements?'

CHAPTER EIGHTEEN

Harry was hit by the buzz in the office as soon as he walked through the door. Beth was on him before he'd even got halfway to his desk.

'We've had a bit of a breakthrough.'

'Oh?'

'I was trawling through the CCTV before I headed off to Daniel Jefferson, and … guess who else was at the seminar that we know – apart from me?'

Harry shook his head. 'Who?'

She allowed a dramatic pause, before saying. 'Michael Sanderson … Juliet's step-father.'

'What?'

Beth nodded. 'Have to say I never noticed him, but there he was on the footage sitting across the other side of the room to me. And talk about stony-faced.'

'Well, well. Have you done anything about bringing him in?'

'No, I wasn't sure how you'd want to play it. We've got his work address on file if you want me to go and pick him up?'

'Get someone else to do it, while you and I catch up. Can you sort that while I get us a coffee?'

Five minutes later, they were in the incident room

updating the board.

'So, names we're interested in so far,' Harry said, scrutinising the board. 'The last people to see Joshua alive. William Blake, Daniel Jefferson, Dean Jordan and now, possibly Michael Sanderson.'

'Plus a couple of other Serenity members that were there. That Brother Fabian for one. Geoff said he'd interviewed him but he didn't have much to add to anything. Still reeling with shock apparently.'

Harry sighed. 'Then, of course, we have over a hundred other possibles from the people attending the seminar. I'll need to get Geoff on to organising that one. But meanwhile, let's concentrate on the ones we do know about. How did you get on with Daniel Jefferson?'

'He's downstairs at the moment, giving a DNA sample and making a statement. He told me he was there for counselling, and that his appointment was at nine forty. He had a drink in the bar afterwards, then headed home. He says Joshua was alive and kicking when he left.'

'Which is what William Blake claims, too.'

'Interestingly, we have footage of both him and William Blake re-entering the corridor where Joshua's room was, a little after ten. Not together mind, but within a few minutes of each other. Could be significant?'

'Yeah, but it could also be that they were leaving the building that way. William Blake said there was an emergency exit open on that corridor and that it was a quicker way out to the car park.'

'If that's true … it means it would be just as easy for someone to *enter* the hotel the same way, without being seen? I'll check it out. How did you get on at Serenity?'

'Waste of time for the most part. Dean Jordan was in

his father's office, taking up residence. Seems like he's heir apparent, although that has to be approved by the elders. I'd have thought he was a bit young myself. What a set-up! How intelligent people get sucked into that sort of thing beats me.'

'Yeah, well, they're vulnerable a lot of them, aren't they? It feels like a security blanket, a way of escaping the pressures of the real world. That's what a lot of the deprogramming people reckon, anyway. They say people like the idea of handing over responsibility for their lives to someone else and they like that they have a structure to follow.'

'Well, seems bonkers to me, but each to his own. Right … looks like the next call is to get Michael Sanderson in, to see what he was doing there last night. He seems to be popping up quite a bit on our radar and he'd certainly have a motive to want to harm Joshua Jarvis.'

⌒

Michael Sanderson faced Harry across the desk in interview room two. He looked tense but not particularly worried.

'What's this about?' he asked.

'Do you mind telling me where you were last night, Mr Sanderson?'

The man hesitated. 'Well, I was at home most of the evening.'

'But not all evening?'

He shifted in his seat. 'I went out for a while, yes.'

His expression became uncomfortable as Harry kept his gaze firmly fixed on his face, and finally Michael Sanderson said, 'If you must know, I attended the Serenity seminar in Borehamwood.'

'And why did you do that?'

'Because I wanted to see what sort of set-up it was –

see the bastard who's been poisoning my daughter's mind against me.'

'Maybe even speak to him about her?'

'Maybe.'

'Did you, or didn't you?'

'I tried, but as soon as I approached him, told him who I was, he brushed me off – said he had appointments waiting for him. Why? Has he complained about me?'

'He's not in any state to complain about anything right now. He was murdered last night. Stabbed.

'*What*? You're kidding?

'It's hardly a joking matter. He was stabbed sometime between the hours of nine and ten thirty last night.'

'Jesus – well, it just goes to show that something's not right at that place. I'm telling you – the way Juliet changed over such a short space of time, the way they poisoned her mind against me ... it was brainwashing, as far as I'm concerned.'

'You realise you're in a difficult position?' Harry said. 'We're trying to find out who might have a motive for killing him.'

'And you think I do?'

Harry's gaze settled on some bruise marks on the other man's knuckles. 'When you say he brushed you off, were you angry?'

'Of course I was, but not angry enough to murder the man.'

'You were picked up on CCTV at nine ten pm leaving the conference hall. Where did you go after that?'

For a long moment, Michael Sanderson held his gaze, then with a shrug, he said, 'I'd tried to speak to Jarvis in the conference hall and as I say, he brushed me off. I wasn't having it. I followed him through some swing doors into a room off the corridor.'

'Did you talk to him there?'

Michael Sanderson shrugged again. 'I tried. It got quite heated though and next thing I knew a couple of his lackeys rushed in and threw me out. And yes, these marks on my hand were from the scuffle. I wasn't about to let them eject me without a fight. I wanted some answers. Not only about Juliet, but where our grandchild is.'

'I take it he had nothing to say on that?'

'No.'

'So this was when, around nine fifteen then, you're saying?'

He nodded.

'Yet there's no CCTV showing you coming back out into reception.'

'That's because they propelled me down the corridor and threw me out of that exit.'

'The emergency one?'

'Yeah.'

'You must have been very upset when your stepdaughter started accusing you of inappropriate behaviour?'

'Of course I was – and please don't refer to her as my stepdaughter; it's not how I think of her. As far as I'm concerned, she's my daughter.'

'There was clearly only one place she was going to have picked up such awful ideas?'

'If you're trying to get me to admit that I had reason to be furious with Joshua Jarvis, then you're right. I was livid and we had quite a slanging match in his room because I didn't believe he was telling the truth about Juliet's movements. But things would have to be really bad for me to attack someone physically and I'm not in the habit of walking around with a knife in my pocket.'

155

'Unless you were so angry that you'd decided to arm yourself beforehand, knowing it would be a confrontation.'

'Oh, come on, do I look like the sort of person who runs around stabbing people?'

'You'd be surprised how many murderers ask that one. Where did you go after leaving the hotel?'

'I was so worked up that I couldn't face going back to an empty flat. I went to the Three Blackbirds and had a beer before heading home.'

'Did anyone see you at the pub?'

'No one I know, but I guess someone might remember me. There was a blonde girl serving behind the bar – she might.'

'We'll need to send forensics around to your flat. I'll get someone on to that now and if you could provide them with the clothes and shoes you were wearing last night – to eliminate you as much as anything else – I'd appreciate that. But first I'll get someone to come and take a formal statement from you, and a DNA sample too. Then you'll be accompanied back to your flat to wait for forensics to arrive. If you want a solicitor, you're free to contact one.'

'Do I need one?'

'It's up to you, some people feel happier having one.'

'You won't find anything to tie me in with Joshua Jarvis's murder.' His look was belligerent. 'But I don't mind saying, he was a nasty piece of work and he probably got what was coming to him. His attitude when I confronted him was disdainful and smug. He told me he was glad he'd warned Juliet about me because now he understood why she'd run away from me.'

'I can see that would have made you very angry.'

Michael Sanderson made no comment to that and, after a moment, Harry rose from his seat. 'Someone will come to take your DNA shortly, and then accompany you to your flat. After that, you're free to carry on as normal, but please be aware that we may need to speak to you again and if you have any plans to go away or leave the country, you'll need to notify us first.'

'Are you saying I'm a suspect?

'I'm saying that at the moment you're a person of interest, as are a couple of others, and until we can eliminate you from our enquiries I need to know your whereabouts at all times.'

⌒

Out in the main office, Beth was glued to her computer. 'How did it go?' she asked, looking up.

'He admits he confronted Joshua but says Joshua had him thrown out and was alive when he left.'

'Doesn't mean he couldn't have come back.'

'True. But what's really odd is why no one at Serenity mentioned it? Who threw him out? He was dispatched via the emergency exit apparently, which we know was open. It means you were right earlier – our murderer could just as easily have come in that way, unobserved.'

'That's a bugger,' Beth said, and Harry's lips twisted.

'And that's an understatement. You'd better check with the hotel if there's any CCTV covering that exit.'

'I already did and no, there isn't. It's due to be upgraded in a couple of months. I compared notes on your interview with William Blake and mine with Daniel Jefferson. Jefferson basically said the same as Blake – he saw Joshua Jarvis regularly for counselling sessions. I managed to get a look at his diary and it seems it was regular as clockwork – once every three months. His session on Wednesday just seems a bit short for a therapy session, and that goes for William

157

Blake's appointment too.'

'What's he like? What's his set-up?'

'Family man, wife and young daughter. A cut above the Blakes, I'd say – he's a top bod in one of the Formula One racing teams – probably more your scene than mine, but quite successful if the house and cars they have are anything to go by.'

'I thought the name was familiar. Did his wife say what time he got back from his session?'

'She couldn't remember exactly but says he wasn't back late. They live in Elstree, so he didn't have far to travel.'

'So, let's run with the idea that it might not have been counselling they were meeting up with Joshua for. If it wasn't that, why else would they be seeing him on a regular basis like that?'

'Some sort of business venture? Dodgy dealings? Blackmail?' Beth came out with the suggestions straight away. 'Or maybe they were converts to Serenity and acted for him in some way?'

'If that was the case, why the apparent secrecy? Why aren't the appointments in Joshua's diary? But some of your other suggestions are worth looking into. The blackmail, for example. Three thousand pounds is a lot of money to be carrying around in your wallet, so what if someone or more than one person, gave it to him that evening?'

'It does seem odd that he'd pay to book rooms in a hotel when he had a bloody great mansion he could use.'

'Agreed. So there must have been a reason why he wanted to keep those meetings separate, or secret. And, in the absence of any explanation, we need to start digging more deeply into him as well as Serenity. Let's start by taking a look at bank statements. Phone Geoff and tell him to make sure that he brings anything related to Joshua Jarvis's and Serenity's bank accounts back with him. What are you doing at the moment?'

'Writing up my report and getting phone checks done on our people of interest. It's also been confirmed, by the way, that there were no obvious sightings on the CCTV of Roy Woolman – Juliet's biological father – at Bowman's Market last Saturday, though to be honest it doesn't prove anything – there's not much coverage of the actual market itself. '

'It was worth a try.' Harry looked at his watch. 'Michael Sanderson's still in interview Room 2. Can you make sure he's had a DNA sample taken from him and then accompany him back to his flat? And then wait with him there while SOCO do their stuff? Make sure they relieve him of the clothes and shoes he was wearing last night and look for Joshua's mobile phone and laptop – or anything else that might tie him into the attack last night.'

'Okay.'

'In the meantime, I'll plough on with my Serenity research to see if there's anything we're missing.'

CHAPTER NINETEEN

'Harry? How's it going?'

Harry looked up from his computer to see his boss, DCI Murray hobbling towards him on his crutches.

'You should have called me in, sir,' Harry said, getting quickly up from his chair.

'Nonsense. Sit down. I may be crippled, but unless I want to die from a thrombosis, they've told me I need to keep moving.'

Harry smiled. 'I feel for you, that thing looks bloody uncomfortable. Can I at least get you a cup of coffee?'

'Now you're talking. I'll head to the gents and meet you back in my office.'

Ten minutes later, they were both seated in Murray's office and Harry was filling him in.

'We've a couple of front runners for the Joshua Jarvis murder, but no one who really sticks out, and I've got people trawling through the one hundred plus attendees that were at the seminar in the hope that'll turn something up.'

'Is his murder linked to Juliet Sanderson's attack do you think?'

'We've not found a definite link yet, apart from the obvious Serenity one, but it seems too much of a coincidence not to be connected. One of our possible suspects is her father, picked up on CCTV at the meeting, who we know argued with the victim. Another angle we'll look into is that Jarvis may have been involved in some sort of illegal activity, such as blackmail. He had over three thousand pounds cash in his wallet –we're thinking it could have come from someone at the seminar. You don't usually walk around all day with that sort of money in your pocket, do you?.

'Or maybe *he* was being blackmailed or was going to use it to bribe someone?'

'Yeah … there are those possibilities too.' Harry sighed. 'I've told Geoff to bring anything related to his finances back here so that we can go through it all. There's just so much to cover.'

'Give that to me when it comes in, if you like? I might not feel so bloody useless if I'm doing something concrete. I was good at financial forensics in my time.'

'Thanks, sir, that would really help.'

'Still no news on where Juliet Sanderson's been living this past couple of months, or what's happened to her baby?'

'No—'

A commotion from the corridor had them both looking towards the open door where Geoff Peterson was struggling to manoeuvre a computer with a pile of files balanced precariously on top of it, into the main office.

'Need a hand with that?' Harry called out, jumping up and heading out of Murray's office.

'No, I'm alright. Plenty more where this came from but don't worry, Dave and Ray are on it.'

'I take it that's the Serenity stuff?

'Yup. I've left Rob copying some of the paperwork that they didn't want moving, but Brother Fabian said I was welcome to take this lot.'

'Find anything significant?'

'Not yet but there's something not right there. Everyone's so cagey, as if they're worried about saying the wrong thing. This is Joshua Jarvis's computer, which the tech guys will need to take a look at. It has a password protect system and no one in Serenity knows his password. You'd have thought at least one other person would know it in case of emergencies, bearing in mind his seniority. One interesting piece of info … sounds like there's going to be a bit of a power battle between Brother Fabian and the son as to who takes over. Fabian reckons Joshua changed his mind about Dean and had said more recently that *he* should be next in line.'

'And they were both with him at the meeting last night.'

'Yeah.'

'Right. Time for another visit then. I haven't met this Brother Fabian yet. He'd left by the time I got to the scene.'

⌒

Brother Fabian was a pasty-looking man, with a beard and shoulder-length hair tied back in a ponytail. He looked to be in his early fifties, though it may just have been that he wasn't ageing well.

'It's a terrible business,' he said now, eyeing Harry over his desk. 'Everyone's in shock. I mean, who would want to kill Joshua?'

'That's what I'm hoping you'll be able to help us with,' Harry said. 'I know you told my sergeant that you didn't know why Joshua was meeting these people last night, but you were there – you must have heard something? I understand there was even a fight with a chap called Michael Sanderson, who was thrown out? Were you involved in that at all? Were you aware that he was Juliet Sanderson's father? Can you tell me what happened?'

The man's eyes dropped down to the desk, as if giving himself time for thought. It was a gesture Harry had seen a thousand times before and he waited patiently for him to speak.

After a few moments he looked up again and sighed. 'I wasn't there to start with. I believe the person you're talking about burst into the room and challenged Joshua about his daughter, even accusing him of having something to do with the attack on her, which of course is ridiculous. Our whole ethos is based on peace and doing good. But the man was enraged. I heard the shouting from the room next door where I was packing away Joshua's seminar notes with Dean. We went in to see what was going on, and managed to throw him out. It was very unpleasant and he threatened Joshua that he hadn't finished with him yet.'

'What do you think he meant by that? Do you think it's possible he could have come back?'

'It's possible, I suppose, now I think about it. We didn't take much notice at the time, just put it down to hot air, but it wouldn't have been difficult for him to come back in.'

'Why didn't you mention this when my sergeant questioned you?'

'Because it happened soon after the meeting ended and Joshua was alive for quite a while after that. It didn't occur to me that the man might have come back.'

'And what did you do between throwing him out and finding out that Joshua was dead?'

'I was in another room, as I say, packing away the seminar stuff and going through some work while I waited for Joshua to finish.'

163

'And you heard nothing?'

'No.'

'What time did you leave the hotel?'

'A little after half past ten. Shortly after the first police arrived. I gave them a brief statement and headed home.'

'Why didn't you wait until I got there? They told you I was coming, presumably?'

'Because we decided that Dean could deal with that, and I should get back to the hall and tell the other brothers what had happened.'

'Didn't it occur to you that we might want to talk to you as you were one of the last people to see Joshua alive?'

'I told Dean I'd stay up until he came back. If you'd needed to talk to me, I assumed you'd accompany him.'

'Who takes over here at Serenity, now Joshua's gone?'

The man's expression became cloaked. 'That has to be decided. It was always assumed it would be Dean but of course we weren't expecting the situation to arise as early as it has. He's young, and recently … well, Joshua had been having second thoughts about him.'

'Why?'

'I think he worried that he wasn't quite as committed to Serenity as the leader of the community needs to be.'

'What do you mean? In what way?'

Fabian shrugged. 'I don't know the ins and outs of it but we have certain ways in our community that are written in stone. They're ways that have worked for many years and Joshua saw no need to change things. I think Dean has maybe allowed … outside influences to sway him, to make him start questioning some of the traditions we have.'

'Specifically?'

'That I'm afraid I don't know. Joshua was always

164

protective of his son, but it didn't blind him to his faults. Recently he'd been saying to me that we needed to keep an eye on Dean's development and he put forward the possibility that it might be better for me to succeed him.'

'The appointments he had last night. You have no idea what they were about? It's not the first time he's booked a room there for that purpose, apparently.'

'I assumed they were counselling sessions – that's what he told me in the past.'

'They seem a bit short for therapy sessions.'

'Well, if they're coming towards the end of their sessions, they may only need to concentrate on a couple of issues, in which case Joshua could have given them a couple of thoughts and handling strategies to take away with them. That wouldn't necessarily take up a complete session.'

'We're finding it difficult accessing his computer to try and learn more. I find it hard to believe no one knows his password?'

'Why would we need access to it? We all have our own access to the main system. I doubt if anyone knows my password either.'

Harry sighed. 'And he had a laptop too, I understand, that his son says is now missing?'

'Yes, so I believe.'

'You say it was you and Dean who threw Michael Sanderson out after his row with Joshua?'

'Yes. We didn't go in straight away but when it was obviously becoming heated, we did intervene. After we'd dealt with Michael Sanderson, I finished what we were doing and then tackled some note-writing, while Dean went to get himself a take-away.'

So why hadn't Dean Jarvis mentioned the ruckus with

165

Michael Sanderson? Harry wondered.

∽

By the time Harry got home that night, it was late and he felt physically wrung out. They'd all waded in to Joshua's stuff but there had been frustratingly little of obvious interest. There were so many loose strands to this investigation, refusing to knit together, but there was a common thread he knew, if only he could identify it. What was the cloak of secrecy that seemed to surround Serenity? Why hadn't Fabian and Dean told them straight away about Michael Sanderson? Could Joshua's murder be unrelated to Juliet's attack? Could it have been Michael Sanderson coming back or an attempt by Dean or Fabian to take over as Lead Brother, brought to a climax by some random action that had precipitated the violence?

He poured himself a beer and made a sandwich out of the stale cheddar that was festering in the fridge. He could do with treating himself to a bloody good meal out, but apart from his work mates these days and a few from the hockey club that he rarely got round to seeing, he didn't have a huge selection of people to socialise with, and it wasn't the same eating alone.

Bright blue eyes and shiny chestnut hair swept up in a ponytail … the image danced in front of him totally without warning.

Claire.

He knew he'd filed her neatly to one side since his grandmother's death, but after his conversation with Beth the other day, he didn't seem to be able to get her out of his head. He'd treated her badly, there was no getting away from that, and maybe it was embarrassment that prevented him from getting back in touch. Or fear of rejection?

He missed her and it seemed ridiculously disproportionate when they'd done no more than kiss a couple of times, and yet …

He reached for his phone, his fingers hovering over the keypad as he hesitated.

Do it!

He could almost hear his grandmother's impatient voice in his ear, spurring him on. She wouldn't be hesitating like he was, analysing everything to death. And Beth was right … asking Claire out wasn't a commitment to marriage, it was simply a commitment to explore their relationship to see if it had any substance … wings to make it fly. The idea excited him and before he had time to change his mind, he hit the call button.

'Hello, Harry.'

She sounded just the same. And was it a good sign that she hadn't deleted his number off her phone?

He cleared his throat. 'Hey. How are you?'

'I'm good.'

Silence followed her words as she waited for him to speak. She wasn't going to make it easy for him.

'I was just eating a crap meal and thinking how much nicer it would be if I was eating out with you,' he said.

She laughed softly down the phone. 'It's a bit late for tonight; I've already eaten. Have you been drinking?'

'One beer. How about another night?'

'You don't speak to me in over six months. And then you just call me out of the blue and ask me out for a meal?'

'I know it's clumsy, but I've been thinking about you.'

'Have you?' He could almost see her shaking her head. 'Give me one good reason why I shouldn't stay well clear of you like my instincts tell me?'

'Because if you dig deep enough, you might find a lone one that's telling you I'm not such a bad guy?'

Silence.

'Are you seeing someone?' He found he was holding his breath as he asked the question.

'No. You?'

He released it slowly. 'No. I've missed you, Claire. We didn't really give ourselves a proper chance, did we?'

Her voice was cool. 'I think it was you more than me that ducked out, Harry. But no, we didn't.'

'So how about we give it another try? Dinner tomorrow at The Hacienda? Claire...?' he added into the silence that followed.

Finally, she let out a long sigh. 'Okay. I'll meet you for old times' sake. But it's not a date. We'll just see how it goes.'

Not a date! But he still felt like punching the air – though he kept his voice calm as they made arrangements.

'I'll see you tomorrow then,' he said, preparing to hang up. 'I'll book the table as it's Friday and get back to you if there's a problem.'

'Okay. See you then.'

CHAPTER TWENTY

Juliet

'What's up?' Dean says, as I find myself stiffening involuntarily in his hold.

He's just back from Northumberland and how can I tell him? The memory of Joshua having sex with me last night is hazy, and I feel so ashamed that I didn't stop him. Even though it's the way of Serenity and Dean also knows that, he's surely not going to be happy about it.

'Jules?' he queries gently.

I feel the tears welling up and bury my head in his shoulder. 'Joshua took me last night,' I whisper. 'You know what I'm saying, Dean? He said he needed to fill my baby with the spirit of Serenity. I didn't want him to do it, but…'

He makes no response and I draw back to look up at him. The expression on his face confuses me as I struggle to read the message in his eyes, but then realisation dawns. 'You *knew* … you knew he was going to do that.'

He looks shamefaced. 'I'm sorry,' he says, taking my hands gently in his.

I shake him off angrily. 'You knew! I can't believe you could stand back and let him do that to me.'

'Juliet, it's part of the initiation – everyone undergoes it. I told you, it's how it works here, there was nothing I could have done to prevent it. But it's done now—'

'I don't want him to do it again. I really don't. You must tell him that.'

I can tell he's warring with himself as he runs his hands through his hair. 'It's difficult—'

'No, it's not. It's you I love, not him. How can you bear to let your own father …'

'Jules, it's hard for me, can't you see that? Of course I don't like it on a personal level, but I was born into this way of life, it's the only one I've known, and Joshua – all the brethren – have looked after me, cared for me. The reason why our community has lasted for so long is because we all love one another equally and accept that we're part of a bigger picture. No one person is better than another. I know that's hard for you to understand when you've been taught a different way, but your way isn't perfect, is it? Look at what happened with your parents and the heartache that caused you and them, when your mother had her affair – because you believe so rigidly in monogamy. You have to understand how hard it would be for me to go against the ones I love.'

'But you said you loved me.'

'And I do. You mean everything to me.'

His draws me into him, and his words mollify me just a little. 'I won't do it again,' I say, into his chest. I'm so upset that he isn't with me on this. How can he bear the thought of another man touching me, having sex with me? It's incomprehensible. I'd scratch the eyes out of any woman who slept with him.

'You can't be ready yet,' he says, a worried look in his eye. 'You'll feel different after a while.'

'I don't want to feel different. And I don't want to stay in this room anymore. I want to come back to the cottage with you. I hate it here.'

'You will, soon, I promise. I'll speak to Joshua about it. But – I've got to go back to Newcastle tomorrow. This is only a quick break to visit you'

'Why can't I come with you? I'm so lonely, Dean. I never see anyone apart from Joshua and Fabian. And I miss Cara … at least I could have a laugh with her.'

'You need to show everyone that you're accepting of our core belief that we are one – one family unit with no divisions. That you're content to place your trust not just in me, but in the whole community. They need to be sure you've converted fully before they allow you to go back to the cottage. It's in your best interests. But let me speak to Joshua,' he soothes, 'and see if they'll let Cara come and visit you. Just pray hard for deliverance and then it won't feel so bad.'

I stare at him in frustration. I want to scream at him not to be so weak – to stand up to Joshua – this isn't the first time he's sided with the brethren rather than me. But just as I'm about to vent, he leans down to gently kiss my lips. 'I know it's difficult, Jules, but you're so nearly there,' he whispers, 'and once you've fully embraced Serenity there'll be a peace in your heart that you've never experienced before. I know it, because I've seen it happen to so many outsiders who join our community. It transforms them.'

He knows which buttons to press. Knows that's all I want – peace, and an escape from the terrible hurt that's been gnawing away at me ever since I found out the truth about Dad. But now, for the first time since I left home, I realise that my anger against my parents is lessening – the need to

171

escape the whole ugly mess no longer such an all-consuming issue for me. It feels good to realise that. At some point, I'll have it out with Mum and Dad and there'll probably be a lot of shouting and tears and recriminations, but we'll work it out like we always do. Just thinking about them gives me strength.

As Dean starts to kiss me tenderly, my anger dissolves as it always does. In some ways I hate this power he holds over me, yet I can't imagine living without him.

I'm losing myself in that kiss, realising that our love is all that's important, when suddenly something disrupts the memory…

'*Jules.*'

The voice is coming from a long way off, pulling me back to the present.

It's Mum – and for the first time in I don't know how long, I realise there's no distortion, no muffling of the sound in my ears … I can clearly hear her.

I crash back to the present and try to turn my head in the direction of that voice. My excitement is crushed as I realise that although I can hear her, I still can't move or talk.

But it has to be a good sign, doesn't it? And for now it's enough, and I cling on to the moment. It's incredible just hearing the soft lilt of her voice, whispering tenderly that she loves me … that they all do … to hang on in there … they're rooting for me.

∽

It's a while later and Mum's gone. It's so good to properly hear the bustle of the nurses doing their jobs around me as they fiddle with tubes and talk to the doctor about IV drips and vital signs – although I'm not quite so comfortable about

172

the vital signs, as I realise from things they say, that they indicate how deep a coma I'm in and the state of my health generally – and the awful thought occurs to me that one day they'll switch me off and let me die, and there'll be nothing I can do to stop it. The thought of that is so terrifying that it spurs a violent struggle inside me as I try to force myself to wake up. But my brain still feels like a concrete block, locked inside my head, and I can't break free from it. It feels as if I'm wrestling against physical restraints, the struggle is so powerful. And from nowhere, that triggers another memory.

I'm lying on a bed, my hands tied to the posts.

'What *am* I going to do with you, Juliet?' A voice says, almost mournfully. 'You really have been most tiresome, and you realise now, I can't let you go...'

CHAPTER TWENTY-ONE

There was a spring to Harry's step as he walked into the office the next morning, and he didn't need to analyse why. The thought of meeting Claire for dinner that night had added another dimension to his life, and he suddenly didn't feel quite such a sad bastard after all.

'Right, listen up,' he said an hour later when everyone, including his boss, was gathered in the incident room. 'Who's going first? Geoff?'

'CCTV has shown a few people entering and leaving the hotel on foot,' Geoff said. 'So we're trawling through the footage for the road outside as well as the car park, to see if we can pick anything up on that. We're working our way through the extended house-to-house search, nothing new yet. The background check on Michael Sanderson hasn't shown anything apart from a couple of his work colleagues saying he can have a bit of a temper on him and that he's been quite depressed since the split with his wife. And we're still searching for Juliet's baby. There are absolutely no leads on that at all.'

'Christ, let's just hope it's being cared for by someone.'

'You don't need to make me feel worse than I already do. We've been all over it but every avenue we go up is a dead end.'

'I've had something interesting come out on the trace by Joshua's phone provider,' Beth said into the uneasy silence that followed his words.

'Oh?'

'Yeah, he seems to have been pretty hot on deleting voicemails and messages apparently, but there's a voice message on the day he died that wasn't deleted, from William Blake, about their meeting that night. He accuses Joshua of bleeding him dry and says they need to talk, otherwise he threatens to dump Joshua in it.'

'Does he indeed? Now we're talking. Sounds like that could well be blackmail to me.'

'But what sort of hold could Joshua have over someone like him?'

'We'd better ask him. As you said before, dodgy dealings maybe?'

'Or maybe something in his past, if he was having counselling? Shall I bring him in?'

'Maybe you can get on to Blake's bank, while I sort it. It would be useful to see if he's been paying regular amounts out to anyone.'

'While we're on the subject of finances,' Murray said, entering the frame, '… looking at Joshua's personal account, he was regularly paying lumps of cash into it – anything from a thousand to three thousand pounds in a week. According to the bank, he told them that a lot of his clients paid him in cash or by cheque, as he didn't want the expense of having a machine to process transactions, but that's a lot of money for a part-time therapist to be banking. It's beginning to sound like we might be on to something. It wouldn't be a bad idea for someone to check the other chap's bank statements too

– the one who had the appointment after William Blake. It would make a lot more sense that their appointments were short if they were just handing over money.'

He paused and looked around the room. 'I know you're all on this full-time and these things can be painfully slow, but we need to remember that there's still a missing child out there and it's been nearly a week. That child has to be our first priority. It's looking increasingly likely that the two attacks are linked, so if we can get Joshua's murderer, chances are we'll have, or be close to, Juliet's attacker. From there it's a step away from finding her baby.'

'I've got one other thing to add,' Beth said as people made moves to pack up. 'The calls logged on Joshua's phone were pretty straightforward but there's one number that shows up quite regularly. Trouble is it's a SIM-only number, so difficult to trace. Some of the conversations were quite long though and whoever it is, phoned him the afternooon he was killed. He or she would be a useful person to eliminate.'

'Right,' said Harry. 'Well, you all know what you're doing and I don't want to hold you up any longer. Anyone not know?'

He looked around the room. 'Anything you want to add, sir?' he added, turning to Murray.

'Not much, but we've got a murder and an attempted murder on our hands and I'd say it's pretty certain that they're linked. You don't need me to tell you to tread with caution. Any concerns, you make sure you have backup before moving in and taking any risks. That's it.'

As people filed out of the room, Harry picked up his folder and sifted through it for William Blake's number. Priority number one – try to find out why he'd left the message about being bled dry.

Harry went through the process of setting up the recorder and stared hard at William Blake over the desk, observing that the man was looking extremely fidgety.

'How long's this going to take?' he asked. 'I'm in the middle of a big job and can't afford to lose any time on it if I want to get it finished on time.'

'That depends on you, Mr Blake, and how quickly you can help us out with some information that's come to light in relation to Joshua Jarvis's murder.'

'I already told you I don't know anything about that.'

'We ran a trace on Mr Jarvis's phone and it revealed a voice message that you left him on the day of your appointment, whereby you accuse him of' – Harry glanced down at his notes – "bleeding you dry", and threatening to dump him in it unless he left you alone. What was it that he was doing that made you leave that message?'

William Blake shifted in his seat. 'Nothing, it wasn't that serious. I was just annoyed at how much the therapy sessions were costing me. Business has been difficult the last few months, I needed to vent.'

'It sounds a bit more than that to me. What about the threat to dump him in it unless he was prepared to leave you alone?'

'Did I really say that?'

'Yup.'

'I don't know what I meant. I was just overreacting. Look, I'd had a bad day. It happens to us all – I was just lashing out.'

'Well, I'm not surprised if, as you say, you've been seeing him for a couple of years or more. It isn't cheap to have counselling. Perhaps you could explain something else for me? We've checked your bank records and it seems that, for the past couple of years or so – the same time you've been seeing him – you've been regularly withdrawing fifteen hundred pounds every quarter, in cash. Do you mind telling me what that money is for?'

His eyes dipped away from Harry's. 'Nothing in particular. I just leave it in the wardrobe for general use if my wife and I need any bits and pieces.'

'Right. So … the last withdrawal was on Wednesday, the day Joshua Jarvis was murdered, and we happened to notice that there was a large amount of money in his wallet – over three thousand pounds. Would any of that have been money that you gave him?'

'Only my consultation fee, seventy-five pounds.'

'That sounds like a lot for what seems to have been only a ten-minute consultation?'

'Maybe it wasn't as much as that now I come to think of it. I think he charged me thirty pounds.'

'Okay. So can I assume that if one of my team accompanies you home right now, the fifteen hundred pounds you withdrew from the bank on Wednesday is still sitting in your wardrobe?'

William Blake blinked. 'Probably not. We went shopping and spent most of it.'

'What on?'

'Food and a few household items.'

'What items did you buy?'

'God, I don't know. My wife does the buying I just cough up the money.'

'So if I call your wife now, she'll be able to confirm all this?'

'Yeah, but she's out with her mates today and she couldn't

178

find her mobile this morning. She might not pick up.'

'Could you write her number on this piece of paper, please? We'll give her a call just in case she's found it. I'm not sure you realise how serious this situation is, Mr Blake. It's our suspicion that Joshua Jarvis may have been blackmailing you and others, because around the same dates that you withdraw your money every quarter, he was regularly paying large amounts of cash into his bank account. It would save a lot of time and trouble if you just told me the truth about what's been going on.'

It was a bluff because Harry wasn't at all sure they were on the right track with the whole blackmail thread, but it was obvious he'd hit some sort of nerve if the look on the other man's face was anything to go by.

'There's nothing going on,' he said aggressively. 'It's ludicrous to think I was being blackmailed. He was helping me deal with some issues, that's all. What would he be blackmailing someone like me over?'

'I don't know, but if he was, it's my job to find out. And believe me, I will. Are you still not prepared to tell me why you were seeing him?'

'No, it's personal. I'm sorry, but there's nothing I can tell you that would be of any help to you.'

His face closed over and it was obvious that was all Harry was going to get out of him. He made a couple of notes, then shut his book and rose from the table. 'Okay, you're free to go for now, but you're not out of the woods yet. Have you got any plans to travel anywhere in the near future?'

'Not until Christmas.'

'Good, please tell us if that changes at all.'

'It's beginning to feel like I'm a suspect.'

'Until we find Joshua Jarvis's killer, no one's ruled out. I'd ask that you don't go anywhere without telling me first. And your wife's mobile number, please?'

CHAPTER TWENTY-TWO

Harry sat at his desk, drumming his fingers as he considered their options.

'How did it go with Blake?' Beth asked, approaching his desk.

He looked up. 'He's hiding something, but God knows what. And whatever it is, the wife's in on it too. She was very evasive and nervous when I spoke to her. What about you with Jefferson?'

'I've arranged to meet him at his home in his lunch hour. His bank account shows the same pattern as William Blake's – regular withdrawals of fifteen hundred pounds every quarter, around the same time as the Blakes', and I've cross-checked Joshua's bank statements with Blake and Jefferson's diary dates and some of his deposits are within a day or so of those dates. We've got to be onto something, haven't we? From the notes the DCI's given me, Joshua's personal bank statement shows that he kept the maximum protected amount of eighty-five grand in his account after which it got transferred to a building society account. Apart from regular top ups, not a lot of other activity has gone on with that account in the last year or so, apart from a lump sum payment of over sixty grand on a Jag – seems he was a bit of a car buff. According to Brother Fabian, the money earned from counselling, their seminars and other business ventures gets paid straight into the Serenity business account, which again keeps a healthy balance of eighty-five thousand pounds, after which, automatic transfers to various savings accounts are made. Most of the money in Joshua's private account was paid in as cash, and here's the interesting bit … one of the things they brought in from his rooms was a safe, which we've managed to open. There was another fifty grand in there. I phoned Brother Fabian about that, but he claims to know nothing about Joshua's private finances. My guess is that whatever Joshua was doing, it was funding him very nicely.'

'It's a lot of money and if it's blackmail, how many victims are there? And what hold does he have over them?'

'Maybe some deep secret from their past, that they've revealed in their therapy sessions? I'll see if Daniel Jefferson is any more forthcoming than your guy when I see him.'

'What about Dean Jarvis? What have you unearthed on him?'

Beth looked over at Geoff Peterson, who was pouring over his computer. 'Geoff's looked into his background. You're probably better off talking to him. *Geoff…* can you fill Harry in on Dean Jarvis?'

'I'm surprised you resisted the temptation to do it for me,' Geoff responded good naturedly, looking up.

'Didn't want to steal your thunder,' Beth said.

'You can steal it any time you like, as long as you buy me a drink afterwards to make up for it. Next one's on you anyway, I seem to remember?'

Beth threw him a quizzical look. She never knew quite how to take Geoff. She occasionally felt, from comments he made, that he got her in a way no one other than Andy ever had, and it unsettled her that maybe he saw through the outer layer she put on for the world.

'Dean Jarvis?' Harry prompted Geoff, breaking her thoughts.

'Right, well … potted version … he was the first child of Joshua and Sheila – one of the women in Juliet's cottage. He's also one of the first children to be born into the commune that was separated from their mothers to be raised entirely by the "chosen ones" or mother hens as they also call them.'

He shrugged at the expressions on Harry and Beth's faces. 'It's an odd setup, we already know that and he was one of the earliest participants in the experiment, that they now seem to have carried on with. It's like an institution – the children are brought up by quasi surrogate parents, with limited input from their real parents. It's almost like trying to breed a super race. He was home-schooled and actually did very well. Nine GCSEs, all grades A to C, three A-levels and he went to Hatfield University where he studied Psychology.

'Hence the counselling.'

'Yes, he did that as an add-on afterwards. That seems to be big within Serenity.'

'I guess it could screw you up, being so institutionalised,' Harry said. 'He told me their way of life hadn't done him any harm but what if it had? What if his learning has made him question what they do? Isn't that what Fabian hinted at? Why he said Joshua was reconsidering who was going to succeed him as Lead Brother?'

'But to kill his own father for power?'

'People have done it for less. He admitted that he wasn't close to Joshua, and I have to say, he was weirdly detached when I interviewed him yesterday. We can't dismiss that he

183

might be involved, although if blackmail's a runner, then the chances are just as high, or higher, that it was someone Joshua was fleecing.'

Harry paused, frowning, his mind obviously going off on a tangent. 'I also think we shouldn't discount the possibility of Dean Jarvis being the father of Juliet's baby. And that gives him quite a strong link to both victims. He denied it when I asked him, but he admitted they'd *paired*, as he termed it, and by the sound of it, that was around the time she would have fallen pregnant. That doesn't mean we should stop questioning her friends and Serenity members to try to establish if it was someone else, either in or outside the community, but I think you should check that we're asking the direct question to the people in the commune – especially the ones she shared the house with – as to how close she and Dean Jarvis were. And also get the names of other members that she may have had a relationship with. What about the missing girls? Anything new on them?'

'Not yet, we're working on it.'

The sound of Beth's phone interrupted them.

'Oops, sorry. My reminder to leave for the Daniel Jefferson interview. I'd better head off.' She looked at Harry. 'Do you want to come?'

Harry hesitated. 'I've got plenty to be getting on with here … but I feel he and Blake could be significant and I'd quite like to get the measure of him. Yes, maybe I will.'

Beth reached over for a file and stood up. 'You can drive for a change and I'll fill you in on what we've got on him so far.'

In the car, Beth reread the notes on Daniel Jefferson. 'Oh, I forgot to tell you this. CCTV footage showed him and William Blake having a drink in the hotel bar together. I'm sure they said they didn't know each other.'

'They did. Let's see what he's got to say about that.'

The Jeffersons lived in a large, detached red-brick house in a road of very similar looking dwellings, with an in-out driveway that circled around the front of the house. Harry pulled into the drive behind a smart looking BMW and climbed out.

A man opened the front door, greeting them with a smile and Harry recognised him immediately as a prominent figure in British racing.

'Hello again,' he said to Beth, standing aside to let them in. 'Come through. What can I do for you?'

'More questions, I'm afraid, Mr Jefferson.'

'I can't think of anything more I can add to what I've already told you in my statement.'

He indicated to a couple of chairs and Harry and Beth sat down. They looked up as the man's wife walked in.

'What's all this about?' she asked. 'Daniel's answered your questions once. He had nothing to do with that man's death.'

'I'm afraid some more information's come to light that we need to clarify,' Harry responded pleasantly. 'We'll be as brief as we can.'

He turned back to Jefferson.

'When my colleague last spoke to you, you said you didn't know a man called William Blake?'

'That's right. Can't say I do.'

'Mrs Jefferson?'

She shook her head.

'After your meeting with Joshua Jarvis that night, what exactly did you do?'

'Came home.'

'Did you come straight back?'

The man hesitated, flashed a look at his wife, and said. 'I had a quick drink in the bar first.'

'Did you drink alone?'

'I can't remember. I might have chatted to people if they were there.'

'What would you say if I was to tell you that we have footage from the hotel CCTV showing you having a beer with William Blake, who you apparently don't know?'

For the first time, Daniel Jefferson looked uncomfortable. 'I *don't* know him. We'd seen each other before, because our sessions with Joshua seemed to coincide, but – I remember now – that night we both ended up in the bar for some reason and got talking. You rarely feel great after a counselling session and I remember thinking it was good to meet up with someone who got how I was feeling.'

'Yet your session with Joshua barely lasted ten minutes by the sound of it. I'd suggest that you weren't there for counselling at all. Like William Blake, you've regularly been withdrawing fifteen hundred pounds from your bank account every three months. Were you and Mr Blake discussing the fact that you were being blackmailed by Joshua Jarvis?'

There was a shocked silence. Then.

'No.'

'What do you do with those regular withdrawals?'

'Spend them. Fifteen hundred quid doesn't go far these days. It's just cash we use.'

'I realise it's personal but it would be very helpful for me to know why you were having counselling with Joshua?'

'I had some issues that I needed to deal with, like most people who go for counselling.'

'He used to have a drink problem,' his wife put in, glaring

at her husband as she said it. 'And there's no point looking at me like that Dan, you promised me only yesterday that you hadn't touched a drop in the last six months, and now I find out you were drinking in that bar.'

'It was alcohol-free beer. You know I only drink that now.'

She pursed her lips but said no more.

'So what were you and William Blake talking about?'

'God, I can't remember. It was just talk. We were both feeling a bit fed up after our sessions and it was good to let it out.'

The man didn't look at them as he answered, and it was obvious he was hiding something.

'Well, the fact of the matter is, both of you are bang in the timeframe for having opportunity to murder Joshua Jarvis before you left for home and if he was blackmailing you, then that would give you a motive. So I'd suggest that this might be another time when it would be good to let it out.'

'I've got nothing else to say. You're barking up the wrong tree. Is there anything else you want to ask? Because if not, I need to get on.'

'Okay.' Harry stood up. 'I don't believe you've been entirely straight with us today, Mr Jefferson. We know something's not right and we'll find out what it is. If you cooperate now, whatever comes out, it will be better for you in the long run than trying to obstruct a police investigation. Think on that.'

'They're hiding something,' Beth said, back in the car.

'I agree. And whatever's going on, both wives know about it. Find out as much as you can about the four of them when we get back. Meanwhile, I think for the rest of today, we need to get that search warrant for Serenity Hall organised and everyone needs to sift through every piece of info we've got on the commune in preparation for an unannounced sweep on them first thing in the morning. There's too much not hanging right there, and I want to question Dean Jarvis and Brother Fabian again about these other missing girls.'

CHAPTER TWENTY-THREE

Harry saw her the minute she walked through the door. She hadn't changed at all, but then why would she have done in six months? She was wearing tight jeans and a jumper, with a jacket slung over her arm. Her shiny chestnut-coloured hair bobbed around her shoulders, a pretty clip holding one side up above her ear. She looked great.

He rose from the restaurant table and, after a moment's awkward hesitation, they kissed on the cheek.

'Hey,' he said.

'Hey,' she replied. 'How are you doing?'

He absorbed her features, every detail, shocked to realise how accurately each angle of her face, every expression in her eye, was ingrained in his memory.

'I'm good,' he said. 'You?'

She nodded, then relaxed the atmosphere with a smile. 'Both of us as sad as each other though – that we're free on a Friday night.'

The arrival of the waiter with the menu gave him time to breathe again, to steady his pulse, to remind himself that this was a dinner, no more.

'So …' she said, eyeing him across the table once their

orders had been taken. 'It was a bit of a shock hearing from you.'

'Yeah, I'm sure it was. We didn't part on the best of terms, I know. I've wanted to get back in touch, Claire, but the last six months…'

'Have been busy?'

He smiled ruefully and nodded.

'And you've been promoted, I hear. Congratulations.'

'Thanks.'

'I nearly didn't come,' she said. 'It felt like too much water had gone under the bridge.'

'I nearly didn't call you for the same reason. Why *did* you come?'

'Why did you call?'

She wasn't giving much.

He hesitated. 'Truthfully? I'm not sure. Maybe because I thought we had a connection and I didn't want to live with the possibility that I might just have thrown away the best thing that was ever going to happen to me in my life.'

He watched as a pink stain crept slowly into her cheek and remembered how he'd liked that about her – how she was easily embarrassed.

'But it took you six months to come round to that way of thinking?' she queried lightly.

'No, I've always known that's how I feel, but I was worried about letting you down if it didn't work out.'

'What's made you suddenly feel you can take the risk?'

'A friend, who told me that committing to explore the relationship wasn't quite as extreme as committing to marriage. And she felt you'd get that.'

She nodded thoughtfully. 'She sounds like a wise friend. And I do get it.' Her eyes were candid as they held his. 'So what exactly are you saying here?'

He took a breath. 'That I really like you, Claire, and I'd like to get to know you better … if you feel the same way … and if we can put all the stuff about my grandmother behind us?'

It was a big ask and he knew it. She stared at him for a long moment, clearly weighing his words carefully. 'I can try,' she said, 'but it was hard, and it hurt when you doubted me.'

Her look was frank as she held his gaze.

'It wasn't you I doubted, or your motives even—' He paused, trying to collect his thoughts, remembering back to that time so that he could give some reasonable explanation of his behaviour.

'No need to go into it all again,' she said quickly. 'In fact, probably better that we don't. I was upset with the way you handled it when you should have known that anything I did for your gran would have come from a place of caring and compassion. What happened was for the best, we both know that. She had the end she wanted and that was all she ever asked. I think we should just close that chapter now and see if we can move on from it.'

'Okay,' he said simply, breathing a sigh of relief and more than happy not to argue with her.

'So how's life—?'

'So what case—?'

They both laughed as they spoke at the same time and Harry gestured magnanimously with his hand. 'After you,' he said.

'I was just going to ask you what you're working on at the moment? I mean it's been all over the news about the girl that was stabbed in Little Ashton. Are you working on that? I 'know you'll be limited as to what you can tell me.'

'Yeah. And it's one of those cases that seems to have tentacles that stretch for miles. Trying to pull them all in is proving difficult.'

'You'll get there.'

'Good that someone's got faith in me.'

'I'm sure that cranky boss of yours does too.'

'Hmm ... I wonder sometimes. So what about you? What have you been up to?'

She grinned. 'Quite a lot, actually. I've just started a course training to be a doula.'

'A what?'

She laughed. 'Haven't you heard of a doula? They're a bit like a midwife except they don't have the same medical training and they focus on the needs of the mother's mental, physical and emotional support, rather than the actual birthing process – though they're often around for that too.'

Harry looked impressed. 'Where did that idea come from?'

'I was just reading about it one day and quite liked the idea. I'm getting really fed up with the care agency I work for. They're so disorganized and I end up travelling miles more than I need to just because they can't plan their work schedules properly. I enrolled on a course and I'm loving it. I'm still working while I'm doing it and it takes two years to qualify, but ...'

'I think you'll be great at it and interesting to work at the opposite end of the market to the elderly.'

'Yeah, well I'll miss some of my regulars – ones like your gran who I've become fond of – but it feels the right thing to do.'

'I'm glad for you. How are all your family?'

'They're fine, except … that's the not-so-good news. My dad died literally a month after your gran, from a heart attack. It was such a shock.'

'I'm so sorry.'

He knew how close Claire's family were, in such contrast to his own, and he could only guess at the heartbreak her father's death would have caused her.

She smiled reminiscently. 'He warned me against you, you know.'

'No.' Harry was indignant. 'You told me your family liked me.'

'They did, but Dad said it would be a nightmare if it developed into a serious relationship because policemen were renowned for working antisocial hours and being unfaithful.'

'Oh, great. Well, the first one of those is probably true – the hours are bad – but as for the unfaithful bit …'

He watched the grin spread on Claire's face as he struggled to find the right words. Okay, so he'd had a varied and interesting love life over the years but he liked to think that if he settled down, that would be the end of it. Like most people … deep down he relished the idea of finding *The One*.

'Don't worry. I told him my hours were as bad as yours and that I reckoned I was a good judge of character. If I thought there was any sign of you being unfaithful, then I'd give you the boot.' She hesitated, then said lightly. 'Of course, we never even got that far, did we?'

'No.'

The atmosphere was suddenly charged, and there was something in her expression as she looked at him…

Then she banked down that expression and looked up as

the waiter approached.

'Ah food's here … and I don't know about you, but I'm starving.'

CHAPTER TWENTY-FOUR

Juliet

'*Ah, Juliet ... what are we going to do with you? You really have been most tiresome and you realise now, I can't let you go?*'

I'm lying on a bed, my hands tied. But why? I'm trying to identify that voice, but I can't. I can't remember anything about the circumstances at all. Who was holding me prisoner? Why? Was I pregnant when I was tied up? Had I had my baby? The questions loop violently back and forth in my head but I can't grab at an answer for any one of them. As always, it's as if I've jumped too far ahead and my brain isn't ready yet to process things out of sequence. But it's a man's voice. Is that relevant?

I concentrate fiercely, stopping myself from trying to force the information ... going back to where my brain feels comfortable, telling myself that all will be revealed if I'm patient.

Slowly, bit by bit, the memories start to filter through. I'm seven months pregnant and have been up in the big house for what feels like forever, undergoing the final phase of my initiation. I feel exhausted, drained. They warned me it would be hard but really I had no idea what I was letting myself in for. It's been non-stop teaching about Serenity's ethos, how its objective is to follow in the footsteps of God to bring peace and love to the world. People say it can't be done but Joshua believes it can – that if we start with small steps the rest will follow. Serenity's membership is increasing enormously, not just here in the UK but all over Europe, the Far East ... the world in fact. The movement for peace has never been stronger and they've shown me the videos, showing hundreds of thousands of people marching in protest against war and greed. He makes it sound so exciting that we're the fore-runners of this new momentum, and I so much want to believe in it. But I've always questioned things – too much for my own good my parents have often said – and maybe that's why it's taking me so long to convert. Fully conform. They seem to think I'm there now though, and it's a big day. Because today, I'm being allowed to go back to the cottage.

I can't wait, even though I feel guilty achieving this by deception. I've not seen anyone but Joshua, Fabian and the elders for the last two weeks, not even Dean, and I've felt so isolated here on my own, that in the end I pretended that I'm ready when really I don't feel any different at all. All I feel is a heavy lethargy and a deep sense of shame that I'm too weary to confront. I can't believe that this is really how it should be – that I'm no better than a zombie most of the time. Joshua and Fabian say it's because I've undergone such an incredible mental cleansing, and that this is what happens when you're stripped back to your bare soul ... that soon, the spirit of Serenity will fill me and it will be like the biggest high I've ever experienced. I don't know what to believe anymore and I don't seem to have the energy to question any of it. I just wish it would hurry up and fill me – give me the tremendous high they're promising, so that I can begin to feel again.

'It's so good to have you back,' Cara says now, giving me a hug as I drop my suitcase on the bed. I hug her back fiercely, holding on to her tight as I realise how much I've missed her. We laugh as our bumps get in the way.

'You're enormous,' I giggle, pulling back. 'When did that happen? Will I get as big as that?'

'Probably bigger,' she grins.

'How are you feeling about it? Nervous?'

She nods, her gaze sliding away from mine. But not before I've seen the tears welling in her eyes.

'What's the matter?' I ask quickly. 'Is everything alright?'

'I think so … it's just …' She looks nervously towards the door, as if expecting someone to be standing there, listening. 'We were out and about the other day and I tried to call my mum from a phone box … but Terence caught me. He got really angry – said that *Serenity's* my family now and was I saying that I didn't trust them to look after me well enough?' She lowers her voice. 'Can I trust you, Juliet?'

'Of course you can,'

'I've changed my mind about this baby. I don't want them to take it from me. I want to bring it up myself.'

'Me too,' I say quickly, the words tumbling out of my mouth before I'm even aware I'm going to utter them.

We look at each other, recognising the enormity of what we've just said.

'It's not just nerves,' she says, and I nod, knowing that we're both scared of where these thoughts might lead us and need time to absorb them. We swing around at the tap on the door, which then opens. It's Paula.

'Terence says for you to move your stuff back into my room, Cara, now Juliet's back. It's for the best, in case you have any problems.'

Cara lowers her gaze and nods her head. 'Of course,' she murmurs.

'I'll help you,' I say quickly, but Paula intervenes. 'Don't worry, I'll help her, you get on with your own unpacking. And then lunch is ready. We've done you a special welcome home meal.'

Lunch is a jolly affair, with everyone really pleased to have me back in the fold. For the first time in a month I feel myself relaxing – part of the family again.

'I sense a difference in you,' Terence says, pouring me a glass of the fruity elixir. 'The initiation went well?'

I nod, taking a large gulp of the drink I've come to love. It does such a good job of soothing me if I'm feeling unsettled – and whenever I think of my initiation I feel incredibly unsettled. My abiding memories will always be those of Joshua's possession of me – and then Brother Fabian's – until I 'happily' accepted giving myself to the *family*. I can't think about it – it's too upsetting – and because of my resistance, they even stopped me from seeing Dean, saying that clearly his hold over me was too strong. Belatedly, I realised the only way I was going to be allowed to return to our cottage was to pretend that I welcomed them in my bed. In other words, to lie. But that goes against everything Serenity is supposed to stand for and leaves me in an even worse state of confusion. Now, I lie again.

'It went well,' I say, 'and I'm happy to be back here with you.' The last bit at least is true.

Terence smiles and I know that was the right answer; but after that day it seems to me that Cara and I are being watched like hawks. It's almost impossible to have any private conversation and on the rare occasion that we manage to slip into each other's rooms to try to talk, someone always interrupts within a minute of us being there. It's obvious we're being spied upon, which feels creepy – could someone have overheard our conversation in the bedroom that day? Most of the time I feel too tired to think about it. The good news though is that Dean's coming back for a few days to see me and I feel so lucky to at least have him, when Cara has no one. She'd been in an abusive relationship and Serenity had saved her. On my more lucid days it strikes me that she's swapped one bad situation for another.

$$\backsim$$

'Quick, come in here.' A hand shoots out from the bathroom and yanks me inside. It's Cara and her face is ravaged from crying.

'What's the matter?' I ask. She hasn't been well this week and now she looks awful.

'I feel so ill, Juliet. The doctor said I was fine yesterday and the baby will come any day now – but I don't feel fine. I'm frightened. I wanted them to take me to the hospital – but they say there's no need.'

'I'm sure they know what they're doing,' I offer tentatively. 'And didn't they say you'd have the baby in hospital anyway, because of your blood pressure?'

'Yes.'

'Well, there you are then, as soon as you start your labour you'll be in the best hands. It's so exciting, Cara, I can't wait to meet little baby Rose after all this time.'

Unlike me, Cara had opted to know the sex of her baby and we'd spent hours choosing the name. As I hoped, my words bring a smile to her face.

'It does seem unreal to think that maybe a couple of days from now, I'll be a mother,' she says. 'But I've made a decision.' She lowers her voice. 'I'm going to tell the hospital doctors that I don't want to come back here. That I want to go home... I reckon that way Serenity can't force me to come back.'

A bang on the door makes us both jump. 'What's going on in there?' Terence asks. 'Is everything alright?'

We exchange looks and I move over to the door and open it. 'Cara's not feeling well. I was just massaging her back for her.'

He looks at Cara suspiciously. 'I hope you haven't been unsettling Juliet like we talked about? It's not fair on her in her condition.'

'No, I haven't,' she says. 'I feel dizzy though – I think I need to lie down. I don't feel too good.'

I slide my arm through Cara's and we walk slowly to her room with Terence following. I settle her carefully on top of the bed and kiss her on the forehead. 'Call me if you need anything, okay?' I say.

She nods.

And that's the last time I see my friend.

CHAPTER TWENTY-FIVE

Harry finished speaking at the early morning meeting and looked round at everyone in the room. 'So … it's obvious that the good brethren of Serenity haven't been entirely straight with us which is why I think they merit another visit. An unexpected one this time. Geoff, you've got the warrant? Right, take Beth and Tom, and as many people as you can round up. First off, I want an unannounced sweep on the nursery and residences to check there are no newborn babies anywhere. While I'm questioning Dean Jarvis and Brother Fabian, I want you to mingle with the community and find out what you can. I want as many people questioned as possible and I want names of everyone you interview plus a comprehensive list of all the commune members who live at Serenity Hall – including those who sometimes spend time elsewhere. Anyone you feel is even mildly suspicious, or might be worth questioning further, you bring them in. I want all hands on deck for this one; we need to catch them by surprise to maximise our chances of actually learning something useful. That baby is somewhere – and I'm sure as I can be, that the answers to our questions lie within the commune. They're hiding something. Let's find out what it is.

As Harry got shown into Joshua Jarvis's old office, Dean was standing by the widow looking out.

'Three police cars and a van,' he commented, turning round. 'That seems a bit heavy.'

'We have a warrant to search the premises. We need to question everyone in the community and as I'm sure you'll appreciate, that will take a bit of time.'

'What about?' he asked, moving back to the desk and indicating a chair to Harry.

'Have you moved in here, now?' Harry asked, ignoring his question.

'Oh no,' Dean replied. 'I'm just going through some of Dad's stuff, trying to prioritise it. So … what do you want to talk to me about?'

'I wondered if you could help me out with something? We've been looking into some women who seem to have disappeared after spending time at Serenity. One of them, Cara Swift, only very recently. I did mention it to your father and we've been trying to trace those women – so far without success.'

Dean frowned. 'Well, I remember Cara, of course, but I wasn't aware she'd disappeared. Who told you that?'

'Her parents. They came forward after they heard the news on television about Juliet Sanderson. They apparently hadn't seen or heard from her in over a year, apart from a phone call a couple of months back where she asked them to meet up with her. When they got there, she'd gone.'

'Look, I'm sorry but I know nothing about that. As I've said before, I've spent most of the last few months up in Newcastle helping out up there. I only know what I learned when I got back on a visit, which was that Cara had chosen

202

to leave. You'd be better off speaking to Fabian about any previous members here. He was my father's right-hand man and knows much more about the day-to-day happenings in Serenity than I do.'

'Is he around?'

'He's probably in the library. I can take you to him.'

'Thank you, if you wouldn't mind?'

As Harry followed him out of the room, he asked. 'Where did Cara Swift live when she was here?'

'In one of the cottages.'

'Which one?'

There was the slightest of hesitations before Dean answered. 'Number four.'

'Isn't that the same one as Juliet Sanderson? And you, when you're here?'

Harry was grateful for Beth's diligent homework in passing that little nugget of information over to him.

'Yes. Juliet and Cara were quite friendly, I seem to remember.'

'Were you and Cara … friendly?'

'If by that you mean did we pair, then no.'

'Why not?'

'I'm sorry?'

'Well, an attractive young woman. If pairing, as you call it, is so free and easy within the commune, that would be quite a natural follow on, I'd have thought.'

'We just didn't.'

'Because you and Juliet were an item? I have to say, I'm finding it increasingly difficult to believe that no one has any idea who the father of Juliet's baby is – and when I look at the information we do have, your name is top of the list of possibles, bearing in mind you were with Juliet both here and over her time in Northumberland.'

'I told you … she wouldn't tell us who the father was.'

'I know you did – I'm just not sure I believe you. I'll be wanting to head over to the cottage after I've spoken to Brother Fabian, to have a word with the other occupants. Can you let them know and ask them to make themselves available?'

They went down the large staircase and doubled back on themselves, coming to a halt outside a solid oak door. A brief tap and Dean opened it.

'Fabian? D I Briscombe would like a quick word with you about Cara Swift?'

The man looked up. His shoulder-length hair was loose today and the way he sat back in his chair indicated his own sense of self-importance. He didn't offer Harry a seat, or get up from his own.

'Cara? Of course, but what about her? She's not here anymore.'

'Yes, well that's what I want to speak to you about,' Harry said, nodding at Dean as he headed off. 'According to her parents, you told them that she'd left Serenity to go and live with her ex-partner.'

'That's right. She came to us originally because she was trying to end the relationship, but we suspected that he was still on the scene, and unfortunately that was confirmed to us when she told us that they'd patched things up and she was moving out.'

'Well, we've now spoken to him and that's not what he says. He says he hasn't seen her since she moved in here.'

'Maybe he's lying – or she was when she said she was going back to him.'

'How did Serenity feel about her going?'

'Sad to lose her, but people come and go as they please – we don't hold them against their will. And if you have any doubts about that, I can supply you with a long list of members who have done just that. Joshua did try to talk her out of going, but …' He shrugged. 'It happens. What more can I say.'

'Strange that the exact same thing should happen with Juliet though? You see why we might want to make sure that Cara is safe?'

Fabian made no response to that.

'On another note, can you tell me what happens to people's money when they join here? With Juliet, we noticed that she had no money going in or out of her account during her time here until a few months back, when three thousand pounds cash was paid in. Almost the entire amount was withdrawn in cash, by a male in a hooded jacket, over the last couple of weeks.'

'A lot of people here donate their savings to the community once they decide to stay, usually because they're committed to our cause and don't particularly want the responsibility of looking after their finances themselves. Someone like Juliet may not have been ready for that step quite yet and we wouldn't have dreamt of pushing her. I have no idea what the three thousand pounds would have been for, or who withdrew it. As far as we're concerned, people's financial situations are their own business unless they choose to hand responsibility over to Serenity.'

Harry bit back on his frustration. 'Well, I have to tell you that quite a few things aren't stacking up as far as your organisation's concerned and we're looking into some matters that we feel warrant further investigation. As well as the fact that three women supposedly left and subsequently disappeared without trace – until one turned up stabbed – we also have reason to suspect that Joshua was involved in some sort of illegal activity, and we're not ruling out blackmail. There was over fifty thousand pounds in cash in his safe. Would you happen to know anything about that?'

Fabian gave a soft, incredulous laugh. 'Illegal activity? Joshua? I never heard such nonsense. Joshua was committed to Serenity and all it stands for. Our job is to help people and spread the Lord's word, not blackmail them. But in answer to your question, no, I don't know anything about the money in his safe. And as for the women disappearing without trace, I'm sure that once you investigate the matter fully, you'll find there's a perfectly reasonable explanation for where they went to from here. I think you're barking up the wrong tree, detective inspector, I really do.'

There was nothing in his manner to reflect anxiety at being caught out in anything untoward, but then again, Harry was beginning to wonder if the man ever showed emotion of any kind. There was something unnerving about the vacancy in his eyes as their gazes met; it felt like there was no connection between them at all.

'What happens with regard to Joshua's Will, do you know?' Harry asked. 'Who inherits his personal wealth?'

'Now there I can help you. If any of us die, any belongings or wealth we may have are bequeathed to Serenity and I happen to know that's the case with Joshua, because I'm his executor.'

'His son inherits nothing?'

'Joshua had fourteen children, most of whom still live within the community – though not all here at Serenity Hall. None of them will benefit personally from his will.'

'Right. Well, I'll need their names and we'll be checking

that out, obviously. Now, I'd like to speak to the occupants of the cottage where Cara Swift lived, please.'

'Of course. If you go out of the front door and go round to the gardens at the back, there's a pathway that leads to the cottages. She was in number four.'

⤳

As Harry drove back to the station an hour later, he couldn't help thinking that none of it felt right. As it happened, there had only been Terence Burrell and the older woman, Sheila, at the cottage, the other occupants having been requested by Beth to accompany her back to the station for further questioning. It was obvious that Terence was incensed at this. He'd apparently insisted that he go with them as they would find it intimidating, but Beth had refused, saying that they were all of age and perfectly capable of answering a few questions by themselves.

Although Terence, who clearly ruled the roost in the house, had seemed fairly unfazed by Harry's questions, the same couldn't be said for Sheila, who'd looked apprehensive, then positively agitated, as he'd dug deeper for information. She'd looked to Terence for guidance on almost everything he asked … but she was adamant that Cara had left a couple of months back and none of them had had any contact with her since.

'You have to see why it all looks a bit suspicious to us?' he said, directing his gaze first at Terence and then at Sheila. 'That both Juliet and Cara suddenly disappear off the scene, supposedly for the same reason, after having lived in this house?'

Again the woman looked to Terence for guidance, but she followed his lead in saying nothing and, on the basis that Beth had already rounded up several people for further questioning at the station, Harry decided to postpone until the following day, doing the same with these two. He'd wait and see what the others had to offer, which might then become grounds for further questioning.

CHAPTER TWENTY-SIX

Juliet

I lie here in the peace of my room, listening to the low, soporific bleep of the monitor beside me, and now I can hardly keep up with the rush of memories that are storming in.

Cara's gone and it's an unspoken cloud that hangs over the house. She apparently needs to be erased from our minds, as she did what she told me she was going to do – the ultimate betrayal – and decided she didn't want to return to Serenity after having her baby. Dean's back for a few days and we'd been woken in the night by her cries but when I tried to get out of bed to go to her, he told me to stay put – he'd go and see what was happening. He was back very quickly.

'She's fine. Sheila's with her and she's in labour. They're taking her to the hospital, there's nothing we can do and we'd probably only get in the way.'

'*I'm leaving here and never coming back*,' I hear her scream. '*Do you hear me?*'

I look at Dean anxiously, but he smiles reassuringly. 'She doesn't mean it. You wait and see what you'll be screaming when your time comes. Giving birth certainly brings out the worst in people! Now go back to sleep … tomorrow you'll be able to visit her and see the baby.'

But that never happened.

'Why can't I go?' I ask Dean the next day as we sit on the sofa in the breakfast room together, and he shakes his head, looking upset.

'Sheila and Paula sat with her all night at the hospital. Then, when she had the baby, she told them that she wasn't coming back to Serenity and never wanted to see us again.'

He looks completely bemused by this and it reinforces yet again the huge difference in our upbringings.

'Maybe she missed not having her mother there?' I query tentatively. I'm beginning to realise that when I have my own baby, that's what I want – Mum and Dean seeing me through it – not Sheila or Paula, kind though they are. 'It's what I want,' I add.

'What do you mean?'

'When I have my baby … I want the two people I love most in the world to be with me, and that's you and my mum.'

He rubs a frantic hand through his hair. 'Jules, you can't do that, surely you can see that? We're your family now – I'm your family. You've made commitments to Serenity, you can't undo all that.'

Now's my chance to tell him that I've changed my mind, and I take the bull by the horns, saying quietly.

'Dean, I get that this is the only life you've known but you know the world outside isn't the awful place you all seem to think it is. There's so much more freedom and independence there – and you can still be a good Christian and lead a good life,' I add quickly.

'What are you saying?'

'I'm saying that I've given your way of life a try for the last year, and I'm not sure it's working for me – for us.

Couldn't you give mine a try for a while? We could live with my mum and dad until we get sorted. You'd really like them. I'm thinking about our baby … how it would be so much better for us to bring it up ourselves. Wouldn't you like that too?'

The look on his face is one of sheer horror as his eyes dart quickly around to see if anyone's listening. 'We can't talk about it here,' he says in a low voice, rising from his chair to help me up. He looks through to where Terence is reading a newspaper in the lounge.

'We're just heading upstairs for a little while,' he says.

'Lunch will be served in half an hour,' Sheila informs us, and looks at me reproachfully as if to say that my condition doesn't exempt me from helping out a bit more.

Up in our bedroom I sit on the bed as Dean paces the room, and I want to go and put my arms around him to comfort him, feeling guilty that I'm the one causing him such distress.

'I don't know what to say to you Juliet, I really don't. I love you, you know that, but why are you always trying to make me choose between you and Serenity?'

'I'm not.'

'You are. I don't get why you have to make things so difficult. Other people who join us embrace the way of life – accept that it's hard turning their back on old ways, but realising they're doing it to better themselves. Doesn't it excite you, the thought that we're the forbearers of things to come? That the children of Serenity will be instrumental in leading the world to a better way?'

I find I just can't admit to him that I no longer believe that. 'I don't get why mothers are happy to hand their children over to the commune to be brought up,' I say stubbornly.

'It's not natural. A child should be with its parents.'

'But a lot of parents are damaged – we all are – far better for them to be raised by people who know what they're doing. Who can bring the very best out in them, surely?'

'Make them perfect followers of Serenity, you mean?'

'Yes. What's wrong with that? You disappoint me, Juliet. I thought you believed in me … in what we do here.'

'I do, it's just that … I've got a few weeks to go before I have my first baby and I want my mum. What's wrong with that? I need to see her.'

'Are you forgetting how she deceived you for all those years? How much she hurt you?'

'No, but I miss her – and my dad and sister – just like you'd miss Sheila if you never saw her again.'

But even as I say the words, I wonder how true that is. It had come out almost by accident that Sheila was his mother – that she'd paired with Joshua all those years ago – and he didn't seem particularly close to either of them, nor they to each other.

'I want to visit them, Dean. Please say you'll take me? I know you're probably worried that they'll talk me into staying with them but I'll come back with you, I promise.'

The words are loosely spoken because I'm not at all sure I'm speaking the truth. I just need to persuade him. I hold my breath, even as my heart goes out to him. I know how difficult I make life for him sometimes, and all he's ever shown me is love. Finally he relaxes just a little, and I know I've won.

'Okay,' he sighs, 'we'll visit them at the weekend as long as you promise me you won't leave me?'

I'm so excited at the thought of seeing my family that I give the promise without hesitation and around the table that night at supper I'm beaming from ear to ear, though I make no mention of our plans to Terence or the others. Terence wouldn't approve, I sense that without being told it and I don't want to say anything that might jeopardise things.

'You seem particularly happy tonight, Juliet,' Terence says and I smile at him breezily. 'I'm feeling at one with the spirit of the community,' I say, knowing it's the sort of language he likes. Paula and I had spent two hours that afternoon undergoing a grueling Bible lesson with him and I'd almost lost the will to live, but now he nods sagely and I know he's attributing my newfound contentment to his teachings. Everyone is smiling at me, teasing me about the bump that's getting bigger now, and as I take a sip of water, my eyes meeting Dean's across the table, I feel myself relax again, settling back into my groove. I do like it here, it's just that I've realised I want to bring my baby up myself.

Time's moved on. My bump is much larger now and there's a horrible atmosphere in the cottage. I feel miserable and I'm beginning to wonder what I'm doing here. I know the real cause for my depression… it's because I never got to see my parents that weekend and I just can't shake off the bitter disappointment of that. Dean and I had kept it our secret – we hadn't told a single person – and then Joshua ruined it all by telling Dean he needed to go back to Newcastle urgently. I was so disappointed I even threatened to go on my own. But even as I said the words I wondered who I was kidding, for I realise now that my life is no longer my own – this baby is no longer my own – and until I have it, maybe in less than a week now, I'm effectively a prisoner in Serenity.

'Please don't go,' I say to Dean as I watch him pack his case yet again.

'I have no choice, Juliet.'

'Of course you do, they can't force you to go, and our baby is due any day now. What happens if I go into labour while you're still away?'

'Joshua will call me, I'll come straight back.'

'Dean…' I take a deep breath but know it's now or never. 'I've changed my mind.'

He looks at me sharply. 'What do you mean, what about?'

'About the baby… about everything.'

I shake my head trying to clear the constant fog that seems to inhabit my brain these days. Am I really considering the possibility of leaving this life, of leaving Dean, if it comes to it?

'I'm sorry, but it's so different to anything I've ever known and I've tried, Dean, I really have. I love you and I can't bear the thought of not being with you, but—'

'Then stop talking like this. What are you saying? That you want to leave Serenity? Leave me?'

'No … yes … I mean, I want to leave Serenity but I want you to come with me. Come to my parents – they'll help us start a new life together with our baby.'

'You know we can't do that—'

'But I've changed my mind. I'm allowed to do that, aren't I? I know at the beginning I didn't want to be pregnant, and didn't want the baby, but now I can feel it moving … it's become a part of me and I don't want anyone else bringing it up. I want to bring it up myself. It's what Cara wanted too – that's why she didn't come back, because she didn't want to give up her baby.'

'Juliet, we talked about this – how things are done here … all the options. We both agreed that apart from anything else we weren't ready yet to settle down and be parents – and even if we were, that's not how it's done here, you know that. Ours is a way of life that's existed for years and sometimes it involves self-sacrifice but it makes better people of us. How can you even think of disrupting everything like this?'

I jump up from my chair. I don't want to hear it all again. 'If you don't want to come with me then fine, I'll go alone,' I say.

'Go where?' A smooth voice enquires from the doorway.

I spin round to see Joshua. How long has he been standing there?

'I want to go home,' I say defiantly. 'To my parents.'

'Of course you can do that,' he says pleasantly, 'but not until after you've had the baby – and if you remember, you signed an agreement about that. It's a child of Serenity now. We decide its future. You won't be able to take it with you.'

I feel the tears spill down my cheek. 'This is my baby. You can't force me to give it to you.'

'And doesn't Dean have a say, as the father? Nobody wants to force you to do anything, Juliet – what I'd like is for you to think about the agreement we made. We did it to help you out because, if you remember, at the time you were considering killing your child by having an abortion? You've taken all the hospitality we've offered you, and become one of us – it's hurtful now that you want to throw it all back in our faces. I think you should spend tonight thinking about that, and all that we've done for you. And pray to God for enlightenment.'

He turned to Dean. 'Take five minutes to say goodbye to Juliet, and then come and see me at the house before you head off. Thomas is hoping you'll get there in time to help with the recruitment session this evening.'

Without another word he turns and leaves.

For a moment nothing is said. Then Dean steps forward his hands reaching out to cup my shoulders as he draws my resisting body towards him. 'Don't leave me, Juliet.' His eyes are intent as they burn into mine. 'Joshua may be running things now but he won't be Lead Brother forever. When I take over I can change things, just be patient.'

'But that could be years away. It doesn't help me now, Dean. Why can't you stand up to him and just leave?'

'Because this is my life and that's not the path God's chosen for me. I'm singled out to be the next leader of Serenity, I know that. I will be Lead Brother. Do you realise how powerful that position is? I can give you whatever you want then, but please, don't let me down now.'

But for the first time, as his lips settle persuasively on mine, I know that I'm going to defy him. Already, the plan is spinning in my mind. When I go into labour and they take me to the hospital, I'll do the same as Cara and tell the staff there that I don't want to come back – that I want to go home to my parents.

The day after Dean's departure I'm desperate to escape the stultifying atmosphere of the cottage. Things have changed, I can sense it. I'm viewed as someone to be suspicious of – almost an enemy now, rather than one of them. Even Paula's wary around me, as if she might be tarnished by association. I miss Cara so much, and I think that's what's unsettled me. It all seemed so easy when I first met Dean and got swept along by my love for him, and the thought of being able to

216

park my troubles so that I didn't need to deal with them. The counselling sessions I had in the early days made me feel so good. It was as if Joshua really got what I was going through, tapped into my deepest unhappiness and showed me that there was a way through it. But the sessions I had in my final indoctrination seem to have done the complete opposite of that. They've unsettled me, made me question everything about myself and realise how flawed a person I am; how I deceived myself, living in a delusion of misguided self-belief that, at the age of nineteen, I knew everything, and could make the right decisions. Now, my brain feels foggy all the time, incapable of making any decisions at all, and I don't have a view on anything. I have no self-confidence, and I still can't come to terms with the fact that the love I'd saved for Dean has been cheapened by the knowledge that I allowed other men to possess me – that he allowed other men to possess me.

Two o'clock is 'reflection' time when we all go to our rooms to meditate and ask God for guidance. We're all reminded by Terence, at lunchtime, that I in particular need guidance, and am suffering a crisis of confidence. Everyone must pray for me. I want to scream my frustration at them. I don't want their prayers, I want to go home. I feel like a prisoner here, and although they've always said I'm free to walk out at any time, I know it's not true. I remember only too well Joshua's words about how I can only leave after I've had my baby.

The house is quiet. Everyone's in their room and all I know is that I need some fresh air. I open my bedroom door and look out. My room's quite close to the stairs and there's no one around. Without stopping for thought, I close the door behind me and slip silently down the stairs and out

217

of the house. Immediately, I feel the weight lifting. It's a lovely crisp autumn day and I find myself walking towards the impressive gardens that back the cottages. They're extensive, leading to a large wooded copse at the bottom, with a lake to one side. It's the woods that I head for, they'll give me more privacy than the exposed lake area. On the border of the woods I sit down on a bench and at last I have time to think. I've been drinking less of the elixir this last couple of days because, although it lessens my anxiety, I've realised it also muddles my thoughts – deadens my senses and emotions – and I don't like how that feels. I'm clearer in my head than I've been in a long time.

I remember how Cara and I used to sneak off down here when all the praying and high worship got a bit too much for us. In those days, it was all a bit of a giggle and we were so glad to have found each other – fellow conspirators who could secretly share their irreverent thoughts. She'd been there a shorter time than I had but, although like me, she struggled with the intensity of some of the teachings, I'd always thought her a committed convert to Serenity, and she'd been my guiding light. Especially when Joshua was always sending Dean off to do other things and he was no longer the constant presence in my life that he had been. The void she's left is huge. I'm glad for her sake that she had the courage of her convictions and got out, but I can't help wishing she'd thought to try and get me out somehow, too. I feel the tears well up in my eyes again and for once, in the privacy of that wood, I give vent to the unhappiness that's been plaguing me for weeks. But even then, out of habit, I keep my sobs low, not wanting to draw attention to myself.

'Hello.'

I jump at the sound of the voice, then relax when I see that it's only Emanuel, the gardener's assistant. He's a couple of years older than me and clearly has learning difficulties, but we've struck up a relationship since I've been here, because we discovered that we have an interest in common. Nature and birds.

'You shouldn't be in this part of the garden,' he says with a worried look around.

I quickly blow my nose and try to look unconcerned. 'How are your nesting boxes? Did you get many birds using them?'

He gives me a shy smile and nods. 'They all got used, even my new robin boxes. Do you want to see them?'

I shake my head, tapping my stomach. 'Another time. I'm tired, and …' I hesitate, feeling the need to offload to someone, yet knowing there's no point sharing my troubles with him. 'I'm feeling a bit sad today…' I trail off with a shrug.

'Is that because you miss your friend?' he asks, and I nod, touched that he should remember my friendship with Cara. 'I'm feeling sad and if she was here, she'd know what to say to cheer me up,' I say,

He stares at me, his soft brown eyes filled with concern. 'I don't like it when people cry.'

I sniff loudly and pull out a tissue to wipe my eyes. 'I'm not crying now, and sometimes it makes people feel better after they've cried.'

'Would it make you feel better if I take you to her?' he asks.

I shake my head, smiling sadly. 'I wish you could, but she's not here anymore.'

He looks frightened then, his eyes darting nervously around as if he's worried that someone might be listening.

'Yes she is. I can take you to her but it might make you

219

more sad and you mustn't tell anyone.'

I look at him in confusion, and the expression on his face sends a trail of ice down my spine.

'What do you mean? Where is she?'

He looks suddenly unsure. 'I thought you knew.'

'Knew what? What's there to know? She left here to have her baby and then decided she didn't want to come back.'

He wrings his hands, looking even more worried. 'I got to go.'

He turns, starts to lumber away from me. 'You're right, she left here,' he repeats woodenly. But there's something wrong. He's lying, I can tell. I jump up and run after him, grabbing him by the arm. 'Emanuel! What did you mean when you said you'd take me to her? Where is she? What aren't you telling me?'

His expression is terrifying me. I shake his arm. 'Tell me, or … I'll report you to Joshua.' It's mean to say that, and I regret the words as soon as they're out of my mouth, but they have the desired effect.

'No,' he says, looking anxious, 'don't do that, he'll kill me if he knows I told you.'

'Told me *what*? I promise I won't say anything to anyone. I'm your friend. You know you can trust me.'

He stares at me penetratingly for a long time and I feel suddenly wary. 'Not quite all there,' Dean had said – and the look on his face is so wild that for a moment I wonder if I'm safe with him.

'*She's dead,*' he whispers theatrically, grabbing my hand. 'Come with me and I'll take you to her.'

'*Juliet!*'

Emanuel drops my hand as if it burns him, and I startle at the sound of Terence's voice. They must have discovered

220

that I'm missing.

'I must go,' Emanuel says quickly. 'Don't tell them I told you.' And before I can say anymore, he's gone, melting into the bushes as quickly and silently as he appeared.

I cast a bewildered glance after him, then sit quickly back down on my bench. Behind me I can hear voices getting closer. My heart's thumping. Cara's *dead*? Can it be true? Suddenly, I'm terrified. For myself, my baby – I just want Mum and Dad to take me away from here back to the safety of home. It doesn't matter anymore about Dad not being my biological father. They love me, I know that – have always known it – and that's all that matters. But how can I contact them? We're not allowed mobile phones in the community and the only way I could call them would be to get my hands on either Terence or Sheila's phones.

'She's here,' Paula shouts out from behind me, sounding relieved, and I turn around to face her. 'Where have you been? We were worried about you.'

I find myself looking at her closely, wondering how much I can trust her, but her concerned gaze seems genuine enough and I relax a little.

'It was stuffy in the cottage. I needed some fresh air and thought I'd go for a walk. I'm fine now.'

But I'm not fine, I'm shaking like a leaf and I try to hide it as Terence strides towards me, his eyes blazing with anger. 'Where have you been?'

'Just here, in the garden. I was walking by the lake; I came over all hot in the   house—'

'Well, it's cold out here and you could get a chill. You should have told someone you were going out, what if you'd fallen or had an accident, in your condition?'

'I'm sorry … I didn't think. I felt a bit faint and just

221

needed to get some air.'

I hope that the fact I'm shaky now adds a bit of authenticity to my words.

'You mustn't leave the house in future without telling someone, do you understand? You don't go anywhere on your own, and Paula, you will move into Juliet's room and sleep with her so that you can keep an eye on her.'

His hard eyes are drilling into mine but it's not concern I see reflected in them, it's suspicion. I summon all the acting skills I possess as I force a tight lipped smile to my face and apologise again, agreeing to do as he says. Inside I'm quaking with fear at what Emanuel's revealed. It was his expression as much as his words that terrified me. Something awful is going on, I can sense it.

As we all troop back to the house I'm filled with despair that I'll never be able to escape – but then a sudden thought comes to me, and with it, a glimmer of hope.

'I ... I've got a hospital appointment tomorrow and I think I'd like to keep it. I've not been feeling too good this last couple of days. It would reassure me to know everything's fine with the baby.'

I see Terence look at Sheila, and then he shrugs. 'I'll speak to Joshua about it for you, I'm sure we can arrange something.'

'Thank you.'

My heart flips. It's my only chance to get away and I'll grab it. Tomorrow, I'll tell the people at the hospital that I don't want to come back to Serenity, and absolutely refuse to budge from that clinic until they call my mum and dad.

Somehow, I manage to hold it together as I make my way back to the house, but up in the privacy of the bathroom, as I stare at my pale reflection in the mirror, I can't stop the tears from spilling over.

Movement from my belly reminds me that my baby's due to be born in less than a week and I've signed away my rights to bring it up as my own, to teach it the values I was taught; to keep it safe. I'm far worse than Mum, who at least kept me close and in her life.

What can I do?

If only Dean was here, he'd know how to handle this. I refuse to believe that he knows anything about what might have happened to Cara.

I hardly recognise the girl staring back at me, the terror on my face mirroring the exact same terror I'd sensed in Cara. It's a huge wake-up call.

I need to escape.

CHAPTER TWENTY-SEVEN

Beth put two heaped scoops of coffee into the pot and filled it up with water, discharging its contents into two cups. 'Sugar, Victoria?' she asked, and the young girl nodded, her face tight with tension. Terence had made a fuss when Beth had insisted on bringing Paula and Victoria in for questioning without him, but it had become obvious very quickly that the only way she had any chance of getting anything out of them was to separate them from him.

They were in a little side room that was set out more casually than a formal interview room, and Beth walked over to where the girl was sitting and put the cups and sugar bowl down onto the table.

'I probably shouldn't in my condition,' Victoria said, scooping a heaped teaspoon of sugar into her cup, 'because I know it's not good, but they say you get cravings don't they?'

'You're pregnant?' Beth was surprised.

The girl nodded, relaxing her face just enough to allow a small smile. 'twenty-two weeks, but it's not showing yet.'

'Congratulations. Is it your first?'

'Yes.' She stirred her coffee and put the spoon carefully back on the saucer, then looked at Beth, waiting for her to speak. She was slightly built and looked as timid as a sparrow, and Beth half expected her to jump up and run out of the room at any moment.

'Okay, pet. I need to ask you a couple of questions, if that's okay? As you know, we're trying to find out who attacked Juliet and who killed Joshua.'

Victoria nodded.

'How well did you know Juliet?'

'Not very. We overlapped in the same house for a short while after I moved in.'

'Why was that? Where were you before that?'

'In one of the other houses, but when you're pregnant the elders try to put you into one of the cottages that has a midwife in it, so that you've always got someone there if you have any problems. It's a reassurance.'

'I can see it would be. Did Juliet have any problems with her pregnancy?'

'Not that I know of.'

'And she was happy there?'

Victoria nodded. 'As far as I know, but you'd be better off talking to Paula. They were quite close.'

'Do you know who the father of her baby was?'

'No … none of us did.'

'I find that hard to believe, Victoria. Have you been told to say that?'

She didn't answer.

'How close was she to Dean?'

'They got on alright.'

'Was he the father of her baby? From what we can put together, he seems the most likely candidate.'

'We don't know who the father was.'

It was obvious she wasn't going to deviate from that path, so Beth changed tack.

225

'What about Cara Swift? Did you know her?'

The girl looked surprised, but shook her head.

'What? You never met her?'

'Not properly. She'd left by the time I moved in. I saw her around, at meetings and the like, but I never had much to do with her.'

'Where did she move out to?'

'I don't know. As I say, she'd gone by the time I moved in.'

'And then Juliet decided to leave too. Didn't that strike you as a bit odd?'

The girl sighed, then said reluctantly. 'Juliet had some issues—'

'What issues?'

'I … I don't know. But she went back to her boyfriend.'

'Yet no one knows who that boyfriend is. Doesn't that strike you as odd?'

'Serenity did their best by her but she threw our help back in our face.'

'Was it because she was unhappy about her baby being taken away from her to be brought up in the nursery? Is that why she was unhappy? That would be a big thing for someone coming in from the outside.'

Victoria's lips clamped together. 'We did everything we could to make her feel welcome and part of our family. That's all I have to say.'

'How old are you?'

'Eighteen.'

'And how long have you been a member of Serenity.'

'All my life. I'm a true blood.'

'A true blood?'

'Yes. I was born into the community.'

'Right. Your baby, when it's born. How does that work?

Will it stay with you, or you both go into the nursery straight away?'

'Usually we both go to the nursery. I was meant to be having a talk with Joshua about it all, but –'

'He was killed?'

She nodded.

'Do you have any idea who might have done that? Did you ever see or hear anything that suggested someone might be out to harm him?'

'No.' She looked surprised at the question. 'I didn't have much to do with him at all. He was Lead Brother.'

'Going back to your baby. Does it bother you that you won't bring it up yourself? That someone else will be doing that?'

'I wouldn't know what to do with it. It's so important that children are brought up properly, and Serenity, as a family, knows how to do that. They turn perfect children into perfect followers, who continue on and spread the word of the Lord.'

The words trotted out of her mouth, a mantra.

'Is that how you were brought up? Are you a perfect follower?'

She looked serious. 'I try to be. Serenity is my life. I know people outside don't understand our community, but they don't realise how far they've strayed from the path and how, when the time of reckoning comes, they won't be among the chosen ones like we will.'

Dear God, Beth really didn't know where to go with all this. It was obvious that the girl believed everything she was saying – and how did you even begin to start picking it apart?

'So you're quite happy about handing your baby over to the mother hens, as I believe you call them? Isn't there a part of you that would like to bring it up yourself?'

There was the slightest of hesitations. 'I've been warned that it might be hard handing my baby over. But we are one family and that is what sustains us. God will help me accept that it's for the best if we want our children to be strong followers and preachers of the path.'

CHAPTER TWENTY-EIGHT

As a consequence of her interview with Victoria, Beth felt she was a little better prepared for what to expect from Paula. There was no doubt the woman looked nervy and on edge but unlike Victoria, she was composed and didn't look to be someone who was frightened of her own shadow.

'Are you okay?' she asked the woman now. 'Can I get you a drink of any sort?'

'No, I'm fine thanks. How's Juliet?'

'She's holding her own, but she's still in a coma.'

'When can I see her?'

'Not for a while, I'm afraid. Her family are with her but until we find out who attacked her, you understand we have to be very careful who we let in to see her?'

The woman nodded. 'I just don't understand who would do a thing like that.'

'We intend finding out, which is why you're here, to see if you can help us at all.'

'I don't see how I can.'

'Were you and Juliet close?'

'Quite.' She smiled. 'She was good fun – bright and breezy, you know? At least—' She broke off.

'At least what?'

'Nothing. She seemed a bit down towards the end. That's all.'

'Paula, we've found no trace of a boyfriend for her to go back to, and I have to tell you that there are a few things coming out of Serenity that aren't stacking up. If there's anything you can tell us at all, to do with her attack or Joshua's murder?'

'I told you, there's nothing.'

'If you're worried you'll get into trouble for talking—'

'I'm not.'

Beth sighed her frustration and started again. 'We're very concerned about Juliet's baby and its whereabouts. Do you have any idea where it is?'

'No.'

'You don't look very concerned about it, which makes me wonder if you're telling the truth. Perhaps you do know where the baby is … that it's safe … and that's why you're not too worried?'

'Why are you saying these things, trying to catch me out? Making out that Serenity's some sort of evil organisation, so that I'll speak against them? I know it's different to what you'd call normal life, but they help so many people – people like me. I was lost and floundering before I joined the commune – ready to end it all. My parents were killed in a train crash when I was ten and I was in and out of foster homes from then until my teens – and you don't want to know what went on or what I got up to. I had nowhere to go, nowhere to call home, until I found the commune. Sometimes it's hard following their beliefs, but I put all my faith in them and I've never had any regrets. They've taken me under their wing and given me security. I want for nothing and I'd do anything for them.'

'Even lie?'

Their eyes locked. 'No one in the commune would have stabbed Juliet, or murdered Joshua. It goes against all our teachings. Whoever it is, you should be looking for someone outside.'

'Juliet had marks on her body, as if she'd been tied up and beaten.'

The girl shook her head and dropped her eyes, but not before Beth saw the tears swimming in them.

'Do you know anything about that?'

'No.' Her voice was husky.

'I'm not sure you're telling me the truth, Paula. Does Serenity dish out punishment if people ... misbehave?'

No answer.

'You say Juliet left – maybe to go back to her boyfriend, maybe not. Why was that – was she unhappy at the commune?'

'I think she struggled with some of our beliefs.'

'Like, maybe the fact she wouldn't be bringing up her baby herself?'

'That may have been an issue as she wasn't used to our ways, but they counselled her a lot about it.'

'Did they counsel you about it? Do you not miss having your children around you, cuddling them at night when they can't sleep? Loving them?'

'Of course I do.' Her voice was husky with emotion. 'But I accept that I know nothing about being a good parent. It's better this way.'

'But is it? Do you really believe that? That it's better for your children? Better for you? It's different for people like Victoria, they've never known another way – just as your children won't. But you do. I don't know what your home life was like before your parents died–'

Paula's gaze took on a far-away quality, fixing somewhere over Beth's left shoulder, and it became obvious that just for a moment, she was allowing herself to remember.

'They were brilliant,' she said simply. 'I have only happy memories.'

'Then you're very lucky and you must have been devastated to lose them.' Beth said gently. 'But if you can remember your relationship with them and how special it was, why would you not want that for your own children? Do you never question any of Serenity's teachings?'

'No.' Paula's response was abrupt. 'We're taught that the present and the future are all that count. I don't let myself think about the past.'

'Well maybe you should, pet – because we're all products of our past. You're lucky to have happy childhood memories to look back on. Not all of us get that. And I've yet to meet the expert who doesn't agree that the best upbringing a child can have is with its own loving parents.'

She allowed Paula to dwell on that for a moment while she reined in her own emotions.

'How much of an item were Dean and Juliet?'

Paula hesitated. 'They liked each other.'

'Was he the father of her baby?'

No answer.

'Did Juliet really leave the commune? Paula?'

'I don't know what to say. You're confusing me.'

'You just need to tell the truth.'

She shook her head. 'I can't. I can't say anything. I *won't* say anything against the people who saved me.'

'Not even if those people turn out not to be the good guys you think they are? Would you still feel comfortable leaving your children in their care if that proved to be the case?'

Paula was looking increasingly agitated, plucking at the folds of her dress. 'Please stop. You're confusing me.'

Beth considered for a moment; then gave a little sigh. 'I'm going to end this interview for the time being,' she said. 'But please think about what I've said. I'll want to talk to you again.' She pulled out a card. 'I know I already gave you one of these, but if ever you want to call me in complete confidence, my mobile number's on here. I'll talk to you at any time, day or night.'

CHAPTER TWENTY-NINE

Harry made his way to the incident room where the whole team was reassembling for the latest briefing. Two large jugs of coffee were perched on the table, and people poured from them gratefully as they came in.

'Where's Beth?' he asked, looking around.

'Interviewing the last of Serenity's finest,' Geoff responded. 'Said she'll be with us shortly.'

'Right. First off, did anyone learn anything new from the Serenity Hall sweep today?'

'They gave us free rein of the entire premises. No newborns anywhere,' Geoff said. 'But no one was giving away anything. The people I spoke to said they didn't have much to do with either Juliet or Cara, didn't know where they'd moved on to and had no idea who might have murdered Joshua. But they were definitely nervy. I reckon they'd all been primed and were terrified of saying the wrong thing.'

'Well, as far as I can see, that goes for everyone we've interviewed so far. The whole place is beginning to feel quite sinister,' Harry said. 'I really don't get how two women and a newborn baby can disappear off the radar like they have. Where have they been? Is Cara being held somewhere against her will? If we find her, will we also find Juliet's baby? It's been a week now since her attack. The worst case scenario doesn't bear thinking about as far as that baby's concerned.'

Harry turned his gaze to Geoff Peterson.

'What about Cara Swift's finances?'

'Her current account has two hundred pounds sitting in it. She had a one-off cash payment of three thousand pounds several months back, all of which was transferred to Serenity's coffers two months ago. No activity on it since.'

'That was the same amount Juliet received.'

'Yes.'

'Anything come back from the search on Sanderson's flat?'

'Nothing obvious to link him to Joshua's murder, apart from a poster advertising the seminar on his kitchen table. We brought the clothes and shoes in that he was wearing that night. There was a small amount of blood on the tee shirt but it's quite possible that it's his own. They're analysing it. Beth said there was nothing out of the ordinary from what she could see.'

'What about the other missing girls?'

Geoff consulted the action book. 'No trace as of yet on either of them. We're waiting to hear back from the Spanish authorities about Louise Riley, it'll take a bit longer getting info back on her. Bearing in mind Sophie's social problems, we're checking out all the usual organisations that she might have turned to – again, it's time consuming, but we've got Susie working solely on that thread.'

'Well, it seems to me that every avenue we go up takes us firmly back to Serenity's front door. And we have no proof from anywhere that any of these girls actually left the commune. I think it would be prudent to do a thorough

235

search of the grounds next, to rule out the possibility of Cara being held somewhere against her will. We know that Juliet was being kept prisoner somewhere. Maybe there are other buildings in the grounds that aren't noticeable from the main complex. We'll get that done this afternoon. They won't like it, but if they're not going to willingly help us with our enquiries then we need to show them that we're serious about finding out what's been going on—'

Before he could say more, the door was flung open as Beth burst into the room.

'I think we've got a breakthrough,' she said, looking at Harry. 'You need to come and talk to this guy… his name's Emanuel and he's one of the gardeners at Serenity Hall.'

She led the way to the interview room. 'I brought him in because he was so fidgety when I questioned him, but he's got special needs, so we had to get an appropriate adult to sit with him through the interview, which is why he was left until last. Just wait till you hear what he's got to say. If he's telling the truth … Cara Swift is buried in the grounds of Serenity Hall. And Juliet Sanderson found out about that.'

CHAPTER THIRTY

Harry didn't bother with niceties as he stood in the entrance of the large house.

'Where's Fabian?' he asked of the brother who opened the door.

The man blinked. 'In the library, I think. Shall I take you to him?'

'Don't bother, I know the way.'

He strode across the tiled hall and opened the library door without knocking. Inside, Fabian was sitting at the desk talking quietly on the phone. He looked up, annoyance on his face at the interruption. When he saw who it was, he hesitated, then said quickly into the phone, 'I'll call you back. Something's come up.'

The look he cast at Harry was hostile, but there was more to that look, Harry was quick to observe. It was also fearful.

'What's the meaning of this?' he demanded. 'Don't the police knock anymore?'

'Not when we've possibly come to arrest you, no.'

'*What?*'

'We have reason to believe that the body of a young girl may be illegally buried within the grounds of Serenity Hall. I have a warrant here to fully search these premises and grounds, and until we have confirmed that one way or the other, I'd ask you to remain in this room where I'll be leaving PC Rainer here standing on guard.'

'Are you *imprisoning* me?'

'If you want to call it that, yes. Until I get back, no one leaves this room or enters it.'

⌒

Emanuel Jacobs looked terrified as he led the small army of police officers and the CSI team through the woods at the back of the cottages.

'I'll be in big trouble,' he kept muttering to himself, wringing his hands. 'Big trouble. Big trouble. I'll lose my job.'

'It's okay, Emanuel,' Beth said, touching his arm as they walked. 'You're doing the right thing. It will be the bad people who did this that will be in big trouble. Not you. Now, as soon as you can see the area where Cara is buried, you must tell us, okay? Because we'll stop anyone else from going further so that we can seal it off.'

It was some minutes later that Emanuel stopped and pointed to the tree trunk. 'There … she's over there.'

Immediately, the CSI team swept into action sealing off the area, the photographer taking pictures of the overview first, then the mid-views, and finally close-ups of the mound of earth and surrounding area clearly visible to the naked eye. Only when all that had been done, did two other gowned-up members of the team move in to start carefully digging into the ground. There was a small clump of flowers on the top and Beth felt sad as it got swept away with the rest of the dirt. Had Emanuel planted that?

Out of the corner of her eye, she saw Harry quietly join

the group, but nothing was said. The scene was eerily silent, the only sound to disturb the air, the relentless hard clunk as spades hit the ground. It didn't take long. The recent rain had softened the soil, making it easier to penetrate, and within a few minutes one of the men raised his hand and stopped digging.

'There's something here,' he said and, without a word, the medical officer moved in as the men proceeded more cautiously.

It was some while later before he straightened up again and moved over to where Harry and Beth were patiently waiting.

'It's a young woman. No sign of physical trauma but there's quite a degree of decomposition. I'll need to get her back to the lab to do a proper post-mortem.'

Harry pulled out a photo of Cara Swift. 'Can you tell me if you think it's this woman?'

The man pulled a face, flicking only a cursory glance at the picture before shaking his head. 'Could be, but I'm afraid the bugs have been feasting quite royally on her soft tissue and the body's in a state of active decay. I certainly can't identify her from that photo. When I get back I can do a DNA test and maybe find other ways of identifying her for you. Dental records might be best if you think you know who she is.'

Harry sighed. 'Okay, thanks. And we can get a DNA sample off one of the parents if we need to.'

He turned to Beth. 'Right. Get Brother Fabian in and everyone who shared the house with Cara Swift, including Dean Jarvis. Until we have confirmation to the contrary, we treat this discovery as a murder investigation.'

He walked over to where Emanuel was watching the proceedings wide-eyed, and smiled at him encouragingly.

'Well done, Emanuel, you did the right thing telling us about this. You told us it was Joshua, Fabian and Terence who buried her here with you, but you said there was another man with them. Have you remembered yet who that other man was?'

Emanuel shook his head, his expression worried. 'It was dark. Brother Fabian rang me and said to come over to dig the hole and then they came out with Cara on a stretcher. The other man went off in a car.'

'Was he from the commune do you know?'

He looked uncertain.

'Could it have been Dean Jarvis?'

'Maybe, but I didn't see his face.'

'Did you see what car he was driving?'

Again, Emanuel shook his head. 'He went to the car park while we went to the woods.'

'And how long ago was this?'

'I don't know.' He frowned. 'Near the end of August maybe?'

'Okay, well, thank you. You've really helped us today. You said that you told Juliet about her friend? She must have been shocked?'

The man's expression had lost some of its anxiety as he basked in Harry's praise, but now it clouded over again. 'She was very sad. I thought it might make her feel better knowing where her friend was, and that I was looking after her, but it didn't. That's why I didn't tell her about the others.'

Harry's head snapped up. 'The others?'

The sudden wariness on Emanuel's face made his heart sink. 'You mean … there are more people buried here?'

Emanuel nodded, his eyes becoming anxious again as he took in Harry's evident shock.

240

'How many?' Harry asked, hardly daring to voice the question.

A pause, then… 'Three.'

He hesitated. 'I can show you if you like? I look after them, make sure they have nice flowers on them.'

⌒

'Read Brother Fabian his rights, then cuff him,' Harry said to Beth an hour and a half later.

'Brother Fabian,' Beth said, realising she didn't actually know the man's surname. 'I'm arresting you in connection with the suspicious death and unlawful burial of Cara Swift and three other people. You do not have to say anything. But it may harm your defence if you do not mention when questioned, something which you later rely on in Court. Anything you do say may be given in evidence.'

She stepped forward, reaching for her handcuffs.

Fabian was looking shocked, his face so pale that Beth thought he might actually pass out.

'You can't do this,' he blustered. 'I've not done anything. I demand to see my lawyer.'

'We can arrange that after we get you back to the station,' Harry said grimly. The image of one of those skeletons, with the tinier skeleton of a newborn baby buried with it, still weighed heavily. He watched as Beth attached the cuffs, then gestured towards the door.

'After you,' he said, reaching for the mobile phone on the desk and slipping it into his pocket.

Out in the car park, Harry turned to Beth. 'I think make a formal arrest of Terence and Dean – give them something to think about – Terence in particular as he's been identified as being involved in the burials. I want everyone from that cottage brought back in – I'll see you at the station. Maybe, finally, we'll find out what really happened to Juliet Sanderson.'

CHAPTER THIRTY-ONE

Juliet

'*Tara's dead.*'

The words are like a mantra going round and round in my head and I'm so scared all the time now, that I don't feel I can trust anyone.

I never got to the hospital to carry out my plan – they didn't even call the doctor in to check me out. Sheila took my blood pressure, listened to the baby's heartbeat and movements, and pronounced that everything was fine and no need to waste the doctor's time. Now, with only a couple of days to go until my due date, I find myself analysing everything and everyone, trying to work out who I can trust … even Dean. Because why isn't he here? If he really loved me, wouldn't he be with me now, sticking like glue to my side until the baby comes, rather than preaching in Northumberland? Sheila tells me it's not Serenity's way; that they'll call Dean when I go into labour and he'll come back. But I still feel abandoned.

The house is quiet. Everyone's attending the regular Friday service up in the main house before supper. I've been given a freedom pass from having to attend because I had a mammoth meltdown earlier today, screaming at them that I needed to see a doctor and that I felt sick. They've left Sheila with me and I can hear her moving around in the kitchen downstairs, getting our supper ready for when everyone's back. I know that it's now or never.

I open my bedroom door and slip quietly down the stairs, pausing to listen. She's still in the kitchen. I can hear her banging pots around as she prepares the food and I move silently to the front door.

It's double locked and there's no key.

I tug at it disbelievingly. Have they done this to prevent me from leaving? It adds a whole new level to my situation that wipes away any doubts that I'm right to try to escape. My eyes dart around the hall looking for another means of exit. The lounge is too close to the kitchen, so I head for Terence's study, closing the door quietly behind me. I rush as quickly as my bump will allow, over to the window and open it, pulling Terence's desk chair beneath it so that I can clamber up and haul myself out through the opening. It isn't easy and I bite back a sob of panic as I imagine myself getting stuck and having to wait for someone to come and find me. But finally, I land in the bushes with a bit of a stumble and look around me.

It's still daylight and even if I stick to the side of the road as I head towards the large gates, I'm clearly visible if anyone happens to look in my direction. But I can't help that. If I don't get away now, I know I never will.

I make it to the large gates and of course they're closed but there's a little entrance door to the side of them and I try that. It opens.

I'm free. With a stifled sob, I set off down the lane, heading in the direction of the village. I move as quickly as I can but it isn't fast by any standards, and I pant heavily, my hands clasping my stomach, trying to support the weight of it. If only a car would come. Even though Mum made me swear never to hitch a lift, I know that today I'd disobey her. I just need to get to safety.

I've half run, half walked, about a mile and I'm just crossing a lay-by when I hear a car behind me. I spin round just as it passes and screeches to a halt in front of me. Before I even realise what's happening, Joshua leaps out.

'Where are you going, Juliet?'

His voice is quite calm but I sense the underlying threat. I try to run past him, but he grabs my arm and I start to scream, struggling violently. '*Let me go. I'm going home.*'

'You're going nowhere,' he says, his grip painful as he stops me from moving. 'Quick, give me the syringe, or you do it,' he rasps to someone over his shoulder.

Two of them. I know I'm never going to be able to fight them off now, but still I scream and struggle in the vain hope that someone will hear. And then a miracle happens.

I hear a second car pull up and a woman's voice enquiring if everything's okay at the same time as I feel the syringe plunge into my arm.

'*Help me,*' I scream. '*They're holding me against my will.*'

'*It's not true,*' I hear Joshua say. I can hear the tension in his voice but I can also imagine the apologetic charm in his smile as he looks at her. '*She's my wife and we're just helping her get home – she suffered a psychotic episode recently and hasn't been well.*'

There's a pause, and I'm aware that the injection, whatever it was, is kicking in and I'm beginning to lose it. I want to scream out for her not to believe them, but their voices are slipping away.

Through a dim haze I hear the woman say, 'I'm sorry but I'm calling the police. If this is genuine, you can sort it out with them,' and I'm so thankful to her, but then I hear the other voice and it becomes obvious that they know each other.

'There's no need for that, Amelia. Really. Hang on a moment, let me just help him get her in here and then I'll be with you. It's fine though, nothing to worry about.'

The voice is muffled to my ears, and I can't process who it belongs to as I feel myself start to slip away. '*It's not fine,*' I scream. But only a slur comes out, as my legs finally buckle under me completely and I feel myself being lifted into the car.

After that, nothing.

I remember nothing.

⌒

I'm back in my room, but it no longer feels like my room … or even looks like it. Black drapes have been hung over my curtains to keep it totally dark and I know that the door is locked from the outside so I can't escape. Not that I could anyway … my feet are tied together and so are my hands.

I'm meant to feel like a prisoner, and I do.

I don't know how much time has passed since they brought me back. One hour? Two? Joshua told me he'd be back later to talk to me and I'd shivered at the tone of his voice. But now, as I lie quietly, unable to move, absorbing all that has happened, I no longer care what he does to me.

I turn my head towards the door as I hear the key in the lock. Joshua walks in, the smile on his face doing nothing to quell my fear, or hide the ruthless expression in his eyes.

'Ah, Juliet … what are we going to do with you?' He

246

sighs mournfully. 'You really have been most tiresome and you realise now, I can't let you go?'

'I want to see Dean,' I say.

He shakes his head. 'You know that's not possible, he's in Northumberland.'

'He's not. I know he's not. I demand to see him.'

'Even if he was here, you haven't been behaving well enough to deserve to see him, have you?'

'*I want to see him,*' I scream. 'He's the father of my baby, I have a right to see him.'

'Do you think yours is the only baby Dean's fathered?' he delivers with poisonous venom. 'It's about time you realised that Dean is not your property, and you are just a tiny cog in a very big wheel – as we all are.'

'Dean loves me,' I say, but I hate myself for the lack of conviction in my own voice.

'How long is it since he last had sex with you? One month? Two months? Three? Do you really think he's been celibate all this time he's been away?'

'He wouldn't betray me,' I say, desperately needing to believe it.

He shakes his head sadly. 'You're very naive, my dear. Young men like Dean need sex on a regular basis and he's a good-looking man. He won't be short of offers.'

'No,' I whisper. The tears are threatening to spill, but I won't give him the satisfaction of seeing them. Instead, I turn away from him to stare at the darkened window.

A sudden pain lurching through my stomach makes me cry out in shock. It's followed almost immediately by a surge of water between my legs.

'The baby,' I gasp. 'I think it's coming. I need Sheila.'

He stares at me as if suspicious that I might be lying, then without a word he spins round and leaves the room.

Sheila's kind and so is Paula, who sits by my side holding my hand, telling me it's going to be fine, I'm going to be fine, the baby's going to be fine. But I know it's not fine.

They've at least removed my binds and the black lining from the windows. The evening light filters into the room and it looks more like my normal bedroom again.

'It's going to be a quick birth,' Sheila tells me encouragingly, after a brief examination. 'You're nearly there already.'

'Joshua's going to kill me after I've had this baby,' I say in a dead voice. 'Like he killed Cara.'

Sheila looks at me in shock. 'Don't be silly. Why are you saying that? He didn't kill Cara.'

'Yes he did. She's dead. And soon I'll be dead too.'

Paula's mopping my brow and her eyes gleam warningly into mine as if trying to pass me a silent message.

Sheila tuts anxiously, her eyes darting to the door, clearly fearful that someone might overhear or walk in. But her voice is firm as she sits down on the bed beside me and takes my hand.

'No one killed Cara, Juliet. But if you know she's dead then I won't lie to you. She died here in childbirth because she had complications with her blood pressure. We did our best, but there was nothing we could do to save her.'

'But you *knew* she had problems with her blood pressure. Why didn't she go into hospital to have her baby like you said she would? That's what you said happened. You said she went and didn't want to come back. Dean told me you sat with her all night.'

'And I did. But here, not at the hospital.' To my surprise, her eyes fill with tears as she remembers. 'I told Terence

248

and Joshua that she should be in hospital, and they called an ambulance – but it never came. I was with her when she died.'

'I want to go to hospital to have my baby. Please call an ambulance for me. Otherwise I'll die, I know I will.'

'Now don't be silly,' she says, taking a breath and squeezing my hand before standing up again. 'Your case is completely different to Cara's. You're perfectly healthy. And I predict you'll have this baby within the next half hour.'

She's right. Twenty minutes later at ten thirty p.m. Theo is born, weighing in at a healthy 7lb 7oz.

'He's perfect,' I whisper, looking down at him tenderly as I clutch him to my breast. Sheila helps me guide him to suckle and it's a clumsy effort at first, but we laugh, as he finally seems to get the message and latches on.

I stroke his head. It's so soft; even though there's a bit of blood matting what little hair he's got. I make as much as I can of this moment, fearful that at any time Joshua will march in and take him away from me, to give him the perfect life that I apparently am incapable of giving him.

They've brought a little cot into the room and put it beside my bed. Sheila makes to take the baby from me and I resist.

'I'm putting him in the cot, Juliet,' she says, not unkindly. 'He needs his sleep as much as you do. He'll wake soon enough for his next feed and you must rest while you can.'

I let her take him, but it's as if she's tearing a part of me away as she lifts him and places him gently in the cot. As soon as she says goodnight and leaves, I look at Paula who's going to be sleeping in the other bed, and say defiantly. 'I want to have him by my side for as long as I can before they take him from me.' I throw back the duvet and swing my legs out of the bed.

'No,' she says, moving towards me. Then adds. 'Not yet. Wait until I'm in bed. Then if it comes out, I can say I was asleep and didn't see you do it.'

Her eyes are soft, understanding … and for an instant, we bond in that moment of conspiracy.

'What can I do, Paula?' I ask.

'Nothing,' she whispers bleakly. 'You can do nothing.'

Ten minutes later, my son is lying on my chest again, his little hand curled into a tight fist against my breast, his steady rhythmic breathing calming my own frantic heartbeat. I lie there, treasuring every breath, every murmur he makes, knowing that each one could be the last memory I'll have of him. And finally I drift off to sleep.

I'm woken early the next morning by Terence coming in to take my baby. He's in and out so quickly that I hardly realise what's happening.

'No!' I scream, clutching Theo tightly to my chest.

'Hand him over, Juliet,' he orders. 'You can't stop it from happening and you know he'll be well cared for.'

'*I've changed my mind.*'

'It's too late for that. Sheila … Paula … hold her still while I take him.'

'*No!*' I struggle hysterically as he's torn from my arms. '*Give him back to me!*'

Theo starts to cry and the tears stream down my face as I fight wildly and hopelessly against the arms that are restraining me. As the door closes swiftly behind them, I know that that cry from my baby will be the last, heartbreaking memory I'll have of him.

And it will stay with me forever.

⤺

Now, as I lie motionless in my bed in the hospital, that same sense of hopelessness and fear swamps me as I try to remember what happened next.

Where is my baby? Where is Theo? Why can't I remember? Dear God, please let him be safe.

CHAPTER THIRTY-TWO

Fabian Glover sat next to his solicitor, facing Harry across the table. Harry had deliberately left him stewing while they'd interviewed some of the lesser members of the commune, in the hope that they'd learn something new. It was a strategy that had paid off, as several things had come to light that he was now able to confront Fabian with.

'I've told you all I know,' Fabian said belligerently, 'and I don't know anything about any bodies being buried in the grounds of Serenity Hall.'

'You can see why we might have a problem believing that when, from what we've heard, you and Joshua Jarvis ran the place?'

'Joshua was in charge, not me.'

'But not a lot happens there that you don't know about.'

'I wasn't aware of any bodies.'

'Fabian, there's no point lying. We have a witness who contradicts that. He puts you firmly in the group of people who he claims carried Cara Swift out on a stretcher and buried her in the woods, and on the strength of that information, we've now dug up the body of a woman we believe to be Cara Swift, and three other bodies.'

Fabian looked shocked but, recovering quickly, he gave

a sneering laugh. 'And who's your witness? Poor, muddled Emanuel? He wouldn't last five minutes under questioning in a court. And he's odd … anyone will tell you that. It was more likely him who killed and buried those poor women.'

'Did I say all the bodies were women? Or that they'd been killed?'

No reply, and Harry let the question hang in the air for a moment before adding, 'Perhaps you know more than we do at this stage. But I can assure you that we'll know soon enough exactly how those women died, and far better for you that you tell us everything you know, now.'

Silence.

'Okay, I'll park that for the moment. Moving on … I want to ask you again about Joshua's death. I find it hard to accept that you were in the room next door and heard nothing. The walls are hardly thick. Now that he's dead and it's between you and Dean as to who takes over, some might suggest, quite reasonably, that you had motive to kill him.'

'Then they'd be wrong.'

Harry glanced at his notes and pulled out one of the earlier witness statements taken by Geoff. 'Another member of your community, who was helping out at the seminar that night, says he heard Dean and his father rowing. He says that he and you were in a room together and that you heard it too. What were they arguing about?'

Fabian hesitated, his sly eyes drooping for a moment, before rising again to meet Harry's. 'Okay. I couldn't hear what they were saying, but yes they did have an altercation.'

'Why didn't you mention it at the time?'

'Because fathers and sons row. It happens all the time and they don't usually end up killing each other.'

'Well, someone killed Joshua, and it's not your job to rule

people out. What time was it when they argued?'

'I can't say exactly … quarter past nine maybe. Joshua was certainly alive when Dean left to get himself some food.'

'And where were you when he came back?'

'In the adjoining room, waiting for Joshua to finish with his clients. Dean and I finished loading up the car and when Joshua didn't come in, Dean went to see where he was. That's when he found him.'

'So you didn't go in with him. When was the last time you actually saw Joshua alive?'

'When he and Dean were … talking. Just before Joshua's first client was due. When Dean came in I left them to it and went next door to make some notes on the meeting. I also made use of the time to prepare my sermon for the following evening's service.'

Harry pulled another piece of paper out of the folder and slid it across the table for Fabian to see. 'You were talking to someone on the phone when I entered your office this afternoon. We've checked your mobile and it was this number.' He deliberately omitted to mention that it was the same SIM-only number that had called Joshua on the day he was killed. He didn't want whoever it was getting wind of the fact they were on to them and ditching the phone. 'Who was that you were talking to?'

Fabian stared at the number circled in red and shrugged. 'Haven't a clue. I get quite a few calls. Unless it's in my contacts I wouldn't know who it was.'

'Think harder. It was only a few hours ago and I heard you say you'd call them back which, according to your call log, you did – shortly after I left you.'

'Sorry. I can't remember.'

'You're only putting off the inevitable, you know. We'll

find the answers to these questions and it won't look good for you that you've not been helpful in our enquiries.'

The man sat there, saying nothing, and Harry sighed.

'Okay. Moving on again. You told us that Cara Swift had left the community a couple of months ago, yet now it appears her body has been found buried in the grounds of Serenity Hall. Why did you lie?'

'No comment.'

'Come on, Fabian, we're not idiots and you know as well as I do, that we'll soon have her identity confirmed, and it follows on from there that it's likely Juliet Sanderson never left the commune either. Did you kill Cara and stab Juliet?'

'No.'

'Then tell me what happened, because from where I'm sitting, frankly your future's not looking too bright at the moment.'

'I want to talk to my solicitor in private.'

Harry was beginning to feel that he was more than ready for a break himself.

'Okay. We're pausing the interview at twenty ten hours,' he said into the recorder, and switched it off. He rose from his seat and nodded at Fabian and his solicitor over the table. 'Ten minutes.'

Out in the corridor, he looked at his watch again and sighed. He still had Dean Jarvis to interview. No way was he going to make the date he'd arranged with Claire for this evening, and he felt unusually deflated by that. Their meal the night before had gone well and he'd been looking forward to taking her out again tonight. But there was nothing he could do about it. He needed to finish this. He pulled his phone out of his pocket and texted her.

'Really sorry, but something's come up at work and I'm

not going to get away for at least another couple of hours. Can we take a rain check? I'll call you later. Harry X'.

He looked at the message, then debated over the X, before finally deleting it. It looked quite bald without it, but not much he could do about that.

Seeing that he'd also had a message from Beth ten minutes ago, he clicked on that.

'I'm in Burger King grabbing a bite to eat if you want to join me? If not, I'll be back in the office around eight thirty and we can catch up then.'

He texted her back. 'Still interviewing Fabian and then moving on to Dean Jarvis. See you back here.'

He was just about to head back into the interview room when his phone pinged. It was a message from Claire, and for the first time that day he smiled.

'You'll be hungry. Head over whenever you've finished if you like? I'll cook.'

⤶

Finishing up her burger, Beth headed back to the station. There was no one around in the office and she made her way up to what they called the overview room, where she could watch the monitor and hear what was going on in the interviews. Interview room 1 was where Geoff was questioning Sheila Bates and she flipped the switch so that she could hear what was being said.

Sheila was seated next to her solicitor and she was looking agitated as she faced Geoff across the table.

'I'm going to ask you again, Sheila, if you were aware that Cara Swift's body had been buried in the grounds of Serenity Hall,' Geoff Peterson said, 'and I'd remind you that it won't look good if you say something now that we later find to be untrue.'

The woman hesitated; then gave a little nod.

'For the benefit of the tape, Sheila has nodded her head. Can you tell me who buried her?'

A quick shake of the head.

'Sheila, I think you do know the answer to that and it would save a lot of time and be very helpful if you could be honest with us about it. We need to find out what happened to Cara. And why her death was covered up. Was she murdered? How exactly did she die?'

'No.' Her response was shocked, her voice distressed as she replied. 'She died of pre-eclampsia. It was no one's fault. We tried so hard, but there was nothing we could do to save her.'

'Pre-eclampsia! You're saying she was *pregnant*?'

The woman nodded.

'So, why was she not in hospital if she had a condition like that? That's a serious complication of pregnancy isn't it? Even I know that.'

Sheila nodded again. 'Joshua called the ambulance but it never turned up. We were forced to deliver her ourselves.

'Couldn't someone have taken her in a car? You're not far from the hospital.'

The woman's expression was distraught, and Beth found herself imagining the chaotic scene they must have gone through trying to save Cara. She guessed from Sheila's expression that she was still haunted by the memory.

'Sheila?'

The woman looked at her solicitor, then shook her head and said quietly, 'I did suggest that, but it was just too late. She died and there was nothing we could do.'

'What about her baby? Where is that now?'

'I don't know.'

Beth could see Geoff trying to hide his frustration. 'Sheila, I understand that you feel a loyalty to Serenity,' he said, 'but you have to understand that things have happened there that we need answers for. So far, we've had Juliet stabbed, Cara dying and buried illegally, three other bodies buried in the grounds of Serenity Hall, and now two missing babies. Plus Joshua has been murdered. Surely you can see that we need to find out what's been going on before anyone else gets hurt? Do you know anything about Joshua's murder? Who might have killed him?'

'No, I wasn't even there. But Joshua was a good man. He was our Lead Brother. Nobody from inside Serenity would have harmed him. We loved him.'

'Except that we now have information that your son Dean argued with him that night. Is it possible Dean might have killed his father?'

'*No*. Dean would never do a thing like that.'

'Then who might? Because someone did. Fabian, maybe?'

No response.

'I understand there's a power battle going on between him and Dean as to who is the rightful person to take over from Joshua. What are your thoughts on that?'

'I don't have any. God will decide and we'll abide by his decision.'

'What about the bodies of the other three women buried in the grounds? Who were they and what happened to them?'

The woman hesitated, looking bemused, then as if coming to a decision, said in a quiet voice, 'I only know about one of them.'

'Right. Well, that's something at least. Can you give me a name and why she's buried there?'

'Sophie Parkhurst. It was a terrible accident a number of years ago. She fell down the stairs in the main house and broke her neck. So sad.'

'She was living in the main house at the time?'

'That was my understanding. I didn't know her well. She'd never lived in our cottage but I heard she had … issues. They were trying to help her through them. When Joshua told us she'd died he said her wish had been to be buried in the grounds of Serenity but that we shouldn't tell anyone as we'd then have to hand her body over, and he'd promised her he'd honour her wishes. We held a proper service for her.'

This last sentence said as if it somehow made everything alright.

'One of the other bodies was a woman, with a very small baby buried with her.'

Sheila's eyes widened. 'How long ago?'

'We don't know exactly. We're waiting on the full post-mortem results, but probably more than five years and less than ten?'

She shook her head, looking bemused. 'I can only think of one person that *could* have been, and that's … Louise. But Fabian said her body had been returned to her parents for burial.'

'Louise Riley?'

She nodded.

'Well, we know for a fact that she wasn't returned to her parents. Her mother hasn't heard from her in several years. Serenity told her that Louise had moved to Spain with a boyfriend.'

'No, no … that can't be right. Why would they say that?' She sat for a moment, looking completely confused, then said slowly, 'Louise wasn't one of my girls – by that I mean I wasn't the midwife in charge of her case – but I know her baby was born prematurely and died. She was so upset … she … she took her own life that very same night. It was tragic and everyone was horrified. But I thought she'd been taken to the hospital to be returned to her parents – I don't understand any of this,' she said again.

'Are you sure about that? You've admitted you agreed to covering up Sophie Parkhurst's illegal burial. You surely must have realised that it was wrong to do that? We've uncovered four bodies in Serenity's grounds and, even as we speak, a wider search of the area is being conducted. Can you think who the fourth and final woman buried there might be? It would have been very recent … within the last two or three weeks.'

'*No*.' She looked shocked. 'It's no one from the community, I'm sure.'

'Is there anything else you feel we should know at this point? Apart from wanting to know who killed Joshua and attacked Juliet, our most pressing concern at the moment is the whereabouts of Juliet's baby – and now, it would seem, Cara's?'

The woman looked from him to her solicitor, anxiety swamping her features. 'I don't know … I can't speak. Serenity is my life. I can't go against what I know the Elders would want me to do. I'm sorry.'

'What happened to Cara's baby?'

Silence.

'Was Dean the father of Juliet Sanderson's baby? That would make it your grandchild.'

No answer.

'Did she really leave the commune two months before

the baby was due, or did you deliver it?'

'I have nothing to say.'

'That's a simple enough question for you to answer, especially if, as you say, she left the commune several weeks before her baby was due. Why won't you answer it? What are you hiding? Where's Juliet's baby now?'

'I don't know.'

'You realise you're obstructing our investigation by not answering these questions?'

'Please … I can't go on. I won't say any more. I need time to think.'

Her voice was cracked, the tears streaming down her face as she gave her replies. Beth couldn't help feeling sorry for her, even though she found it astonishing that someone could be so brainwashed by the commune that they were totally unquestioning of the terrible things that seemed to have gone on there. She doubted Geoff would get much more out of her tonight and he was obviously of the same mind, as he said into the recorder: 'The time is eight forty in the evening and I'm terminating this interview, but we will continue with it tomorrow.'

He fixed Sheila with a penetrating stare over the desk. 'You can go home tonight, Sheila, but think carefully about your situation. I understand your loyalty to Serenity, but I can't believe that you'd risk perjuring yourself, or condoning murder and illegal activities. That certainly wouldn't be God's way. I hope that, by tomorrow, you'll have thought things through and will have come to the decision to do the right thing and tell us everything you know to help us establish the truth as to what's gone on.'

Beth's attention was diverted by a noise outside in the corridor and she opened the door to see Harry grabbing a quick cup of water from the machine. He looked weary, as she was sure they all did.

'How's it going?' she asked.

'Slowly,' he sighed. 'How did you get on with Terence and Emanuel?'

'Same story. Terence is still claiming that Juliet left the commune a couple of months before her baby was due, but I could tell that he was freaked out by our discovery of the bodies and the fact that he's been identified as one of the people who buried Cara. He refused to comment on that or the other bodies, and says he knows nothing at all about Joshua's activities or who would want to kill him, but he's shaken. I've left the transcript of my interview on your desk. Emanuel's a trickier problem because of his special needs. He's clearly deeply unsettled by everything that's going on – especially the realisation that he's broken the law burying the bodies and, when I asked him what he knew about Juliet, he became very agitated and kept saying he wanted to go home. The appropriate adult accompanying him felt it was too much for one sitting and we've arranged that he'll come back in tomorrow to complete his statement.'

'Right. Well, we'll hold on to Terence and Fabian overnight. Fabian for one definitely needs a rocket up his backside. The only useful piece of information I've got out of him was confirmation that he heard Joshua and Dean arguing on the night Joshua was killed and he only admitted to that when he knew someone else had already told us. He clammed up after speaking to his solicitor and everything was no comment after that, but he knows what went on, I'm sure of it. Maybe a night in the cells will be enough of a shock to make one or both of them talk. They'll be worried about what's coming out from other people, even if they have put the fear of God into the women.'

'I was just listening in on Geoff's interview with Sheila. Sounds like hers might be the most enlightening interview of all, quite a lot came out of it. For one … it seems Cara was pregnant and died of childbirth complications – pre-eclampsia.'

Harry frowned. 'Did she now? How come no one ever mentioned she was pregnant?'

'They'll probably say it was because we never asked them. Anyway, she reckoned Joshua called an ambulance but it never turned up. I'll check that out with the emergency services. At least we definitely know now that Cara never left the commune, which backs up Emanuel's statement.'

'And it might go some way to explaining why they buried her in the grounds if she died in childbirth. I can see that Serenity might not want anyone looking too closely into their practices. Find out which hospital she was under, and we'll need to speak to that consultant and GP again tomorrow to see if they can throw any light on anything. It's finally beginning to feel like the net's closing in. We don't want to miss anything.'

'There's more. That other body … the one with the baby? Sheila thought that might be Louise Riley. Apparently she went into premature labour, lost the baby and was so distraught that she took her own life. They were told though, that Louise had been returned to her family for burial. I think Sheila was shocked that wasn't the case.'

'So the Spain story was a complete lie. What about the other two bodies? Did she have anything to say about them?'

'She said one was Sophie Parkhurst – and before you

ask – no, she wasn't pregnant. And neither was the fourth woman, remember – the most recent one? Sheila said they were told that Sophie fell down the stairs in the main house and broke her neck. We've not had confirmation of that yet from the post-mortem.'

'And the last woman? Did she know anything about her?'

'Nope. She claims to have no knowledge of her at all.'

'She hadn't been buried there that long – a couple of weeks or so, is Edwards guess. I'll chase him up on any preliminary findings first thing Monday morning. He said he'd work on them tomorrow. I'm heading down to interview Dean now, if you want to come? Or maybe, unlike me, you've got a life outside of all this?'

Beth fell into step beside him. 'I wish – but anyway, there's far too much going on here to abandon it now. One last thing, I interviewed Paula earlier … the girl who shared a room with Juliet? She's also being very economical with the truth but I think it's like you said – she's terrified of speaking out. I think she's probably the weakest link in that house – she was clearly fond of Juliet. Having said that, I think they're all fragile – I reckon if we can crack it open, it'll be like a stack of cards tumbling once people start to talk.'

'Let's find the crack then and set that process in motion.'

⌒

Harry let Beth set up the tape and go through the formalities, and when she was finished he sat down and fixed his gaze on Dean Jarvis.

'How about you just save us all a lot of time and tell me what's been going on?'

Dean sighed. 'If something's going on, I don't know what it is, and that's the truth.'

264

'So how come I don't believe you?'

'I can't help that.'

'Well, we have an even more serious situation now in that we've uncovered four bodies from within the grounds of Serenity, one of whom is Cara Swift. Are you telling me that you knew nothing about any of them, or who put them there?'

The briefest of hesitations before he replied. 'I've told you over and over, that I haven't been around half the time this year. I've spent most of my time up in Newcastle, helping out up there.'

'But you've been backwards and forwards between there and Serenity Hall, and some of those bodies have been there years rather than months. You can't have been totally unaware of what was going on? You said you knew Cara. Why didn't you mention that she was pregnant? Or that she'd given birth at Serenity? Why did you say she'd left the community to go back to her boyfriend?'

'Because when she died Joshua was worried it could backfire on the commune and that they might stop us from doing the home births. He told us to say she'd left to go back to her boyfriend and not to mention the pregnancy.'

'And did you always do everything he told you?'

'Usually, yes.'

'What about her baby? What happened to that?'

'I don't know.'

'*Nobody knows it seems!* It's vanished into thin air, just like Juliet's!' Harry felt like thumping the desk. 'Do you really expect us to believe that no one knows?'

Dean made no answer and they stared each other out for a long moment before Harry finally turned back to his notes.

'We have a witness who overheard you arguing forcibly

265

with your father the night he was killed. What was that argument about?'

'Who told you that? Fabian?'

'It doesn't matter who it was; it's been substantiated by another person. Answer the question, please.'

'My father and I had differences of opinion sometimes, that's all. It was more a heated discussion than a row. I don't even remember what it was about now.'

'Could it have been because you'd heard you weren't going to be the one to follow in his footsteps? That he was having second thoughts about that?'

'No. He hadn't said any such thing to me, and it wasn't something that I thought about. I was expecting him to be around for years and I know I still have a lot to learn.'

'We have reason to believe that your father was involved in some sort of illegal activity, possibly even blackmail. Did you know about that?'

Dean shifted in his seat and it didn't take an expert in body language to see that he was getting uncomfortable with this line of questioning. 'No.'

'He would have learnt some quite intimate secrets from the people he was counselling, for example?'

Dean gave a dismissive laugh. 'We all do and he took his counselling work as seriously as the rest of us do. You don't seem to get that the work we do in Serenity is about making people feel happier with their lot, making them feel part of one big family. Our community is spreading all the time and the more people get disillusioned with the world, the more they're turning to communities like ours to teach them a better way.'

'I know that Serenity has grown enormously over the last ten years since your father took over. I've been researching it, and the *WeAreOne* hash tag on Twitter and your social media presence, have an impressive following. But it must be expensive to run an organisation like yours. Do the revenues you get from the seminars and counselling sessions you run really cover it all?'

'Fabian would be better able to answer that than me. He ran the place with my father and is a senior elder.'

'And how would you feel if he took over the running of Serenity now, and not you?'

Dean's expression hardened, without, Harry suspected, him even being aware of it.

'I accept that he's older than I am with more experience, but life is very different these days and I feel that both he and my father have been stuck in an outdated mode that could end up holding us back. I'd do things differently to capitalise on the huge strides forward we've made. So yes, I'd resist it. That doesn't mean, however,' he added smoothly, 'that I'd ever use violence to achieve my ends.'

Harry made a note. 'Okay, turning now to Juliet Sanderson. I'm going to ask you again, how involved were you and Juliet?'

'I told you, we paired.'

'Just casually? Was she one of many?'

'She's not the only woman I've slept with if that's what you mean.'

'No, that's not what I mean. While you were sleeping with Juliet were you also sleeping with others? And, if so, I'd like some names please?'

There was a significant pause before Dean answered. 'I don't remember.'

'Come on, Dean, I'm sure you can if you put your mind to it. You've talked about pairing with more than one person before. How did Juliet feel about that? That wouldn't have felt natural to her, I'm guessing. Did it bother her?'

'She accepted it was our way – and the ethos behind it. That we love everyone in the community, with no bars, distinctions or jealousies to interfere with our ultimate aim of total oneness and loyalty to each other.'

'And I'm guessing that works quite well until people develop feelings for each other. You're still human, after all, and I'd argue that when you develop feelings for a person, it's natural that you want only to be with them and might not like the idea of sharing them. Were you in love with Juliet? Is that one of the things you'd like to change, because maybe you didn't like the thought of her pairing with other people and you were starting to question the way things were run?'

'I don't see what any of this has got to do with my father's murder or the bodies you say you've found.'

'Don't you? You must see the link, surely? You're wanting to change things because you feel their ways are outdated. Your father – and Fabian, presumably – are resistant to that change, and things get out of hand. Happens all the time and next thing you know, someone's dead.'

'That's not what happened.'

'What can you tell us about Juliet and Cara? You shared a house with both of them. Two women, both of them pregnant, who subsequently give birth. One of them is now lying in a coma in intensive care and the other is even more unlucky – she's dead, buried in the grounds of Serenity Hall. And both their babies are missing. Where are they?'

'I don't know.'

'Well, you know what? I'm getting fed up hearing that answer, because I don't believe you. I think you – and Fabian, and Terence, and God knows who else – *do* know

268

where those babies are. You're just choosing not to tell us. And now we've discovered three further bodies buried in Serenity's grounds, two of whom are likely to be Sophie Parkhurst and Louise Riley – who we were informed, had left of their own free will. You see where this is going? On that basis, it gives us strong suspicion to believe that Juliet Sanderson never actually left Serenity either and that her attacker, therefore, was someone within your community.'

Dean's face had gone a paler shade of grey, but he shook his head stubbornly. 'I don't know anything about any of that. I keep *telling* you. I've spent a lot of my time up in Northumberland – and I can prove that. I've not been involved in what goes on down here.'

'That last body, who is it?'

'I don't know.'

'Well, we'll find out, you can be sure of that.'

Harry looked at his notes. 'You have a programme within Serenity of separating babies from their mothers. Is that right?'

Dean nodded.

'Tell me how that works and the ethos behind it.'

'We believe babies fare better being brought up as part of one big family community by women who are trained in child-rearing. You have to understand that quite a few of our members come from difficult backgrounds and obviously children need the best start in life they can get. Joshua started that programme when I was born. My mother had been a victim of domestic violence before she came to the commune and she and Joshua decided the commune could do a better job of bringing me up than she could.'

'And your mother was happy with that?' Harry's voice was raised in disbelief. 'Not many women would be. It's an unusual decision for a woman to take.'

'Not when you believe in a higher cause. Our community is our life and our unity is our strength, the bond between us unbreakable. Look at the world outside – your world. It's full of greed, jealousy and hatred. Those are characteristics that aren't tolerated in Serenity and Joshua believed that if we started young enough with the children, guiding them in a structured way – in the future we'd have a more caring community and even stronger, more dedicated followers to preach the word,

'A sort of super breed? Like, for example, the Nazi breeding programme for a master race?'

'That's a loaded way of putting it. And no – obviously that would be going to extremes.'

'You don't see yourself as being special or a chosen one then, because you were the first to be a part of this programme? You can see the similarity of concept, I'm sure?'

Harry had chosen his words deliberately, but Dean had a ready answer, either because he'd been questioned on this before or maybe because he'd questioned it himself. From his response, Harry guessed it was the latter.

'It's totally different. Hitler followed the path of eugenics, which as it happens, I studied as part of my psychology degree. You may or may not know that eugenics is the application of Darwinian evolution – to produce better offspring by improving the birth rate of fit and healthy babies and reducing that of the less healthy. That's not how Serenity works at all. There's no selection – women get pregnant by a partner of their choice – it's just that the children are brought up together within the commune, instead of with individual families.'

'So where are Juliet and Cara's babies now? We've

already established that Cara gave birth in the cottage and then died of pre-eclampsia, but clearly her child survived or it would have been buried with her. What happened to it?'

Dean shook his head.

'The same goes for Juliet. She had no child with her when she was stabbed. Where are those babies, Dean?'

When Dean just stared at him tight-lipped, he carried on, 'You see, I can't help wondering if maybe some sort of super-race programme *might* be going on here, where some babies are sifted out and given an even more rigorous upbringing than the one you had, to turn them into perfect followers? Is that what's happened to Juliet's and Cara's babies?'

'How many times do I have to tell you, I don't know where they are.'

'You can say it as often as you like, I don't believe you. Now we know that Cara didn't leave the commune, we seriously have to consider– despite what you and others have said – that Juliet didn't either. And it's clear that wherever she was, she was being held against her will and was being physically abused. There were marks around her wrists indicating that she'd had them tied or handcuffed, and significant wheals on her back, suggestive of beatings with a leather belt or similar. What have you got to say about that?'

'Nothing. I have no knowledge of any of that and I feel terrible that I wasn't there to help her.'

'Well, I'm sure Juliet would be very happy to hear that.'

The other man glared at him, but Harry was unmoved. 'Is beating a form of punishment within Serenity?'

'Of course not.'

'I'll ask you again, are you the father of Juliet's baby?'

Dean hesitated, then finally gave a little sigh. 'It's not impossible when you look at the timings. But I don't know where that child is now.'

'You don't seem particularly concerned about its whereabouts?'

His words fell into a silent room and, after a moment, Harry closed his folder and signalled to Beth to stop the recorder. Unlike with Terence and Fabian, although Dean was clearly obstructing the investigation, they didn't have anything concrete to hold him on overnight.

'Have you got any plans to return to Northumberland in the near future?'

'I'll have to go at some point.'

'Well, I'd rather you stayed put down here for the time being, where we can contact you if we need to. So please don't go anywhere without notifying us first.'

CHAPTER THIRTY-THREE

The hustle and bustle of the incident room had died down by the time Harry and Beth had finished questioning Dean Jarvis. Only Geoff Peterson was still there, hunched over his computer. He looked up as they walked in, took one look at their faces and said, 'You two look whacked. You still up for a drink Beth? Want to join us, Harry?'

'Not tonight. I have other plans.'

'How have your interviews gone?'

'It's a maze. We just need to keep following the trails. You?'

'Same. I've just finished typing up my notes and updating the action book. I'll print them off and leave them on your desk with the book.'

'I'm too tired to think straight tonight, that's for sure. Beth, I'm sorry, but I think tomorrow I'd like you to head back to Newcastle to question Thomas White again. And maybe you can go with her, Geoff? If you can get them I want the exact dates that Dean Jarvis has been up there over the last year. If he's involved in all this and has spent most of his time there, then it's quite possible that Thomas White's involved in it all too. Juliet's baby could even be there. Don't let him know you're going though. Then, while

Beth's interviewing Thomas, you can head over to Serenity's Hexham HQ and check that out at the same time. The one thing I'm going to do tonight, before I head off, is look up every address they occupy and tomorrow we'll organise a sweep of the lot of them. If there are any more up your way, I'll let you know. Those babies have got to be somewhere and we need to find them.'

'I already made a list,' Beth said, heading over to her desk. She flicked through a folder and pulled out a piece of paper. 'Here it is. There are fifteen properties countrywide. I'll copy it for you, and Geoff and I can deal with the ones around Newcastle.'

'I'll get on to that first thing in the morning and involve as many of the local forces as I can. I'll let you know if there are any outside of Thomas White and the HQ that you need to search.'

It was ten o'clock when Harry finally drew up outside Claire's house. He sat for a moment in the car, absorbing the familiarity of it and trying to analyse his feelings. Why was he here, and why did he suddenly feel terrified of locking himself into something and having it end up in disaster? Claire had been special, he knew that, and he was looking forward to seeing her again. But why did it feel such a big deal? He had to keep reminding himself that seeing her wasn't committing to anything. It was simply an exploration of their relationship. He thought back to the handful of counselling sessions he'd had, feeling the usual mixture of irritation at becoming someone who'd needed counselling and a deepening sense of calmness as he remembered some of what he'd learnt about himself. People laughed about commitment phobias but when you had it broken down as to the whys and wherefores, it made sense – and understanding it was the start of dealing with it. But he was way too exhausted tonight for any great depth of analysis. He was just looking forward to seeing Claire. He took a couple of deep breaths and opened the car door.

'Smells good,' he said, thrusting a bottle of red wine into her hand as they exchanged kisses on the cheek. 'Sorry – are you sure this isn't too late?'

She was wearing jeans and a sweatshirt, her hair loose to her shoulders and, unlike him, she looked great.

'It doesn't matter. I've only done bangers and mash.'

'Sounds perfect.'

Claire already had a bottle of wine open with a half empty glass resting on the kitchen worktop, and she filled another glass for Harry before taking the sausages out of the oven and serving up.

'Thought we'd eat in here if that's okay with you?'

'Yeah, fine.'

Once they were seated, she took another sip from her wine and it occurred to him that maybe she was just as nervous as he was. The thought was oddly reassuring.

'So, a late night. Does that mean something new has come up on the case you're working on?'

Harry hesitated, but it would be all over the morning news anyway.

'We've had a massive breakthrough. Four bodies buried in the grounds of Serenity Hall. All women.'

'My God, that's terrible. Were they ... murdered?'

'We don't know all the details yet but for two of them at least, probably not. We've got two men in custody at the moment, awaiting the formal autopsy results.'

'When did all this happen?'

'This afternoon. We'd taken a number of people from

275

the commune in for questioning and randomly the gardener tells us there's a body buried in the grounds – and it just so happens that it turns out to be a woman reported missing by her parents.'

'Bloody hell.'

'Then, as we're about to head back to the station, he calmly lets slip that there are three others. It was grim. That's what I've been doing all evening … questioning everyone involved. And it's a conspiracy, I'm not kidding.'

'God I can't believe that. Could there be more, do you think?'

'I hope not, but we'll be searching the entire grounds now and God knows what we'll find. This is very welcome,' he said, changing the subject as he scraped the last of his meal off his plate. Sorry I was so late.'

'It doesn't matter. I wasn't going anywhere.'

Their eyes met across the table and the atmosphere was suddenly charged.

'More sausages?' she asked, jumping up to remove his plate.

His hand reached out for hers as she would have taken it. 'No,' he said, curling his fingers around hers and pushing his chair back to stand also. Very slowly he drew her towards him, giving her every opportunity to pull back. But she didn't.

'I'm really sorry about your dad,' he said softly. He pulled her into his arms and just held her, and after the exhausting day he'd had, it felt so good. The tension seemed to seep out of him and when she turned her face upwards to return his look, they stared at each other for what seemed an age, before it seemed the most natural thing in the world for him to lower his mouth to cover hers. And once he'd done that, it was game over.

'Oh, God,' Claire said, pulling back, her hands on his shoulders. 'I promised myself I wouldn't let this happen tonight.'

Her voice was breathless and husky and only served to heighten Harry's need as he looked down at her. 'Me too,' he whispered huskily, teasing her lips with his before deepening the kiss again.

'I think we have to do it though,' Claire said between kisses. 'Otherwise, how will we ever know if we're compatible? We'll just be left wondering.'

He slid his hands down over her hips and pulled her into him, enjoying the physical buzz that shuddered through him.

'Couldn't agree more. Your place or mine?' he growled.

'Definitely mine.'

She gasped as he suddenly manoeuvred her back against the wall, pressing her into it as he continued to kiss her.

'Upstairs,' she whispered after a few moments. 'I hope you've got some protection?'

He groaned. 'Oh, God. No. I didn't think …'

She gave a wicked little laugh, grabbing hold of his hand and leading him confidently towards the stairs. 'Good thing I have then.'

CHAPTER THIRTY-FOUR

When Beth woke the next morning, it was to the unusual sound of someone in her shower. She froze for a moment and then remembered. Geoff.

They'd gone for their drink and after that it had seemed sensible that he pick up a few bits from his place and stay over at hers so they could get an early start in the morning. Although Whetstone, where he lived, wasn't that far away from Enfield, it was long enough when an early start was called for. He'd slept on the sofa, which she knew wouldn't have been that comfortable and for a moment she lay there trying to analyse how she felt about having someone else in her flat. It was strange. When she'd first come down to London from Northumberland, she hadn't been able to cope without someone in her life and she'd done one or two things that she looked back on with something less than pride, but since moving into Harry's flat, she seemed to have undergone a metamorphosis. Having her own place, her own space, had become important to her and discounting Harry and her grandparents, Geoff was the only other person to set foot in that space.

She looked at her phone and groaned. Six fifteen. They'd agreed to head off at six thirty. Why hadn't her alarm gone off?'

She jumped out of bed, got her clothes ready and listened. No sounds coming from the bathroom now, but the sudden, soft tap on the other side of her bedroom door made her jump.

'Beth, are you awake?'

'Yup, I'll be out in a minute.'

'Bathroom's free. Hope it's okay that I'm frying some egg and bacon? One egg or two?'

'Uh …' She wouldn't normally have egg and bacon in a million years. She was surprised she even had any and wondered how long they'd been there, but she found her mouth watering unexpectedly at the thought. 'One, thanks. It'll only take me a few minutes to grab a shower and get ready.'

By the time she emerged from the bathroom, showered and fully clothed, the smell coming from her little kitchen was tantalising.

'I found some mushrooms and baked beans too – hope that's okay.'

'Oh God, it smells great. I don't bother much with cooking for myself.'

'To be honest, your bacon looked like it had seen better days, but it smelt fine.' He grinned as he handed her a plate. 'I doubt we'll die of food poisoning.'

She sat down at the table and watched as he poured two cups of coffee.

'It should be me cooking for you. You're the guest.'

'Yeah, well I'm just grateful that I got an extra hour on your very comfortable sofa. Thanks for that.'

Yup, she liked him, she decided – an opinion that had been gradually growing these last few months. From the careless sweep of his brown hair to the twinkling warmth of his interesting hazel eyes, there was something about the unprepossessing Geoff Peterson that drew her. And it felt nice having him here in her flat. Not as a lover but as a friend. They were chalk and cheese in many ways and she knew a relationship wouldn't work. He was confident, popular with everyone, and she was sure would have had a very normal upbringing, whereas she knew that although she got on reasonably well with people, she had a tendency to put their backs up with her chippy character that she'd been told more than once, matched the spikiness of her hair. No, it would never work as a romantic pairing but maybe, as he'd suggested again only last night, as friends they could have fun together.

'So I think the best plan is for you to drop me near the Serenity HQ and then head off to interview this Thomas White chap,' Geoff said, scooping a forkful of food into his mouth. 'That way, I can hang around for half an hour and when you get to White's, you can call me and we can hit them both at the same time. I won't make any mention of you seeing White in the hope that, if either of the babies are there, they won't think to phone ahead and warn him.'

'Okay, sounds like a plan. It's going to be a pretty full-on day and not exactly how I was planning on spending my Sunday. My grandparents were meant to be coming for lunch today so I had to cancel them … but there you go. That's the job we chose.'

'Yeah – and you wouldn't change it, would you?'

'Not in a million years,' Beth said.

⌒

Harry was down in Claire's kitchen, making coffee while she scrambled some eggs. He was still adapting to waking up in her bedroom. Did all this feel as weird to her as it did to him?

'Milk and sugar in your coffee?' he asked.

'Milk, no sugar thanks. Right …' She turned off the gas. 'This is about ready now.' She tipped the eggs onto two slices of toast and carried them to the table.

'Looks great. My mouth's watering.'

She laughed. 'Your turn to cook next time – if you want there to be a next time, that is.' She threw him a cheeky look.

'I think you could twist my arm! How do you feel about meeting up later this afternoon? I'll need to check in at work this morning, but if you've got any thoughts about where we could go–?' He broke off, frowning, as his mobile went off. At this time of the morning it could only mean one thing.

'Damn,' he muttered, picking it up and seeing Murray's name flash up on the screen. 'Excuse me a minute, will you?'

'Boss?' he said into the phone.

'Where are you?' Murray said. 'Second thoughts, you don't need to answer that on a Sunday morning. Something's come in. A missing woman report. Can you get over to Watford asap? I'll text you the address. Uniform got in touch because they thought we'd want to know. They were contacted by a Mrs Morrison, who was under the impression her sister was trekking in the Himalayas for the past three weeks – until it turns out, she never went on that holiday at all. The woman's worried. Says it's not like her sister to disappear like that. On a whim Uniform asked her if she had any connections to Serenity and, guess what?'

'She does?'

'She apparently attended a couple of their seminars and was impressed by them. The sister doesn't know if it went any deeper than that.'

'You're thinking she might be the final body?'

'It's possible. We don't have an ID on it yet and I've just spoken to Edwards. He hasn't done proper PM's on them all, but says that cause of death for the unidentified body is probably from a stab wound. I've asked him to prioritise her autopsy and let us have any info he gets as soon as possible. The address you're going to is where the missing woman lives. The sister and her husband are waiting for you there.'

Harry ended the call and looked at Claire.

'Don't tell me … something's come up.'

'Sorry. I need to deal with it, but with a bit of luck I might still be able to make it over later – if you're free?

'Yeah, that would be cool.'

'But, meanwhile–' Harry pulled out a chair and sat down at the table '– nothing and no one is going to make me miss out on this breakfast you've cooked. Even a bloody policeman needs to eat.'

The ping of his phone confirmed Murray's text coming through and thirty minutes later he was being shown into the lounge of 29a Meakin Road, Watford.

Pulling out his notebook, he looked at the distraught woman facing him as they sat down. 'In your own time Mrs Morrison, can you confirm your sister's name and when you last saw her?'

He looked up as the woman's husband came in with a cup of tea and handed it to his wife. She took it from him and sipped shakily for a minute before clearing her throat. In the far corner, two young children sat absorbed watching *Tom and Jerry* on the television.

'Mrs Morrison?' Harry prompted gently.

'Her name's Amelia Watkins and I saw her just over three weeks ago, before she went on holiday.'

Harry frowned. Why was that name familiar?

'And was that the last contact you had with her?'

'Yes. I tried to WhatsApp her a couple of times while she was away but I never got through. It was a trekking holiday in the Himalayas and she'd warned me that reception out there wouldn't be good – so, although I was a bit concerned, we put it down to that. She was due back yesterday afternoon. We left it until last night, after the kids had gone to bed, to call her but she didn't pick up. I messaged her to call me on WhatsApp and that message hasn't been looked at. So this morning we came here to her flat. When she didn't answer the door we let ourselves in with the spare key.'

She broke off and tears filled her eyes. 'You can see for yourself if you go into her bedroom. It looks like she never even went to Nepal. Her cases are there packed and all ready to go, her passport, tickets, currency – all of it still sitting on her bed in her documents wallet.'

'What about her car? Does she drive?'

'Yes. It's still parked in the drive. A silver golf.'

'Okay, any idea who she booked the holiday through, so we can talk to them?'

'Exclusive Getaways.' She allowed herself a small smile. 'She only ever travels in style.'

She lifted a shaky hand and sipped her tea. 'I can't believe this is happening. Where can she be? I keep calling her phone but it goes straight through to her voicemail.'

'We'll do our best to get to the bottom of it. What about work? What did she do for a living?'

'She's a medical secretary – does private work for a couple of consultants.'

Immediately, Harry's ears pricked up and now he remembered where he'd heard the name.

'Is one of them a gynaecologist, called Jonathan

283

Anderson, by any chance?'

'It could be – that name's familiar and one of them is a gynaecologist. The other is an orthopaedic surgeon, I think. How did you know that? Is she alright, do you think?'

Harry hesitated but knew the only way to confirm the dead woman's ID for sure was to get a genetic match.

'I hope she is, but …' He looked at her husband, who luckily seemed to pick up on that look and moved over to sit next to his wife on the settee.

'Has something happened to her? Just tell us if you know something.'

'I don't know for sure – and I mean it when I say, it could well not be your sister. But … we discovered the body of a young woman yesterday who we're trying to identify. I'm sorry to have to put you through this, but if we could take a DNA sample from you, it would help us get an answer quickly, either way?'

'Oh, God, no.' The woman buried her face in her hands, and collapsed into her husband.

Harry gave them some space and then said quietly. 'As I say, it might not be her.'

She raised her head, took a breath and said. 'Can't we just come with you now – and identify her one way or the other?'

'It's not that straightforward I'm afraid. She was buried about three weeks ago. Better that we do it through DNA or maybe dental records?'

'It might not be her though, you say?'

'It's possible.'

'But if it's not, then where is she?'

Harry didn't answer.

'She goes to the same dentist as me – Mr Ruben in Bushey. You can get her dental records from there.'

284

She pulled a tissue from her pocket and dabbed at her eyes. 'I should have gone round yesterday, when she didn't pick up my calls. Why didn't I? But she could be funny if she thought we were checking up on her. And it never occurred to me that she might not even have left the country.'

'You mentioned to the police when you reported her missing, that your sister had some connection to the commune in Bushey … The Brethren of Serenity?'

'Yeah, but I don't know how involved she was with them. I just know that she went to a couple of their meetings and then signed up for some therapy sessions.'

'Do you know what that was for? The therapy?'

The woman sighed. 'She had an abortion when she was seventeen –she never forgave herself.'

Harry pulled his phone out. 'I'm going to give someone a call and ask them to come over and check the flat for any obvious forensics. It's probably best that you head home now. We'll try to prioritise things so that we can tell you the results as soon as possible.'

'You don't want us to wait here for them? I might be able to answer any questions they've got.'

'No … we know where you live. You take your family home – someone can call on you there if they need to ask you anything.'

He dreaded to think what forensic evidence might already have been destroyed by two adults and a couple of children crashing around the place.

After they'd gone, he headed into the bedroom. It was exactly as the woman had said. All of Amelia Watkins' belongings were carefully piled together on the bed in anticipation of her holiday. The fact that they were still there, untouched, three weeks later didn't bode well for her.

285

But the two really significant factors that gave him food for thought in all this were her connection to Serenity and the fact that she was Jonathan Anderson's private secretary – the one they knew was away on holiday.

He pulled out his phone and dialled the office, knowing that someone would be in even though it was a Sunday. It was Susie who picked up.

'Earning brownie points?' Harry quipped.

'Nah … just a boring home life. Sad isn't it, when I get more enjoyment coming in here than I do staying home alone in my flat.'

'Well, it's good for me that you're there. Can you look in the file for Jonathan Anderson's home address and phone numbers – the consultant that Juliet Sanderson was under? I need to pay him a visit. Oh, and while you're at it, get me the GP's details too. I might drop by on him as well if I've got some time, see what he's got to say about Cara Swift.'

⌢

Half an hour later, Harry was pulling up outside Jonathan Anderson's rather nice detached home in the suburbs of Northwood. He'd had the forethought to phone ahead this time and consequently Anderson himself came to the door, leading him through to a large, comfortable study where he offered him a chair.

'So what can I do for you?' Anderson asked. 'It must be urgent, coming on a Sunday?'

'We've had some developments in the Juliet Sanderson case and I wondered if you might be able to throw some light on a couple of things?'

'Of course, if I can.'

'You told us your private secretary was away on holiday,

due back yesterday?'

'That's right. I'm seeing her tomorrow to update her and hand over some clinic typing.'

'So you've spoken to her since she got back?'

'No. We arranged it before she left.'

'Right. I'm not sure how to tell you this, but it seems she never went on her holiday – her sister rang and reported her missing this morning and we've been round to her flat. All her pre-holiday documents and luggage are still there, sitting on her bed.'

'What?' Jonathan Anderson looked astounded. 'I don't understand. She definitely said she was going away. Where's she been these last three weeks then?'

'That's what we're trying to find out.' Harry hesitated. 'You might have seen on the news yesterday that four bodies were discovered in the grounds of Serenity?'

Anderson frowned. 'Yes, I did see that. What the hell's going on there—?' He broke off. 'You're not saying … one of those isn't Amelia?' He looked horrified.

'We'll be conducting tests to find out. But she apparently had links to the commune. Did you know that? How involved was she with Serenity – or Juliet – do you know?'

'Uh … I'm not sure.' He pushed a hand through his hair, clearly trying to get his head around this new information. 'She's a great people's person and interested in everyone and everything – all my patients love her. I'm quite sure she'd have built a relationship with Juliet – and others before her, but I'm sure it would only ever have been professional. As for Serenity, I did know that she went to some of their seminars and was impressed by them, but how deep that went…'

'When did you last actually see Amelia?'

'The Friday before she went on holiday. Her flight was

the next day. She brought the message book and some other stuff to the Oakfield to give to the girls in the office while they were covering for her.'

'So they would have seen her too?'

'Yes.'

'One of the other bodies we found yesterday is that of another Serenity member called Cara Swift.'

'*Christ* ... she's another patient of mine that I was told had left the commune.'

'What can you tell us about her?'

'Well ... only things related to her pregnancy, obviously. I was more concerned when they told me she'd left, because unlike Juliet, things weren't quite so straightforward for her.'

'In what way?'

'She had problems with high blood pressure, which I'd prescribed medication for. I stressed to her and Serenity that she needed bed rest, and that we'd be monitoring her bloods and urine to get a better picture. We were keeping a close eye on her to make sure she didn't develop pre-eclampsia. When she missed her appointment and Amelia called Serenity to ask why, they said she'd left without leaving a forwarding address but that she'd told them she'd inform her new doctor about her medical condition. I wasn't happy about it, but in the absence of knowing where she was, there wasn't much else I could do. I stressed to them again that her condition was potentially dangerous and that it was important that she carry on being monitored, but they seemed to be in the same situation as me, in that they didn't know where she'd moved on to. Amelia told me that she then rang to say she'd forward her new hospital and GP details once they were confirmed.'

'It was definitely Amelia who relayed that message to you?'

'Yes.'

'Do you remember when that was?'

'Not exactly, but … hang on a minute.'

He reached for a somewhat battered briefcase, withdrew an A4 book and started to flick back through the pages. 'This is my message book. It should say in here when she phoned in.'

Harry waited as Anderson went back through the pages. 'Ah … here it is.' His expression was bleak as he turned the book round so that Harry could see.

The entry was scrawled untidily at the bottom of the page, simple and to the point. *Cara Swift (hospital No: P249621) – moving away and will be having her baby at another hospital. She'll let us know the details in due course. No further OPA required – thanks for your help!* In the narrow left-hand column was the date, 1st July 2019. And at the end of the message the scribbled initials, AW.

Amelia Watkins.

'OPA?' Harry said, looking up from the book.

'Outpatient appointments.'

In the right-hand column marked ACTION, was a comment from Jonathan Anderson. *Chase up for new GP/ Hosp details asap so I can send medical report.*

'So didn't it strike you as odd that both Juliet and Cara decided to have their babies elsewhere?'

He frowned. 'In retrospect, maybe, but not at the time. It happens. Usually, I'd do a medical report on the patient's pregnancy for her to take to her new doctor, but obviously I couldn't do that with Juliet or Cara because they hadn't left Serenity their forwarding addresses and when we tried the mobile number we had for Cara, which we did several times because of her condition, it just went to answerphone. All we could do was leave her a message to get in touch. Are you saying that she never left Serenity?'

'That's what it's looking like.'

'But why would they tell me she had?'

'That's what we're trying to find out. Apparently, she died from the complications you've spoken of. Who did you deal with at Serenity if there were any issues?'

'Joshua Jarvis. Everything was done through him.'

'And how long have they used your services?'

'A long time. I took over as the main consultant about ten years ago when my colleague retired, but they'd been coming here to him for at least ten years before that. Most of their deliveries are home births, I only tend to get involved with the more complicated ones, and generally those patients would come in to the Oakfield – or Watford if there were more serious complications. Sheila's a qualified midwife and there's another woman there who's also trained. They say they like to give their members a home birthing experience if they can, and I have to say they do a pretty good job of it.'

'Have there been other cases of their members moving away before they have their babies?'

'There may have been. I could go back through my records if you like and check it out?'

'That would be helpful.'

'What's going on? Do you have any idea? '

'Not yet,' Harry said, standing up to take his leave. 'But as I've said, we have had some developments. Can I have a copy of this message book for our files?'

'Of course. In fact, if it's just that page, I can copy it for you now.'

'We'll need to go through all the messages I'm afraid.'

'In that case, I'll ask one of the secretaries at the hospital to photocopy it tomorrow if that's okay, and someone can drop by to pick it up from there?'

'Watford or the Oakfield?'

'I'm at Watford tomorrow.'

'Okay, thanks for your time.'

'You're welcome.' He shook his head. 'I can't believe it. I see enough of death that can't be avoided in my job and it's always tragic – but there was no need for her to die. Not if she'd been monitored properly.'

‿

Harry pulled up outside the attractive detached house in the leafy private road in Elstree, and got out of his car. There were two cars parked in the drive and, as he walked up to the front door, he stopped in surprise at the leaflet stuck to the rear window of the black Mercedes.

WE ARE ONE! JOIN US AND TAKE A WHOLE NEW VIEW ON LIFE

It was one of the many Serenity posters he'd seen dotted around Serenity Hall. But why would Dr Janner be advertising Serenity and its teachings?

At the front door, he rang the bell and waited, his brain still fixed on that sticker.

'Yes?'

The man who stood in front of him was mid-fifties with grey hair and a beard. His appearance was nothing out of the ordinary. His voice was crisp, as if slightly irritated at the intrusion on a Sunday morning.

'Dr Janner?'

'Yes.'

'I'm Detective Inspector Briscombe from Hertfordshire police? I'd like to talk to you about Juliet Sanderson and another woman who I believe might have been one of your patients … Cara Swift?"

'Oh ... Right.' He looked nonplussed, glancing at Harry's card before opening the door wider. 'You'd better come in.'

In the lounge, he offered Harry a chair and waited for him to speak.

'I believe my sergeant's already spoken to you about Juliet Sanderson?'

'Yes. How's she doing?'

'Still not come round yet, but the doctors seem hopeful.'

'Good, good.'

'But, Cara Swift … what can you tell me about her?'

Janner frowned, as if trying to recall the name and Harry filled him in briefly. 'She was also a Serenity member but apparently had issues with high blood pressure, so was being kept an eye on?'

'Ah yes, I remember. Well, it's exactly as you say and a similar story to the other girl. Serenity informed the surgery that she had moved away and would pass on her details in due course. She never did. We tried to chase her up a few times because of her medical issues but our messages kept going to answerphone. There's very little else we can do in those circumstances. People have to be responsible for themselves to a certain extent. She knew she needed to be monitored.'

'Well, it's now looking like she may not have moved away at all. Yesterday, we found what we believe to be her remains, buried in the grounds of Serenity Hall and obviously that sheds a very different light on things. We're also not convinced that Juliet left their premises either.'

'Good God, what are you saying?' The man looked shocked as he stared at Harry.

'Just that,' Harry said. 'We're looking into the possibility that rather than leaving – they were both held at Serenity against their wishes, and that Cara Swift died in childbirth, probably from pre-eclampsia. It looks like her baby survived though, but there's no sign of where it is now. Talking of which … do you want to see to yours?'

From another room, Harry had become increasingly aware of the sound of a baby crying, with no one as yet, going in to it.

'No, no …' The man looked horrified at the thought. 'He's fine … just a bit colicky. You know what young babies are like.'

'I don't actually … not married.'

'Ah, right … well, enjoy your freedom while it lasts, because it's exhausting once a baby comes onto the scene.'

'Your baby?' Harry couldn't quite hide his surprise, as it was clear the doctor was well into his fifties.'

'Good Lord no … our daughter's. We're giving her a break and looking after him for the afternoon so she can catch up on some sleep. As I say, it's a tiring time for young parents. My wife will go into him in a minute if he doesn't settle.' He shook his head dismissively. 'But going back to what you were saying … I can't believe Serenity would be involved in anything underhand. It goes against their whole ethos.'

'I noticed on my way in that you had one of their stickers in your car window? Are you involved with them in some way?'

Just for an instant, Janner looked disconcerted, but then he said. 'Well … yes, on the fringes, you know? I see their members in my professional capacity and I'm a great supporter of what they do. In fact, I did used to be quite an active member when I was younger. I met Joshua in my university days and got swept along by his enthusiasm for it all … the idea of making a difference. Their business arm is quite big now – they run excellent courses and seminars to help individuals and companies get the best out of themselves – and of course that funds their mission to do good in the world and spread the word. I find it very difficult reconciling the Serenity I've known all these years with the picture you're painting of an organisation that holds people against their will.'

'How well did you know Joshua Jarvis? You're aware, obviously, that he was murdered a few days ago?'

'Yes, I heard it on the news. I was appalled. As I say, I used to know him quite well in our younger days but I only ever saw him in a professional capacity over more recent years.'

'We have reason to believe that he may have been blackmailing some of his clients who he was seeing for counselling.'

'What? Joshua? No … from what I do know of him, I can't believe that. That would be a terrible thing to do.'

'Yes, it would.' Harry rose to go. He didn't feel he'd learnt anything new here but he was glad he'd finally met the doctor.

And the fact that he was an active supporter of Serenity, was definite food for thought.

CHAPTER THIRTY-FIVE

Thomas White looked taken aback when he opened the door to Beth later that morning, but his expression seemed to ease when he realised she was on her own.

'Ah remember you, gal. You're Mitch MacGaskell's sister, isn't that right? How are you doing?'

'DC MacGaskell, Mr White. And this isn't a social call, just so you know.'

'Ah, right.' His smile was unnerving. 'You'd better come in, pet. I've been wanting to talk to you.'

'Before I talk about anything with you, I'll need to do a thorough search of this house, Mr White. Two babies have gone missing from Serenity. Do you have any young babies here?'

'No, no, Pet. We don't keep 'em here. All pregnant women go down to Serenity Hall or across to Hexham to have their babies.'

'I'd like to search the house, if that's okay.'

'I should probably be asking you if you've got a search warrant?' he quipped. 'But don't let it be said that I'd obstruct the police. Feel free. I'll get Mary to escort you around whilst I get the kettle on, eh? Tea wasn't it?'

She wished she could tell him what he could do with his

offer, but she was gasping for a cuppa. 'Tea would be good, thanks,' she said.

A few minutes later, following a fruitless search, she was seated opposite Thomas White, a steaming mug of tea on the table in front of her.

'Right, Mr White. First off … Dean Jarvis,' Beth said. 'Does he spend most of his time here or down South?'

'Well now, mostly here I'd say, though he nips back and forth when they need him, like. I couldn't do without him.'

'When Juliet was up here, we understand they had a relationship. How close were they?'

'Now, that I couldn't say. They paired but then she went back down South. I don't know what went on after that.'

'Are you aware that four bodies have been found buried in the grounds of Serenity Hall?'

'No, lass, I'm not. Whose bodies would those be?'

'That's what we're trying to find out. We think one of them may be a girl called Cara Swift. Did you know Cara?'

He shook his head and took a sip from his tea. 'Nope, can't say I did.'

'You don't seem too disturbed. Most people would be horrified at learning something like that.'

Thomas shrugged. 'If there were bodies discovered at Serenity Hall, I'm sure there'll be a right enough reason for it.'

'There can be no right enough reason for it, Mr White. Serenity could be in big trouble over this and my advice to you would be to tell us anything you know.'

'Which 'ah would if 'ah had anything to say about it. You're not like your brother, are you, Pet?' he said, his voice suddenly softening intimately. 'Apart from the colour of your hair – which looks much nicer on you than it does on him, by the way. Do you see much of Mitch?'

Beth stiffened, aware of that shift in tone. This was a path that every instinct in her body warned her not to go down, yet she had the sickening feeling that it was out of her hands and she could do nothing to stop it.

'Mitch has nothing to do with this, Mr White,' she said calmly. 'I need you to focus on what I'm saying to you about Serenity.'

'Ah, but that's where you could be wrong, see. Thinking your brother's got nothing to do with all this.'

It was Beth's worst nightmare, but she shook her head, determined not to be drawn in. 'If my brother has anything to do with this, then you need to talk to one of my colleagues. It's not appropriate that you talk about him with me.'

'Well, I could do that, of course, but that might mean you see your brother in jail for murder. Don't think that would go down too well in your family now, would it?'

Beth stifled a gasp, feeling the colour draining from her cheeks. 'What are you saying?'

'Ah, now, I thought that might get your interest. Let's just say your brother has connections with us. That we've done the odd bit a business with him and maybe if you was to investigate us too close like, you might suddenly find he was popping up on your radar, too.'

Everything screamed at Beth not to go there, but she couldn't help herself. She needed to know if her brother was caught up in all this.

'What sort of business? What did you mean when you said he could go to jail for murder?'

'Well, perhaps that last one was a bit strong – though some might not agree – but better not to even run the risk of it, eh? Much better that you put the brakes on things now. There's people out there might want to get their own back, and you wouldn't want your lovely little sister caught up in anything like that now, would you?'

Beth jumped up from her chair, ashamed to realise that she was trembling. 'I don't want to hear this. Are you threatening me, Mr White? I'm a detective constable – not a chief superintendent. There's bugger all I can do to halt an investigation, even if I wanted to. And if a single hair on my sister's head gets hurt, then I won't rest until I have you.'

'Just speak to your brother, pet. He'll tell you what you need to do. Other than that, I'm afraid I got nothing to add to what I already told you.'

All the way back to Hexham on her way to pick Geoff up, Beth's brain was spinning. It was her worst fear come true, that her chosen career would one day clash with the lawless activities of some of her family. The truth was she'd never been close to her older brother, Mitch. He was a thug and a bully and she had no illusions about him at all. But Isi, and even to a lesser degree, her other brother Ryan, were a different matter. They'd all united in childhood against the actions of their parents and even though they seemed to have turned their back on her since she'd chosen the police force as her career, those bonds weren't easily severed.

By the time she and Geoff were heading towards the first of the houses Harry had texted them to search, she'd made up her mind. She listened while Geoff talked her through the various interviews he'd done and DNA swabs he'd requested on two babies he'd seen there that were young, but not young enough, he reckoned. Then she gave him a censored version of her own interview with Thomas White. When she'd finished, she drew a breath, then said. 'Geoff, there's something I need to do once we've finished with these houses. It's a family matter. Do you mind going back without me? I can catch a train back later.'

'No need for that. I can hang on. By the time we've checked out these addresses, the day will be done. I'll call Harry and just say we'll catch up with him tomorrow.'

'No. Thanks, but there's no need. You get back. I don't know how long I'm going to be or even what my plan is at the moment.'

'Are you okay? You've been very quiet.'

'I'm fine. There are just a couple of things I need to do and it seems stupid not to do them while I'm up here.'

He shrugged. 'Okay, if you're sure?'

He pulled the car over and parked. 'Well, this is the first of the houses. Let's see what they've got to say for themselves and if they're hiding any babies.'

⌒

What a complete waste of time, Beth thought, as they finally exited the last house two hours later. Each building had been a replica of the previous one, both in the way it was run and the number of people living in it. They all had what she now termed as a 'dominant male' running the place, usually with one other man present and up to four women also living there. The women seemed to have no standing at all within the community, giving the impression that they did as they were told and were seemingly happy to do so. She found it both fascinating and horrifying that such women existed in this day and age, and couldn't begin to understand it.

'Are you sure you don't want me to hang on,' Geoff said, after she'd asked him to drop her off at an address within Newcastle city centre.

'Quite sure,' she said firmly. 'I don't know how long I'll be, but I need to see my brother and it could take a while. I'll catch up with you tomorrow.'

She turned away from him and headed down the path to the house that Mitch rented. Or at least, she hoped he still rented it. Her heart was pounding. She hadn't seen her brother in five years and it angered her that he still had the power to instill fear into her. But there was no getting away from it; she needed to know if he was linked in any way to Serenity.

The door opened and there he was. They stared at each other for a long moment, as if neither of them wanted to be the first to speak. Then raising an eyebrow, her brother drawled. 'Well, well … if it isn't our Beth. Finally remembered you've got a family, have you?'

'I need to talk to you, Mitch. Can I come in?'

He rubbed his chin. 'Well, now, I'm not so sure you can. I seem to remember the last time we spoke you told me what I could do with my life. That you were cutting me completely out of yours.'

Beth forced herself not to rise. She shrugged. 'We all say things in the heat of the moment.'

'No uniform. Have you left the police?'

'No. I'm CID now.'

'Oh, fuck.' He went to close the door, but Beth managed to ram her foot in the gap to jam it.

'I need to talk to you, Mitch. After that I'll go. I can do it like this in private, or I can come back later with a warrant and a colleague. Your choice.'

She saw the indecision in his eyes and waited. Finally, he stood back with a scowl. 'You've got five minutes.'

She heard talking coming from the lounge. 'Is there somewhere private we can go?'

He didn't answer, but led her away from the voices into

the dining room. There, he closed the door behind them and leant against it, arms folded against his chest. He was a tall man, solidly built like their father, but with the same auburn hair as her and their mother. She wished she didn't still find him intimidating.

'Go on then.'

'I've just been questioning a man called Thomas White. He belongs to a commune, cult, whatever you want to call it … The Brethren of Serenity? He tried to get me to back off from investigating them by saying that if I dug too deep, I might find that my enquiries led to you. And that I might not like that.'

'Did he now? Well, why would he say that I wonder, when I hardly know the man.'

'Now's not the time to play games, Mitch. We're investigating the deaths of four women and the near-fatal stabbing of a fifth. Thomas White insinuated that links to you could possibly even lead to you going to jail for murder. I need to know if you're involved in this.'

'Do you think I'd tell you, even if I was? I wasn't born yesterday – and I'm not going to jail for anyone. But for the record, that's rubbish and I don't know anything about these women. All I'll tell you is that yeah, for a while I was involved a bit with Serenity. I liked what they preached, you know?' This last was said with the mocking sneer she remembered so well. 'But I severed links with them a few years back – realised there was a real criminal element in that organisation that small fry like me didn't want to get involved in. So you can fire away with any questions you want into this investigation, pet, because I doubt any of it'll come back to me.'

'He also threatened Isi.'

301

Mitch's eyes narrowed. 'Did he, by heck? They won't dare harm a hair on her head, 'cos they know that if anything happens to her, they'll have me to answer to. Reckon he was just trying to put the frighteners on you.'

And he'd succeeded, Beth thought, though she wasn't going to share that with her brother.

'You'd better be telling the truth, Mitch, because as I said to Thomas, there's nothing I can do to halt this investigation now. And I wouldn't even if I could.'

'You always were too plucky for your own good. It'll be your downfall one day.'

The words hung between them for a few moments, a threat or an observation? Then, levering himself off the door, Mitch turned and opened it.

'Now … as I already know what you're doing these days, and you really don't want to know what I'm getting up to, I think it best you go. I'll say hi to Mam and Dad for you – unless you're planning on visiting them, too?'

'No.' Her voice was curt.

'I thought as much. Dad's not been well, though. Heart attack a couple of months back. Of course the old bugger won't slow down, so …?'

He let the sentence hang unfinished between them, but Beth's expression remained unmoved at the unspoken suggestion that she might not see her father again. Too much water under that particular bridge.

Out on the street again, she took out her phone and searched her contacts. While she was breaking the self-imposed family estrangement, she might as well take it one step further – and there was one other person who might be able to help her out on this one.

The phone rang several times before it was finally picked

up and a man's voice answered.

'Hello, Beth.'

It felt easier this time around. Her other brother wasn't as intimidating as Mitch, although she knew she had to be careful as he'd always been in awe of his older brother and dominated by him.

'Ryan. How are you doing?'

'I'm okay. What's up?'

'Where are you? I need to talk to you. I'm in Newcastle at the moment, I can come over.'

'You might have a bit of a problem there.' She could hear the chuckle in his voice. 'I've moved to Glasgow.'

'*What?*'

'I'd have thought you knew that, doing the job you do.'

She let that pass. 'What are you doing up there?'

'I live here now, with my fiancée.'

'You're *fiancée*?' She knew she must be sounding really thick, but she was flabbergasted.

'Aye, and my son, Charlie. He's eighteen months now.'

She had a nephew … and he actually sounded proud of being a father, when a few years back he'd sneered at friends he saw as being 'caught in the trap'.

'I had no idea,' she said lamely. 'I just saw Mitch. He never said anything.'

His tone hardened. 'That's because he don't know and I want it to stay that way. Mitch and I fell out big time over all that business with Br—'

He broke off and immediately Beth was on full alert. The way he'd said it sounded as if he'd been about to talk about something that she might have known about.

'Business with who … or what?'

'Don't matter now, Beth. Best you don't know.'

Far from reassuring her, that only added to her worry. 'Ryan, what are you talking about? I'm on an investigation – a murder investigation – and someone's implicated Mitch. I need to know if he's involved in any way, because if he is, I need to take a step back. In fact, they'd probably take me off the case.'

'Murder, you say?'

'Yeah. Two in fact. And there could be more.'

'Is it to do with the girl on the news this morning? The one found at the commune?'

'Yeah.'

There was a long silence.

'Ryan?'

'I don't know anything, Beth, and that includes whether or not Mitch has any involvement. If I had to put money on it, I'd say it's unlikely. He fell out with them big time, the same time as I did with him. I can't see him getting involved with them again.'

'So what did you fall out over?'

Her brother sighed. 'We rowed, that's all I'm prepared to say, and seriously, pet, I wouldn't go digging if I was you. You don't want to go opening old wounds.'

'What the hell does that mean?'

'Nothing. And I'll not say any more on it now. Have you seen Isi recently?'

It was a clear change of subject, and although Beth didn't want to let go of it, she knew her brother well enough to know he wouldn't be pushed.

'No, I haven't. She's made it clear she doesn't want anything to do with me.'

'She was broken when you left – you know what the atmosphere in that house was like. How could you have done that to her?'

'I was broken too.'

'I get that. But she didn't. You were the only one she had.'

'Stop it! Just stop.'

She didn't need this. If she could have taken Isi with her, wouldn't she have done just that? But she couldn't, not with all the police training she'd had to undergo, let alone the fact that Isi was underage and her parents would have had something to say about it. Her tone was distraught as she said, 'Do you think I wanted to leave her? It was the hardest decision I ever made. I tried keeping in touch with her, but Mum and Dad made it impossible and she stopped answering my letters years ago. Last Christmas she wrote saying she didn't want anything to do with me.'

'That's because she was hurting.'

Beth knew it was. It didn't make her feel any better but she still trotted out the excuse she'd used to herself these last few months. 'I tried to talk her into meeting up with me after that letter, but she didn't even answer. What else am I supposed to do? She's nearly eighteen. Old enough to be making her own decisions.'

'She's a mixed-up kid. She don't know what she wants. I've not been the best of brothers, but maybe, like you, I'm seeing that now. I've got a kid. It makes you see things differently.'

'You sound worried about her. Is there something you're not telling me?'

'I have my own family now, Beth, and I'll not do anything to put them at risk. Keep an eye on her is all, and while you're at it, check out she's not involved in this religious sect you're investigating. And no one must know we've had this discussion. Not Mitch … not anyone. I've moved on with my life. Going straight for one thing. Had a stint in prison that I didn't much enjoy and was lucky to meet Eleanor when I got out. We moved to Glasgow, where her dad's given me a job at his garage, selling cars. Who'd have thought it, eh – me, a car salesman? But I'm doing alright and I won't mess it up for anyone. You'll think it's typical of me I'm sure, that I've dumped Isi in your lap. But there you go … someone needs to look out for her. Just go and see her, eh?'

Beth was bemused. Was she missing something here? How did Isi fit into what was going on at Serenity? She put the question to her brother.

'I'm not saying she's got anything to do with them. I'm just saying that it might be worth checking it out.'

'I don't have her address and she won't pick up the phone if she sees it's me.'

'I'll text it to you … and a couple of photos of Eleanor and Charlie, if you like? But Mitch, Mum and Dad don't know about him, and I want to keep it that way.'

As Beth hung up and waited for her brother's text to come through, her expression was worried. She needed to see her sister, make sure for herself that she was okay. And why had Ryan been worried that she might have a link to Serenity? That was what was sitting most uneasily in her mind, because it was another thread linking her family to the commune. And she didn't like that one bit.

She glanced down at her phone as it pinged. There was an address and four photos – and she had to smile when she saw that her laughing little nephew had inherited the auburn hair. He wouldn't be happy about that one as he grew older.

She started to walk purposefully down the road towards the bus stop, then spun around startled as a car hooted and slammed to a halt alongside her.

'Taxi?'

It was Geoff, a rueful smile on his face as he waited to see her reaction.

'From the few bits you've let drop about your brother in the past, I was worried about you,' he said through the open window. 'Just wanted to make sure you came out in one piece. Come on, hop in. I'll drop you wherever you want to go.'

She sighed, stooping down to open the car door. 'Do you ever do as you're told?' she said, sliding on to the seat next to him.

'Not often. Contrary Joe, that's me. I won't pry, but did your meeting with your brother go okay?'

'As okay as it can ever go.'

She looked at her watch. It was five o'clock and her tummy suddenly gave a loud rumble, reminding her that she hadn't had anything to eat since breakfast. 'Well, now you've waited this long, I've got one more visit to my sister to make if you're still happy to wait? But shall we grab something to eat first? I don't know about you, but I'm starving. And I suppose it's only right that it's on me.'

'Now there's an offer I can't refuse, Geoff said, starting up the engine. 'Where to?'

CHAPTER THIRTY-SIX

Juliet

'Come on Juliet, you must eat.'

Paula's voice is kind as she tries to encourage me to eat the stew on my plate, but I have no interest in eating. No interest in anything since they took Theo away. I toy with the food, averting my eyes from the bruises on my wrists where they handcuff me at night, to make sure I don't try to run away again. I can't believe that my life has come to this – that I'm being held prisoner and no one outside Serenity knows.

For the first few days after Theo was taken, I was hysterical, screaming and shouting for my baby, swearing that if I broke out I'd expose them all for what they've done. Their answer is to make me drink more of the elixir I used to love. I realise now that it drugs me, makes me incapable of thinking straight, and for a while it's a blessing and I drink it freely. I don't want to think about the terrible thing I've done to my son – abandoned him to some life I know nothing about, when my instinct tells me I would have given him a much better life myself, with the love that only a parent can give.

I'm broken.

On the few lucid occasions I have, I'm gripped with terror for my future, because I'm sure that if I carry on like this, I'll end up in a hole next to Cara. Even Dean's given up on me. At first, after they took Theo, he moved back into the house for a few days and tried to console me. I'm sure they only allowed it because they thought he could control me, make me conform again – but I could see that he didn't know how to handle me and that only upset me more. He tried to talk me round, saying that we could have another baby and that he'd talk to Joshua to see if next time we could keep it, but I don't believe him. I don't trust him anymore.

'You'll never stand up to Joshua,' I throw at him. 'You're too weak. You're brainwashed. You all are … how can you not see it?'

'Juliet, stop it. Why don't you understand? Serenity's a loving, compassionate community, but our unity with God and loyalty to each other comes before anything else. People who violate that – violate our trust in them – have to be punished to make them see the error of their ways. I don't want to see that happen to you.'

'And what about your loyalty to me? You told me you loved me.'

'I do, but I don't understand you. You came into this with your eyes fully open. You were grateful that we took you in at a time when you were at your lowest and now you repay us like this. It's hurtful. I don't know what to think.'

'Have you been faithful to me while you were up in Newcastle?'

The question comes from nowhere and he blinks. 'Of course I have.'

'Well, that's not what Joshua said and I don't feel I can

trust you anymore. I'm going to end up dead, like Cara. Why don't you just admit it?'

'Cara's death was a tragic accident because the ambulance didn't come in time.'

'It didn't come, full stop. I bet they didn't even call it, and they could have taken her in a car. They killed her. And then they buried her – probably without even telling her family. That's illegal, Dean. You could go to prison for that.'

'Stop talking like that. We look after our family, we don't kill them.'

He's angry, like he always is when I criticise his beloved Serenity. 'And you're part of our family,' he says in a gentler voice. He pours me a glass of the elixir. 'Here, have some of this, it'll calm you.'

But as his arms encircle me, drawing me to him to comfort me, I find myself stiffening. I used to feel safe in these arms, cherished; but now when I think about feeling safe and cherished, it's my mother's arms that I long for.

After a few days it's as if he's washed his hands of me – whether it's because I make him feel guilty, or because he *is* guilty, I don't know. But we're arguing the whole time and he moves out, and Terence tells me that he won't be moving back in *until I pull myself together* and move on from what's happened. I tell him that I'll never give in, never forgive them for taking my baby. That's when I'm moved from the house to the shack – which is basically a large shed with a toilet in it. And the beatings begin.

When Terence and another man took me there, I thought, this is it … they're going to kill me. But I was so groggy and confused from the elixir, that I barely registered the fact, or what they were doing as they handcuffed me to a wooden post.

Then Terence took off his belt. The first lash across my back shook me out of my stupor and made me scream out with pain, the cotton of my dress doing nothing to protect me from the brutal, searing agony of the leather as it cut into my skin. That was followed by four more lashes and by the end of it, I could hardly stand.

'I take no pleasure doing this, Juliet, but you have to realise that by betraying your fellow brethren, you are not only betraying Serenity and all it stands for but also God, whose light we follow in this otherwise dark and corrupt world. It's not always an easy path, and I hope this will give you food for thought, but if it doesn't, next time it will be ten lashes. And so it will continue until you reaffirm your undying loyalty to Serenity. You must understand that we can never allow you to return to your old life, and therefore it's imperative you fully embrace the community and all it stands for. I'm sure when you've had time to think about it, you'll rediscover the joy and contentment you knew when you first came here.'

'And what if I don't?' I hurl at him defiantly.

'We won't even think about that. You'll stay in here alone tonight and reflect on your situation. There's a mattress on the floor over there.'

He undoes my handcuffs and attaches them to a sort of pulley affair on a chain that enables me to walk the length of the shed. After they've gone, through my tears, I test it out and realise that there's just enough length to the chain to allow me to reach the toilet, and lie down on the floor. I look at the bucket in the corner in disbelief. Am I really expected to use that to wash? Then I drop gingerly down onto the mattress and lie on my side, trying to avoid the painful mess that is my back.

Later as Paula gently bathes my wounds and she sees me wince, there are tears in her eyes. 'Oh Juliet,' she whispers. 'Just do as Terence says. I can't bear to see you like this.'

The beating seems to have shocked me out of my constant state of daze and for the first time I realise that if I have any chance at all of escaping from here, I need to keep my wits about me. Which means no more elixir.

'I need to get away from here, Paula. I'll never give into them. Never. How can you bear to stay?'

'Don't. They warned me you'd try to corrupt me. I have nowhere to go if I leave here. I'm *happy* here.'

She pulls out the flask with the elixir in it and pulls off the top. 'Here, have some.'

I take it from her and pretend to take a couple of sips. 'It's so soothing,' I say, 'but I feel sick at the moment. Can you leave it with me so I can drink it in an hour or so?'

She nods and gets slowly to her feet. 'Think hard about your situation, Juliet. There have only been a couple of people who I've seen resist like you and I don't want to see you go through what they did. Joshua, Fabian, Terence … they can make life very difficult here for you, and believe me, it's not worth it.'

'And what about Dean?' I blurt out. 'Where does he fit in all this? Does he know what they've done to me here today?' I can't bear to even think he might.

She shakes her head. 'I don't know … and that's the truth.'

I jump at the touch of a hand on my arm. Or at least, it feels like I jump although I'm sure I've made no movement at all. But my heart pumps with excitement because I *felt* that

312

touch which I've never done before.

'Hey honey,' my mother's voice murmurs softly. 'Dad's here and he's brought a playlist that Lisa's put together for you. She says it's all the stuff that she and you used to listen to when you pranced around the bedroom together, and you'd better appreciate it because it took her hours to do.'

If I could cry with emotion, I would. They come every day, all of them, and they've always got some of my music, or an old family video to play to me, trying to bring me back to them the only way they know how. It must be early evening, because Mum sits with me all day and Dad and Lisa join her after work. At first, he'd take over and Mum and Lisa would leave when he got here, but I've noticed the last couple of visits that Mum's stayed when Lisa's gone, and as I listen to them talking quietly by my bedside, I realise that if nothing else, my accident seems to have drawn them closer again. I'm so glad about that. I hate thinking that my childish tantrum – because that's what it was – had driven them apart.

I feel Mum's fingers now, lightly stroking my face, so much tenderness and love conveyed in that single action that I want to cry for the child who will never know the tenderness of *my* touch. Where is he now? Are they being kind to him?

I wish I could respond in some way, any way, that would let her know that I can hear her, that I love her – and I have to believe that one day I will. But it's not today.

To suppress the crushing panic that always wells up in me at the thought I might never escape the trap my body has become, I turn my thoughts back to Serenity and the final pieces of the puzzle that I know are coming together.

There's something dark and horrible in the recesses of my mind. It's been trying to surface for a while and it's as

313

if I couldn't let it, but today an image flashes into my mind unbidden, and once revealed, there's no going back.

I've been in the shack for three days now, and it's been three days of hell. Each morning, Paula brings me a bucket with water in it and a towel to wash, and she bathes my back, which is agony. All I can think about is escape and how it's just a hopeless dream. I even hatch a plan – one I feel ashamed over. But I'm desperate and terrified. The only thing keeping me going is the thought of finding my son – and the memories of my mum, dad and Lisa – and the warmth and laughter that is home.

Every evening, Emanuel comes with a fresh bucket of water, and the one good thing about that is that I've been able to tip my elixir into it without anyone realising I'm not drinking it. As a result I'm feeling almost back to normal now, alert and aware of what's going on around me, though I make sure no one else realises that.

Today, I smile at him as he walks hesitantly into the over-sized shed. I'm surprised because it's still morning. 'What time is it?' I ask.

He looks at his watch. It takes him a moment to work it out. Then he smiles his lopsided smile, looking proud of himself. 'It's half past eleven.'

'And what day? You're early.'

'Saturday. I'm going to the football this afternoon with my dad so I won't be here to do it later. I didn't want to leave it till tomorrow. The water would be dirty.'

His kindness brings the tears to my eyes. 'Thank you, Emanuel. That's very thoughtful. And you'll enjoy the football.'

He nods and goes to pick up the dirty bucket.

'How are your nest boxes?'

'They're all empty now, but I had some late nesting robins and they've become very tame.'

I sigh heavily. 'I wish I could see them. You're such a kindhearted man, Emanuel.'

He flushes with pleasure and I hate myself for what I'm doing. I know he likes me and although I must look a dreadful sight with my unbrushed hair and lack of general hygiene, I'm at least wearing a clean dress while my other one is being washed.

'I love robins. Will you show me?'

He shakes his head frantically. 'I can't.' He looks at my handcuffs. 'Anyway, I don't have a key for those.'

'I think they keep them on a hook outside the shed, don't they? I've heard them hang them there. You know they're keeping me prisoner here?'

He doesn't answer, his eyes intense and bright.

'Do you think that's right?'

He shakes his head but still says nothing.

'All I want is to go for a little walk and see your robins. No one need know and it would make me really happy. I'd think you were the best man in the world. Actually, I already think that.' I flash him one of my brightest smiles and watch the colour fill his cheeks again.

'Please?' I say. I hate myself for taking advantage of him but I feel this is my last chance, my last hope. And decency is a poor substitute for desperation. I'll do anything to escape.

'I mustn't,' he mutters. 'They told me I shouldn't even talk to you.'

'I know,' I say. 'But we're friends, aren't we?' I can feel the moment slipping away and I want to grab it back but don't know how. I hold out my hand to him and he hesitates before reaching out slowly to take it in his grasp. His fingers

315

are muddy and calloused but I relish the warmth as they curl around mine.

'Think about it,' I whisper softly. 'They need never know.'

That evening, Terence comes back. He looks at me piercingly, stroking the leather belt in his hand. I'm sitting slumped on the floor and as I look up at him I pretend that I'm having trouble focusing on him, trying to remember how groggy I felt when I was under the influence of the elixir.

'How are we feeling, Juliet? Now you've had time to reflect on your situation, are you ready to be welcomed back into the house or do you need more punishment?'

The thought of that belt slicing into wounds that still haven't healed is enough to make me capitulate instantly. I'll get nothing by holding my ground defiantly out here in this shed. I'm realising that I need to play them at their own game if I'm to have any chance at all of escaping. I try not to think about the fact that it might be months, years even, before I'm given back the freedom I used to have.

'I'm ready to come back,' I slur, shaking my head as if to clear it. 'I'm sorry I've been such a nuisance.'

He stares at me hard for a moment. 'Maybe you need one more beating to remind you what happens when you let us down?'

'*No.*' My fear is genuine and I hate myself for my weakness. 'Please … I'll mend my ways.'

'Very well. We'll give you one more chance. But if you let us down again … well, you understand we just can't let that behaviour continue?'

I shudder at the tone of his voice, as I imagine another hole in the ground next to Cara's.

CHAPTER THIRTY-SEVEN

Harry skimmed the abbreviated preliminary post-mortem report on Cara Swift.

'I've put the obvious findings in there,' Edwards said from his position next to where another body lay partially covered on a trolley. 'The more detailed report will take longer.'

'Thanks for prioritising it – and working on it yesterday when I'm sure you had better things to do with your weekend. We need to crack this. What started out as a random stabbing is now ballooning out of all proportions.'

He lapsed into silence as he continued to read. It confirmed that the body was that of a young woman of medium stature who appeared to have been buried for a period of approximately 2–3 months. "On section of the cranial contents," he read, "signs of extensive haemorrhage were found involving the brain stem and pons. The only other feature of particular significance on general investigation of the thoracic and abdominal organs was the presence of extensive haemorrhagic areas in the liver, characteristic of eclampsia. Cause of death: spontaneous cerebral haemorrhage (brain stem and pons), arising from pre-eclamptic toxaemia."

He sighed, folding the report and slipping it into his

pocket. 'So it definitely was pre-eclampsia. What about the others?'

'I'll do them as quickly as I can but I can't sacrifice accuracy for expediency.'

'Point taken.'

'The only thing I can say with any certainty is that the most recent victim's death was definitely foul play. She was stabbed.'

'Right.' Harry absorbed that. 'Thanks.'

'You're welcome. I'll let you know straight away if I find anything else significant.'

∽

Back in the office it was a hive of activity.

'Morning,' Beth called out as he hung his jacket on one of the pegs. 'How was it for you yesterday?'

'Interesting, but you go first. How did you and Geoff get on in Northumberland?'

She shrugged. 'It didn't feel very productive. We searched all the houses but no babies anywhere and Thomas White denied all knowledge of any bodies being buried at Serenity – or of what goes on there. I get that he doesn't live down this way, but …' She shook her head. 'I don't trust him. He's not as straight as he'd like us to believe.'

'The famous woman's intuition?'

Beth suppressed a twinge of guilt. Her sister had been out when she'd called, so she'd never got to see her and had had to settle with leaving a voice message. She felt very unsettled by the apparent link between Serenity and her family.

'Something like that,' she said. 'What about you? Anything new?'

Harry indicated the report on his desk. 'We're checking

dental records and DNA on Cara Swift to confirm the match, but there's not much doubt it's her – she was wearing a ring that her mother gave her. The PM's confirmed that she died of pre-eclampsia, which fits in with my conversation with Jonathan Anderson yesterday and we've had a bit of a breakthrough on the unidentified body at Serenity.'

'Oh?'

'Looks like it could be a woman called Amelia Watkins – name ring a bell?'

Beth thought for a moment, then her brow cleared. 'Yeah … isn't she the secretary that works for Jonathan Anderson? The one who's on holiday?'

'Yup, except it seems that she never went on her holiday. All her luggage and documentation are still piled on her bed ready to go. And as well as working for Anderson, she also apparently had some involvement with Serenity, which gives another link to Juliet and Cara. It feels too much of a coincidence for it not to be her.'

Harry dug out his notebook. 'She booked her holiday through a company called Exclusive Getaways – check them out will you and see what they've got to say about the fact she didn't show? I spoke to Anderson yesterday. He was expecting to meet up with her today after her holiday. He said he knew she'd been interested in Serenity – and I don't know whether it's relevant or not, but she's also the one who supposedly took a message from Cara Swift that she'd left Serenity and was being seen elsewhere.'

'You think Serenity may have influenced her in some way to lie about that?'

'It's possible. Or someone else could have called pretending to be Cara.'

'Maybe Cara said something to Amelia that put her

in danger? That she hadn't really left the commune, for example.'

Harry sighed. 'That too is possible. I didn't get very far with Fabian yesterday – they're still clamming up and we're running out of time before we need to charge or release them.' He looked at his watch. 'I'm going to head back to Serenity and check how SOCO's doing there – see if they've got anything new to report. I'll round Dean Jarvis up for more questioning at the same time. I wasn't happy about letting him go just as things were beginning to break, but we didn't have enough to hold him on.'

'Did Emanuel come in yesterday to give his statement?'

'Yeah. I took it myself.'

'What did he say about Amelia Watkins' burial, if it is her?'

'That it was Joshua who called him and the body was already wrapped in a sheet and laid on the ground near where she was to be buried. Joshua told him she was a member who'd died of a heart attack, who wanted to be buried in Serenity's grounds. He never opened the sheet. Just buried her. It doesn't seem to have occurred to him that there was anything wrong in that, but I think he'd be easy to manipulate, especially as they've obviously got him to do it before. Right … are you coming with me?'

'Sure. Give me two minutes.'

CHAPTER THIRTY-EIGHT

'Have they found anything? Anything at all?' Harry asked the young police officer standing on duty while the SOCO team were making a thorough sweep of the woods.'

'Nothing more from the gravesites, sir, though they're extending the search area. What they have found has been bagged up and taken away. But they've discovered a couple of outbuildings that look like they could have been used to imprison people. They're still checking them out.'

'Where?'

'Up through the trees that way...'

Without another word Harry headed off in the direction indicated. 'Anything significant?' he asked, sticking his head in the door of the first oversized shed they came to.

'I definitely think we'll pick up some DNA from in here,' the gowned up individual said, turning to look at them. 'There are blood splatters on the floor and on some cloths over there and look at these...' He held up a pair of handcuffs. These were attached to that pulley up there – I reckon to give someone the capability of walking the length of the shed without being able to leave it. We'll also be taking that mattress and various other items away for investigation.

Obviously we'll draw up a full inventory for you. The other outbuilding looks like it's just for garden equipment and the like but we'll check it out to make sure.'

'Great stuff,' Harry said. 'At last … some concrete evidence, with a bit of luck.'

'And good news there's no more bodies,' Beth said, as they turned and headed for the main house. 'I was living in dread of that one.'

'Let's not get ahead of ourselves. There's a lot of land here to cover yet.'

They got to the front door of Serenity Hall and rang the bell. 'Is Dean Jarvis here?' Harry asked the brother who opened it. The man looked at his watch and shook his head. 'I don't believe he's come over yet. He's probably still in the cottage. Number four it would be.'

But when they got there, the house seemed remarkably quiet and empty and only Sheila and Paula were present. They both looked nervous as Harry and Beth followed them into the lounge, and Paula looked as if she'd been crying.

'Dean's gone out,' Sheila said hesitantly. 'When will you be releasing Terence and Fabian?'

'When we're satisfied that they've told us the truth about the bodies buried in your grounds. Where has Dean gone?'

Sheila hesitated and Harry's look became impatient.

'Sheila, now is not the time to be stringing us along. You must realise that all this isn't just going to melt away. We need answers and we'll get them one way or another. If you're organisation has any chance at all of surviving this, you need to be honest and open with us.'

She and Paula exchanged glances and Harry saw Paula nod.

Sheila's expression was anxious as she said. 'He didn't

say, but I think he's gone to the hospital to see Juliet. He heard on the news that the doctors are hopeful that she'll come round any time now. He was fond of her, you know … I think he just needed to see her.'

Immediately, alarm bells sounded in Harry's brain.

'When was this? How long ago?'

'About half an hour?'

He'd turned away from her before she'd even finished speaking, heading briskly for his car. 'We need to get over there, now,' he said to Beth, unlocking the door and climbing in. 'Who's watching over her?'

'I'm not sure. But I'll ring through to the ward.'

⌒

Juliet

It's quiet here in my room, and I've come to recognise the different types of quiet that happen throughout the day. This is the morning quiet, before things have really woken up and started to happen and I lie here, breathing in the silence – in a weird way enjoying the solitude. Later, I know, Mum will arrive. Her reassuring presence is the only thing that has kept me sane for however long it is that I've been lying here. I think I'd have gone mad if it hadn't been for the reassuring warmth of her fingers curled around mine. Sometimes she talks to me as if we're holding a normal conversation, seeming not to notice that I make no response. At other times she reads to me or sits in silence, perhaps reading her own book or paper. But always there. The times I hate the most are when her emotions get the better of her and she blames herself for what's happened to me, and asks if I can ever forgive her. Because it's her who should be forgiving me, for acting like a spoilt child instead of the near adult that I am.

My thoughts halt as I suddenly become aware that someone has entered the room. It's probably one of the nurses and I wait to see which of my tubes she'll fiddle with today, but nothing happens. I can sense that whoever it is, is standing very still and a prickle of unease trickles up my spine as I imagine their eyes on me. They move closer. It's amazing how alert my senses have become – as if aware of how vulnerable I am without movement or sight.

'Hello, Jules.' The words are whispered, as if he doesn't want anyone else to hear them. I feel the soft touch of his finger on my cheek, drifting slowly downwards in a caress over my jawline, down the side of my neck, and I recognise that touch, my senses responding to the familiarity of it even though I can't move.

Dean…

⸙

'No one's picking up,' Beth said, disconnecting the phone and redialling.

Harry put his foot down on the accelerator. 'Don't we have a direct number for ICU?'

'Yes, that's the one I'm using.'

'Shit. Just keep trying, we're still at least ten minutes away.'

'I'll ring the office; see if they've got another number. Look, let's not panic. Somebody will be there on duty. They're not going to let a complete stranger in.'

'I know. I'll just be happier when we get there.'

⸙

Juliet

I can feel his breath on my face, he's that close. And suddenly, I don't know why, but I'm fearful. Part of me just wants him to take me in his arms and hold me, but there's another part, in a darker recess of my brain, that doesn't trust him. *Why?* Why can't I remember what happened to me? Was Dean involved? Is that why I'm suddenly frightened?

I feel both his hands cup my cheek and then he's pressing his lips oh so softly against mine.

'Look at you. This should never have happened.' he whispers. 'You need to know that this was never part of the plan…'

⤳

By the time Harry and Beth threw themselves out of the elevator and raced into ICU, it was over.

Marie Sanderson was there looking grey with anxiety and PC Carter was looking shamefaced, even though he'd managed to apprehend Dean Jarvis who was now locked in the relatives room.

'It was a call of nature,' he defended himself, 'and he managed to slip past the staff while they were dealing with other patients. As soon as I saw him in there I arrested him and called you.'

'Good thing you did,' Harry snapped. 'Christ, do you realise what a security lapse that was? How's the girl?'

'She's fine. He didn't hurt her.'

'It was me who found him,' Marie Sanderson said, glaring angrily at the young policeman. 'And if I hadn't come in early this morning, God knows what might have happened. I saw him leaning over her and just rushed in.'

'He's distraught,' PC Carter said. 'Says he loves her and just needed to see her.'

'Well, it's lucky for everyone that nothing worse happened. We'll get him back to the station and question him properly. In future, if you need a call of nature, you make sure you ask a member of staff to watch over her while you're away.'

He turned to Marie Sanderson. 'I'm sorry that happened, but thank God she's okay.'

'It's just good I came in when I did.' She hesitated. 'He started to cry as your chap took him away. I don't think he meant her any harm.'

'Maybe,' Harry said.

Or maybe he was just a good actor.

～

Juliet

He's gone and I don't know whether I'm sorry or glad. But oh my God, my mother! She came rushing in like a virago, shrieking at him to get away from me and launching herself at him without hesitation. I think she actually frightened him and if I could smile I would at that thought, except that I wish she'd left it just a little bit longer before she launched her attack, as I still don't know where Dean fits in to all this.

I can hear them out in the corridor talking and before I know it, I'm slipping back into that half-awake, half-asleep state of mind where I'm back in the past. There's no stopping it I know, so I just let it happen. In fact, I'm embracing it now – impatient to put the final pieces of the puzzle together, so that at least I know who I can trust and who I can't. But above all – desperate to remember what happened to my baby.

◞

I've been out of the shack for a week but they're not stupid. They still don't trust me and as part of my punishment they've sent me to Coventry. Every night I'm handcuffed to the bed and during the day I'm locked in my room, where the windows have had wooden planks put over them to contain me. Last night, Terence came to my room and made me pleasure him. A test, he said, to see if I was as penitent as I claimed. Somehow I hid my revulsion but I can't break through the despair I feel. I can't see that I'll ever escape, and after he leaves me I cry myself to sleep.

My meals are brought up on a tray and at first Paula can't even look me in the eyes as she puts it down on the little table in the corner. It's as if she's scared I might contaminate her in some way just by looking at her. This morning she offers me a little nod of acknowledgement.

'Where's Dean?' I ask, desperate for conversation and equally desperate to know why he seems to have abandoned me.

'Northumberland,' she says in hushed tones, turning to leave.

'Please don't go, Paula. Stay with me for a while?'

'I can't. We're not allowed to talk to you.'

'I need the toilet,' I say desperately. Even when I go to the bathroom now, either she or Sheila accompany me. I don't know what they think I'm going to do in there. Slit my wrists? Jump out of the window?

She hesitates, then opens the door for me to precede her.

'I thought you were my friend,' I say when the bathroom door closes behind us.

'I am.'

'Then help me get out of here. They'll kill me if you don't, because I can never go back to how I was. Do you want that on your conscience?'

'Don't…'

'I mean it, Paula. I can never settle back into this life.'

'*Paula!*' It's Terence's voice coming from the stairs. 'What's taking you so long. We're waiting to say our prayers before breakfast.'

'Coming. I'm just in the bathroom with Juliet.' She lowers her voice. 'Your room is bugged. Terence can hear everything we say.'

My eyes widen in shock and she gives me a long look before turning to open the door. But there's something in that look that gives me hope.

That night, as she gently handcuffs me to the bed, her manner is nervous.

'I can't help you escape, Juliet,' she whispers so quietly I can barely hear her, 'but all I can say is that everyone apart from Terence will be going to the crematorium tomorrow at eleven o'clock for Brother Simon's funeral. If you have a plan, that would be your best chance to escape.' She gives me a warning look. 'You didn't hear that from me.'

I think about it all night and though what I'm contemplating terrifies me, I know I have to do it. When Paula comes in that morning to undo my handcuffs and take me to the bathroom, I whisper urgently. 'If I don't make it … if anything happens to me …'

'I don't want to know,' she whispers back, shutting me down. 'I still have to live here after you've gone. I was happy here until you started putting doubts in my mind. It might not be perfect but I've known a much tougher life than this. I just want things to get back to what they were. I love you, but the brothers are right. You're a disturbing influence on us all. It's better that you go.'

When I'm alone again, I run my plan over and over in my head, unable to believe I'm really considering it, let alone intending to carry it out. But I am. I check that the bedside lamp is unplugged, and wait.

I hear them saying their goodbyes, hear the front door slam and know it's just Terence and me.

I leave it ten minutes before I bang on the door and ask Terence for the bathroom. He tells me that he's busy and I'll have to wait. It's over an hour before he finally comes up and I'm getting agitated. How long do funerals last? I've dressed with care, leaving the buttons of my tunic open at the neck exposing bare skin – something the women of Serenity never do. My heartbeat increases as I see Terence's eyes drift to my cleavage – still bigger than normal, although the milk is at last beginning to dry up.

'Thank you,' I say demurely, brushing past him as I make my way to the bathroom. 'I just need to freshen up a bit.'

When I come out he's there waiting for me and he follows me into the bedroom.

'Lie down on the bed,' he orders, undoing his trousers. 'You can pleasure me again.'

I hate the feel of his hands on me, rough skinned and clumsy through the material of my robe, but I force myself to actively participate, just grateful that it's too soon after the birth for him to expect intercourse.

When it's over, he rolls sideways off the bed and sits up, reaching for the handcuffs that are lying on the table.

There's a moment of sheer panic. *I can't do it.* I'm frozen into immobility – too terrified to push myself through the boundary I've set. But then, as his hand settles on the cuffs, it spurs me into action, my right hand reaching out so that my fingers curl tightly around the lamp on the other bedside table. He pauses in his actions to turn and see what I'm doing. I have no choice now. Lifting my hand quickly, I smash the base of the lamp as hard as I can onto his head, then drop it as he slumps sideways onto the bed, blood seeping ominously from his temple. I stare at his unmoving form, horrified by what I've done; then before he can come round, I scramble off the bed and grab the discarded handcuffs that have fallen onto the floor. He's heavy but somehow I manage to hoist him far enough up the bed to handcuff him to the wrought iron bedhead. He's totally still. Have I killed him? I stifle a sob, knowing that there's no point worrying about that. If I wasn't dead meat before this, I certainly am now. I need to get out of here before everyone gets back. I reach for the package on top of my wardrobe – my old clothes, jeans and a tee shirt, that I haven't worn since I came here. I can't do the waist up, but just putting them on boosts my confidence. I can do this.

At the front door I hesitate. What if Paula was wrong and everyone hasn't gone to Simon's cremation? Or even now, the minibus is driving back through the gates? I'm sobbing, knowing I'm on the verge of losing it. But I mustn't. I must hold myself together for just a little longer. *Think!* Turning on my heels, I head for the kitchen. Better to go out of the back door rather than the front, where there's always more activity.

I unlock the door and I'm *free* – racing for the trees, hugging them tightly as I make for the gates. And after a while, there they are in front of me – and they're *opening*. My initial joy is blown apart as I can see the front of Joshua's sleek car, waiting patiently to enter. I dive behind a tree.

No! No!

I stand there helplessly, fighting back the sobs, praying no one can see me – knowing that my only chance is to run through those gates before they close. But I can't do it without giving myself away, and I stifle another sob as I watch them swing shut again – my only chance of escape slipping away in front of my eyes. I realise this is madness. The gates are tall, at least eight-foot high, with spikes on the top. I can never climb over them. And the little side gate that I escaped through last time now has an enormous padlock on it.

I wait for his car to disappear up towards the main house, holding my breath as it approaches our cottage.

He's pulling over. That can only mean one thing. He's going to call in on Terence. Without allowing myself time to think, I turn away from the gates and dive back into the trees.

Where am I going? Which direction should I take? I'm panting, my heart fit to burst, and I let out a shriek as a pair of hands suddenly grabs me from behind.

It's Emanuel and I clutch at him in relief. 'Emanuel,' I sob, 'you must help me. I need to get away from here or they'll kill me.'

For a long moment he says nothing and I see uncertainty warring with his desire to help me. Then without a word, he turns and pulls me into the bushes.

I have no choice but to trust him. We don't speak as he hauls me along a little path through the woods, and finally, a few minutes later, we come to a boundary hedge.

'Through there,' he says quickly, already pushing me through a small gap. 'It leads out to some trees and then the road.'

'Thank you.'

I'm so grateful that I hesitate only for the briefest of moments before I grab him by the shoulder and kiss him on the cheek. His embarrassed pleasure is something that even in those circumstance, warms my heart and will stay with me forever. If I get out of this, I vow, I'll buy him something really nice. Like a nest camera, which I know he'd love.

I squeeze through the gap in the hedge and don't look back.

The memories are flooding back with unstoppable force now. The mad scramble through the undergrowth until I get to the road – which I quickly cross in the hope that if they come searching for me they'll concentrate more on the other side – the race alongside it, hugging the trees, as I head for the shops. The terrifying chase through the market. And finally – the blade, glinting in those fingers before it was thrust into me.

And suddenly the final pieces of that puzzle slip into place as I remember it all. Who it was that plunged that knife into me – what happened to my baby – my utter shock and sense of betrayal.

And then a new fear grips me. Because I know it's not over.

He'll be back.

CHAPTER THIRTY-NINE

Back at the office, Harry snatched a quick coffee and skimmed his notes, before heading down to interview Dean Jarvis.

'Good to let him stew,' he said to Beth. 'Are you coming?'

'No, I'll get on with looking into stuff here. There's stacks to follow up on.'

Harry took his time sitting down, setting up the recorder and sorting through his notes. When he was ready, he looked at Dean over the utilitarian table, pleased to see that the man was looking ruffled.

'Right,' he said. 'How about you start off by explaining exactly what you were doing sneaking into Juliet's room this morning?'

'Is my solicitor on the way?'

'Yes. You have the right to wait for him if you want to.'

'No. It's okay.'

'So?'

'I wasn't sneaking … I just needed to see her. They said on the news that she was improving and they were hopeful she'd come out of her coma. I thought if she heard my voice, it might help.'

'And why would hearing your voice be any different to

hearing her parents' or her sister's voices?'

'Because she loves me. And I love her.'

'That's convenient new information. Up to now you've been denying she was anything special. So … you love Juliet. How come it's taken you so long to admit it, or go and see her?'

'It's complicated. I needed time to think.'

'What about?'

He sighed. 'I've let her down badly all the way along, I know that and I'm not proud of myself. When you told me about the marks on her back … I knew straight away what they were. Beatings for being disobedient or disloyal to the Family. That's one of the things I'd change if I was Lead Brother. I knew Juliet wasn't happy; she struggled with some of our beliefs and ways, but I thought she'd come round.'

'That they'd beat her into submission, you mean?'

'That her love for me would be strong enough to help her conform,' he said firmly. 'I realise now that it was just too much of a change for her and was never going to work. Just as her way of life could never work for me.'

Harry studied the other man carefully. 'Let me get this right. You're saying that if people don't agree with Serenity's teachings in some way, they're beaten? We've found the shed that they probably imprisoned her in, by the way.'

Dean looked uncomfortable. 'It's extremely rare, you must understand that, but we acknowledge that sometimes, if we step out of line and cause disharmony within the community, then we need to be punished – the pain helps to concentrate our minds on the consequences of what we've done. Everyone accepts that, you won't get anyone who'll speak out against it.'

'Except Juliet, perhaps? Which is another reason why

you could have been there this morning – to silence her.'

'That's not why I was there. I love her. Why would I want to hurt her?'

'I don't know, Dean, but I intend to find out. You've just said that your worlds are incompatible and intimated you wouldn't give up yours to be with her. Isn't love about compromise? She tried your way. Why wouldn't you be prepared to try hers – if you really loved her?'

Dean's face closed over. 'As I said before, it's complicated. People like you would never understand.'

'Try me.'

But he just shook his head, and they both turned as the door opened and his solicitor walked in.

Harry terminated the interview. 'I'll give you some time with your solicitor to get him up to speed and we'll resume this interview shortly. I suggest you tell him everything – and do the same with me when I get back.

As he left the room he literally collided with Geoff Peterson who was about to enter it.

'Harry. I've been questioning Brother Fabian like you said, doing my "good cop" against your bad cop bit, and I think we've got a breakthrough. He's running pretty scared now, especially after the identification of the fourth body, which he swears he knows nothing about. And while I haven't got it all out of him yet, he's given some interesting information about the events surrounding Joshua's death.'

'What's he said?' Harry asked as they fell in step up the stairs.

'He's admitted that Joshua told them he had one more person to see before he was ready to leave, and that he wasn't to be disturbed under any circumstances. He said he was trying to calm Dean down after his original row with his father, which was apparently because Dean had found out that Joshua was thinking about appointing Fabian as his successor. Dean was still seething about that when things apparently started to get heated in the room next door. They moved closer to the wall to hear what was going on. He said it became evident that the two men had some sort of business dealings going on and that the other man was livid because he'd had a phone call from someone who'd said that Joshua was blackmailing him – and that they could no longer afford the payments. The man told Joshua that his greed was in danger of blowing up the whole enterprise and exposing everything, and he wasn't prepared to stand by and let that happen. Joshua apparently responded that there was nothing he could do to stop it because, if he exposed Joshua, they'd both go down – so he'd better get used to the idea. That's when it seems to have got violent. Fabian said they were trying to figure out if a tussle was taking place when they heard what sounded like a chair going over. At that point, Dean ran out to investigate. According to Fabian he looked livid. Fabian says he wasn't so quick to follow, remembering what Joshua had said about not being interrupted but then, after a while, felt maybe he should go in. He says by the time he got in there, Dean was bending over his father, who was dying in his arms. He said he'd seen a man running down the corridor as he'd intervened, but Fabian didn't see that himself.'

'So how come he's only told us this now? None of that implicates him in any way, why wouldn't he speak sooner?'

'Because they were worried it would ruin Serenity's reputation if it came out that the commune was involved in illegal activities. Well, he's right there – you can imagine the publicity. He also implied that he couldn't rule out the

336

possibility that it could have been Dean who stabbed his father. He said Dean was ambitious and was always arguing with Joshua about being old-fashioned and the need to change some of their ways if they wanted to carry on attracting new members. He says Dean has anger management issues and had still been completely wound up from his previous argument with Joshua, and hearing now what his father had been up to, Fabian reckoned, made him see red – he flew into that room in a rage, although he also said that Dean seemed genuinely distraught afterwards as he held his father in his arms. At that point, Fabian called for an ambulance and went out to inform the hotel staff what had happened.'

'Which, if it was Dean, would have given him time to hide any knife.'

'Yes. Fabian said that when he got back, Dean had disappeared, but came back shortly after, saying he'd needed to wash his hands to get rid of the blood.'

'No knife was found by forensics.'

'Nope. And they will have done a thorough sweep.'

'Of the surrounding area, certainly. I'll get Beth to make sure they checked all accessible areas in that part of the hotel. He could have nipped up a floor and hidden it somewhere.'

'Okay. I'm going to grab myself a drink, and head back in there … see what else he's got to say for himself.'

'In particular, about Cara, Juliet and Amelia. And we need to establish if it's the same person who attacked both Joshua and Juliet, or two different people.'

'A message on that came through from Edwards this morning, while you were out. He reckons the same knife was used on them both – a six-inch kitchen knife most likely.'

'Well, that's useful. And we still need to find the owner of that SIM-only mobile. Until we have him or her, we don't know the full story.'

'That reminds me, Beth's just told me that Fabian's phone records showed that he rang William Blake around the same time as you were interviewing him at his house.'

'He took a call while I was there – said it was business.'

'Well, Blake had no other incoming calls two hours either side of your visit, so that must have been Fabian. He also rang Daniel Jefferson on the same day.

'So he knows more than he's letting on if he had their numbers. I think you need to get back in there and turn up the heat. Forget Mr Nice Guy and go for the jugular. We need to know if he knew about the blackmailing – and get Blake and Jefferson back in for questioning.'

'Found anything useful yet?' Harry called over to Beth, turning away from Geoff and approaching her desk. 'In particular, with regard to Dean Jarvis? I've left him with his solicitor but I'll be going back in a few minutes.'

He filled her in on what Geoff had said. 'So it looks like Joshua was murdered, either because this other chap found out about the blackmailing or because Dean lost his rag – a theory favoured by Fabian now, it seems.'

Beth consulted her notes on what she'd been doing that morning. 'Dental records have confirmed that one of the bodies buried in the grounds of Serenity Hall is definitely Cara Swift, so someone's gone round to see her parents. We're still awaiting confirmation on Amelia Watkins' ID. Preliminary findings on the other two women show that they've been there for several years. One had a broken neck, possibly from a fall, and he says cause of death for the other one will take longer. The baby's skeleton found with her was newborn, so she probably died in or soon after childbirth. He's still working on them and will send a provisional report asap but the official reports on all of them, won't be for some time. It ties in with what Sheila told Geoff though when he interviewed her about the two other women reported missing from Serenity.'

'Well, we need to get formal confirmation of their identities, we've been caught out on those sorts of assumptions before. You'd better start by taking DNA samples from family members, and get dental records if you can.'

Beth nodded. 'A couple of other interesting things. According to the emergency services, no calls were received from Serenity about Cara Swift needing an ambulance for her pre-eclampsia, and I'm not sure how relevant it is, but it seems the Blakes use Serenity's GP – Dr Janner – although they see him privately, not on the NHS. It's a coincidence.'

Harry frowned. 'Yes, it is. And when I visited him yesterday, he had a Serenity sticker in his car, which links him to the commune. What about the Jeffersons' GP?'

'He's different.'

'Okay, well, give Dr Janner a call and see if he's got anything useful to say about the Blakes. And maybe Jonathan Anderson as well, for the sake of completeness. Also, can you get another team over to the hotel to do a sweep of the public places on the upper floors? If Dean killed his father, he needed somewhere to dump the knife. Toilet cisterns are always a good place to start.'

⌒

Back in the interview room, Harry took his seat again, nodding at Dean's solicitor.

'So,' he said to Dean. 'Are you going to tell me now, what's been going on?'

339

Dean glanced at his solicitor; then looked back at Harry. 'I can only tell you what I know, and I don't know all of it.'

'Well, maybe I can help you out a bit, by telling you what we already know and giving you a chance to comment on that. According to Fabian, the circumstances surrounding your father's death weren't quite as you both originally stated.'

Dean's eyes narrowed. 'Oh?'

'He says your original argument with your father was much more than a heated discussion. You were livid because you felt your father's ways were outdated and you'd just discovered that you were no longer next in line to the throne, Fabian was.'

Dean sighed. 'I was angry, it's true. I do think there's room for change and I've often told my father and the Elders that. They go around with their heads buried in the sand, not realising that people today are very different from twenty years ago.' He hesitated, before seeming to come to a decision. 'That night my father was in a foul mood. He'd just been confronted by Juliet's father, demanding to know what had gone on with her. The man had gone for him just as I walked in. I pulled them apart and we threw him out, but he was shouting that he'd be back and he'd do us for what had happened to his daughter. Joshua was furious and rounded on me for not noticing he'd been in the audience. As if I'd have had a clue who he was – I'd never met the man. I was already upset with him about his treatment of Juliet and it just fired my anger. I blamed him for the breakdown in my relationship with her because he kept sending me off to Northumberland all the time, and he told me she was a threat to my commitment to Serenity. That nothing and no one should be more important than our cause, and he was no longer sure that I was fit to be Serenity's leader. I don't know what made me say it, but I accused him of having something to do with Juliet's attack – and he didn't deny it. Just stood there looking at me. And then he said, perfectly calmly, that they'd had no choice. It had to be done, to protect Serenity.'

'What did he mean by that?'

'I don't know. I was dumbfounded. I realised I hardly knew my father at all and I had to get out of there before I lost it completely. I turned and left the room and went to get some food. I needed the walk to calm down and sort out what was going on in my head.'

'Fabian says you still hadn't calmed down by the time you got back.'

'Well, what do you think? Of course I hadn't. I knew I had to tackle Joshua about it. If he'd had anything to do with Juliet's attack, it undermined everything we stood for – everything he preached. And then … Fabian and I overheard raised voices through the wall. My father and another man. It wasn't difficult to hear and it became apparent that my father was blackmailing people. It was just going from bad to worse. I'd spent my entire life being in awe of him – trying to live up to his expectations – and he was no more than a cheap crook. When we heard what sounded like a piece of furniture going over. I realised it was turning violent. I rushed from the room and saw a man running off down the corridor. When I entered the room … my father was lying on the floor in a pool of blood.'

'Why didn't you tell us all this before, if you had nothing to hide?'

'I was in a state. Fabian told me we mustn't say anything because it would be the end of Serenity and all we stood for. He said that we had an opportunity now to rebuild it as we wanted. I didn't trust him though. He and my father have always been thick as thieves and I couldn't imagine Joshua doing anything that Fabian wasn't aware of. But I needed time to think, so I agreed not to say anything. Now I've realised I just want justice for Juliet.'

'Better late than never, I suppose. She'll be grateful for that, I'm sure. So, I'll ask you again, where is her baby?'

He hesitated. 'I genuinely don't know. When Juliet found out she was pregnant, she didn't want the baby but equally she couldn't bear the thought of living in the community and watching it grow up. So I spoke to Joshua and he said he'd deal with it once it was born. Find it a new home. I don't know where that new home is, but Fabian might.'

'Oh?'

'I've asked him several times about it and he says he doesn't, but I think he knows more than he's letting on. He was my father's right-hand man and why would Joshua appoint him over me, unless it was because Fabian knew more about what was going on than I did?'

'Fabian says it's because you have anger management issues and are too ambitious. Not to mention your desire to change things.'

Dean's lips tightened. 'I don't have anger issues. If he's saying that he's lying. But it's true I'd change things, which is why they might not have wanted me as Lead Brother. I can't help wondering if there are more illegal activities going on that he's trying to hide.'

'Which of course you know nothing about?'

'I'm telling you the truth.'

'But still not all of it, is my guess. For clarification here, are you now admitting that you're the father of Juliet's baby?'

The slightest of pauses, then. 'Yes.'

He waited to see if Dean was going to add to that, and

when he didn't he turned to the next question on his list.

'This person being blackmailed … was a name mentioned?'

Dean frowned. 'William someone, maybe?'

'Does the name Amelia Watkins ring any bells with you?'

'Maybe. But I can't put a face to the name.'

'It might interest you to know that we now believe her to be the fourth body discovered at Serenity Hall and she'd apparently been to some of your meetings. This is a photo of her. Does it jog your memory at all?'

He slid the picture across the table and Dean looked at it. 'Yes, she does look vaguely familiar. As you say, I think she came to some of our meetings.'

'We believe she was murdered.'

'Christ.'

'Is that all you have to say?'

'Isn't it enough? I don't know what else you want me to say – I know nothing about her apart from the fact that I've seen her at a couple of meetings.'

'She's an attractive woman, educated, good job … I'm guessing she would have been an asset to Serenity if someone could have taken her under their wing … given her special treatment to encourage her in?'

'That's not how we do things.'

'Yet you'd have me believe that you're ignorant of how things *are* done – you apparently have nothing to do with the running of the organisation.'

'That's true.'

'Well, we have people from forensics going through all of Serenity's paperwork and we'll find out from that just how involved you are. Obviously it would speed things up if you freely volunteered information that would help us with our enquiry.'

'I'm sorry, there's nothing else I can think of that might help.'

'Okay. So, for clarification, you don't know who stabbed Juliet, you don't know who murdered your father – but it wasn't you – and you don't know where Juliet's and your baby is?'

'That's right.'

'You also know nothing about any of the bodies found buried in the grounds of Serenity.'

Dean hesitated, then sighed. 'That's not quite true.'

'Oh?' Harry waited.

'It was tragic – a few years ago now. I don't remember her name but one of our members had drink issues. They were keeping an eye on her over in the main house and she tripped and fell down the stairs – killed outright. Only a few of us knew about it and Joshua said better for it to stay that way. She had a habit of coming and going so they just said she'd left one day and not come back.'

'And they buried her in the grounds.'

'Yes.'

'Didn't that seem strange to you?'

'Maybe, but … I had no real reason to question anything.'

'What about Cara Swift? We have identified her body as one of those buried at Serenity.'

'I knew about her too. She died in childbirth. They did everything they could for her but she had some medical condition and although they called the ambulance, it didn't come in time.'

'That's because no one actually called it.'

Dean looked at him in shock.

'You weren't aware of that?'

'*No*. I wasn't there during her labour. I was with Juliet. Are you sure about that?'

'Quite sure. So she died and they buried her in the grounds. Were you present at that burial?'

'No. Joshua told me the next day that they'd been unable to save her but not to tell anyone because the fact she'd died of childbirth complications could have repercussions on Serenity delivering home births in the future. Only a few people knew about it and the rest would be told she'd decided not to come back to the community after giving birth.'

'So why put out the story that she'd left two months previously?'

'To create more distance between her disappearance and us, I assume.'

'She had a clear medical need for monitoring and by the sound of it, she didn't get that for the last two months of her pregnancy.'

'Sheila would have looked after her.'

'But Sheila's a midwife, not a doctor.'

'It looks bad, I know. God knows how we're ever going to recover from this.'

'Some might consider that to be the least of your problems. Right … we'll stop the interview here for the time being.'

'Is my client free to go?'

Harry had spoken to Murray about that, who'd commented that unless they had enough proof to charge him, they needed to release him. 'Sometimes it works better that way,' he said. 'Gives them more rope to hang themselves.'

He gave a frustrated nod. 'Yes, for the time being. But please make sure to be on hand if we need to question you again. You're not off the hook yet. And stay away from the hospital. If we catch you there again, you'll be arrested on suspicion of wanting to harm Juliet Sanderson.'

⌒

It was nearly lunchtime and Harry's stomach was rumbling, but he wanted to update the information in the incident room before he headed off for something to eat. It didn't surprise him to find Beth in there, doing the same.

'How are you getting on?' he asked.

'I rang Dr Janner's surgery to ask him about the Blakes, but they said he was tied up and would have to call me back. I said it was urgent. I'll try again when I've finished in here.'

'And Jonathan Anderson?'

'He's operating. His secretary said she'd pass on the message and get him to call me when he finishes. I just had a phone call from uniform, by the way. They've done a thorough sweep of the hotel ... no knife found.'

'Well, it was a bit of a long shot, I suppose.'

'What about you? Anything new?'

'I'm not sure ... I've learnt some useful stuff, some of it from Dean, some of it from Geoff's interview with Fabian, but it's still a minefield pulling it together.'

'So what facts have we got?'

'Well, we now know that Joshua was definitely blackmailing people – and I think that can quite safely lead us to assume that William Blake and Daniel Jefferson were two of his victims. Now, they were both in the bar having a drink and talking. They both had motive and opportunity, but if Dean and Fabian are to be believed, they overheard Joshua arguing with a third man who said he'd received a phone call from someone, claiming he was being blackmailed by Joshua. He could well have been referring to William Blake because we know Blake phoned Joshua that day too and

346

Dean thought the blackmail victim's name was William.'

'I think it's definitely him they're talking about,' Beth said, 'because when I went through his phone records again, that SIM-only number was on there, and he rang it the day of his appointment.'

'So it's very possible, that if it isn't Blake or Jefferson, then the owner of that phone is Joshua's murderer. We need to get Blake in and get the name of the person who owns that phone from him. Can you do that, and get Jefferson in too?'

'Next on my list to do.'

'Good. And while you're doing that, I've got some more digging of my own. I've got a hunch.'

CHAPTER FORTY

He stood in the hospital corridor, blood racing through his veins. This was by far the riskiest thing he'd done so far, and certainly the most premeditated, and if he failed it would all be over. He suspected it was all over anyway – it wasn't rocket science to work that out after his conversation with the police. For a moment he allowed himself to dwell on all that would mean. Quite simply, he'd lose everything.

But, no... he straightened up. He wouldn't go down without a fight.

And the dead couldn't speak.

Pulling his phone from his pocket, he dialled the number for the intensive care unit.

'Yeah, this is car park maintenance here. We've had a car vandalised in the car park and think it belongs to one of your visitors? A Mrs Sanderson? Ah, good. Can you ask her to come to the management office on the ground floor of the multi-story? Yeah, that's right. Thanks.'

It was done and there was no going back. Slipping the phone back into his pocket, he walked swiftly through the hospital doors and headed for the lift. He'd already got hold of a white coat, so now he put that on and by the time he exited the lift on the sixth floor, he was transformed into a doctor again. This wasn't the first visit he'd made to ICU, he'd made a point of being seen there on a couple of occasions, so that hopefully, his presence wouldn't raise suspicion. But this time he could feel the sweat breaking out, knowing that he wouldn't have much time to act, and luck needed to be on his side. But he had no other choice.

A swift glance around was enough to inform him that lady luck hadn't deserted him quite yet. The clerk on the desk had her head buried in paperwork and threw him no more than a cursory glance as he walked swiftly past. Up ahead of him he could see the policeman sitting outside her door, but instead of entering her room, he walked past it into the next one, as if visiting that patient – clocking, on the way past, that the mother was no longer sitting by the bed. He made a pretence of reading the patient's notes, then exited that room and walked past the policeman, face averted, straight into Juliet's room.

'Morning, Juliet,' he said, walking to her bed and removing something from his pocket. 'And how are we this morning…?'

‿

Juliet

My heart freezes. This is the moment I've been dreading ever since I remembered who it was who plunged that knife into me. *And now he's here.*

I struggle to open my eyes to see him – to let him know that I know – but, as always, they're as paralysed as the rest of my body.

I tense as I sense him leaning over the bed, studying me. Then I feel him withdraw.

349

'I'm sorry to have to do this Juliet, I really am,' he whispers. 'If Joshua hadn't been so greedy …'

I've got used to the sounds of the nurses fiddling with my IV tubes and monitors and I realise with horror that he's doing something to them. I sense him unplugging something and then fiddling with something else. He leans over me again and whispers quietly, almost kindly, 'I promise, you won't know a thing about this, and hopefully neither will anyone else. It will be painless for you.'

He's going to kill me. The adrenalin is surging through my veins like a torrential river. Is that because of my fear, or because of some awful drug he's just inserted into me? My panic swells to gargantuan proportions – I'm helpless inside this bloody body that won't move. I *need* to wake up. Every fibre of my being is trying to burst free from the paralysis, but it's like I have marble weights on all my limbs – none of them will respond. In my head I'm screaming with terror. I don't want to die. I want to live. I want to see my parents – tell them how sorry I am, how much I love them. I want to open people's eyes as to what really goes on within Serenity. But most of all … I want to see my son.

He leaps back from the bed as if startled, and – *Oh my God* – I suddenly realise that the scream in my head is not in my head at all … it's real – the sound bouncing gloriously off the walls; filling the entire room.

I turn my head to look at him, and *it moves.* I can *see.* Behind him, the door is flung open and a policeman rushes in.

'Quick, get the nurse,' he orders. 'This is excellent news. She's come out of her coma.'

'*No!*' I scream, but already the policeman is running from the room.

'Breathe a word and I'll kill your baby,' he says. 'I've

already killed Joshua, so don't think I won't do it.'

And he's gone – a flash of white coat the last I see of him, as he disappears through the door.

CHAPTER FORTY-ONE

Harry slammed down the phone and jumped up from his seat, heading straight into Murray's office. 'I've just had a call from the hospital. Someone's tried to kill Juliet Sanderson.'

'What! You'd better get over there. Did they catch him?'

'Don't think so,' Harry said, already turning to leave. 'I'll call you as soon as I know more. Beth, with me,' he shouted, exiting the office.

As they got to the bottom of the stairs and strode across the reception area, Katie on the desk, intercepted them. 'Harry … there's a young couple here, say they need to talk to you urgently.'

Harry looked over to where the couple were sitting in the far corner. The woman was in tears and the man doing his best to comfort her. He really didn't have time for that now.

'Sorry, Kate. I'm on an emergency call. Take their names and get someone else to deal with them, or tell them I'll get back to them later if you take their details?'

'I'll drive,' Beth said, flicking the fob. 'Then you can fill me in.'

'I don't know much,' Harry said. 'Just what Carter told me. He was sitting outside her door, when what he thought

352

was a doctor went in. Said he was wearing a white coat and he'd seen him before, so he had no reason to be suspicious. But then suddenly, Juliet started screaming.'

'You mean she's come round?'

'I assume so. He said they're testing her now. Carter said this doctor told him it was great news, she'd come out of her coma and for him to get one of the nurses quickly. You can't blame him for doing that, but when they got back, the doctor was gone.'

'Has Juliet told them who it was?'

'No, not yet,' Harry said in grim tones. 'And of course, it may well not have been a real doctor.'

⤚

There was a quiet buzz in the intensive care unit. As soon as they arrived, they were shown into one of the relatives' rooms where several people were standing around talking. A mixture of medical staff and management, Harry guessed.

He pulled out his card and showed it to them. 'Who's in charge here?'

'I am,' a man with a bald pate said, stepping forward. 'Arthur Hawkins, I'm the Directorate Manager, and I can assure you we've lodged this matter as an SUI and are giving it our utmost priority.

Harry blinked at him. 'SUI?'

'Serious Untoward Incident,' the man replied, and Harry barely managed to suppress a groan. 'This fake doctor somehow got into her room and fed what would have been a fatal dose of insulin into the saline bag attached to her. If she hadn't woken up and told us she'd sensed him doing something to her drip …' He stopped there, his unfinished sentence leaving them in no doubt as to what would have happened. 'We've got people searching the hospital and the grounds at this very moment,' he continued, 'but obviously it's going to be a forward-moving challenge.'

'Yes, well perhaps you could be getting on with overseeing this forward-moving challenge, while I have a word with Juliet Sanderson? Do I take it that she's come out of her coma now?'

'Yes, but I'm not sure we can allow you to interrogate her before Dr Breesh arrives,' Arthur Hawkins said. 'He's her consultant, and I've bleeped him. She may not be well enough for—'

'I think she'll be fine as long as you go gently with her,' another voice interrupted. 'I'm Andrew Neave, Dr Breesh's registrar. I'll need to accompany you, though.'

In the small quiet room, Marie Sanderson was sitting next to her daughter, who appeared to be sleeping. She looked up as Harry walked in, her face etched with anxiety.

'She's sleeping,' she whispered, watching as the registrar moved around to check her pulse with his fingers.

'Has she said much about what happened?' Harry asked.

She shook her head. 'She's saying she doesn't know who it was, but I don't think I believe her. I think she's terrified and doesn't *dare* say anything.'

'I need to question her,' Harry said. 'I promise I'll be gentle with her.'

'Juliet?' Marie turned back to her daughter and reached for her hand, squeezing it lightly. 'Darling, can you wake up? I know you're tired, but it's important.'

It felt as if they were all holding their breath as, for a moment, nothing happened.

Don't let her have slipped back into a coma. For a minute, Harry feared he'd said the words out loud, but then with a

354

small sigh, Juliet's eyes opened and turned to rest on her mother's face.

'Darling, this is Detective Inspector Briscombe. He's here to help you. Do you think you can answer a couple of questions for him?'

Juliet's eyes switched to Harry.

'Hello, Juliet,' he said quietly, moving forward. 'You've been through a rough time, and I want to help you put that behind you and arrest the people responsible. Can you help me with that, do you think?'

Tears filled her eyes and she shook her head.

'Do you know who it was that came into your room today?'

She shook her head again, her hand clutching her mother's tightly.

'I think maybe you do,' Harry said, 'but perhaps you're frightened because he's threatened you in some way? He's good at doing that, and you know there are several other people in your position, too scared to talk because of what they fear he might do. I want to put an end to all that – and stop him from doing it to the next person.' He hesitated. 'I think I might know who this person is, in which case all you have to do is nod your head. Once we've got him, everything will fall into place and he'll be put away for a very long time. I can promise you that.'

Her eyes had locked to his.

'I'm going to say two names now, and if one of them is your attacker, all you need to do is nod your head.'

⌒

He was in a state as he turned on the engine of his car and headed for home. He'd messed up, but it didn't necessarily mean curtains. She might not have realised that he'd

355

interfered with her drip – she'd been unconscious after all, and if that was the case he could still get away with it. There was no reason for anyone to check the contents of that drip. But he couldn't rely on that. She'd woken up screaming, which suggested that she knew something untoward was going on. So he had no choice now but to move to Plan B.

Inside the large house, he went straight up the stairs to his office, pulled out a couple of black bags from the stationery cupboard and tipped the contents of three drawers from his filing cabinet into them. Then he grabbed a box of matches and headed outside to the bonfire site. Tossing the contents of the black bin liner onto the previous charred remains, he set fire to them with a flourish and watched as the fire leapt greedily into life, eagerly lapping at the paper – the golden flames turning to a burnt orange as the sides of the papers curled inwards, and finally to a charred black, as the fire finished its job. Gone. There was no written proof now to link him to what had gone on, unless people talked. And they wouldn't do that. They had too much to lose.

He walked swiftly back into the house and was about to head up the stairs to pack his bag in case he needed to flee quickly, when the doorbell rang. He froze. He could see a man's head through the small pane of glass at the top of the door.

'Jonathan Anderson, this is the police. We know you're in there. Please open up. You're under arrest.'

Like hell he was going to open up. Spinning around, he headed quickly for the kitchen, grabbing a knife from the block as he went. Then he opened the back door and cautiously peered out.

'Grab him.'

'Mind the knife.'

356

'I've got him.'

It happened so quickly he barely had time to register the fact, as three burly men suddenly appeared from nowhere and overpowered him – swiftly relieving him of the knife and escorting him back into the house.

They opened the front door to let Harry in.

'Caught him just trying to escape out of the back door, boss,' Peterson said.

'Planning on going somewhere were you?' Harry said conversationally, and Anderson frowned at him. 'I was on my way back to the hospital as it happens. I'm late for my afternoon op list.'

Harry shook his head. 'Well, that's a real shame, because I don't think you're going to be doing any more surgery for a very long time … in fact I doubt you'll ever be operating again after we've finished with you.'

'What are you talking about? What's going on? You can't just storm in here like this.'

'Oh, but I can, Mr Anderson. I have a warrant here that says exactly that. Read him his rights and take him back to the station,' Harry said, nodding at one of the uniform officers. 'I'll question him there when I get back. Take his phone off him and make sure he talks to no one, other than his solicitor, until I'm through here. In fact, wait a minute…'

From his pocket, he pulled out his little notebook and flicked through the pages. Then pulling out his own phone, he tapped a number into it. A pause and then, clearly coming from up the stairs, came the ringtone of a mobile.

'Ah, The mysterious SIM-only number.' Harry said with a satisfied smile.

'I'll get it,' Beth said, taking the stairs two at a time.

Less than a minute later she was back down again and

holding it out towards Jonathan Anderson so that he could see Harry's number on the display. 'Yours, I believe?'

'I want a solicitor,' Jonathan Anderson said. 'And I won't say anything until he's present.

Harry saw them off, then walked back into the house where Beth was presiding over the forensic sweep. 'Found anything?'

'Give them a chance, boss.'

'Sir … there are recent signs of a bonfire out in the garden. Looks like he could have been burning evidence,' a young PC said, coming into the hall.

'Damn. Anything salvageable?'

'Doesn't look like it, but someone's sifting through it.'

'Okay, well, not much we can do here until everything's recorded and brought back to the station, so we might as well head back. Give us a shout if they find anything significant, and in particular, anything that might connect him to Joshua Jarvis's murder. Jarvis's phone or computer would be a great start. Someone better contact his wife as well – let her know that we're here, and why – and also the hospital to inform them that he won't be going in this afternoon.'

'How come you suspected him?' Beth asked as they walked out to the car. It was a question that had been bugging her ever since he'd said his name and Dr Janner's to Juliet.

'What you said this morning, about the Blakes being registered under Janner. Seemed one too many coincidences. I wondered if Blake's wife might also have been seeing Anderson for some reason, so I phoned the Oakfield and they confirmed it. What with that and his secretary turning up dead, suddenly, there was a huge red flag showing on him. He was telling the truth when he said he took over from another guy as Serenity's private obs & gynae consultant

358

over ten years ago. It was 2007 to be precise but, when I got Susie to dig into his finances over the last few years, it shows they're in a mess. We've still got info coming in on that but it seems he lost a small fortune in the 2008 market crash, which basically broke him; and as a result, his personal life is in tatters with him and his wife on the verge of divorce. That made me look at our notes on him more closely and, when I took another look at the pages from his message book, I noticed that the handwriting for Amelia Watkins' supposed message saying that Cara Swift had moved away, wasn't quite the same as in previous messages from her – and that message had been squeezed in at the bottom of a page. I'm sure any decent handwriting specialist would quickly be able to confirm that that message wasn't written by the same person.'

'So Cara Swift never rang to say she'd left Serenity?'

'No.'

'Not just a pretty face, are you?'

Harry smiled. 'That's the easy part. Getting it out of him is going to be the hard bit.'

As Harry and Beth walked into the reception area back at the station, Harry hesitated when he saw that the young couple from earlier were still there. The woman still looked very upset and the man jumped up as soon as they re-entered the building.

'We need to speak to you,' he said. 'And it can't wait, it's urgent.'

'What's it about? I'm sorry but this really isn't a good time. I'm in the middle of an ongoing investigation and I have some urgent interviews—'

'It's to do with the woman who was stabbed in the market and if you don't speak to us now, we'll walk out of here and not come back.'

Harry blinked. 'Okay,' he said. 'You'd better come with me.'

'Right,' Harry said, sitting back in his chair once the initial details were completed. 'So what is it that you need to talk to me about so urgently, Mr Dawson?'

The man hesitated, looking at his wife, whose swollen eyes and defeated demeanour spoke of a misery that pierced the very depths of her being.

'You'll have to bear with us,' the man said. 'It's taken us a long time to pluck up the courage to come and see you. If we tell you everything, can you give us some sort of immunity against any charges?'

'I can't guarantee that,' Harry said cautiously, 'but obviously if you help us in a significant way, that will count in your favour in any resulting prosecution.'

'We were desperate,' the woman broke in. 'Or we'd never have done it. I'd been trying to have a baby for six years before they told us it wasn't going to happen because of fertility issues on my side. We were heartbroken at the thought of never having our own family. We'd had several failed rounds of IVF, and were considering adoption, when our consultant, Mr Anderson, told us that he knew someone who was pregnant and desperate to find a loving home for her baby. We couldn't believe our luck.'

Her voice broke and her husband took over. 'He said he knew someone who could arrange it for us so that it wouldn't even involve adoption, which could take years and still not guarantee us getting the baby. It would cost us sixty thousand pounds, but the birth certificate would be registered in my name with the mother's and the baby would be handed over to us straight away on a type of surrogacy basis. He told us that he'd arranged several surrogacies like ours and it cut through all the red tape.'

Finally … the key to it all.

'When was this?' Harry's expression was intent.

There was a long pause. The woman was sobbing quietly and the man looked at her, before finally saying. 'We got him three weeks ago. And before you say anything, we know that our baby belongs to the woman who was stabbed in the market.'

'But how do they know it's Juliet's baby?' Beth asked as they made their way to the interview room half an hour later, where Dean was waiting for them.

'Because they met her. Anderson told them that Juliet wanted to see the people who were going to be raising her child and they subsequently met up with her, Joshua and another man, who sounds very much like Dean.'

'What's made them come forward?'

'They're scared and I think it's only now that they're realising the enormous implications of it all. The publicity surrounding Juliet has freaked them out.' He shook his head. 'I feel sorry for them. They're not crooks. They were just desperate to have their own child and they thought Juliet was happy for them to have her baby. They weren't to know she'd changed her mind. I've left them with Geoff, making a full statement.'

'Do you think they'd have become the next targets for Joshua to blackmail? Is that how it worked do you think?'

'More than likely. While I'm interviewing Dean, now that we know roughly what's gone on from Juliet, do you think you and Geoff can tackle the other members of cottage four and get as much information out of them as you can?'

'Sure. And I still need to speak to William Blake who's waiting in one of the interview rooms. Now we know that SIM number was Anderson's, I'd say it must definitely have been Blake who was complaining to him about being blackmailed.'

Harry's expression sobered. He was remembering the Blakes' little boy playing so happily in the garden. What a can of worms this was about to unleash. Did the same apply to the Jeffersons' child?

'Yes, we need to get the truth out of him – and the Jeffersons. Stress that we'll be taking DNA from them and their children. I know …' he said when he caught Beth's expression. 'But it's not for us to decide what happens about that. It has to be done. Meanwhile, I'll head on down and start with Dean Jarvis.'

CHAPTER FORTY-TWO

'Right ...' Harry said, sitting down and looking ready for business as he faced Dean Jarvis and his solicitor across the table. 'Why don't you just make it easy on everyone and tell us, from the beginning what's been going on, because we know most of it now and it's just the loose ends that need tidying up. We've arrested Jonathan Anderson and will be questioning him regarding your father's murder and that of Amelia Watkins. We also know for a fact that he stabbed Juliet Sanderson. You look shocked by that?'

'*I am*. Do you mean Jonathan Anderson, the gynaecologist?'

'Yes. You know him, of course?'

'Yes, but ... you're saying he stabbed Juliet?' His brow cleared. 'I thought, after what my father said that night, that it was *him* who'd done it. I'm glad it wasn't.'

'Fill us in, Dean, will you? Tell us what's gone on. It's all going to come out now so there's no point trying to hide anything. How about you start at the beginning when you met Juliet?'

Dean seemed to give his words some thought, then sighed.

'Okay. I've done a lot of thinking and I've made some mistakes. But none of it was deliberate. I met her at a meeting

363

we were holding in a local hall. She was looking lost and so unhappy that she caught my attention. We got talking and she confided some of what had gone on at home to me. I suggested she come to one of our meetings at Serenity. I told her I was a counsellor as well, and maybe I could help her.'

He shrugged. 'It grew from there. She's different to anyone I've ever known, and even though she's quite a bit younger than me, we just got on. She loved everything about Serenity at first. She came to stay in the main house and attended lots of meetings and classes, saying she really liked the idea of it all, the simplicity of our life. The way everyone supported each other. She'd been betrayed by her family. They'd lied to her about her birth and I understood how upset she was feeling.'

'A lot of people have stuff to deal with. It's usually better for them to face their problems and air them rather than run away from them. She was young and vulnerable and your organisation took advantage of that.'

'We're there to help people,' Dean said simply.

'And abuse them, it would seem.'

'No. I was furious with Joshua when I found out about that. I realised too late that he saw Juliet as a threat to my commitment to Serenity. I've done a lot of thinking this past couple of weeks. I'm not a stupid man, but I have been stupid over all this. Or maybe naive is a better word. People on the outside would never understand, but I've been raised not to question anything, to believe that Serenity … our community … is above all, the most important thing in my life. We Are One. That's our motto. To go against Joshua – the Elders – was unthinkable. If he told me to do something, I did it. I believed him when he said I was needed up in Newcastle and that he'd call me when Juliet went into labour.

364

I knew she was unhappy but I couldn't deal with it, because I couldn't change her mindset and I couldn't alter my own to accommodate hers; even though she made me question, for the first time, whether how we ran things was really for the best. The way she talked about her parents, the family life she'd had, made me realise what I'd missed out on. But to acknowledge that was huge. It was easier for me to take the coward's way out and remove myself from the scene.'

'I might as well tell you that a young couple have come forward admitting that they paid sixty thousand pounds to Jonathan Anderson for Juliet's child. How much do you know about all that?'

He shook his head. 'Very little as I already said. I knew Joshua organised for some of the Serenity babies to be adopted and that people usually made a donation to the commune by way of thanks, but I had no idea as much money as that was involved. Juliet was paid £3,000 to seal the contract—'

'Which then made it very difficult for her to change her mind? It's a lot of money to a girl of her age.'

'I guess.'

'And the rest we assume was split between Serenity and Anderson?'

'I don't know how it worked.'

'But you were quite prepared to hand your child over to complete strangers? Was that the first time you'd done that?'

'No. I've done it once before. I see it as a charitable deed. It makes me feel good to know I'm helping people out who couldn't otherwise have babies of their own.'

'Do you feel no emotional attachment for those children of yours that you've basically sold?'

He shrugged. 'I knew they were going to a good life,

to couples desperate for a child – I never thought beyond that.' He hesitated. 'I can guess what you're thinking – that it's not natural – and maybe you're right. I covered issues such as attachment disorders and the like when I was doing my degree, and to be honest, some of that stuff resonated with me. It's possible that the upbringing I had has made it difficult for me to … bond with people. That's why my relationship with Juliet felt special – I had genuine feelings for her that I'd never experienced before.'

'Yet realising that, you still weren't prepared to give her way of life a try?'

'It was too big a leap of faith – and I felt I could do more good changing things from within, if I could.'

'Okay, moving back to Juliet, tell me from the beginning what happened.'

For a moment, Dean buried his head in his hands; then he raised it again and looked directly at Harry. 'Juliet was devastated when she found out she was pregnant. She was adamant she didn't want it. She was talking about having an abortion and I couldn't let that happen, it goes against everything we stand for. But she said if she had it, she couldn't do what we do and watch it being brought up in a nursery by someone else. So I spoke to Joshua about having it adopted and he said it would be easy to arrange. It seemed the perfect solution. I put the idea to Juliet and she seemed quite taken with it initially. She wanted to meet the couple – which we did – and she was really happy to be doing something selfless to help people who were clearly having such a difficult time. But then she changed her mind. The nearer she got to giving birth, the more she was talking about wanting to keep the baby. Joshua said it was quite normal for women in the last stages of pregnancy to have wobbles – that it was part of the hormonal changes going on in their bodies, and that I shouldn't worry about it. He said he'd handle it if things got really difficult – but the bottom line was that she couldn't change her mind because we'd received a very generous donation and had signed a contract. Not to mention the fact that it would break the prospective parents' hearts. He also said …' He took a breath. 'That it would be awkward for Serenity if news leaked out, because when we did these deals we sometimes cut a few corners.'

'What did he mean by that?'

'I don't know. It worried me – it's why I didn't tell you about it in case it reflected badly on Serenity. I buried my head in the sand, I suppose, and just kept reminding Juliet how desperate that couple had been for a baby, and how she was doing a really kind thing helping them out. But it wasn't enough for her, and she kept on saying how we could both leave Serenity and start a new life outside it. She didn't get that that would be stripping me of the only life I'd known – one that was so different to the one she'd led. She said it would do me good to step out of my comfort zone – and maybe she's right – but I just couldn't do it.'

'So you took yourself off to Northumberland when she was at her most vulnerable?'

'I'm not proud of myself, and I had no idea they were subjecting her to violence to bend her to their will.'

'And yet you say that punishment is accepted within the community. Maybe you just turned a blind eye to what was going on in the hope that it might work?'

'I was weak, I admit it. I've been trying to atone for my sins ever since.'

Harry suppressed a snort and turned back to his notes. 'What happened with Cara?'

367

'I can't add anything to what I've already said. Juliet was upset when she heard her crying out, and I stayed with her to comfort her. After a while it all went quiet and we assumed Cara had either had the baby or been taken off to the hospital. It was only the next day that Terence told me she'd died of complications to do with high blood pressure. I couldn't tell Juliet that, because her baby was due a few weeks later and it would have terrified her. As I said, Joshua was worried the authorities might stop us from doing our own home births if the truth came out. So the story was put around that Cara had chosen to leave Serenity when she was at the hospital.'

He paused, then said, 'I can see it's hard for you to understand my role in all this, but the only life I've led to any significant degree outside Serenity, was when I was at university. And even then I was still living at the commune. I was like a square peg in a round hole, it all felt so wrong – the drinking and drugs, the lack of discipline and courtesy. I did my degree and couldn't get back to my old life quickly enough. That's how I knew I could never live happily in Juliet's world…'

⤶

'Do you think he's telling the truth?' Beth asked, a while later, greeting Harry as he emerged from the interview room. 'I've been listening in the viewing room.'

'Who knows? We're taking a break while I see what else unfolds. What do you think?'

She shrugged. 'You can't believe people can be so naïve, can you? And yet, I can see how, if you're brought up in that sort of environment, it might become automatic to take the easy way out and just do as you're told. People will put up with the most terrible abuse because they've been programmed into thinking they're not deserving of any better – it takes a eureka moment to break a pattern like that. And I know that's one of your words … but it fits the bill.'

She didn't add that she'd had her own eureka moment, after she'd met Andy.

'You could be right. How have you got on?'

'I questioned Paula, Sheila and Victoria – and Geoff's doing Terence. He was going to tackle him about his head wound, which he said he got falling down the stairs, whereas we now know, from what Juliet told you, that she hit him with her bedside lamp. And he was also going to confront him with the fact that the jacket he was wearing when he came in yesterday, matches the jacket worn by the man seen on CCTV taking money out of Juliet's bank account. I didn't learn anything groundbreaking from the women but at least they're talking now, and they confirmed what Juliet said about the baby being taken away from her to be adopted. Paula's opened up the most. She said Juliet had been desperate to escape because she believed Joshua and Terence were going to kill her. I think she and Juliet were close. She said she was the one who told Juliet that the house was going to be empty on Saturday morning; that it would be a good time to escape if that was what she wanted to do. But she was adamant she wouldn't speak out against Serenity in court. Said that while it wasn't a perfect life, she felt safe there. Can you believe that?'

'Right now I'd believe anything,' Harry said. 'It *all* beggars belief.'

'Yeah, well, she was quite agitated by the end of the interview – after I told her some of what we suspect Joshua's been up to. I'm not sure she feels quite so safe there now and perhaps it'll give her something to think about.'

'What about the other girl, Victoria?'

Beth rolled her eyes. 'She's a *true-blood* and doesn't seem capable of having an original thought in her head. She's an ideal candidate for deprogramming if ever I saw one. It's tragic. She's pregnant too, and when I asked her if they'd ever talked to her about having her baby adopted, she said no, but if they did she'd be happy to help someone less fortunate than herself. I guess it is quite a selfless thing to do, isn't it?'

'Except that people like her are being manipulated and taken advantage of – and it's not quite as altruistic as they'd have us believe, if they're charging sixty grand a pop for it. Right … I want to hear for myself what Brother Fabian's got to say on the back of all this new information.'

~

When they brought Fabian into the interview room, he looked agitated. 'How long can you keep me here?' he demanded. 'Surely by now you need to be charging me or letting me go?'

Harry eyed him for a long moment over the table, before saying. 'You need to know that Juliet Sanderson has come round from her coma and we've arrested Jonathan Anderson in connection with the murders of Joshua Jarvis, Amelia Watkins, and the attempted murder of Juliet Sanderson. The field is still wide open, however, with you as one of the front-runners as far as other accomplices go so you might want to think about that. We know that you were Joshua's right-hand man, and my instincts tell me that you're involved in this up to your ears – interestingly backed up by this message that you left on Jonathan Anderson's SIM-only mobile the day we arrested you. The one you claimed to know nothing about.'

He hit play and waited. 'It's Fabian,' a voice said. 'Call me back. The police are on to us and I don't know what to say. I need to know how to handle this.'

Harry watched as Fabian's face visibly paled.

'You also didn't get to hear his reply, as we took your phone off you shortly after that. Do you want to hear it?'

Fabian shook his head, but Harry played the message anyway.

'Just remember that you're involved in this up to your neck too, because of the adoptions. Keep your nerve and make sure Dean doesn't say anything that might drop us in it. We need to let things cool down for a while, and it'll be fine. Call me.'

'So …' Harry said, putting the phone back down on the desk and looking directly at Fabian. 'From that message it's clear that you knew about the adoptions.'

He looked at his solicitor, who nodded.

'Yes, but I didn't know anything about Joshua blackmailing people. As far as I knew, we provided the occasional baby and got a very generous donation. Usually around ten thousand pounds, three thousand of which we would pay to the surrogate – who would normally then choose to donate it back to Serenity. But Anderson subsequently told me it was sixty that was paid … split two ways between him and Joshua. So Joshua was obviously keeping most of it for himself, as well as blackmailing people.'

'So how come you phoned William Blake and Daniel Jefferson after Joshua's murder if you didn't know about the blackmailing? Where did you get their numbers?'

'Anderson gave them to me. He had Joshua's diary with their details in. No names, he said … just initials. I called them and told them that if they kept quiet about everything there would be no more blackmailing and they could live their lives in peace.'

'I'm tempted to believe you, because we've checked your personal financial records and you don't seem to have benefitted personally from any of this. But I think the time's come for you to consider your own position. You can make things better or worse for yourself, the choice is yours.'

He sat back and watched as Fabian cast an anxious look at his solicitor, who leant forward and whispered something to him, before turning to look at Harry.

'If my client cooperates, can we do some sort of a deal here?'

'You know how it works,' Harry said. 'It depends on what he gives us and how implicated he is. But whatever happens, it will look better for him if he tells us everything he knows.'

He switched his gaze back to Fabian, who met that look for a considerable time before finally relenting.

'Alright … I'll tell you what I know.'

CHAPTER FORTY-THREE

When Harry finally faced Jonathan Anderson and his solicitor across the same table that Dean had sat at earlier, it was seven o'clock in the evening and, with the information that now seemed to be pouring in, he knew he already had enough to charge the man. But he still needed to persuade Anderson to fill in some of the gaps.

'First off,' he said, 'I might as well save us both a lot of time and trouble by letting you know that I believe we've more or less got the whole story,'

'Oh?' The other man leant indolently back in his chair and crossed his legs.

'Yes. Your associates have been pretty frank with us, and putting all the facts together, it would seem that you matched parents desperate for a child, with donors from Serenity willing to give up their babies – making yourself a tidy little sum into the bargain. A pretty good scam one way and another.'

'I wouldn't call it that.'

'Wouldn't you? What would *you* call selling people's babies for a shedload of money, then?'

Jonathan Anderson's mouth tightened, and for a moment Harry could almost see the cogs going round in the man's head, trying to work out how much they knew and what he could get away with.

'I'll tell you what,' Harry said, trying to head off a protracted interview, 'why don't I tell you some of what we already know, so that you hopefully realise there's nothing to be gained from prevaricating further? It's over. My team and I have spent the last few hours sifting through the evidence, and we already have enough to put you away for a very long time. We intend charging you this evening with the murder of Joshua Jarvis and the attempted murder on two occasions, of Juliet Sanderson. I expect that very shortly, we will also be charging you with the murder of your secretary, Amelia Watkins.'

'And what evidence do you have to support these charges?' the solicitor at Anderson's side, enquired.

Harry looked briefly at the other man. 'As your client is aware, Juliet Sanderson's come round from her coma. She's confirmed that he told her he'd murdered Joshua and that he threatened to do the same to her child if she said anything to the police about what's gone on. She also confirmed that it was him who stabbed her in the marketplace after she'd escaped from Serenity Hall, where they'd been holding her prisoner – and him who entered her room this morning and tampered with her drip, which on later examination was found to contain insulin. The policeman on duty also identified him from a selection of doctors on one of the hospital's information boards.'

He switched his gaze back to Anderson. 'You must have been pretty desperate to risk that. I'm assuming you must have heard the bulletin on the news this morning, saying they were hopeful she'd come round soon?'

No response, so Harry continued.

'With regard to your secretary, Amelia Watkins, it's obvious now that the message you showed me in the message book was in someone else's handwriting, and I'm quite sure that any handwriting expert worth his salt will be able to match it to yours. CCTV of the street she lived in has a very clear image of you returning her car to her drive the night before she was due to go away on holiday, and then getting into Joshua Jarvis's car and being driven away. Her car has been picked up and is undergoing forensic testing as we speak, and I'm pretty confident we'll be able to match clothes fibres or DNA to strengthen our case that you were in that car. We'll also be conducting tests on DNA samples taken from you today, which I'm confident will match hair particles found clutched in Amelia Watkins' hand, from where she presumably grabbed at your head trying to fight you off. Add to that the fact that her phone was found in your house, and there's some pretty comprehensive evidence there that would take some explaining away. And that's just for starters. We also have witnesses who overheard you arguing with Joshua seconds before he was murdered and a knife seized from your possession earlier today matches the type of knife that was used to stab both Juliet Sanderson and Joshua Jarvis. We're running forensic tests on it, and the logo on the handle matches that shown on CCTV footage of Juliet's attacker as he slips the knife under his jacket. Put all that together with the discovery of Joshua's phone and diary in your safe at home, and I think you'll agree – you've got a lot to answer for.'

Harry gave a brief pause for breath, then picked up the notes from their interview with Fabian. 'On further questioning, Brother Fabian has admitted that he knew about the adoption operation you and Joshua ran, and he's confirmed that it was you he overheard arguing with Joshua the night he was killed, because you'd found out that Joshua was blackmailing some of the adoptive parents.'

He put the sheet of paper down on the table and looked at Anderson. 'I could go on … mention the couple who have come forward admitting that Juliet is the biological mother of their baby, or another witness, William Blake, who's admitted that Joshua was blackmailing him over that very same issue, but all that will come out in the brief we put together. For now, it's been a long day for all of us, and I hope you can see that trying to make things more difficult for everyone, isn't going to go down well in court. So why don't you just fill me in on the details? I must admit, it seems to be an impressive piece of organisation you've had going on.'

He chose his words deliberately, knowing that for some criminals that was what they got off on … the fact they could outsmart the system … and by the self-satisfied glint in Jonathan Anderson's eyes, he suspected he could be one of them.

The man sat for a long moment, rubbing his chin pensively with his fingers, before finally shrugging and saying. 'To be honest it's a relief to get it out in the open.' He sighed. 'Things just snowballed and got out of control somehow. I never for one minute envisaged people dying as a result of what we were doing.'

'And what were you doing exactly?'

'Helping people who were unable to have children of their own,' Anderson said simply. 'Women from inside Serenity saw it as an act of charity and were happy to help those poor parents out. The two dovetailed perfectly – until Joshua got greedy and broke the tried and trusted mould we'd established.'

'How long's it been going on? '

The other man hesitated, flicked a quick glance at his solicitor, and said. 'More or less since I took over from my predecessor. Joshua and I go back years. We grew up together … Children of Serenity.' This last was said with a sardonic lift to the lips. 'Unless you've gone through something like that, you can never understand how that sort of life affects you. So restrictive in many ways, but that very restrictiveness creates a bond that's virtually unbreakable. As young children, we were inseparable, like brothers, but as we grew older, rivalry kicked in. Joshua was ambitious. He always intended taking over as Lead Brother and he had that extra something that made you know he would.'

He shrugged. 'I found that hard to swallow … that he was destined for better things than me. So when I was eighteen, I did the unthinkable in those days. I left. Serenity agreed to fund me through university studying medicine, as long as I agreed to stay involved and make regular donations to the commune once I qualified. On the face of it I was doing well – wife, house, children – but I found it hard adapting to the outside world. Then, in 2008, the crash happened, and I'd invested heavily in a new property development that went bankrupt. He shook his head. 'That was a bad time, and I found myself going back to my roots … to Serenity, to explain why I couldn't keep up with my contributions to them. I was an obs & gynae consultant by then, and Joshua had realised his dream of becoming Lead Brother. I told him about my financial problems and he told me about his. How they'd made a massive investment in the new nursery facilities they were extending, and with the economic downturn, how it was proving a burden servicing that.'

He paused, as if remembering, then said, 'I don't

377

remember exactly when we came up with the idea – or even how – all I remember is thinking, *yes, this could work.* I was a consultant specialising in fertility problems, with a constant stream of women desperate for a baby in a world that makes it so hard for them to adopt. And he had women who would thrive on the idea they were doing a charitable deed by either handing over their babies for adoption or acting as surrogates. It was the perfect match.'

He shrugged. 'That's how it started and it was so easy – especially back in those early days when the laws surrounding surrogacy weren't properly formulated or policed. I'd treat the Serenity surrogate with IVF using the sperm of the prospective father, Joshua and I split the fee, and everyone was happy. Do you know how heartbreaking it is for parents when they can't conceive? We were glad to be helping them, and what we were doing wasn't exactly illegal – we just cut a few corners, enabling people who were prepared to pay, to jump the queue.'

'It was totally illegal what you were doing.'

Anderson's eyes narrowed. 'I'm not sure what you mean.'

'I think you do. Apart from the fact that it's illegal to pay more than reasonable expenses to a surrogate and you were charging sixty thousand pounds – I'm referring to people like the young couple who received Juliet's baby.'

Harry's words hung in the air between them and he could see the solicitor was intrigued as well as perplexed. 'You don't have to respond to that,' he said to Anderson.

Harry almost groaned his frustration as the man hesitated. But then he gave a dismissive shrug. 'You've obviously done your homework,' he said. 'I know I'm going down for a long time. You might as well have the full story. You're right, we did step over the line, which of course is why Joshua was able to make even more money out of it by blackmailing people.'

'In what way?'

'In some cases, like the couple you mention who had Juliet's baby, both parents are infertile, and in those instances we tweak things a bit, using a birth mother and father from Serenity, who hand over the baby when it's born. I preside over the birth...' he hesitated for a moment but then gave another shrug. '... so that I can issue the Certificate of Live Birth in the name of the "adoptive" father, rather than the Serenity one – as if it was a Surrogacy arrangement. We also help prevent any potential issues by registering the adoptive fathers with Serenity's GP. That way I have complete control over what goes into their medical notes and can cite them as the donors.'

'So, just to make sure I've got this right – in those cases, you document the adopting father as being the biological father, when he isn't?'

'Correct.'

"Has no one ever questioned any of it?'

'Why would they? We usually only do a couple a year like that and as far as the system is aware, the adoptive father is the biological father because that's how I've signed off the certificate of live birth. As long as his medical notes reflect that, it's a fairly simple procedure signing it off with the authorities and the new parents can then register the birth in the normal way. You see, it's when neither parent is the genetic parent that the system becomes more protracted and complicated – with no guarantees at the end of it that they'd be allowed to keep the baby, so it was simpler for everyone the way we do it. It worked perfectly, until Joshua ruined it all by using newcomers to the commune who weren't so committed to our ways.'

'So, in effect, you forged the certificate of live birth?'

'Yes.'

'You must have known you'd get caught out one day?'

'At first I expected that knock on the door all the time, but when it didn't come, I realised that it's actually quite easy to trick the system if you know what you're doing. Of course the risk was always there that some child would need medical treatment for example, and they'd find out the father wasn't their real father, but we've never had a problem so far.'

'Was it Dr Janner, the GP you used?'

'Yes, he was a friend of Joshua's from way back. Obviously, he already treats the Serenity patients.'

'So, just for the record, you're confirming that he was involved in all this?'

Anderson nodded. 'On a more minor scale. We paid him two and a half grand for every patient he agreed to take onto his list.'

'When did you find out that Joshua was blackmailing patients?'

'The day he died. I had a phone call from one of the adoptive parents, saying he was at his wits end because Joshua was extorting money from him and he couldn't afford to keep paying. I was livid that Joshua could jeopardise the whole operation like that, especially after the risk he'd taken using Cara and Juliet. If he'd stuck to using established Serenity women, who are so institutionalised they wouldn't think of disobeying his orders, none of this would have happened.'

'So, what exactly did happen with Cara and Juliet?'

'They both changed their minds about giving their babies up for adoption. Of course that would have made things very difficult for us, as we'd already received a substantial amount

380

of money up front and signed a contract – as had they.'

'Did they talk to you about it?'

'No. They didn't know I was involved. But I noticed a change in both of them in the latter trimester and queried it with Joshua. He said they were fine and it wouldn't be a problem, but with Cara it was more complicated because of her potential pre-eclampsia issues. They called me when she went into labour and I told him she needed to be in hospital. He said they couldn't take her there because she was hysterical – saying that when she went into hospital she'd tell them she'd been held against her will and was being forced to hand her baby over for adoption. I rushed over but by the time I got there, it was too late. She was dead. There was nothing I could have done to save her.'

'Except call the ambulance yourself when you first got that call?'

'Yes. I could have done that.'

'Were you involved in her burial?'

'Good Lord no. I helped them carry the stretcher downstairs so they could bury her and then I went home. There was nothing more I could do.'

So, the fourth man Emanuel had seen, Harry thought.

'And Juliet?'

He shrugged. 'She changed her mind too and was being difficult after they'd taken her baby away. I'd attended the funeral of one of the Elders of Serenity – someone I'd known since childhood. When Joshua and I got back to Serenity Hall, Juliet had attacked Terence and escaped.'

'Juliet's confirmed that it was you who stabbed her.'

She was a threat to everything,' he said simply.

'And had to be disposed of?'

No response.

381

'So when you'd done it once with Amelia, was it easier the second time – the attempted murder of Juliet? And the third time with Joshua?'

'Look, I'm a doctor. My job's to save people, not kill them. But I had no choice. Everything just spiralled out of control. I really regretted having to kill Amelia, but she witnessed Juliet's first attempt to escape when she was still pregnant, when Joshua and I were struggling to get her into the car. I admit, I panicked.'

He dropped his head into his hands and for the first time, Harry detected a hint of remorse. He looked up again. 'I didn't enjoy doing it – I'd known her a long time.'

Harry let the man digest his own words before changing tack.

'Fill me in on what happened with Joshua.'

'I was so angry when I went to see him. I told him he was in danger of exposing the whole setup and how dare he go behind my back, blackmailing people like that.'

Remembered anger flared in his eyes. 'He had the gall to threaten me – said there was nothing I could do about it because if I exposed him, then we'd both go down. When he refused to see sense –'

'He too had to be dealt with?'

'It took me a long time to claw back all the money I lost and it was me who was taking most of the risk. I gave him his chance.'

'What did you do with his laptop?'

'I dumped it somewhere you'll never find it. I daresay he had details of all the people he was blackmailing on there so that's good news for them, isn't it? We can't have all those poor parents worrying that their children are going to be taken away from them. Think of the unhappiness it

382

would cause.'

Harry sighed, thinking again of the Blakes and their little boy – knowing that that side of things was going to be hideous to unravel. There was a part of him that couldn't disagree with the man but it wasn't something that could be glossed over. Someone was going to have to dig deep and hard to find out what had gone on over the last ten years – he was just glad it wouldn't be him.

'Maybe you should have thought about that before you started playing God with people's lives,' he said.

CHAPTER FORTY-FOUR

It was gone nine o'clock before Harry finally closed off the interview with Jonathan Anderson. And of course it had been the most enlightening interview of all.

Up in the large office, he was surprised to see not only several members of the team still hard at it, but also DCI Murray. He suppressed a sigh, realising he'd have to go in and report back to his boss now, rather than nip off to see Claire, which he'd been hoping to do.

'I think you all ought to head off home soon,' he said to the room as he made his way towards Murray's office. 'Everyone's done really well today, but there's plenty more still to do and we need to keep fresh eyes and alert minds about us.'

Murray looked up as the younger man walked into his office and smiled broadly. 'Well done, Harry.'

'Thanks, Sir. Team effort, as you know – and we've been taught by the best.'

'Well, I wasn't much help to you this time around, with this bloody thing holding me back.' He waved his foot in the air, before returning his gaze to Harry's face. 'I listened to some of it in the viewing room. He's a hard case, that Jonathan Anderson but at least he's playing ball.'

'You're telling me – for a doctor, the empathy gene is sadly lacking. How much did you hear?'

'Enough to realise he was confessing.'

'I think he realised we'd got most of the story before we even questioned him. I also think he's the sort to enjoy the fact that he beat the system for as long as he did, and couldn't resist sharing that with us.' Harry shook his head. 'It's hard to believe that communities like Serenity still exist on our doorstep, living in a world that's totally divorced from reality.'

'That's the appeal, is my guess.'

'Certainly for Juliet – for a while – but then her common sense kicked in and she saw it for what it was.'

'So how was he working it, exactly?'

'On a wing and a prayer, by the sound of it. It's all here in his statement if you want a read. Beth's added a note to the file saying she's found an off-shore bank account for Joshua and suspects that he was blackmailing others over all sorts of sensitive information they revealed during their counselling sessions. She thinks that must be the case with the Jeffersons as the little girl is definitely theirs, but they're still refusing to say what hold Joshua had over him, and it may be that we never find out the truth on that one.'

'It's a huge abuse of power by Joshua,' Murray said, taking the folder from him. 'I wonder what scam I could pull out of the hat to line the pension fund with?'

'You'll have to think of something quickly if you're still thinking of taking the early retirement option. Not that much longer to go, is there?'

'No.' Murray's face became thoughtful. 'Six months if I do it.'

'Well, for the record, none of us want you to go, sir. Can't imagine this place without you.'

'The job changes as you go up the ladder, Harry. It's not what it was.'

'I get that but you still have a lot to contribute. And if you go, God knows who they'll fill the void with.'

'Is there a compliment in there somewhere?'

Harry laughed. 'Don't want to embarrass you, guv.'

'Well, practice what you preach and get off home now. Sounds like all this is the tip of the iceberg and as you said out there, you're going to need your wits about you sifting through it all. We need to make sure we present an airtight case to the CPS.'

⌐

As Harry pulled up outside Claire's house forty minutes later, he switched off the engine and leaned his head back against the headrest with a sigh. He felt a mixture of exhaustion and pure exhilaration as he always did at the end of a case, and the buzz in his blood was still high. Normally when a case was solved, there was a celebratory gathering in the pub, where congratulations were passed on, outstanding issues debated and more than a fair share of alcohol consumed by some. That hadn't happened tonight, partly because there were still a lot of loose threads to tie up and partly because it had been such a long day that everyone had agreed they just wanted to get home.

Now, as he looked at the porch light twinkling outside Claire's front door, he felt a renewed surge of energy, glad to be heading back to a warm welcome and good company rather than the solitary silence of his house. The realisation caught him by surprise. Having been an only child brought up mainly by his grandparents, he was used to and liked his own company and had often found the expectations put on him by others a challenge. But not so with Claire, somehow.

When she opened the door, he swung her energetically into his arms and kissed her soundly, laughing at her protestations. It was only as he put her down and stared over her shoulder, that he caught her mother staring at him from the kitchen doorway.

'Uh, Mum was passing and dropped by,' Claire said, a mischievous glint in her eye.

'But I'm off now,' her mother said quickly. 'Leave you two love birds to it.'

'Mum!'

'Sorry. Good to see you, Harry,' she said as she sidled past him into the front garden.

'You too,' he said feebly.

When she'd shut the door, their eyes met and they both burst out laughing. 'Well, that was embarrassing,' Harry said.

'Nah, don't worry about it. She's seen me with enough boyfriends over the years. No need to worry that she'll be demanding you make an honest woman of me. Not yet anyway!'

'How about I make a dishonest one out of you first, then? Like right now?'

She entwined her arms around his neck and kissed him soundly.

'That,' she murmured softly, 'sounds like a perfect idea to me. Good thing it's only chicken salad and a baked potato for supper.'

CHAPTER FORTY-FIVE

Beth finished tidying her desk and looked around the deserted office. It was nine twenty and she was the last one to leave. Harry, she knew, had gone off to see Claire, Geoff had said he was going round to his sister's, and what did she have to rush home to?

A big fat nothing.

Her mobile rang and she looked at the display, not recognising the number but guessing who it was, as she answered it.

'It's Paula,' the girl said on the other end.

'Hey, Paula.' Beth's voice was soft as she spoke. 'Thanks for calling back. We need for you to come in again tomorrow, I'm afraid … we've had some new information come to light today, that I need to talk to you about.'

'What is it?' The girl's voice was anxious.

'I think maybe you know, pet.'

There was a long silence. And then … 'Is it about my baby?'

'Yes. We brought a man in for questioning today, a Mr & Mrs Blake, who told us that you were the biological mother of their little boy. Is that true?'

Another long silence.

'Yes, it is.'

'Do you want to tell me about it?'

She heard a gentle sigh down the line. 'What do you want to know? They were a lovely couple, and she was so sad not to be able to have a baby of her own. It was heartbreaking and I was happy to do it for her – really happy. I felt like that for once I was doing something worthwhile, you know? I couldn't imagine what it must be like not being able to have children – I fell so easily with my two – and though it was hard handing my baby over, when I saw the happiness in their eyes, I was proud of myself, knowing I was doing something really good. There was nothing wrong in it.'

'I'm afraid there was. The way they did it was illegal, though I'm sure you knew nothing about that. It needs to be sorted. Can you come down in the morning to give us a statement?'

'I suppose, but … what will happen to my little boy? He won't be taken away from them?'

'I hope not, but that'll be for the courts and social services to decide. Can you get here tomorrow around ten o'clock? That way I'll be able to speak to you myself.'

As she ended the call, she let out a sigh. She loved her job, she never questioned that, but she did regret the knock-on effect their investigations sometimes had on people who didn't really deserve to have their lives turned upside down and laid so bare.

Getting up from her desk, she moved over to where her jacket was hanging on the wall and slung it over her arm as she headed for the door. The cool day had eased into a crisp autumnal evening and she was ready now to head home, grab a shower and slump in front of the TV with a nice glass of wine. She didn't regret moving South, but sometimes she missed having friends to call on. Especially at times like

389

this, when she felt elated and deflated at the same time, and would have liked having someone to share that with.

The drive home to Enfield was quicker now the clog of rush hour commuters had passed. As she parked her car and crossed the road to her flat she relished the little uplift of spirit that she still felt every night when she headed home … so grateful to Harry that she was no longer sharing with a random bunch of girls she had nothing in common with.

She came to an abrupt halt at her gate, staring up the path in dismay. Some down-and-out was slumped in a tight ball on her doorstep, head bowed as if they were out for the count. That was all she needed.

She approached the front door, slipping into police officer mode like a second skin.

'Alright, mate … you need to move on I'm afraid. You're trespassing here—'

She broke off as the figure raised its head and clear green eyes, just like her own, looked up at her.

'Isi!' she exclaimed.

Isi jumped up from where she'd been dozing on the doorstep, those eyes cool now as they surveyed her sister. 'Hey, Beth.'

'Oh, my God … this is great. What are you doing here? How long have you been sitting there?'

'About an hour. I was beginning to think you weren't coming back.'

'Long day,' Beth said, slipping the key in the front door and opening it. 'Come on in. I'll get the kettle on.'

She led the way into the open-plan kitchen, her mind teeming. Why was Isi here? It was so out of character. Was something wrong? But the fact of the matter was, she didn't care. She was just so happy to see her. To know that she was

390

okay and finally, for whatever reason, she was reaching out and breaching the estrangement between them.

'Nice place,' her sister commented, dumping her rucksack on the floor and looking around.

'Thanks. Are you hungry? Do you want something to eat?'

'I wouldn't mind. I've not eaten since lunch.'

'I haven't got a lot in the fridge but we can go out. Get a nice meal.'

'No.' Her sister's voice was firm. 'I need to talk to you and it's best done in private. Can I use your bathroom?'

'Sure, it's just through there.'

By the time Isi had returned, Beth had made the tea and put some biscuits out.

'Thanks,' she said, sitting down on the settee.

Beth put her own cup down and sat opposite her. 'Is everything alright?'

Her sister nodded. 'Right enough, but I want you to know, I wouldn't have come off my own bat. Ryan asked me to see you because he's too scared of Mitch to do it himself. Says he's been doing a lot of thinking since he spoke to you – a lot of worrying by the sound of it, about what might come out in this investigation of yours into those young women at the commune.'

Beth found herself filling with a sense of dread. 'He's not involved in that? Please don't be saying that.'

'No. But there was stuff went on, over that time Bryony died, that he thinks you should know about.'

Beth stared at her in disbelief. '*Bryony*? What's she got to do with any of this?'

'Nothing, according to Ryan. But he reckons you need to know the full truth of what went on.'

'I thought I did know the truth and I'm not liking the

sound of this. I'd better warn you that if anything you say incriminates him, I'd have to pass that on.'

'He says it won't, so I hope he's right. He just wants you to know the facts so that if anyone gets a nose about it you can shut it down before it causes any trouble. Anyway, he decided it's best you know the truth, because he knows how much Bryony's death ate away at you.'

For a moment Beth didn't answer, images of her friend and Andy suddenly swimming in front of her. She'd shut the memories down so completely and for so long, that she was dismayed to find it took a while to picture them both clearly, and that pierced her heart. But what could they possibly have to do with the Juliet Sanderson case?

'Go on then. You're right, it did get to me … nearly broke me. But what are you trying to tell me, and how come you know about it all when I don't?'

'Because Ryan told me.' Her sister hesitated. 'Bryony and Mitch were an item … you didn't know that, did you? Because she knew you'd disapprove, Ryan says, so she didn't tell you. But not only that, she was pregnant by him, and Mitch had talked her into giving the baby up for adoption – he got paid a tidy sum for that.'

Oh no. Beth's heart plummeted, because now she knew exactly what was coming. 'Go on,' she said grimly.

'That day Bryony and Andy died; Mitch and Ryan were there too. Up on the cliff path.'

'*What?* They never said.'

'Of course they didn't. They weren't gonna broadcast the fact. But they were there. And so, apparently, was that Serenity weirdo, the one that was murdered recently. Mitch was quite involved with them at that time.'

'Joshua Jarvis?' Beth's stomach flipped sickeningly.

'What do you mean? What did he have to do with any of it?'

'I only know what Ryan told me. He said that when Bryony first found out she was having a baby, she was so scared of how her dad would react, that she was only too quick to be talked into giving it up and earning a bit of money out of it, but as time went on, she and Mitch argued more and more because she wanted them to be a family … keep the baby, like. But there was no way he was wanting that. He wanted her to move down this way to the Serenity HQ so they could look after her properly and he could get her off his case. That day she called you from the cliff, she called Mitch too, told him she was going to jump. That Joshua bloke had come up to collect her. He said to Mitch he'd go with him and Ryan. When they got there, Andy was already there, talking to her on Cliff Leap.'

Beth knew it well – a locally nicknamed, narrow path that ran along the side of the cliff.

'Ryan said there was a confrontation, and it seemed to him like there was only ever going to be one ending as far as that Joshua was concerned. He told her she couldn't back out, money had been paid, people were waiting on her baby and if she let them down they'd sue her for thousands of pounds. Mitch was trying to talk her round – saying they could have another baby – one they could keep, but she called him a worthless piece of shit and said she wanted nothing more to do with any of them. That she'd go to the papers with her story about them. After that Ryan said, that Joshua changed tack … pushed her into jumping, Ryan reckoned. Not literally, but verbally … told her she was just bluffing to get attention – and that pathetic women like her never had the balls to actually do it.'

Her sister paused and Beth waited…….

'Your Andy was apparently doing good, telling her that there was no way they could sue her; that it was her baby and if she wanted to keep it she could … that you and he would help her. But she was getting more and more hysterical. And Ryan said that bastard kept on shouting at her that she didn't have the guts to do it. *Go on then, jump…* he kept saying. *Show us you mean it.* And then suddenly – she just let herself tip over, backwards.'

Beth's hand flew to her mouth in horror. 'And Andy?'

She hardly dared ask the question. She could picture them both so clearly now, up on that cliff-top path that she'd walked so many times. And it had always struck her that in a country that had gone red-tape mad over so many issues, there were no safety barriers there to prevent people from falling or taking that one step to jump.

'Ryan said that he remembered thinking there was no way Andy was going to be allowed to walk away from that lot alive. He'd heard too much for sure. That Joshua was evil, he said. He turned on Andy, and Ryan thought he was going to push him, but at the same time as he did that Andy apparently grabbed at Bryony, trying to save her. Ryan said she grabbed his arm with both hands, as if she'd suddenly realised what she was doing and changed her mind. But it was too late, and she pulled him over with her.'

Beth was trembling so much she felt sick. It had been bad enough believing the path had given way and crumbled … but for Andy to be dragged over like that …

'You okay?' Her sister's voice was gruff as she asked the question.

Beth shook her head. 'I thought it was just a terrible accident, but now you're saying it was more than that.'

'No, I'm not, not really – it *was* an accident. He egged

her on, but it were her that jumped. And her that took Andy with her.'

'What were Mitch and Ryan doing all this time?'

'Freaking out by the sound of it. Mitch is a thug but it shook him up. He cut his ties with the commune after that and made Ryan swear he wouldn't tell anyone what happened that day, or that they'd even been there. It was Ryan that was the anonymous caller though, telling the coastguard he'd seen someone going over the cliff. He said he couldn't have them just disappearing off the face of the earth like that, with no one the wiser.'

'He should have told me the truth.'

'Oh, yeah ... you a policewoman and all. Mitch would have had his guts for garters. And you hated them both, anyway.'

'Not always, I didn't. And not Ryan. We used to get on alright before he joined Mitch's gang. When did he tell you all this?'

'When I first left home and moved in with Mitch. Him and Mitch fell out after the Bryony business and he said he didn't want me being caught up in Mitch's activities. Thought I should know the sort of life I was letting myself in for.'

She shrugged. 'I got myself a job and a mate offered to let me share with him. I took him up on it. And it's not like that,' she added, seeing the glint in Beth's eye. 'It's Al from school. Remember him? Al Collins?'

'Yeah, I do. Little chap with curly hair?'

For the first time since she'd arrived, Isi's manner relaxed a little. 'Well, he still has the curly hair but he's six foot two now. A sports coach. You wouldn't recognise him.'

'I'm glad you came, Isi.'

Her sister's expression closed over again. 'I did it for

Ryan. He's freaking out that his new life's gonna be ripped apart over all this.'

Beth considered what her sister had told her. It didn't really change any of the facts surrounding Bryony and Andy's death but it could be significant if Bryony had been sucked into the baby surrogacy scam that Joshua was running. On the other hand, Bryony – and her baby – were dead. There was no baby out there that they could trace – no proof of any of it. It was all just hearsay from Ryan. Her sister had just made the first tentative step in closing the gap between them. Was she really going to risk estranging her again by dropping her brother in it on the basis of no evidence?

She sighed. 'I think Ryan's probably safe enough. Technically, I should probably report what you've said, but … he's right … what happened with Bryony isn't going to affect our ongoing investigation. They'll be looking into Serenity's wider activities, I'm sure, and if that leads them to Mitch or Ryan they'll have to deal with that at the time – and so will I. But it won't come from me.'

'Right then,' Isi drained her mug and got up from her chair. 'I'd best be off.'

'Where are you staying?'

'I'm not. I'm going back tonight. I've got work in the morning.'

'It's late. You won't be back until gone midnight.'

Her sister shrugged. 'Don't matter.'

'Stay. Please. I can drop you off as early as you like at the station in the morning. It would be good to talk.'

She could see her sister was hesitating.

'Isi, I know I let you down leaving like I did.'

Her sister's eyes glistened suspiciously. 'It was like the lights went out in the house when you left, Beth. I had no one.

396

And Mam and Dad were so angry they took it out on me.'

'I wasn't thinking straight with Bryony and Andy dying like that. I had to get out of there. Can you understand that?'

Isi didn't answer.

'Can't we start over, pet? You, me … maybe even Ryan? We could be a family, a *proper* one. Not make the same mistakes that we grew up with.'

Her sister shrugged, pulling a tissue from her pocket to blow her nose fiercely. 'I don't know, Beth. I don't believe in fairy tales. And I manage fine on my own.'

'So do I, but I'd be happier if I had you in my life. We could make it work, Isi, if we want it bad enough. I've never stopped loving you. You must know that.'

Her sister looked like she was about to crumble and Beth held her breath. Then …

'I'm tired, Beth. Maybe I'll take you up on that offer of a bed if you're sure you can take me to the station in the morning? We'd need to leave early though.'

Beth jumped at the opportunity. 'No problem. You can have my bed and I'll sleep on the sofa.'

'There's no need—'

'I insist,' she said firmly. 'You've had a long day and you've got an early start in the morning. I can catch up on my sleep any time.'

'We could share, if you like … like we used to?'

Beth grabbed the olive branch with both hands. 'Done! But first, I'm going to knock us up something to eat.'

In the end they'd talked into the early hours of the morning. She'd learnt that neither Isi nor Ryan saw anything of their parents now, or Mitch. But they saw each other.

'He's changed so much, you wouldn't recognise him as the same person,' Isi said, with her sad smile. 'That Eleanor's turned him around and that's a fact.'

Just like Andy had with her, Beth thought. Except Ryan's partner was still alive.

She'd looked at photos on Isi's phone of his Eleanor and their son, and realised that for the first time ever, her brother looked happy.

'He is,' Isi said when she commented on it. 'He adores his little Charlie and Eleanor.' She pulled a face. 'It's a bit sad, if you ask me, but maybe I'm just jealous. They're not rolling in money or anything, but they're happy. She's very close to her family and he struggled with that at first because, as he said, we've all spent our lives trying to break the ties with ours. But he says her lot are different.' She shrugged. 'They sound nice.'

That night, as her sister slept beside her, Beth relived their conversations in her head. Everything she'd said to Isi about being shattered after Andy and Bryony's deaths had been true and if she'd stayed in the toxic atmosphere of her family home, it would have broken her. What she hadn't been able to say was that, at nineteen years old, she'd been living at home with a bully of a father and still sharing a bed with her eleven-year-old sister. She'd needed her space.

Now, as she listened to Isi's steady breathing, she was filled with a hundred different emotions. The warmth of her sister's body, even the scent of her, was familiar. She remembered the laughter they'd shared, Isi's cheekiness … such a contrast to the constant weight she seemed to carry on her own tired shoulders.

I hid Dad's whisky so he can't get drunk tonight, Isi had giggled one night when Beth had gone up to say goodnight. *I put it on the floor behind his chair. When he finds it, he'll just think he left it there last night.*

Isi, he'll be furious.

He's always furious. You can find it for him if he gets too cross.

It was her way of getting her own back – little victories that she chalked up, and Beth had admired the spirit that even at eleven years old, wouldn't be crushed. She reached out and touched her sister's sleeping face.

'Night, night,' she whispered.

～

Six thirty the next morning Beth waved her sister off at Kings Cross, suppressing the emotions that made her want to cling on to her and not let go. They'd taken the first tentative steps forward in re-establishing their relationship last night, but the gulf was still huge. She'd made a private resolution though. She'd do her damnedest to help recreate some sort of family unit for them … her, Isi and Ryan. Just because they hadn't had the best of starts in that direction didn't mean they couldn't work it out for themselves if they wanted to. She'd had the most contented night's sleep knowing that Isi was there beside her, the wall of silence finally broken. And they could build on that.

CHAPTER FORTY-SIX

Harry slipped quietly out of the bed, careful not to wake Claire. He showered, dressed, and after checking that she was still soundly asleep, crept quietly down the stairs. He needed to get home for a change of clothes before heading into work.

In the kitchen, he made himself a coffee and sat down at the table. He looked around him and realised it felt good being here – good being with Claire. For once he didn't seem to be spending more time worrying about how he was going to end things than actually enjoying being in the relationship. He looked up as the door opened and Claire walked in, her dressing gown tied tightly round her waist.

'Oh, you're here,' she said. 'I thought you'd sneaked off on me for a minute.'

He smiled. 'You don't get rid of me that easily, but sorry it's so early. I was going to leave it another ten minutes and then wake you up with a cup of coffee before I left.'

'Tea! You'd better know what I like if you're planning on sticking around.'

It was said light heartedly but he sensed a half question in there that made him wonder if she really had thought he'd done the dirty on her and left without saying goodbye.

'I'll remember that for next time,' he said, getting up. 'Now you sit down there and I'll show you how good I am at making tea, before I go.'

'How are your parents?' she asked, as she watched him reheat the kettle.

'They're good, as far as I know. Dad's still doing his digging in Egypt and Mum's still by his side, making sure he behaves himself.'

'Do you hear from them often?'

'We video call every couple of weeks. Nothing ever changes, we always seem to talk about the same things. They're coming back for Christmas – they asked after you, funnily enough, the last time we spoke. I think they'll like that we're seeing each other.'

It was a thought that came back to him as he opened his front door a while later and picked the mail up off the mat. If he and Claire were still seeing each other, maybe she'd like to come over for Boxing Day.

He looked at the post in his hand. One envelope stood out from the others in that it was neatly handwritten and unfamiliar. He studied it curiously before turning it over and opening it.

There was no letter inside, just a short obituary that took him seconds to read.

ROSEMARY ANNE FOX

FOX Rosemary Anne on Thursday 7th November 2019, after a long illness. She will be greatly missed by her beloved family and remembered by many for her courage in the most difficult of times, her loving warmth and zest for life. Her funeral will be at New Southgate Crematorium, on Thursday 28th November, at 2.30 p.m. No flowers, but donations to Cancer

Research would be much appreciated.

Harry's brows knitted together. Was this meant to mean something to him? Did he know a Rosemary Fox? The answer to that was a resounding no, he was pretty sure of that. So why had someone gone to the trouble of sending him her obituary?

He turned it over in his hand but nothing was written on the back. There must be some mistake – someone had misdirected it. Yet … it was his name on the envelope. His address. It was no mistake.

He shook his head, looked at it for a bit longer, then finally screwed it up into a ball and threw it into the waste paper basket. Then he looked at it, hesitated and retrieved it. This was what he did for a living … solve mysteries. It went against the grain to ignore it. He took it through to the lounge and put it on the coffee table. Maybe he'd hang onto it for a bit.

Just in case anything else came through …

CHAPTER FORTY-SEVEN

Juliet

I've been dozing on and off all morning. It seems ridiculous, after the amount of 'sleeping' I've been doing for the past couple of weeks, that I should still be tired. But I am. I'm exhausted. It's still such an effort even to talk, but I have to find the energy from somewhere as DI Briscombe is apparently coming back to see me later today to take a formal statement. Now I'm away from it all I can see how toxic Serenity was, yet why is there a part of me that feels I'll be betraying them if I do that? Mum says it's because they've brainwashed me and when I think of my induction, which I try not to do, I get what she's saying.

Now as I become more aware of the familiar sound of machinery and monitors around me again, I brace myself to open my eyes. Each time I do this, I'm terrified that yesterday's breakthrough will prove to be a fluke, that I'll find that once again I can't move. I hardly dare try, but … my eyes are open and relief swamps me. I realise that someone is holding my hand and I don't need to look to know who it is. Mum was with me every day when I was in the coma, why wouldn't she be here now?

403

'Hey, sweetheart,' she whispers, leaning forward to kiss me.

'Hey,' I respond, squeezing her hand.

'How are you feeling? Is there anything I can get you?'

I shake my head. 'I love you, Mama.'

'I love you too.'

Yesterday, she wouldn't let me talk about what had happened between us, what had led up to all this. But today I'm determined to get it out in the open.

'I'm so sorry,' I say.

'There's nothing to be sorry about.'

'Yes there is. If I hadn't been so childish, stomping off like that—'

'It was a shock. You had every right to react the way you did. It's me who should be apologising, not you. What I did was a moment of madness, but how can I regret it when it gave me you?' She sighs. 'We all make mistakes. I've learnt to live with mine and I'm just so thankful that dad loved me enough to forgive me.'

'Until I split you up.'

'Call it more a temporary respite,' Mum says with a little smile. 'We needed our space for a while, but I can't help feeling that if we could survive being unfaithful to each other all those years ago, it'll take more than this to split us up now.'

'Does he really love me as if I was his own? As much as he loves Lisa?'

'He loved you from the moment he set eyes on you, and you don't need me to tell you that.'

'That's how I felt about Theo …' I break off, the tears welling up as I remember my son. Those precious few hours I had with him. 'How could I even have thought about giving him away? It'll be my punishment forever more if we can't find him. And I deserve it.'

'What did I say about making mistakes? You need to forgive yourself. But as it happens –'

She breaks off as the door opens and my dad walks in, holding something carefully in his arms.

'Well, just look what the stork left behind,' he greets me, a twinkle in his eye. 'A bouncing little boy, desperate to see his mum.'

I gasp, my eyes locking on the tiny bundle in disbelief as he approaches.

'Is that... is it really?'

'You'd better believe it,' he answers, handing Theo over to me. 'We've had to go through a few hoops to get him released to you, but the young couple who had him came forward voluntarily and have convinced the powers that be that this is your child. They've taken DNA just to be absolutely certain, but just look at him … he's the spitting image of you when you were born, isn't he, Marie?' Mum smiles, peeling back the shawl to take a peek. 'Oh yes. Just look at him. Here …'

She rummages in her handbag for a tissue and passes it to me. 'Now come on. The poor little lad doesn't want you crying all over him. This is meant to be a happy reunion…'

But suddenly I'm not listening, my eyes fixing instead on the man who has just walked into the room. Instinctively, my hold on Theo tightens.

'Dean!'

'Hello, Juliet.'

'What do you want?' I can hear the hostility in my voice, and by the despondent expression on Dean's face, so can he.

'Just to talk to you … and meet my son.'

405

'Would you like us to leave you alone, or would you rather we stayed?' Mum asks.

'I won't upset her,' Dean says. 'If you could give us a few moments together, I'd appreciate it?'

'Jules?'

I nod. 'It's okay. I'll call you if I need you.'

'We'll be just outside.'

After the door clicks behind them, Dean moves closer to occupy my mother's chair and leans forward to get a look at his son.

'He looks like you,' he says with a strange little smile.

'That's what Mum and Dad said. What are you doing here?'

He runs his hands through his hair and the eyes he turns on me are tortured. 'It's been a hell of a time. You know Joshua's dead?'

I nod.

He looks lost. 'He was never much of a father to me, but he was still my father. And all the stuff that's coming out about him … I need you to know I wasn't involved in the bad stuff he was doing.'

I want to believe him, and I find I do, about all the illegal stuff Joshua was apparently up to, but the way they treated me towards the end? Was he really in total ignorance of all of that, or did he turn a blind eye, hoping it might work?

'You said I'd left the community,' I say, remembering what Mum's told me.

'Because Joshua told me to. He said he didn't know what had happened to you or who'd stabbed you, but he didn't want the commune coming into disrepute. People were suspicious enough of us already.'

'And our baby? You could have told them earlier

about him.'

'That was another thing he said to keep quiet about. I was still trying to get my head round it all when he was murdered. That's when Fabian told me some of what they were up to. He said I'd be fully implicated because I was the baby's father and I'd assented to it being handed over. You and I didn't know the full names of those people, or where they lived. I couldn't really tell them anything about where he was.'

He pauses, and when I say nothing, adds. 'They want me back in this afternoon for more questioning. I don't know what the outcome of all this will be, but ...' He reaches for my free hand and I see the determination in his eyes. 'Everyone in the community's reeling at the moment. They're rudderless. My lawyer's trying to get me off with a suspended prison sentence, but I'm not sure how hopeful he is. Either way, when I can, I want to rebuild Serenity. I feel I owe it to them to make up for what Joshua's done. But it's going to be hard. I'll need to convince the elders that I wasn't involved in any of Joshua's dealings, and there are those who think I'm too young.'

His gaze rests on where his hand is covering mine for a moment, and then shifts to my face. 'I'm not sure I can do it on my own – I know I let you down badly, staying away when you needed me, but I'd never been in that position before – where something, *someone*, was more important to me than Serenity. And I didn't know how to handle it. If you come back and bring our son, I promise you it will be different. It will be as it was always meant to be, a loving, caring community where we look out for each other and the vulnerable. Where we can have one partner for life if we choose and bring our children up within a proper family

407

unit, as God intended. Can you do that with me, Juliet?'

I look into his face and feel the tension in my own soften. I believe every word he's saying. I have no doubt that he can rebuild Serenity if he gets the chance. There's more of Joshua in him than he realises. I also have no doubt that he loves me in his own way, but is it enough? Because he was right … he's made monumental mistakes as far as our relationship is concerned. Can I trust him to always be there for Theo and me? Do I have what it takes to help him rebuild Serenity?

It takes all my effort to look him in the eye, as I say, 'I can't come back, Dean. For a while I thought maybe I could make a life within the community, but the differences between us are too big. I'd only cause you grief when what you need is support. I'm sorry.'

'I thought you said you loved me?'

'I do—' My voice chokes and I stop, then start again. 'But I have to be practical too – and sometimes love isn't enough.'

'It is for me.'

'No, it isn't. Not really. Otherwise you'd be choosing me over Serenity.'

We stare at each other for a long moment and I think, finally, he sees the truth in my words.

'Where will you and the child live?'

I'm relieved that he's not going to fight me for custody. 'I don't know. With Mum and Dad to start with, probably. It won't be easy, but I'll get a job and work it out somehow.'

'I'm not sure I'll be in a position to help support it financially.'

It! Not *him*, or our *son*, or *Theo*, just *it*. I feel the weight of my decision float away as something clarifies in my mind. Not once has Dean shown interest in Theo since he walked

408

into this room … he hasn't wanted to hold him or cuddle him – just one brief look when he first came in. I realise it's because he doesn't feel the same sort of love that most fathers would feel for their child. He was so estranged from his own parents that he never had that sort of bonding with them and probably has no *idea* how to attach to his son – and it's something I'm not sure can be taught. The realisation eases my mind. I'm making the right decision. Life won't be easy but I can bring my son up my way and we'll manage.

He squeezes my hand then lets go of it. 'Probably best that I don't visit. As you say … our worlds will be too different.'

Part of me wants to say that of course he must keep in touch with his son, knowing that's the usual mantra trotted out to separating parents, but I'm ashamed to admit that the other part is stronger – the one that wants nothing to do with Serenity's way of life, or run the risk of Theo being sucked into it. The less noble side wins out and I keep quiet.

I watch as Dean rises from his chair. 'Bye, Juliet. I do love you, and if you should ever change your mind…'

I don't answer and we both know that won't happen. He touches my hand briefly and then he's gone.

I look down at my son lying contentedly in my arms. I feel like I've learnt a lot this past year since I stormed out of my parents' house in such a strop, but the biggest knowledge I've gained is about love and what it is – the ability to forgive, as my father did my mother when she conceived another man's child; the physical pain of having a part of yourself ripped out as your baby's wrenched from your arms … and perhaps most importantly, the realisation that while the bonds of love can be uncomfortably stretched, they never snap. Instead, they cocoon you from a wider distance, allowing you your space – waiting for you to recognise the value of their worth, before moving in again to embrace you.

It's not over yet, I know that. There'll be a court case and my story will be laid bare for the world to know – and God knows what will happen to Serenity. But eventually, it will pass and I'll pick up the pieces of my life and move on.

Theo opens his eyes and they fix on mine in fierce concentration. He's probably wondering who I am. His little fist is clamped around my finger and I find myself thinking about his other mother … the one who was so desperate for a baby of her own, who held him in her arms just like this, looked into his eyes and loved him for the few, precious short weeks that she had him. How must she be feeling now? I feel guilty about that and silently thank her, suspecting that I'll move on from this a lot quicker than she will. I'm just so grateful that I've been given this second chance – worth every hour, every minute of the darkness and terror I endured.

'I'll never let you down again,' I whisper in his ear, as the door opens and my parents walk in.

'I promise you that.'

THE END

You've Finished!

BEFORE YOU GO … A little gift for you

Have you read my prequel novella to the series, *Behind Closed Doors?* If not, you can download it for free from my website at: **www.carolynmahony.com**

Thank you so much for taking the time to read *No Escape* – if you enjoyed it, I'd love it if you'd pop over to Amazon and leave a Review. Reviews are so helpful to authors.

Other books featuring Harry Briscombe:
Behind Closed Doors
Cry From The Grave
The Jagged Line

OR Shadow Watcher … a standalone Romantic Suspense novel to prove that love and crime do mix!

You can take a look at them on Amazon or on my website above.

With very best wishes,

Carolyn

Printed in Great Britain
by Amazon